THE
FANTASTIC
FAMILY
WHIPPLE

THE FANTASTIC FAMILY WHIPPLE

MATTHEW WARD

razOr
bill

AN IMPRINT OF PENGUIN GROUP (USA) INC.

A division of Penguin Young Readers Group
Published by the Penguin Group
Penguin Group (USA) LLC
345 Hudson Street
New York, New York 10014

USA / Canada / UK / Ireland / Australia / New Zealand / India / South Africa / China
Penguin.com
A Penguin Random House Company

ISBN: 978-1-59514-690-8

Printed in the United States of America

1 3 5 7 9 10 8 6 4 2

*For Wendie and
Henry & Miles,
who continue every day to secure my
records for Luckiest Husband on Earth and
World's Luckiest Dad, respectively.*

THE MOST EXTRAORDINARILY
ORDINARY BOY ON EARTH

All the members of the Whipple family had managed to be born in the same month on the same day: March the first. All, of course, but one.

Arthur Whipple had been so eager to join his amazing family that he decided to make a surprise arrival into the world at eleven thirty-four P.M. on February the twenty-ninth, just twenty-six minutes ahead of schedule. But to Arthur's astonishment, his family was not as delighted by the surprise as he had hoped. When the doctor placed Arthur in his mother's arms, she smiled lovingly down at him—but he could sense a hint of sadness in her eyes. And when the nurse came and carried him out for his first bath, he turned back to catch a glimpse of his mother quietly crying as the door shut behind him.

Arthur's father sent the marching band home early that night, after they had performed but one song. Charles Whipple was a good man, but he found it hard to conceal his disappointment in his new son's poor sense of timing.

Seeing that something was troubling the baby's father, the doctor sought to reassure him. "Congratulations, Mr. Whipple. You have a healthy baby boy. His heart rate is normal, and he is breathing very well. Furthermore, he has the proper number of fingers and toes, and—"

"Really?" Mr. Whipple interjected. "Well, that *is* good news! I was under the impression he only had ten of each, but . . ."

"Well yes," replied the doctor. "Ten fingers and ten toes. That's generally considered to be the proper number."

"Oh. I see," sighed Mr. Whipple. "No one must have told you."

"You were expecting a different number of digits?"

"We were really hoping for *at least* fourteen of each. . . . Are you quite sure there were only ten?"

"Uh, yes. Quite sure."

"And there is no way he might sprout a few extras in the near future?"

"Um. No," replied the doctor, who was beginning to look noticeably uncomfortable with Mr. Whipple's questions.

"Oh, well, there you have it," said Mr. Whipple with more than a hint of despair. "This is just a disaster."

The doctor made an expression that was somewhere

between a smile and a grimace, then turned, whispered something to the nurse, and walked out of the room. One could hardly blame him for feeling uneasy. He was used to people being overjoyed when he gave them the news that their child was healthy and normal.

But, of course, the Whipple family was anything but normal, and Arthur's being so had shocked his parents to their very cores. In truth, they would have been less surprised if Arthur had been born a duck-billed platypus. For the Whipples had long been regarded as extraordinary, due to one simple fact: the Whipple family had broken more world records than any family on earth.

After a few minutes, Arthur was brought back into the room and returned to his mother. Perhaps sensing he wasn't measuring up to his family's expectations, the baby looked as though he might be trying to think of something remarkable he could do to prove himself worthy of the Whipple name. Unfortunately, he had just been born, and apart from gurgling, there wasn't a whole lot he was capable of. In the end, he apparently decided on attempting the world record for Longest Time without Blinking—but only made it forty-two seconds. Luckily, no one really noticed. He didn't know it then, but this was the last time his shortcomings would go undetected. From that moment on, each of Arthur's failures would be documented, analyzed, studied, and graphed.

Outside the hospital room, the crowd of well-wishers was buzzing with anticipation. In some parts of the crowd, there was a rumor circulating that the latest addition to the Whipple family had been born with polka-dotted skin and a full set of teeth. In other parts, it was whispered the baby had weighed 22½ pounds and was covered with fur. Some people were even saying the infant had refused the doctor's help and simply delivered itself.

A crack of the door sent a hush over the crowd.

Mr. Whipple stepped into the hallway. He stood smiling awkwardly for a moment and then addressed the onlookers.

"Thank you all so much for coming. I am happy to report that my wife has given birth to a son—and that he is healthy, happy and . . ." Mr. Whipple paused, grappling with the next word. "Normal."

The crowd looked puzzled. Surely he was exaggerating. He couldn't have meant *normal* normal. After all, this was a Whipple they were dealing with. Certainly the word "normal" had an entirely different meaning in that family.

One man spoke up. "So what records has the little one broken in his first hour? Birth weight? Shoe size? Arm length?"

"Actually," replied Mr. Whipple, his smile straining a bit, "Arthur has not broken any records at this time. We are sure, however, that with the proper guidance, he will soon join his siblings in the pages of *Grazelby's Guide to World Records and Fantastic Feats.*"

"But what about your streak of Coincidental Birth Dates? This marks the sixth member of your family born on the first of March. Surely, *that* is a world record?"

Mr. Whipple's smile grew even more strained. "Unfortunately, Arthur was born several minutes before midnight, giving him an actual birth date of February the twenty-ninth. But we are perfectly satisfied with continuing to share our record of five coincidental birth dates with the Nakamoto family in Osaka."

The crowd looked stunned. They had come to rely on the Whipple family's unbeaten track record in the realm of world-record breaking. Nothing was certain anymore.

Stepping forward through the crowd, a grizzle-faced reporter peered out from under a dark-brimmed hat.

"Mr. Whipple," said the man, "do you think this setback might be explained by—how shall we say—*other-than-natural* means?"

Mr. Whipple arched his brow, his smile vanishing altogether. "I'm afraid I don't take your meaning, sir."

"My apologies, Mr. Whipple. What I mean to say is: Mightn't your son's unremarkable quality be the result of a certain *family curse*? A curse that has gone so far as to claim the life of—"

"Who is this man?" cried Mr. Whipple. "Who let him in here? Wilhelm!"

A burly, handlebar-mustachioed man rushed forward, clapped the reporter about the shoulders, and proceeded to drag him down the hall as the crowd looked on with wide eyes.

When the two men had disappeared from view, Mr. Whipple straightened his shirt and cleared his throat.

"Terribly sorry about that," he addressed the onlookers. "We can't have just anyone attending the births of our children, you understand. But please, let me assure you—the so-called Lyon's Curse has nothing whatsoever to do with my son's momentary recordlessness. Any family tragedies resulting from such a curse are all in the distant past." Mr. Whipple wiped his brow with his handkerchief. "And besides, this is hardly a tragedy: I have every confidence Arthur's unfavorable status won't last more than a matter of days—certainly no more than a month or two."

The crowd said nothing.

Amidst some awkward shuffling of feet and a few nervous glances, Mr. Whipple thanked everyone again for coming.

It was not until Mr. Whipple's valet and butler, Wilhelm, returned with a forklift—and presented the men with the World's Largest Box of Cigars—that the memory of the strange interruption faded.

After distributing the seven-foot, three-hundred-pound cigars into giant cigar holders, Wilhelm—whose title of World's Strongest German had made him uniquely suited to the task—promptly donned a flamethrower and proceeded to light them.

The men sat about smoking their colossal Cubans through large funnel-shaped tips while the women formed gossip clusters and flitted from one to the next. Just before dawn, when all had had their fill of gossip and smoke, the guests offered their closing compliments and bid the Whipple family farewell.

Mr. Whipple gazed out of the maternity ward window onto the procession of cars leaving the hospital, each with a giant half-smoked cigar strapped to its roof or secured to its tail, as the sun rose in the distance, drenching the whole scene in a warm amber glow. He looked back toward the hospital room where his wife lay holding their recordless newborn son, and thought about the past. He couldn't help but wonder if his family's incredible legacy had come to an end.

• • •

When the octuplets arrived—on schedule—the world could finally relax. The Whipples had returned.

Seven years after Arthur was born, Eliza Whipple was in labor again. The doctors had told her she was to have plain old quintuplets—but Abigail, Beatrice, and George had been hiding behind their siblings in order to surprise the family. It was true, of course, that Arthur had tried to surprise the family at his own birth—by arriving early— with unfavorable results. The octuplets, however, proved to be masters of surprise. They waited until the last minutes of March the first—and then made their move.

The world had expected a repeat of Arthur's recordless birth, but when the quintuplets showed up just before midnight and brought three extra Whipples with them, everyone was astounded with joy. At the moment they were born, the Whipple octuplets broke two world records: Highest Number of Healthy Babies in a Single Birth, and Highest Number of Coincidental Birth Dates.

The Nakamoto family soon telephoned to concede defeat.

THE DAWN OF DISASTER

On the morning the curse came back, Arthur was jolted awake by the Whipple family breakfast bell. He found himself lying on his bed—on top of the bedding—still wearing his clothes from the day before. He was filled with the sinking feeling this was not the morning he had planned for himself—but he could not remember why. Then Arthur noticed the sound of accordion music coming from the next room, and it all came rushing back to him.

The music was being performed by Arthur's older brother Simon, who was now six days into his attempt at the Longest Continuous Time Playing an Accordion.

On the first day, Arthur had found the music coming from his brother's room enchanting and beautiful—that is, until he had tried to go to sleep. Arthur then found the music rather loud and entirely sleep prohibitive. But the boy soon saw it as just another opportunity to finally break his first world record. He got out of bed and decided to attempt the Longest Time without Sleeping. He knew if he could just stay awake one day longer than his brother's projected seven-day accordion-playing streak, he would set a new record for sleep deprivation—and just maybe earn the respect of his family in the process. Nothing could stop him now. . . .

And yet, there he was on the present morning, waking up to the realization he had fallen asleep after only five days.

Arthur looked up at the slowly clicking time-lapse camera, which had been set up in the corner of his room to verify his state of wakefulness—and gave a frown. The boy was not unfamiliar with failure, but he could not help but feel a bit disheartened. He'd really thought he'd had this one.

Still, the Whipple family breakfast bell was ringing—and it took excuses from no one, disheartened or otherwise—so Arthur stood up and walked to the mirror. He straightened his shirt and did his best to flatten the clump of light brown hair that was sticking straight out on the side of his head. Nothing seemed to work, so he cut his losses and went to the wardrobe. The finely carved cabinet—one in a matching set of thirteen made for the Whipple children by champion woodworker Alan Splinterson—had once been part of the World's Thickest Tree Limb, before it was severed from its trunk by the Most Powerful Lightning Storm in Recorded

History. These days, it simply held Arthur's clothes. Opening the wardrobe, he promptly found his robe, put it on over his matted clothing, then walked to the bedroom door.

Now, if Arthur had known the chain of catastrophic events that would be set into motion that day, he might have turned himself right around and opted instead to attempt the record for Longest Time Staying in Bed. But since he did not have the luxury of a working crystal ball or a subscription to *Tomorrow's News Today*, he simply turned the doorknob and stepped through the threshold.

● ● ●

Once inside the corridor, Arthur joined the procession of Whipple children as they made their way toward the sweet smells wafting up from the kitchen. They had all lined up in age-descending order, just as they always did at meal time. Leading the way was Henry Whipple, who, at seventeen, was the eldest.

Henry, being the most athletic of his siblings, was never quite comfortable unless he was competing at something. Because his parents had recently banned hurdles, bicycles, and horses from the upstairs passageways, he was presently in a contest with his brother Simon to see who could hold his breath the longest. Simon, a thirteen-year-old musician/ mechanical engineer, was at a slight disadvantage, as he was, of course, still playing his beloved accordion as he walked. Graciously, Henry had agreed to give him a five-second delayed start to compensate for this, but Simon had already begun devising plans for a "breath-holding machine" in his head.

Next came twelve-year-old Cordelia. She was the over-achiever in a family of overachievers. Not to be outdone in music by her brother Simon, Cordelia had already mastered both the violin and the harpsichord. She also dabbled in brain surgery and model-rocket science. But her true passion was for architecture. On her back, she carried a T square like a barbarian battle-ax; in her hand, she carried a perfect $1/1000$th scale model of the Taj Mahal, constructed entirely out of toothpicks.

And then came Arthur. He was eleven. Already trying to make up for his most recent failure, Arthur was now hopping on one foot in another attempt to break a world record.

At the end of the breakfast procession were the octuplets: Penelope, Edward, Charlotte, Lenora, Franklin, Abigail, Beatrice, and George—all age four.

Penelope wanted to be an entomologist when she grew up. She carried a small cage in which she had just the day before captured the Largest Common Housefly Ever Recorded.

Edward was an explorer. That summer, he had become the Youngest Person to Summit Kanchenjunga, the third-highest mountain in the world. He had indeed considered climbing the *Very* Highest, but after a bit of soul-searching and a stern chat from his mother, he'd decided he should wait until he was at least five before he attempted Everest.

Charlotte was the Most Accomplished Four-Year-Old Painter on Earth. One month earlier, she'd had her first exhibition at the Metropolitan Museum of Art. The reviews were impressive: "Exquisite!"; "A tour de force!"; "The finest collection of teddy bear paintings since Victor Flambeau's Stuffed Bear series!" Her hands were usually stained with paint, and today was no exception.

Lenora was destined for the opera house. Under the tutelage of the esteemed Madame Bellissaria, she had recently hit the Highest Note Ever Sung in Live Performance. She carried out her usual vocal exercises as she walked.

Franklin belonged at sea. He wore an eighteenth-century naval lieutenant's bicorne hat, with one of its points jutting out over his face and the other shielding the back of his neck. It had been a fitting birthday present from his parents one year earlier, when Franklin had disappeared off the Whipple family frigate during a sailing excursion and was feared dead. Amazingly, he had turned up three days later in one of the ship's dinghies and recalled to his family how he had set off alone to venture a closer look at some sea caves on the coast of a nearby island.

Abigail had a way with animals. She had recently returned from a semester abroad in Saskatchewan, where she had lived with a pack of wolves through a nursery school exchange program. She was now riding on the back of one of the Whipple family dogs, a giant Great Dane called Hamlet, who held the record for Tallest Dog in the World.

13

Beatrice was a champion competitive eater, but one would never have known it by her size. She was a petite girl with a shocking appetite who astounded bystanders and participants alike by winning every eating competition she entered. But unlike most competitive eaters her age, she had refined tastes well beyond her years. Though it was true she held the record for Most Frankfurters Eaten in One Minute, it was her filet-mignon and crème-brûlée trophies she cherished most.

And then there was George—the youngest of the octuplets by two and a half minutes. Instead of gravitating toward one or two main interests, as most of his brothers and sisters had, George gravitated to whatever held his interest at any given moment. At that particular moment, it was finding out how long he could hang a spoon on his nose without aid from any other part of his body.

The only Whipple child unaccounted for in the breakfast procession was Ivy, who, at twenty-three months, was not quite old enough to be left to her own devices. She had been collected a short while earlier and was now waiting outside for her brothers and sisters near the rear terrace of Neverfall Hall, the Whipples' historic family home.

• • •

The breakfast procession wound its way down the spiral staircase that led to the drawing room and then proceeded out through the huge garden doors that led to the east lawn. Mrs. Whipple was already seated at the outdoor breakfast table. She busied herself fastening a bib around the neck of little Ivy, who in turn—barely able to see over the table-top—busied herself fastening a bib around the neck of the stuffed toy bear seated beside her, thus furthering the pair's record for Highest Number of Matching Outfits Worn by a Stuffed Toy and Its Owner. Mr. Whipple stood behind his wife, chatting with Mrs. Waite, the housekeeper, and Mervyn McCleary, the world record certifier from *Grazel-by's Guide to World Records and Fantastic Feats*. All six of them, including the bear, were wearing safety goggles.

Mr. McCleary, a tallish man with a short, grayish beard, had been certifying the Whipples' world records for almost thirteen years. As a result of the Whipples being such pro-lific record setters, Mr. McCleary had found himself in the company of the Whipples nearly every day of his life since he had been assigned to document their achievements. There had been an instant kinship between them, and Mr. McCleary had soon become known to the Whipple children as Uncle Mervyn. He had since been made the children's godfather and traveled with the Whipple family wherever they went.

Mrs. Waite, on the other hand, had only worked for the Whipples a week and a half. A plump, silver-haired woman with aged but fiery eyes, she had been hired on as the new housekeeper after the prior position-holder, a Mrs. Scrubb, had been stricken with the World's Rarest Strain of Malaria and forced to take an early retirement. The Whipple chil-dren did not object to the change in the least. Where Mrs.

Scrubb had been fussy and ill-tempered, Mrs. Waite was warm and friendly and did not scold them for the many record-breaking messes they tended to leave about the house. Having never had children of her own, she was happy to care for the younger Whipples whenever needed, and had even begun serving unofficially as Ivy's nanny.

At present, Mrs. Waite turned to greet each of the Whipple children as they approached the table, handing each child a pair of his or her own safety goggles, shaking her head dubiously as she did so.

"My my," she murmured. "What ever will it be today?" After little more than a week, Mrs. Waite was still far from comfortable with the Whipples' rather unconventional customs.

When the children had all found their places, Mr. Whipple took his seat beside his wife. "Good morning, children," he said. "A very fine Rueing Day to you all."

Arthur's heart abruptly sank. In the morning's confusion, he had completely forgotten it was Rueing Day. Of all the days he could have chosen to fail a week-long attempt, there was no worse one than this.

"As you know," continued his father, "today is the day we Whipples remind ourselves to squeeze every last ounce of success from every moment of our lives. And this particular Rueing Day is a most historic one indeed. It is twenty years today since your grandfather's death. Sadly, his life was cut short in its prime, leaving, well—certain things never to be accomplished. To honor his memory, we must treat each day as though it is our last—and never settle for achieving anything less than the very best."

Arthur let out a melancholy sigh.

Oblivious, Mr. Whipple gazed out at the horizon for an odd moment, then resumed. "Right," he declared. "That's the last bit of looking back we shall do all year. Now, to the present. Sadly, it has come to my attention we are a bit behind schedule in our current record tally. Would you be so kind as to clarify, Mr. McCleary?"

Uncle Mervyn stepped forward and folded back a page of his notepad. "Indeed, Mr. Whipple. With the Unsafe Sports Showdown only a few weeks away and the World Records World Championships hardly two months after that, I'm afraid the time for casual record breaking has passed. According to my records, on this same day two years ago, during the prior championships season, you already had some forty-seven additional records on the books. As you know, the eligibility deadline for the championships' top prize happens to fall on your birthday this year, so you'll have to bring your two-year total up to the thousand-record minimum by the first of March if you're to be eligible for this year's championships. Of course, I've no doubt you're more than up to the task. Your ability to rise to challenges has always been nothing short of astonishing, and I'm sure this'll be no different!"

"Yes—thank you, Mervyn," Arthur's father broke in. "So, children, you heard the man; unless we can double our efforts in the coming weeks, we are all clearly doomed."

Slowly, his scowl faded. "But let's try to focus on the positive, shall we? Simon, I see your accordion playing is still going strong. Keep up the good work, Son. And Arthur, I've noticed you are hopping on one foot. . . ."

At the mention of his name, Arthur caught his father's gaze—but promptly glanced away as the man continued.

"What a fantastic idea to break two records at once! Surely the challenge of keeping one foot off the ground at all times will help you stay alert enough to break the record for Longest Time without Sleeping. And you're only, what, two days away from that? Just the sort of boost we need during this critical time. I've got to tell you, Son—your mother and I are extremely proud of you. Sure, you've disappointed us in the past, but what really matters is that you've somehow managed to put all your failures behind you, however embarrassing, in order to finally achieve something. Son, you're going to break your first world record! How does that feel?"

Arthur felt sick. He didn't want to speak, but he knew he had no choice. "Well, actually, Father—about that Longest Time without Sleeping record. Um . . . I don't think I'm going to break it."

"What?!" gasped Mr. Whipple. "Son, you really mustn't doubt yourself now—not when you're so close to your first success. I'm sure you feel you'll never achieve anything with the sort of track record you've got—I mean, I myself have wondered that about you for years—but Son, you're almost there. Don't give up now!"

"Well, you see—the reason I don't think I'll be breaking the record for Longest Time without Sleeping is that, um, well . . . I've already fallen asleep. Last night, actually."

"Oh," said Mr. Whipple, the sparkle escaping his eyes. He tried to keep smiling, even though it was obvious he wanted to stop. The result was somewhat disturbing. "Well, that's all right, Son. Better luck next time. At least you've still got the Hopping on One Foot record to shoot for. Well done. Yes, better luck next time. . . ." Clearing his throat, he eagerly changed the subject. "Well then—enough business for now. . . . Who's hungry?"

The Whipple children all raised their hands.

Beatrice gripped her fork and knife in either fist and sweetly snarled, "Bring it on."

Their father signaled for Mrs. Waite to fetch the chef—and soon everybody had forgotten about yet another of Arthur's failures.

Arthur was glad the focus was off him and onto more important matters, like breakfast. But still, he couldn't shake the dull, aching feeling in his heart that he would never be good enough for his family.

His heart was instantly cheered, however, at the sight of the Whipple family chef emerging from the house.

The chef, dressed in the traditional white, double-breasted jacket and tall, puffy hat, waved to the group, then proceeded to push a large serving cart toward the break-fast table. His face was clean shaven with a bright, child-like smile, but its deep grooves and thick, sinewy features suggested a somewhat rougher past than the man's current position implied.

In fact, Sammy "the Spatula" Smith had been a well-known London gangster before giving up his life of crime and coming to work for the Whipples. Though he had been born with exceptional skills in the culinary arts, he had also been born exceptionally poor. So in order to put himself through cooking school, he began dabbling in some less-than-legal business ventures. It started with changing the dates on a few bottles of Scotch in order to increase their value—and ended with half a ton of stolen caviar being seized by Scotland Yard. Sammy was sentenced to ten years in prison, but was released after serving only two. It was rumored he had bribed prison officials with a lifetime sup-ply of his cinnamon caramel custard tarts. Though no one ever found solid proof of this claim, several postmen had reported mysterious packages regularly leaving the Whip-ple estate, all smelling suspiciously of cinnamon.

Unfortunately, Sammy's past habits still got him into trouble from time to time, and Arthur had heard whispers that the chef was actually in a fair bit of it now. Arthur had always done his best to offer encouraging words and friendly advice whenever Sammy's old ways caught up to him, but it seemed the chef's most recent troubles would require more than just moral support.

Upon approaching the table, Sammy gave a cheerful nod to Arthur, and the boy wondered if the chef had received the anonymous gift he had left for him. The thought was promptly interrupted, however, by a loud rumble behind him, whirling Arthur and his family around to face the house.

The noise grew louder and louder until two flying objects appeared over the rooftops of Neverfall Hall. The first was clearly a helicopter, but the other was harder to identify. Arthur soon recognized it, however, to be a giant piece of French toast, dangling from the helicopter on cables.

• • •

It was not every day a helicopter was involved in the preparation of the Whipples' breakfast. It was far more often a construction crane or a cement mixer or a team of elephants. Mrs. Waite couldn't help but gasp.

"My goodness!" the new housekeeper cried above the aircraft's din. "Have we come to breakfast—or an air show?"

Uncle Mervyn smiled. "You'll get used to it, my dear."

"Yeah, this is nuffing, luv," chuckled Sammy the Spatula. "Should've seen the crop duster we used for the Christmas gravy."

Soon, the gigantic piece of French toast was dangling directly overhead, and the helicopter began to lower its cargo. As the hunk of eggy bread came to rest on the table, the chef unhooked the cables and gave the all-clear signal to Wilhelm (World's Strongest German, Mr. Whipple's valet, butler, and now helicopter pilot), who winched up the cables and headed off over the treetops.

The table itself was round and very large—about fifteen feet in diameter—but the piece of French toast was so enormous, its corners drooped over the table's edge and nearly touched the ground.

Arthur now recalled the smells he'd detected wafting out from the World's Largest Bread Oven when he'd gone to the kitchen to leave a package for Sammy the day before. It seemed this was but one slice of the Largest Loaf of Bread Ever Baked.

Patting the shoulder of Mrs. Waite, who looked on with eyes agog and mouth agape, the chef stepped forward to introduce the dish. Though Sammy the Spatula was known for his colossal cuisine, he prided himself not in its size, but in its quality.

"Got the recipe off an old Canadian mate of mine—'Syrupy' Curtis Carmichael," the chef explained, "but I like to fink it were me who perfected it. Not only is it the *Largest* Piece of French Toast Ever Made, this—it's also the *Tastiest*." Opening the doors on his steaming serving cart, he retrieved a spray nozzle attached to a thick rubber hose. "And 'ow else do you finish off the World's Largest, Tastiest Piece of French Toast but wiv the World's Creamiest Butter—and syrup from the World's Oldest Living Maple Tree?"

Sammy moved his safety goggles into position, lifted the hose, and began spraying melted butter over the face of the French toast. When he was satisfied with a generous golden coat, he retrieved a second hose and began dousing it with warm maple syrup.

By the time he had finished, a mixture of maple syrup and butter was dripping over the edges and onto the ground. Returning the syrup hose to its receptacle, Sammy closed the serving cart doors.

"And now," he declared, "the finishing touch: a sprinkling of the Finest Ground Icing Sugar on the Planet." Removing the lid from a large, long-handled pot, he grabbed the handle with both hands, then flung it forward like a massive lacrosse stick, emptying its contents into the air.

When the cloud had settled, the Whipples raised their goggles, revealing large white circles around their eyes, and got their first look at the finished culinary work of art that lay before them.

"Couldn't have painted it better myself," Charlotte said matter-of-factly.

It was truly a masterpiece of French toast. Its dark, golden-brown edges stood in stark contrast to the snow-white sugar that had settled on its summit. Giant crannies on its upper face formed tide pools of butter and syrup. Steam curled off its surface as the hot glaze met with the crisp morning air.

"Incredible . . ." gasped Mrs. Waite.

"Indeed," Uncle Mervyn replied, glancing affectionately at the new housekeeper. As he extracted a tape measure from his jacket pocket, he added, "I'd—er—I'd be happy to give you a tour of the estate's other wonders sometime—away from all these young whippersnappers—I mean, if you'd like, of course."

"Why, Mr. McCleary," grinned Mrs. Waite, "I'd be delighted."

Uncle Mervyn gave a blushing smile, then flashed a thumbs-up to Arthur—and set about obtaining French toast measurements and marking them down on his clipboard. He then snapped several photographs of the Whipple family and their giant breakfast, to be used for publication exclusively in the *Grazelby Guide*, as per the Whipples' long-standing and highly lucrative sponsorship contract.

With all the official business completed, Sammy cut off the bread's crust with a machete, then simply said, "Enjoy."

The Whipples moved their chairs up to the table—and proceeded to follow the chef's orders.

● ● ●

Despite his past criminal leanings, Sammy the Spatula had never lied to them about food. This truly was the best French toast they had ever tasted.

In twenty minutes' time, most of the Whipple family had eaten all they could, which left the giant piece of French toast still looking relatively untouched, apart from having lost maybe three inches on each side. The only Whipples still actively eating were Simon, Arthur, and Beatrice.

As Simon could not feed himself, on account of his hands being unable to leave his accordion during his record attempt, Arthur had been assigned to cut Simon's food for him and raise it to his mouth. Arthur, still balancing on one foot, alternated between serving a bite of French toast to his brother and serving a bite of French toast to himself, which meant it took them nearly twice as long to eat their breakfast. Beatrice, on the other hand, had already eaten twice as much as both the boys put together, and was showing no signs of slowing down.

"Very good, dear," coached her father, "but pace yourself. It's only a training session. The last thing you need is a hyperextended stomach before the competitive eating season has even begun."

As Beatrice grunted her acknowledgement through bulging cheeks, Sammy the Spatula approached Mr. Whipple and said, "I trust your breakfast was satisfactory, sir?"

"More than satisfactory," smiled his boss. "Truly *excellent*. You've really outdone yourself, Sammy."

"Why, fank you, Mr. Whipple," Sammy smiled back. "Plenty more bread where that came from, of course. The loaf's the size of a bloomin' railway carriage, it is. 'Ope you'll not mind 'aving the World's Largest Sandwich for lunch and the World's Largest Bread Pudding tonight for dessert?"

"Not at all, Sammy. That'll do nicely."

"Very good, sir."

The chef hesitated a moment. His smile faded away, then he lowered his voice and added, "Sir—I was wondering if you'd given it any more thought, what we talked about the uvver day."

Mr. Whipple exhaled slowly then looked up. "Yes—I'm afraid I have, Sammy," he said. His voice was nearly a whisper, but Arthur, hopping on one foot between Simon and his father, could just make out the words over his brother's accordion. "I'm afraid we just can't do it this time," Mr. Whipple continued. "We've been happy to help you in the past, but I worry if we keep bailing you out whenever you get in over your head, you'll never learn from your mistakes. I'm sorry, Sammy—really, I am."

The chef nodded and gave a sad smile. "It's all right, guv. I understand. I'm sorry to come to you like this at all—it's just when I get round the lads from the old days, I start acting a bit like me old self, I'm afraid. But I am trying to do better. If only I might've stayed away from the drink this time, I'm sure I'd never have set that record for Largest Losing Bet on a Backroom Game of Hangman. Ravver ironic the word were 'whisky' in the end, weren't it? Serves me right, though, I reckon. Just hope I can convince 'Meat Cleaver' Mike to agree to a long-term payment plan."

Mr. Whipple smiled warmly. "You're a good man, Sammy. When you're ready to get help, we'll be happy to assist you."

"Fanks, guv. You done so much for me already, just letting me come work for you lot. Honestly, there's nobody in this world I'd ravver cook for."

"And there's nobody we'd rather have cook for us."

Sammy smiled, then—catching Arthur's gaze for a split second—returned to his serving cart.

Arthur sighed. He had not realized before how badly his personal plan to fix Sammy's money troubles had hinged on his father's contributions. The only other donor he had secured was one of rather modest means. He would have to rethink his strategy.

As Arthur racked his brain for new ideas to help Sammy, Mrs. Waite appeared at his father's back, holding little Ivy in one arm and a three-inch-thick newspaper in the other.

"Paper, sir?" offered the housekeeper.

"Oh, yes—thank you, Mrs. Waite," Mr. Whipple replied, taking the hefty newspaper and unfurling it before him. "A little light reading might do me some good at the moment."

The front page of *The World Record* (the Most Circulated Newspaper on Earth) was scattered with record-breaking headlines from across the globe, including: **SOVIET BEAR "BORIS" BECOMES FIRST ANIMAL IN SPACE—BEATING AMERICAN EAGLE "KEITH" BY LESS THAN FOUR MINUTES**; and **LARGEST EVER EXPEDITION TO SOUTH POLE VIA ICE CREAM VAN ARRIVES ON SCHEDULE**; and **FIRST NUCLEAR POWER PLANT HAS FIRST NUCLEAR REACTOR LEAK.**

What Arthur's father failed to notice, however, was the tiny picture of a certain smiling man in the paper's lower half.

Mrs. Waite hesitated a moment before turning to carry Ivy and her matching toy bear off for their post-breakfast activities—but then turned back to Mr. Whipple. "Pardon my asking, sir," she said, pointing to the thumbnail photo at the bottom corner of the paper, "but who's this fellow on the front page here? Says he's returning to the world-record-breaking scene after nearly two decades—like it's meant to be news. But I can't say I've ever heard of him. What's his name—*Rex Goldwin*, is it?"

Mr. Whipple gave a violent cough as he nearly choked on his last bite of French toast. Even from across the table, Arthur could see the color drain from his father's face.

"Sir?" said the housekeeper. "Are you quite all right? Why, you don't look well at all. I hope I've not done anything to upset you."

Arthur's father swallowed hard, pounded twice on his chest, and shook his head. "No," he wheezed, "not at all, Mrs. Waite."

Mrs. Whipple gave a concerned look to her husband. "What ever is the matter, dear?" she said.

"Nothing," the man replied gruffly. "It's just—it's . . . nothing." He crumpled the newspaper shut and rose from his chair. "Excuse me." And with that, he turned and strode off toward the house.

His family looked on in puzzlement.

"Dad really ought to have that indigestion checked out," said Cordelia. "If he'd ever make an appointment, I'd be happy to diagnose him."

"Well," said Arthur's mother some moments later, "it was a bit of an odd exit, but I believe your father has the right idea. We've all got a busy day ahead of us if we're to make the eligibility requirement for the championships by our birthday, so let's get a move on, shall we? Simon, Arthur, Beatrice—you may finish your breakfast; everybody else—you are excused. Mrs. Waite," she added, rising from the table and turning to the housekeeper, "you may fetch Mr. Mahankali for leftovers distribution."

As usual, there was a sizable amount of food remaining, and the Whipples saw to it that nothing went to waste. As a matter of procedure, they donated half of every uneaten meal to a nearby orphanage, to help feed those less fortunate than themselves (and to secure the record for Most Food Donated to a Charitable Organization by a Single Donor)—while saving the other half to feed the Whipple animals.

Mr. Mahankali, who trained and cared for the animals in the Whipple family menagerie, arrived promptly at the table on the back of Shiva, the World's Largest Indian Elephant. It was a common mode of transportation for him, but visitors to the Whipple estate seldom remembered the enormous beast he rode on. They were too busy staring at the rider himself.

At first glance, it was unclear whether he was the animal caretaker—or actually one of the animals. On closer inspection, it became apparent he was in fact humanoid, but every inch of his face was covered with long, dark, silver-streaked hair—which was parted in the middle and pulled back into a bow. Owing partly to the three-piece, pin-striped suit he wore and partly to his large, dark, twinkling eyes, he looked at once savage—and completely civilized. He was Phoolendu Mahankali, the legendary "Panther-Man of Pandharpur" and Hairiest Man Alive.

Mr. Mahankali dismounted his elephantine steed and

exchanged greetings with Sammy the Spatula as the two prepared for the important task of leftovers distribution. Those who had finished eating had already gone back into the house to prepare for that day's various record attempts—except for Abigail, who had been going through a sort of wild-animal withdrawal ever since returning from her semester abroad with the wolves, and naturally wanted to ride on the elephant. She politely asked permission from the beast's caretaker, who smiled and said, "Of course, my child," then picked her up and hoisted her onto Shiva's back.

The Panther-Man then retrieved a long, wooden-handled length of wire from the elephant's saddlebag and gave one of the handles to Sammy.

Positioning themselves at opposite sides of the table, the two men pulled the wire taut, then brought it down like a giant cheese slicer to cut the French toast into two triangular halves. With a set of handheld meathooks, they promptly grabbed the farther of the two halves and slid it off the table, onto the broad trailer cart that was harnessed to the elephant.

"Thank you most kindly, Mr. Sammy," said the Panther-Man. "The animals will be most pleased to have a breakfast so delectable."

"No trouble at all," smiled the chef. "You know, Mahankali—it's a long way back to them animals, innit? Hate to see you starve to deff before you make it to the uvver side of the estate. Guess you'll just 'ave to stop and 'ave a bite yourself, eh?"

"Oh, please, Mr. Sammy," cried the animal caretaker, "I could not possibly!"

Sammy waved the sweet aroma to his nostrils, shut his eyes, and inhaled dramatically. "Very well," he smirked. "Don't say I didn't warn you then."

A mischievous smile broke through Mr. Mahankali's genteel expression. "Okay," he whispered. "Maybe just a little bite."

Smiling to Arthur and the other children, he walked to the elephant's side, signaled to Abigail, who shouted, "*Chalō*!"—which is Hindi for "Let's go!"—and in an instant, they were off—the little girl riding on top of the elephant, the Panther-Man walking alongside, and half of the World's Largest Piece of French Toast trailing behind them, on its way to feed Mr. Mahankali's beastly dependents.

When Sammy had packed up his serving cart, he turned toward the table and said, "Right, you kids. Enjoy the rest of your breakfast. . . . Oh—Arfur—may I speak to you a minute?"

Arthur, startled by the request, looked to Simon—who shrugged at him behind his accordion. "Of course, Sammy," Arthur replied dubiously. He wiped his mouth with his napkin, then hopped over to where the chef stood.

As soon as Arthur had arrived there, Sammy retrieved a sack of coins the size of a coconut and dropped it into the boy's hands. "Fanks for this, mate," he said. "But I can't take your money."

Arthur lowered his shoulders and gave a sheepish grin. It seemed his "donor of modest means" had been discovered. "How did you know it was me?" he said.

"After I found this sack in the kitchen wiv me name on it, I found *this* in a nearby dustbin." Sammy held up a pink ceramic shard, on which the lower half of the word "Arthur" was clearly visible. "This were the piggy bank you were using for your Largest Coin Collection attempt, weren't it?"

Arthur nodded.

"You really shouldn't have, mate. I've caused me own troubles, and it's me who's got to fix them."

"But Sammy, what will you do?"

"Don't worry 'bout old Sammy, mate. I'll find some way to make everyfing work out." The chef gave a warm smile. "Right then," he said, mussing the boy's hair. "Get back to your breakfast before it's completely cold. . . . See you at two for knife-block stocking practice?"

"Yes, sir," Arthur smiled over his shoulder as he hopped back to the table, coins clinking with every bounce. "See you then, Sammy."

"Very good," the chef grinned. "Got some new knife-grip techniques to show you. We'll get you a trophy yet, we will."

With a cheerful wink, Sammy then turned and headed back to the house to begin work on his next colossal culinary masterpiece, otherwise known as "lunch," leaving Arthur, Simon, and Beatrice alone at the table.

It was then, of course, that the horrible thing happened.

• • •

Now into the final stretch of her competitive-eating training session, Beatrice had begun "sprinting" to shovel as much food into her mouth as she could before exceeding her half-hour time limit. She was standing at the right-angled corner of the now triangular piece of French toast—which hung well over the edge of the circular table—while the two boys were positioned about fifteen feet to her left at another of the corners.

As Arthur cut off his next bite, he felt the table wobble slightly and noticed the entire piece of French toast shift to one side.

That's odd, he thought. I'd better mention this to Beatrice so she doesn't . . .

But it was too late.

As Beatrice took one last lunge at her breakfast, the nearby table legs buckled beneath its weight, tipping the table toward her and setting the unstable piece of battered bread in motion.

Arthur and Simon watched in horror as the massive breakfast food slid toward their sister on a river of syrup and butter. As its corner hit the ground, the perilous piece of French toast flipped over and began to fall face down—directly on top of Beatrice.

For a split second, it loomed over her like a tidal wave—and then, she was gone. The little girl with the huge appetite vanished beneath a hulking mass of bread and egg and butter and syrup.

Arthur could not believe what he had just seen. He

turned to his older brother for guidance, but found Simon with his mouth wide open and a look of terror on his face.

Being two years younger than Simon, Arthur had expected his brother to lead any sort of rescue effort they might have launched, but he now saw a tragic conflict in Simon's eyes. Simon glanced down at his accordion—then back up at Arthur with a desperate gaze.

Arthur knew instantly what he had to do.

His brother had been playing that accordion for six days straight, which was no easy task. If Simon were to stop playing it now, all of his hard work would have been for nothing.

It was up to Arthur to save their sister.

Sure, he was in the middle of his own record attempt—for the Longest Time Hopping on One Foot—but who was he kidding? He was never going to actually break it—and everyone knew it. He had never broken any of the records he had attempted. Indeed, with such a history of incompetence, he didn't see how he could possibly help his sister, but there was no time to find someone better suited to the task.

Arthur planted both feet on the ground and ran to the place where his little sister had once stood, his brother following just behind him.

While Simon played a suspenseful piece of music on his accordion, Arthur dug his fingers into the edge of the bread and lifted with all his might. When he had raised the French toast to waist-level, he rested it on his thigh and grabbed a nearby chair. Tipping the chair onto its front side, he forced it underneath the slab of dough, creating a small crevice between the bread and the ground. He then dropped to his stomach and thrust his way head-first inside.

With every inch forward, he drove the chair nearer to the French toast's center, deepening his crawl space as it advanced.

The doughy mass pressed down about him on all sides. But just when it seemed he could go no further, Arthur felt a set of tiny fingers—and grasped hold of them.

If Beatrice had been unconscious, she quickly snapped to when she felt her brother's touch—and was soon wriggling toward him as he pulled her out through the makeshift tunnel.

As Simon's tense accordion tune reached an unbearable peak, Arthur emerged from underneath the rogue piece of French toast, still clutching his sister's arms. He gave one last tug, and Beatrice's head finally appeared, dripping with maple syrup and butter.

Her first gasp of syrup-free air was shortly followed by coughing and spluttering, as she cleared her throat of the sticky sludge that had nearly claimed her life.

By this time, the other Whipples had noticed the commotion and come running to Arthur's aid.

Dashing onto the scene, Mr. Whipple scooped up his daughter and wiped the goo from her nose and mouth. Slowly, Beatrice opened her eyes, and everybody breathed a sigh of relief.

"It was Arthur!" Simon exclaimed. "Not only did he save Beatrice's life—he saved my world record as well!"

Mrs. Whipple hugged Arthur and kissed him on the forehead, drenching her clothes with syrup in the process.

Simon played a hero's theme on his accordion, while other family members showed Arthur their gratitude with hugs and handshakes and pats on the head.

"Nicely done, Brother!" cried Henry. "A few seconds quicker and you might've set a breakfast rescue record!"

"Yeah, Arthur," Cordelia nodded. "Though your form may have left a little to be desired, your use of available structures was completely exceptional!"

Their father, however, looked rather disconcerted. "How did this happen?" he said.

"The table legs just collapsed," said Simon. "One moment they were fine—and the next, *bang*! Beatrice never had a chance."

"Goodness," their mother sighed. "The safety advocates will have a field day with this once the report is published. I've had to cancel our last two table-leg inspections due to our hectic schedule. But at least everybody is all right."

Standing between Arthur and his mother, Mr. Whipple clutched his brow and shook his head.

"What a morning this has been," Arthur heard him mutter. "First, I discover *he's* returning—on the twentieth Rueing Day, no less—and now, this. It's almost as if . . . Oh, God," Mr. Whipple gasped. "It's happening all over again, isn't it? The Lyon's Curse—it's, it's finally come for us. . . ."

"Please, dear," Arthur's mother whispered to her husband, "I'm sure it's not as bad as all that. Really, I don't know why you should be so upset by news of some second-rate record-breaker, and this breakfast business, well—nothing more than a minor mishap in the end, was it? We're all still alive, aren't we? So, clearly, it's not anything like the *curse*. . . . Now, try to pull yourself together, dear—and go commend your son."

Mr. Whipple slowly exhaled, then straightened his shirt. "Yes," he nodded. "Of course, dear. You are no doubt right. Do forgive me. I'm afraid—I'm afraid I'm simply not myself this morning."

He stepped forward and offered his hand to his recordless son, then cleared his throat.

"Well done, Arthur," he smiled, the usual confidence returning to his voice. "By saving your sister's life, you have allowed her the opportunity to continue training for the competitive eating season and the chance to add more trophies to the Whipple Hall of Records. And *that*, my boy, is the greatest gift of all.

"Now," he added. "About your own record attempts: I see you are no longer hopping on one foot. I believe that makes two records in one day you have failed to break. Surely you'll never help us close our critical record gap like this. But don't worry, Son. In honor of your bravery, I shall schedule an extended one-on-one training session for the two of us to discuss your mistakes and analyze the choices which ultimately led to your downfall!"

Mr. Whipple ended in a tone that made it seem he had just offered his son a shopping spree to a sweet shop, when he had really only offered him a lecture on his inadequacies.

With syrup dripping off his nose, Arthur simply smiled.

Little did he know, the darkest era in the history of his family had just begun—with one oversized piece of French toast.

THE SPECTER SPECTACLE

Arthur sat in a chair made entirely of wooden matchsticks. Mounted on the wall behind him, the head of the World's Smallest Moose peered over his left shoulder, while the World's Largest *Mouse* gazed over his right. The two heads were roughly the same size, which would have been rather disconcerting had they been hanging anywhere else but in the Whipple household.

Mr. Whipple stood at an easel, studying an elaborately detailed line graph that charted his son's "failure quotient" for the current calendar year.

This figure was determined by dividing the number of target units in a given world record attempt by the number of actual units achieved. For example, if Arthur needed to crush forty-four raw eggs with his elbow to break the record for Most Raw Eggs Crushed with Elbow in Fifteen Seconds, but he only managed to crush eleven raw eggs, he would be given a failure quotient of four (because of course, forty-four divided by eleven equals four). For timed events, the formula was reversed, and Arthur's failure quotient was determined by dividing his actual time by the target time. For example, if Arthur needed to complete a five-hundred-piece jigsaw puzzle in 136 minutes to break the record for Fastest Time to Complete a Five-Hundred-Piece Jigsaw Puzzle While Blindfolded, but it ended up taking him 408 minutes, he would be given a failure quotient of three (408 ÷ 136 = 3). The higher the number, the bigger the failure.

Lately, Arthur's failure quotients were at an all-time high. Holding a pointer up to the graph, Mr. Whipple looked befuddled. "Now, Son. I'm not entirely sure how you've managed to raise your figures past the already startling levels at which they typically reside, but now you'll have to try even harder if you ever want to get a plaque on that wall."

Arthur's father motioned to the massive glistening wall of plaques behind him. It was truly an awe-inspiring sight. Several symmetrically placed ledges held a vast assortment of trophies, while the rest of the wall was almost completely covered in shimmering plaques, so that the wall itself was barely visible.

In Arthur's dreams, the multitude of plaques graciously spread out to make room for a shiny new comrade—a polished brass plate inscribed with Arthur's name. In his nightmares, the legion of plaques swooped off the wall and attacked him like a swarm of vampire bats. But whatever scenario was playing out in Arthur's head, he could not imagine anything greater than to see his own name on that wall, surrounded by his brothers and sisters and father and mother.

"Our family's under more pressure than ever," Mr. Whipple explained, "what with our current record shortage and the unfortunate press from the 'French Toast Fiasco,' as they're calling it. We've got a reputation to mend—and we can use all the help we can get. Understand?"

Arthur nodded.

"All right, Arthur," said Mr. Whipple. "Just remember what we talked about. There is nothing in this world more rewarding than being the absolute best at one's endeavors. Excellence is in your blood, Son—and I am fairly certain that somewhere deep down inside of you, there is a success- ful boy trying desperately to escape. Now, let's get out there and break some records—or at least not fail so miserably at them, shall we?"

"Yes, Father," replied Arthur. "I'll do my best."

"It's nice to do your best, Son. But it's infinitely better, of course, to *be* the best."

"Yes, sir," said Arthur.

"Very well then," Mr. Whipple concluded, turning back to the easel to pack up his son's charts. "You may—"

A sudden, impulsive thought struck Arthur. "Father?" he said.

"Yes?" Mr. Whipple replied, still fussing with the easel.

The boy bit his lip. "What," he ventured, "is the *Lyon's Curse*?"

Mr. Whipple stopped, then whirled around. "Where have you—?" he stammered. "Who's been—?"

"On Rueing Day," Arthur spluttered. "After the French toast fell—you said . . ."

The hysteria slowly faded from Mr. Whipple's eyes. "I see," he said, letting out a deep sigh. "I—I wish you hadn't heard that."

Sighing again, he peered up at the portrait of the solemn, mustachioed man smoking the World's Longest Pipe in a framed photograph that stretched across the entire rear wall.

"The Lyon's Curse," Arthur's father began, "marked a dark time in our family's history. A time, I'm afraid, whose end your distinguished grandfather never saw. It was a time of fear and of catastrophe—and of failure. . . . But thank God it is all behind us now. There is no use in looking back, Arthur. We must look forward. What you heard the other day, it was just, well—a momentary lapse of clarity. I shan't let it happen again." He cleared his throat and straightened his jacket. "Now, I trust you will leave such matters alone. Surely, you've enough to worry about in your future—such as improving your failure quotients—without bothering about the past."

"Yes, sir," the boy replied. "But I just—"

Arthur's father gave him a stern look.

"Yes, sir," said the boy.

"Very good, Arthur," Mr. Whipple replied. "You are excused."

Arthur's rare, one-on-one meetings with his father never seemed to last long enough—and this one had somehow left him with more questions than it had answered. As the boy exited the Whipple Hall of Records, his mind swam with budding hopes and nagging doubts swirled together in a cloud of nameless fear.

Fortunately, the Whipple estate did not lack for distractions. Glancing at the tiny bonsai-wood clock on the mantel, Arthur was consoled to see he might still catch his sisters' trial attempt at the Highest Hamster-Piloted Model Rocket Launch Ever Recorded.

• • •

Indeed, as the boy stepped out onto the south lawn, he came upon several of his siblings gathered in a semicircle. Wearing a white lab coat, Cordelia was hunched over at its center, tinkering with her custom-built rocket, while Abigail stood beside Penelope, Beatrice, Franklin, and George, clutching an adorable and utterly unsuspecting hamster with both hands.

If he had only been given the luxury of a mirror, the fluffy little rodent might have had a better clue as to what the near future had in store for him.

He was wearing a tiny astronaut suit.

"Is our daring space explorer ready?" inquired Cordelia as she made one last adjustment with a socket wrench.

Abigail kissed the top of the daring space explorer's furry little head, then placed a tiny astronaut helmet over it. "Aye. Ready, sir. Ready and eager to serve his country," she replied.

"Excellent," said Cordelia. "I trust the pilot has been checked for enemy bugs?"

"Aye, sir," said Penelope, holding up a stoppered tube with three bouncing black dots inside it. "Pilot is now certified flea-free."

"Very good, Private," said Cordelia. "Unlocking cockpit." She flipped a latch on the side of the rocket that allowed the nose to hinge outward, revealing a miniature control room with pushpins for dials and tin foil for navigation monitors. "Pilot may now take position."

Abigail stepped forward and handed the miniature pilot to Cordelia, who placed him in the miniature pilot seat and buckled him in with a tiny seat belt.

"Pilot secured," announced Cordelia. "Sealing cockpit."

She hinged the nose of the rocket back into launch position. The little hamster astronaut looked a bit worried beneath his space helmet.

Cordelia and Abigail took a few steps back. Abigail put her tiny arm around Hamlet, her towering canine companion and typical mode of transportation, who was sitting on his haunches and waiting patiently for the launch sequence to commence. Beatrice swallowed the last bite of cider-braised lamb chop she'd been having as a light snack and tossed the bone at the dog's feet. With a tip of his bicorne hat, Franklin handed the remote control switch to Cordelia, who stood up straight and proud and said, "We are cleared for launch."

A wave of excitement rushed over Arthur. He had made it just in time.

"Ten. Nine. Eight. Seven . . ."

Cordelia began the countdown, and Arthur made his way around his siblings to get a clear view of the launchpad.

"Six. Five. Four . . ."

By the time Cordelia had called out "Three," Arthur had walked to the end of the line of onlookers and could see the rocket perfectly. What Arthur did not see, however, was the spool of fishing line that had been anchored into the ground behind him—and the single strand that had been attached to the side of the rocket as a way of measuring the height of the launch.

"Three. Two. One. Ignition!"

As Cordelia pressed the big red button on the remote control, Arthur took one last step to his right—and caught the strand of fishing line with his foot. To the shock and horror of all who had gathered, the rocket suddenly jerked toward them, its nose pointing menacingly in their direction—as flames began to stream from its thrusters.

Arthur, realizing what he had done, yanked his foot off the line and threw himself onto Penelope and George, who were standing nearest to him.

Just as the three siblings tumbled to the ground, the

rocket launched off its base at a 45-degree angle and shot over them—whizzing through the space that, only moments earlier, George's head had occupied.

The children spun around to watch, as the Uncontrollable Flying Object sped away over the treetops.

When the rocket was only an orange speck against the evening sky, the children could just make out the profile of a parachute, attached to a small shiny blob drifting on the horizon. It seemed the tiny ejection seat had functioned properly, and there was, at that moment, an uncommonly confused hamster floating through the troposphere, considerably more world-weary than he had been just thirty seconds before. The children watched it for another moment, before the parachute descended behind the trees and out of sight.

Arthur picked himself up off the ground, and immediately felt the icy glare of his sister piercing through him.

"Arthur!" squealed Cordelia. "What have you done?!"

"I'm terribly sorry," Arthur stammered. "I didn't see the string, and—"

"Our official attempt is scheduled to launch at 0900 tomorrow morning, and thanks to you, we no longer have a rocket! You know we can't afford the slightest setback if we're to make our record quota by our birthday—it's like you're *trying* to lose the championships for us!"

"Please, Cordelia—don't say that. The attempt's not spoiled yet, is it? If we just follow the string, shouldn't it lead us to wherever the rocket's landed? Perhaps we'll be able to retrieve it fairly easily."

"If it hasn't landed in a lake!" cried Cordelia. "And even if it hasn't, what about our daring space explorer? How do you propose to retrieve *him*? He could be anywhere—and how are we going to launch a hamster-piloted rocket without a hamster pilot?!"

"What about one of the other hamsters?" Arthur suggested.

"Don't be silly, Arthur. Corporal Whiskerton is the only hamster trained for this mission. Do you really think just any old hamster can be a successful rocket pilot?!"

Arthur shook his head. The training to which Cordelia referred consisted solely of persuading their twitchy subject to sit still while wearing a seat belt attached to a tiny chair. It had truly been a breakthrough in hamster conditioning.

"I'm really very sorry, Cordelia. But I'm sure he can't have gone too far—what with the space suit and parachute and all. We're bound to find him before the sun goes down."

"Well," said Cordelia with a sigh of resignation, "if we don't find him soon, he'll run off and join a pack of wild hamsters, and we'll never see him again."

Arthur had not been aware of the apparently enormous population of wild hamsters in the neighborhood. As a matter of fact, he couldn't remember seeing a single wild hamster in his entire life—not even in books. But he figured the tame ones had to come from somewhere.

As the group set out from Neverfall in search of the missing rocket and its furry little pilot, Arthur kept a constant lookout for any uncivilized hamsters who might have absconded with the good corporal. The thought of savage hamster packs roaming the streets was really rather unnerving—albeit in an adorable sort of way.

• • •

Surprisingly, Corporal Whiskerton proved much easier to find than anyone had expected.

His parachute had caught in one of the elm trees on the neighboring Nesbit estate, on a branch just out of reach of Mrs. Nesbit's Irish terrier, Fergus, who was now leaping up and down beneath the tree, barking furiously as he tried to catch the hamster's dangling feet in his slobbery jaws.

Corporal Whiskerton wore an expression that suggested he had become rather disillusioned with space exploration. Luckily, help was not far off.

Upon spotting their downed comrade, the children rushed to his aid, appalled that a hero of such courage should be made to suffer such abuse. One bellowing bark from Hamlet sent the once-intimidating terrier cowering toward the Nesbit house with his tail between his legs.

"Enemy unit eliminated," announced Cordelia. "Prepare for retrieval."

The giant Great Dane, still carrying Abigail on his back, stretched out his neck and removed the parachute from the branch with his teeth, then dropped the traumatized hamster into his rider's hands. Corporal Whiskerton looked relieved. Arthur shared his sentiment.

The boy stroked Hamlet's shoulder. "Thanks, Hammie," he whispered. "I owe you one."

The dog licked Arthur's face in reply.

Having completed their first objective, the Whipple children set out once again after their vanished aircraft, following the strand of fishing line to the far edge of the Nesbit estate.

From there, they continued across the estates of their next two neighbors—until they came to an imposing stone wall, which brought their recovery mission to an abrupt halt. Over the wall's crest, between two of the spear-shaped iron shafts that jutted up from it, the line disappeared from sight.

It was far worse than they had feared: the rocket had landed on the Crosley estate.

• • •

Maxwell Crosley had been the president of the Rikki-Tikki Toffee Company—the Largest Toffee Manufacturer in the World—whose confections had once been loved far and wide by children of all ages. Ironically, Mr. Crosley detested children—but there was a lot of money to be made in the toffee business, so he purchased a majority stake in the company when its original founder had died. To cut costs, Mr. Crosley proceeded to alter the century-old family recipe to include substandard ingredients and barely edible industrial chemicals. After several children died upon ingesting his company's products, Mr. Crosley avoided financial ruin by slightly altering the recipe again and changing its name to Miracle Mud®, a product that went on to revolutionize the tiling and grout industry. In a bizarre twist of fate, Mr. Crosley met an untimely but fitting end when he fell into one of the Miracle Mud® vats while giving a factory tour to a group of potential investors.

In the six years since its owner's demise, the Crosley estate had fallen into disrepair and was said to be haunted by the ghosts of the unfortunate children killed by Mr. Crosley's greed. Needless to say, it was not the sort of place one would want her custom-built, hamster-piloted model rocket to crash-land.

The previously plucky band of rescuers stared up at the unwelcoming wall of stone.

"So what now, Arthur?" demanded Cordelia.

"Um . . . well, maybe it landed just past the wall," the boy suggested. "Could we try to reel it in?"

Cordelia rolled her eyes and tugged halfheartedly on the line. To her surprise, the line actually moved. "I can feel the rocket on the other end!" she exclaimed, grinning to the others as she began pulling it toward her.

Arthur could hardly believe his luck. It appeared there was still hope for the rescue team after all.

But when Cordelia had reeled in four yards of the line, it refused to give any further.

The girl arched her brow and gave a tug. "I think it's snagged on something," she said.

After all they had been through, Cordelia was not about

to be thwarted by such a minor detail. She pulled harder and harder on the line—but still, it would not budge. She leaned back on the line with all her weight and gave one last tug—and with that, the string abruptly gave way, sending Arthur's sister tumbling to the ground.

Somewhere on the other side of the wall, the line had snapped.

"Are you all right, Cordelia?" asked Arthur, running to help her.

"I was—until you decided to ruin *everything*!" she shouted. "It took me months to perfect that rocket, and now we'll miss our launch—and we'll never break enough records in time!" She put her head in her hands and started to cry.

It broke Arthur's heart to see his sister crying; it was even worse knowing he was the cause of her tears.

"I'll get it for you, Cordelia," he said.

Cordelia sniffled and glanced up at her little brother. "But how? That wall must be twelve feet high."

"It doesn't look completely unclimbable," replied Arthur, sounding far more confident than he actually was.

He glanced down to find his little sister, Beatrice, tugging at his shirt. Ever since he had rescued her from the rogue piece of French toast, he wondered if she didn't look at him just a bit differently somehow.

"But Arthur," Beatrice whispered, "what about the ghosts?"

"Oh, right. The ghosts," said Arthur.

In his eagerness to atone for losing the rocket, he had momentarily forgotten about the Crosley estate's ghastly reputation.

"Um . . . they don't come out until dark, do they?" he asked, gazing up at the fading light of the now heavily clouded sky.

Beatrice shrugged.

This was not the response Arthur had hoped for.

"I'm pretty sure ghosts can more or less come out whenever they please," remarked Cordelia, who had perked up considerably after evaluating her brother's offer. Then, sensing his growing discomfort, she added, "But don't worry, Arthur. Ghosts don't generally murder mortals whose hearts are pure. And you're fairly pure of heart, aren't you?"

Arthur looked puzzled. "I suppose so," he said.

"Yep. You'll be fine," said Cordelia. "But you should probably be heading out now—if you want to make it back before dark."

"Oh. Right," said Arthur.

His soul-searching cut short, the boy stepped up to the towering wall and began searching for a handhold. But before he started his ascent, he turned to his sister one last time. "Oh, um, Cordelia," he added, "do you think you might be able to time me?"

Cordelia shot him a bewildered glance.

"It's just that, well," Arthur explained, "it's not every day one gets the chance to break the record for Fastest Time to Scale a Twelve-Foot Stone Wall. I was just reading about wall scaling in the *Grazelby Guide* the other day. I believe the current record is forty-nine seconds—which doesn't seem like it should be *too* difficult to break."

But Arthur wasn't being entirely forthcoming about his motives. The truth was, he could not bear the thought of being murdered by ghosts before he had broken even a single world record.

With a sigh, Cordelia removed a stopwatch from her coat and held it at the ready.

"Thanks, Cordelia. I really do appreciate it," said Arthur, his mind slightly more at ease as he turned to face the wall once again.

Luckily, the wall was quite rough, with stones of different shapes and sizes protruding from its face, thus providing plenty of footing for Arthur's benefit. Considering the wall's perilous height, however, it did not seem to him the sort of climb that should be overly rushed.

"And, go," said Cordelia, long before her brother was ready.

Arthur clutched at a stone far above his head and scrambled to jam his right foot into a crevice between two stones at the base of the wall. Heaving himself up with his arms, he straightened his right leg and shifted his weight onto it. As Arthur's other foot left the ground, he realized there was no turning back. He would have to retrieve the rocket or die trying.

After several harrowing moments of hunting for handholds and hoisting himself higher and higher up the wall, Arthur briefly paused to catch his breath. He had always heard that one should refrain from looking downward when climbing at extreme heights, so he had been careful to avoid all eye contact with the ground below. But the more he thought about it, the more curious he became, and the more tempted he was to peek. He fought back and forth with the destructive impulse to look, until finally, he could no longer contain his curiosity, and the impulse prevailed.

Arthur peered over his shoulder—and started at his distance from the ground. It was only three feet away.

He glanced back at his siblings, and found—instead of the impromptu cheering squad he had been imagining in his head—a row of perplexed faces, baffled by their brother's ineptitude at timed stone-wall climbing.

Apparently sensing the awkwardness surrounding him, Hamlet trotted up to Arthur and licked him on the cheek (which still wasn't much higher than the dog's normal eye level)—as if to say, "It's all right, little friend—you can start climbing now."

Arthur turned back toward the wall and did his best to resume the ascent, hoping that by focusing on climbing, he might forget about his recent embarrassment. Finding a solid handhold to his left, the boy pulled himself up a few more inches.

• • •

After an exhausting climb (and more than a few near falls), Arthur finally planted his feet on the murky turf of the Crosley estate.

"I made it!" he shouted back over the wall.

There was a strange silence, and for a moment, Arthur wondered if his siblings had left him behind. But then the comforting sound of his older sister's condescending voice met his ear.

"Eight minutes, seventeen seconds," called the voice. "I don't think you quite broke the record there, Arthur."

He had suspected as much, but now it was official. His last possible record attempt before his impending doom had failed. Miserably.

"I can't see the rocket from here," Arthur called back. "I'm going to try and follow the string."

"Best shove off soon," urged Franklin. "There's a stiff breeze blowing nor'-nor'-west with a bit of the old 'sea smoke' on it."

"Looks like prime spider habitat," added Penelope. "Bring me back a specimen if you can."

"Be careful, Arthur," Beatrice warned in a loud whisper.

"And try not to anger the ghosts," called George.

Arthur turned toward the Crosley grounds. In the haze of the setting sun, he could hardly make out the glint of the fishing line through the tangled branches overhead—but he did his best to follow it as it led away from the massive stone wall behind him.

. . .

Though the Crosley estate was horribly overgrown with gnarled trees and twisting vines, it was—at least so far—surprisingly ghost free. This, of course, was no small comfort to Arthur.

Perhaps it isn't haunted after all, he thought. *Perhaps I'll actually make it home alive.*

But after walking through mud and brambles for several minutes, the boy's doubts came swiftly racing back. Hard as he tried, he could no longer see the guiding string above him. Glancing backward, he found he could no longer see the wall either. A thick fog had rolled in and surrounded him on all sides, not only inhibiting his quest—but his escape, as well. Not knowing what else to do, Arthur pressed forward, hoping he might regain sight of the line further up ahead.

There was only one problem with this course of action: Arthur no longer had any way of knowing which direction "forward" was.

By the time he realized this, however, it was too late. He'd become completely and utterly lost. From where he stood, the scenery looked eerily similar from every angle as dark, contorted branches stabbed at him through the grayish fog.

Arthur thought of all the stories he'd read in which some poor child has found himself lost in the woods and suddenly discovers that the trees have come to life, their branches mutating into massive spiky hands, clawing at the poor child in an attempt to pull him into a gaping, fanged mouth that only moments before had been merely an oversized knothole. Luckily, Arthur was not so gullible. He knew that such stories were largely exaggerated, and that trees—however sinister they might appear when you were lost amongst them—did not generally eat children. He had learned long ago from Dr. Twigg, his Record-Breaking Botany instructor (and one of the Whipple children's many tutors), that trees gained the vast majority of their nutrients through the process of photosynthesis, while receiving water and minerals through the soil. Indeed, the amount of a tree's diet that was composed of lost children was so minuscule, Dr. Twigg had explained, that really, it was almost not worth mentioning.

And so, feeling he had a far greater chance of falling into a bottomless pit or being murdered by ghosts than he ever had of being eaten by a tree, Arthur decided to sit himself against the nearest trunk and wait for the fog to clear.

With each passing minute, Arthur fell deeper and deeper into despair. The fog was not clearing. And with fog so thick, and daylight fading so quickly, he had no idea how he would ever find the rocket and escape before nightfall. Cordelia and Abigail would be forced to cancel their official launch the next morning, and in the days to follow, someone would find Arthur's cold, lifeless, recordless body still leaning against the spookiest tree on the Crosley estate—with no rocket to show for his efforts. Once again, he would prove to be an utter disappointment to the Whipple family name.

In a fit of desperation, Arthur flung his head back against the tree—and was suddenly filled with hope.

There, in the branches above him, was the faint outline of what appeared to be a model rocket.

• • •

Until that moment, Arthur had felt so down, he had entirely forgotten to look up—and now he could scarcely believe his eyes. But there it was, on a branch about eight feet up— the rocket, in all its miniature glory, waiting patiently to be found.

The boy leapt to his feet. Though he was no record-breaking tree climber (unlike his brother Edward, who held several records in the sport), the thought of actually living to see his twelfth birthday gave him a sudden boost of energy.

Arthur made light work of the trunk and quickly clambered through the tree's lower branches—until he reached the limb that held the object of his quest.

The rocket was positioned toward the end of the branch, a good three yards from the trunk—and well out of Arthur's reach. With great care, the boy wrapped his arms and legs around the limb and began to inch his way forward.

Soon he was out on the branch, completely separated from the security of the trunk. As Arthur neared the rocket, he felt the branch creak beneath his weight and sensed that if he ventured much further, it would no longer be able to withstand the strain. But he was almost there. Just another foot or so, and he would be within reach of the rocket.

The decrepit limb bowed further and further as Arthur made one last push forward. With his index finger fully extended, he barely brushed the tip of the rocket's nose—but he dared not move any closer. Inhaling, he strained to use every bit of stretchiness left in his body—and just managed to grasp the rocket's nose between his thumb and forefinger. As he pulled the rocket toward him, Arthur felt the tension in his bones melt away. He had done it.

Before he could climb off the branch, however, he was startled by a peculiar noise. In an instant, Arthur forgot all about his recent accomplishment.

A strange swirl of mist rose up from the ground below. And then, as Arthur watched in surprise and terror, a ghostly figure emerged from the fog.

• • •

Arthur froze. He had never seen a ghost before; he could only hope the ghost would never see him.

The figure continued its advance and then stopped a few yards from the base of the tree, almost directly below the boy's position.

His view obscured by the branches beneath him, Arthur could just make out the vague features of the wraith's terrifying form.

It appeared to be a girl. And she appeared to be crying.

His heart racing, Arthur watched as the ghost sat itself on a tree stump and put its head in its hands. Despite his terror, he could not help but pity the poor spirit. How awful it must have been to be killed at such a young age by ingesting toxic toffee. But Arthur was no fool. He knew that malevolent spirits often assume sympathetic forms as a way of luring in their victims. If he allowed it to get close enough, it would no doubt transform into its true monstrous self and devour his soul.

As this was not an acceptable outcome for Arthur, he decided to remain perfectly still and wait for the ghost to pass.

But instead of returning to the foul mist whence it had come, the ghost lingered. It sat on the stump and continued to quietly sob, as if nothing else existed. The more Arthur watched it, the more enchanted he became. Its sympathetic guise had taken its effect, and the boy was powerless to stop it.

Convincing himself his current vantage point did not offer the clearest view, Arthur leaned his head out for a more suitable perspective. That was all it took. There was a sudden crack. The ghost girl looked up. And then Arthur was falling through the air.

In a dreamlike state, the boy crashed through the branches below, until the ground provided an unwelcome wake-up call. Arthur struck the earth with a gut-wrenching thud.

He gasped for breath and peered up—only to find he was now lying at the phantom's feet. Unable to look away, he locked eyes with the sinister spirit. Its face was pale and streaked with tears, which streamed from two sparkling green eyes pink at the edges from so much crying.

It began to move closer.

Paralyzed by fear and still gulping for air, Arthur watched helplessly as the demon-in-disguise approached its fallen prey.

Then, from out of the night, came a distant yet familiar voice.

Arthur! it called.

Arthur and the wraith turned toward the voice with a start. There, shining through the fog, was the far-off beam of a flashlight.

This was Arthur's chance.

Summoning his will to live, the boy leapt to his feet, scooped up the rocket, and bolted toward the light.

As he tore through the undergrowth, Arthur dared not look back. Soon he could see the shape of the wall looming before him, the battery-powered beacon gleaming down from its spiked ridge.

"Arthur, is that you?" asked the voice behind the beam.

Standing atop the wall, Cordelia shined her flashlight in the boy's face.

"It's him!" she shouted down the other side of the wall. Turning back toward her brother, she added, "Where in the world have you—"

"Catch!" yelled a breathless Arthur, tossing the rocket up to his sister as he approached the base of the wall.

Cordelia—who incidentally held the record for one-handed arrow catching—effortlessly caught the rocket with her free hand, examined it in astonishment, then dropped it behind her for the other members of the search party to retrieve.

Arthur's lightning pace slowed only slightly when he reached the wall and began to climb. Soon he was passing Cordelia at the top and scrambling down the other side.

It was not until he'd planted both feet safely on the ground—and off the Crosley estate—that he stopped to catch his breath.

"You did it, Arthur," whispered Beatrice as she wrapped her arms around his waist.

"Woof!" said Hamlet.

"My thoughts exactly," smiled Abigail.

"Glad to see you all as well," panted Arthur.

"One minute, sixteen seconds!" called Cordelia, holding the flashlight to her stopwatch as she peered down at her brother from the top of the wall. "Quite an improvement, Arthur—but still not quite good enough. I'm afraid stone-wall climbing just isn't your event. On the plus side, it seems you've managed to preserve our record quota by retrieving the rocket you lost—though you certainly took your time about it. We walked all the way back to Neverfall to fetch a light, and you still weren't here when we got back. I climbed up the wall for a closer look—and then suddenly, there you were, charging at me like a wounded wildebeest. What in good Grazelby happened over there to make you run like that?"

"You mean you didn't see it?" gasped Arthur.

"See what?" said Cordelia.

"Never mind," Arthur replied, too exhausted from the ordeal to recount it.

Cordelia shot him a skeptical glance, then tossed him the flashlight and started down the wall.

As Arthur held the light for his sister, he began to wonder if he had simply imagined the entire thing. But when he recalled the spirit's tears and sparkling, swollen eyes, he became convinced it could not have been just a dream.

It was certainly a relief to be out of the haunted grounds of the Crosley estate, but Arthur had not escaped entirely unscathed. Now, he too was haunted—by the memory of his mysterious encounter.

As the rescue team headed home under the moonlit sky, Arthur did his best to push the otherworldly images to the back of his mind. Traumatic as the day had been, it had not been entirely fruitless. His second attempt at the wall had garnered him a failure quotient of 1.55, which—while still technically a failure—was a vast improvement over any of his recent numbers. He could hardly wait to tell his father. He had finally returned to only failing moderately, instead of miserably. And all it had taken was the threat of having his soul devoured by a shape-shifting poltergeist.

ARTHUR WHIPPLE'S BIRTHDAY WISH

It **is more or** less common knowledge that a leap year occurs once every four years, and that in this year, an extra day is added to the end of February, creating a twenty-ninth day when there are usually only twenty-eight. The reason for this is simple: a long time ago, some very clever scientist types discovered that it actually takes the earth slightly longer than 365 days to travel around the sun— about 365.242375 days, to be exactish. Of course, that extra 0.242375 of a day is pretty close to 0.25, or a quarter of a day, and four quarters equals one whole. So instead of tacking on an extra quarter of a day every year, which would just be a headache for everyone involved, these very clever scientist types decided to add one whole day every four years. It must have seemed a good idea at the time.

They probably even won some kind of science award for it. But with all their intelligence and test tubes and telescopes, they failed to realize one fatal flaw in their solution: from then on, every child born on the twenty-ninth of February would be doomed to only having a birthday once every four years. These ill-fated individuals have come to be called "leaplings," and, of course, Arthur Whipple was one of them.

It is suspected that some leaplings' families have tried to soften the blow by celebrating their luckless child's birthday on the twenty-eighth of February or the first of March in non-leap years, but unfortunately for Arthur, the thought had never occurred to the Whipples. And so he became accustomed to celebrating the day of his birth rather infrequently. It didn't help matters that, besides Arthur, every person in the Whipple family shared the same birthday—on the very day which, by all good sense, should have been his own.

Every non-leap year, at the end of February, Arthur would get the thrilling sense that his birthday was coming very soon. But every non-leap year, to his dismay, the first of March would arrive instead—and with it, the Whipple Family Birthday Extravaganza.

It certainly wasn't all bad, though. On that day, Mr. and Mrs. Whipple always let Arthur have an extra piece of cake to make up for his lack of birthday parties. Indeed, Arthur very much enjoyed his family's enormous yearly celebration—but celebrating someone else's birthday, however fun it may be, is never quite the same as celebrating one's own.

Unfortunately, leap years did not seem entirely his own either. Though the boy finally got his own party on his actual birthday, everyone was so preoccupied with planning the next day's festivities, Arthur's party tended to be a bit rushed. He tried not to notice. Truly, he was happy just to have a party at all. Arthur was turning twelve years old, and this was only his third birthday party.

• • •

Arthur's party had been relegated to the study, which was virtually the only room in Neverfall Hall not bustling with preparations for the ensuing extravaganza. On the table in front of him was one last unopened present. He had just finished unwrapping the World's Quietest Noisemaker, which had been a gift from his parents, and before that, the Tiniest Model Train Set on the Planet, which conveniently came with its own microscope, so that the train's owner might actually see what he was playing with.

Seated around the table were Arthur's parents and siblings, as well as Uncle Mervyn, while Mrs. Waite, the housekeeper, and Wilhelm, the butler, stood dutifully behind their employers. It was a meager gathering, but one could hardly expect such important friends of the Whipples to attend two parties in two days at the same location—and so the foreign dignitaries and millionaires and movie stars had only been invited to the family's Birthday Extravaganza, leaving the guest list for Arthur's party terribly short.

Arthur picked up his last unopened gift. It was wrapped

in brown paper and tied with a leather cord. Sticking out from beneath the bow was a small card. It read: *To Arthur. May this bring you luck in times of need. Your devoted uncle, Mervyn.*

The boy was intrigued by the inscription, but he hesitated for a moment. It would be another four years before he would get to open another birthday present. . . .

His youngest brother, George, checked his watch.

"Arthur, dear," prodded Mrs. Whipple, "we've still got a dozen records to break tonight if we're to make the championships eligibility requirement by the end of the extravaganza tomorrow—not to mention the additional preparations and inspections to be done in light of the French Toast Fiasco. If we wish to silence our critics, we must take time to ensure there are no further incidents. So, do you think we might hurry it up just a bit?"

"Oh—sorry, Mother," said Arthur.

He slid his finger along one side of the package and peeled back the paper. After revealing a well-worn cigar box, Arthur flipped open the lid.

There, in the middle of the box, sat a single domino tile with three white dots on one end and four on the other.

Uncle Mervyn grinned. "During my brief foray into record breaking—when I was just a few years older than you are now—this domino was in the lineup that secured my record for Most Dominoes Single-Handedly Toppled. There were 378,000 dominoes in that setup, but this one has special powers."

"Really?" said Arthur. "Was it the first in the chain—the one that started it all?"

"No, it wasn't the first," replied his uncle.

"Then was it the last—the one that actually set the record?"

"It was neither the first nor the last. In fact, I don't remember which number it was. Somewhere in the eighty-thousands, I think."

"But what's so special about this one, then?" puzzled Arthur.

"This domino is just as remarkable as the first or the last. Because without *this* domino, the whole thing would have stopped dead. And that's what gives this magical domino its power."

Arthur's brother Henry rolled his eyes at the word "magical."

"Magical?" said Arthur, his eyes growing wide.

"All right, Arthur. That's quite enough," interjected Mrs. Whipple. "Now what do you say to your uncle Mervyn?"

"Thanks, Uncle Mervyn. Thank you very much."

"Really, Mervyn," Arthur's mother added with an uneasy smile, "you didn't need to get him anything—you're too generous!"

This was not the first "magical" gift Arthur had received from his uncle—and Mrs. Whipple had not forgotten the troubles the last one had caused. After Uncle Mervyn had given the boy a magical gardening trowel (which, he'd explained, when used to dig a hole, had the unique power to increase the size of something by actually taking away from it), Arthur had been inspired to attempt the record for Most Holes Dug in One's Own Garden. The north lawn had never quite looked the same since.

"It was no trouble at all, Eliza," Uncle Mervyn replied with a smile and a wink to his godson. "Surely a boy of Arthur's age should never be without a magical object in his possession."

Arthur smiled back, then turned reverently to his domino. As he reached down to pick up his uncle's latest gift, he half expected a surge of electricity when he touched it—but the little black tile remained still as the boy gently dropped it into his shirt pocket.

• • •

The door opened and the lights dimmed. As Wilhelm carried in Arthur's birthday cake alongside Sammy the Spatula, the dancing candlelight illuminated the butler's thick handlebar mustache and cast large spiral shadows upon his rosy cheeks.

The cake, iced in plain white and topped with twelve slender candles, was neither very large nor very small, yet distinctive in a way currently quite obvious to the champion strongman who carried it.

"How do you like it, Arthur?" Mr. Whipple grinned. "At one ounce per cubic inch, it's the Densest Cake Ever Baked—with a total weight of sixty-three pounds! Sammy tells me he devised the recipe in prison for use as a bludgeoning tool. Thrilling, isn't it?"

Wilhelm set the cake in front of Arthur. The table groaned in protest.

"Yes," replied Arthur, turning to the chef. "Thanks, Sammy. It's really, um—monumental."

Smiling uncomfortably, Sammy the Spatula leaned in to Arthur and whispered, "Sorry 'bout the cake, mate. Afraid we got our signals crossed, your parents and me. In the mayhem of party planning, I somehow got the impression they wanted a birthday-themed doorstop. Honestly, mate, if I'd known it were for you, I'd've suggested somefing a good bit tastier."

"No, really, Sammy," Arthur assured him, "it's perfect."

"No it ain't, Arfur. And I aim to make it up to you. Bake a whole nuvver one tomorrow, I will—World's Tastiest—just for you," the chef winked cheerfully. "'Ow's that sound?"

"Well," Arthur smiled, "if you insist."

"Indeed I do," Sammy said with a nod.

At this, Simon and Cordelia launched into an accordion/ violin rendition of "Happy Birthday to You" (less, perhaps, because it was Arthur's birthday, than because it held the record for Most Popular Song in the English Language). Before long, they were playing the last note, and Arthur realized the moment he had dreamt about for four long years had finally arrived: it was time for his birthday wish.

In order to stretch the moment out as long as he could, Arthur pretended to be thinking of what to wish for—but in truth, he had known all along exactly what his wish would be. He did his best to continue stalling, until he noticed the octuplets fidgeting in their chairs. It seemed he had delayed as long as his family would allow, so he closed his eyes and began his wish.

I wish, Arthur thought to himself, *that I was a world record holder.*

But as soon as the wish had entered his mind, his heart became troubled. As Arthur grew increasingly aware of all the eyes fixed upon him, he was struck by an unsettling thought: everyone had known all along what his wish would be.

And how could they not have? Of course he would wish for the one thing that constantly eluded him.

Arthur had always known his failures were a matter of public record, but he had assumed his dreams belonged to him. At that moment, however, he realized his well-known failures had betrayed his most secret hopes, and that the one thing he thought he had achieved on his own—his very dreams—had been predicted by everyone else, even before he had dreamed them himself.

The boy glanced around the table at his restless siblings. They each had an expression that seemed to say, Come on, Arthur—make your wish, already. The whole world already knows what you're going to wish for. . . .

Cordelia tapped her foot and glanced toward the ceiling, while George stared at his own nose, apparently practicing for an eye-crossing record. Even Beatrice peered hungrily at the cake, willing Arthur to finish his wish so she could dig in.

Arthur looked back to the cake. He was no birthday-wishing expert, but he was pretty sure it was fair to alter a wish at the last moment—and that it was the last wish made before blowing out one's candles that actually counted. He had half a second to think of a less obvious wish—before his family tore him limb from limb.

I wish . . . that I belonged, thought Arthur.

It was something his family might not guess right away, and that gave Arthur a new boost of confidence. He opened his eyes and took a deep breath—deep enough to ensure victory over the twelve trembling flames before him. There was no chance of failure now. All he had to do was extinguish a few tiny candles and surely, his wish would be granted.

With his lungs filled to capacity, he pursed his lips and prepared to blow. But before any air had left his mouth, the study door flew open, creating a gust of wind that snuffed out Arthur's candles in an instant.

"This will do," said the short, chubby man who had barged into the room. "Just wheel it into that back corner over there. We only need to get it out of the way for a few minutes while they load the giant squid steaks into the refrigerator."

Two men entered the room pushing a large cart. Sitting on the cart and wrapped in cellophane was a life-size statue of the Whipple family, sculpted in Gouda cheese. Each family member's likeness had been painstakingly carved into the enormous cheese block in honor of their birthday celebration the next day—each, of course, but Arthur's.

At the sight of the World's Most Intricate Cheese Sculpture, the Whipples sprang from their chairs and rushed over for a closer look.

"That looks just like you, Daddy," declared Penelope as she pointed to the Whipple patriarch's cheesy bust.

"I dare say you're right, Penelope," Mr. Whipple replied. "The resemblance is uncanny. Why, we may as well be looking in a mirror!"

Still seated at the table, Arthur looked down at his cherished birthday cake as tiny wisps of smoke escaped from the blackened candlewicks.

THE WHIPPLE FAMILY
BIRTHDAY EXTRAVAGANZA

Using a small fork, the Cannibal King of Manawatu carved a chunk off of Mrs. Whipple's arm and spread it onto a sesame cracker. The life-size cheese sculpture of the Whipple family had proved a huge hit amongst the guests of the Whipple Family Birthday Extravaganza. Much of Mr. Whipple's head was now dispersed throughout the party on appetizer plates in the hands of various guests as they mingled on the east lawn.

The Cannibal King, who politely abstained from his usual customs whenever he was fortunate enough to be invited to the Whipple estate, added one last mini quiche to his plate before stepping away from the hors d'oeuvre table. Every visible part of his body—including his large, clean-shaven head, his weathered face, and his massive, sinewy hands—

was covered with the tribal tattoos of the Māori, the bold native people of New Zealand. He was in fact the World's Most Tattooed Man, with tattoos covering 99.9 percent of his skin. At the present moment, however, most of his tattoos were concealed by his dinner jacket and black tie, which was common attire for all the male guests that evening.

The brutish gentleman made his way toward the bar, where he brushed past a brown-haired boy carrying two glasses of ginger ale.

"Pardon me, little man," the cannibal said in a deep primal voice.

Arthur glanced at the man's face, then quickly looked away. "N-no trouble, sir," the boy stammered as he walked past.

But it wasn't so much the Cannibal King's diet that intimidated Arthur—as it was his celebrity status. Unbeknownst to everyone else at the bar, there was a Cannibal King poster hanging upstairs on Arthur's wall and a mint-condition Cannibal King rookie card framed on Arthur's bookcase. Arthur, who could hardly handle a flu shot or eat a bite of liver without wincing, couldn't help but be fascinated with the tattooed man's seeming imperviousness to pain and impossibly strong stomach.

His heart beating a little more quickly now, the boy made his way through the crowd and headed off across the lawn.

The grounds of Neverfall Hall were strewn with dozens of small stages, and crowds had formed around each of them to watch various persons perform various record-breaking feats. The current crop of performers consisted of those fortunate guests and Whipple associates who had been invited to attempt records in the family's honor—though Mr. Whipple had made certain, of course, that none of them posed even the slightest threat to his family's championship hopes.

The Whipples themselves had taken to the stages the previous hour and—amidst Arthur's exuberant cheers—had set about breaking record after record in pursuit of reaching their critical quota before midnight. Indeed, with Charlotte's record for Fastest Family Portrait Painted on the Head of a Pin and Penelope's record for Most Fireflies Employed in Spelling Out a Floating Message (HAPPY BIRTHDAY TO US!), not to mention little Ivy's record for Fastest Viennese Waltz with a Stuffed-Toy Partner without Falling Over or Being Sick, Arthur's family had nearly managed to meet the eligibility requirement already, with several hours left to spare.

Unsurprisingly—though he'd spent countless hours preparing an attempt of his own—Arthur had not been asked to participate.

The boy's only consolation was the high honor of helping with his family's birthday cake later that evening. Having never been entrusted with any sort of official birthday duty before, he was thrilled to finally get the chance. If he could not join his family in sharing a birthday, at least he might help them to celebrate it.

Until that time, however, his sole responsibility was to enjoy the party. With his family now on break to perform various birthday activities, such as showing guests around the estate and posing for photographs in the Whipple Hall of World Records, the boy had been placed in the care of Uncle Mervyn and Mrs. Waite, whose drinks he was presently on his way to deliver.

After passing by a woman on stage who was in the process of eating a school bus, piece by piece, and was at that moment gnawing on the gear lever, Arthur passed a man who had clipped 167 clothespins to his own face and was reaching for another. The next act, however, so piqued Arthur's curiosity that he put his errand on hold and stopped for a closer look.

On a stage surrounded by over three dozen onlookers stood two suspicious-looking clowns.

Arthur was aware, of course, that many people regard *all* clowns with a great deal of suspicion, without any other reason than the simple fact that they are *clowns*. Indeed, it was a stereotype the IBCPC (International Brotherhood of Circus and Party Clowns) had been trying to quell for years. It seemed to Arthur, however, that these particular clowns—judging on appearance alone—warranted at least some minor misgivings. Their faces were coated with thick, pasty makeup that was cracking in the creases of their skin—and though each of them had a big crimson smile painted around his mouth, neither of them was actually smiling.

What had really caught Arthur's eye, however, was not the appearance of the clowns' faces—but the sizes of their bodies. The clown on the right was so tall that on first glance he appeared to be standing on stilts—and it was only upon further observation that his proportions proved otherwise. The clown on the left was standing on a large wooden crate, but he was so short that the tip of his head barely reached his partner's waist.

There was a sixty-foot pole jutting up from behind the stage, which was labeled in big bold numbers with incremental measurements of height. According to the pole's markings, the giant was roughly nine feet tall, while the dwarf's height measured at just over two feet. Each clown's height was further exaggerated by the close proximity in which they stood—the giant's massive stature causing the dwarf to seem more like a doll than a man, and the dwarf's tiny body causing the giant to appear as large as an oak tree.

As Arthur gazed onto the stage, the clowns performed stretching exercises, in apparent preparation for some forthcoming feat. And then, without a word, the giant clown picked up his dwarfish partner from off the wooden crate—and threw him straight up into the air.

The crowd gasped as the tiny clown shot up like a bullet, ascending higher and higher—passing the twenty-five-foot marker—and then thirty—thirty-five—forty—forty-five. He had climbed over fifty feet in the air before his speed began to slow, and he peaked at the fifty-six-foot marker before plummeting back toward the stage.

It appeared for a moment that the dwarf might slam into the stage's wooden planks on his way back to earth, but the giant, who had not taken his eyes off his partner since hurling him into the air, extended his arms at the last second and plucked the falling dwarf out of the sky. The giant clown then set his partner back down upon the wooden crate, and the two turned toward the audience to take a well-deserved bow.

The crowd erupted in applause. Suspicious or not, these two clowns had just set a new world record for Greatest Height Reached by One Man Thrown into the Air by Another.

Just as Arthur began to clap, however, the small clown looked straight at him—and grinned in such a way that Arthur's blood ran cold.

The boy stumbled backward. Generally, he was exceptionally fair when it came to clowns and always did his best not to judge them too hastily. He would continually remind himself that beneath all the creepy makeup, a clown is just a pleasant, if misguided, fellow in oversized shoes trying to make people laugh—against increasingly difficult odds. But this time, Arthur felt no such sympathy. His only thought was to get as far away from these clowns as possible.

Arthur sneaked behind the crowd and walked quickly away from the stage and its suddenly sinister occupants. When he felt he had reached a safe distance, Arthur's curiosity got the better of him. He turned to venture a glance back at the stage and found—to his horror—that not only was the dwarfish clown still staring at him, the giant had now joined in as well.

A chill ran down Arthur's spine, and he quickly turned away. He continued on his path and did not look back again.

• • •

Uncle Mervyn held a stopwatch an arm's length from a man on stage who was currently juggling five circular saw blades.

"Forty-one minutes!" cried the world-record certifier as Arthur approached the place where Mrs. Waite stood, just behind the crowd of daring party guests.

Arthur handed a well-traveled glass of ginger ale to the housekeeper. "Sorry it's not entirely full, Mrs. Waite. I did have a few sips myself," he admitted.

Mrs. Waite smiled. "Think nothing of it, dear. What a treat to have somebody waiting on *me* for a change! I'm just glad to see you found your way back; I was starting to worry you'd been kidnapped by gypsies."

Arthur smiled back awkwardly. Unlike some children his age, Arthur never worried about being kidnapped. Indeed, it seemed quite unlikely that, of all the Whipple children, any kidnapper would ever decide to kidnap *him*. Surely a kidnapper would not expect half the ransom he could get for one of Arthur's brothers or sisters. Of course, it was nice to have one less thing to worry about—but deep inside, Arthur longed to be worthy of kidnapping.

"Forty-two minutes!" shouted Uncle Mervyn up at the stage.

With that, the juggler let each saw blade fall to the stage floor, one after the other. The razor-sharp blades stuck into the floorboards in quick succession, landing in a perfectly spaced line. The juggler bowed low and the crowd cheered.

After filling out the proper paperwork certifying this latest world record, Uncle Mervyn hurried to the back of the now dwindling crowd, to the place where Arthur and Mrs. Waite stood waiting for him.

As Arthur watched his caretakers exchange fond glances with each other, he recalled Cordelia's assurances that, since Uncle Mervyn was a bachelor and Mrs. Waite a widow, the two were perfect for each other. Arthur, being no expert in such matters, was not so certain—though he had noticed the pair spent a considerable amount of their free time together.

"Ah, there you are, Arthur," declared Uncle Mervyn as the boy handed him his drink. "You've made it just in time! While you were gone, your family achieved the Highest Number of Uniquely Posed Photographs in Ten Minutes, putting them just one record away from their quota. So—as there's nothing scheduled on this stage for the next half hour—how would you like to get up and have a go at your latest attempt? Think of how thrilled the others will be when they find it's you who's ensured their eligibility for the championships!"

Mrs. Waite nodded. "Won't that be wonderful, Arthur?"

"Oh," said Arthur in surprise. He had in fact been secretly hoping for just such an opportunity—but to be asked to make an attempt on such short notice in front of so distinguished a crowd suddenly gave him pause. "Well," he said, "I don't have my bullwhip or my milk bottle with me—and I'm afraid it will take at least fifteen minutes to go and get them, and by that time . . ."

"Mrs. Waite's been kind enough to fetch them for you already," retorted Uncle Mervyn, grinning warmly at the housekeeper. "You'll find them over there, just next to the stage."

"Really?" said Arthur with a nervous smile. "Thanks, Uncle Mervyn; thanks, Mrs. Waite. I've never really performed an attempt on stage before."

"Well, here's your chance then, lad. But I've a feeling," Uncle Mervyn added with an encouraging wink, "this may end up being more than just an attempt for you." He had a twinkle in his eye that made it difficult for Arthur not to believe him.

Arthur went to retrieve his bullwhip and milk bottle while Uncle Mervyn took to the stage to gather the crowd. There were only a few stragglers still milling about from the previous act, as most of the audience had since moved on to the next stage, where Mr. Mahankali's high-diving dogs were attempting a new synchronized diving record.

"Ladies and gentlemen, lads and lasses," Uncle Mervyn called to the six audience members who apparently did not care for canine acrobatics, "prepare yourself for an act like none you have ever witnessed before. Watch in amazement as this rarely seen member of the Whipple family strives to break his very first world record and secure his family's position at this year's championships by cracking a bull-whip 932 consecutive times while balancing a milk bottle on his head. Please welcome to the stage—Arthur Whipple and his magical bullwhip!"

Arthur's heart was pounding through his chest. He had not expected his uncle's boastful introduction, and now he didn't know how he could possibly live up to it. The time for backing out, however, had long since passed—so he put one foot in front of the other and started up the stage steps.

Reaching into his pocket, Arthur grasped the magical domino his uncle had given him for his birthday—and began rubbing it with all his might. He could only hope some of its magic would now rub off on him.

The tiny crowd clapped indifferently as the boy with the bullwhip stepped onto the stage.

When he had reached the middle of the platform, Arthur placed the milk bottle on top of his head, and the half-hearted applause died down. He suddenly found himself stranded in a sea of silence and realized it was up to him to fill it.

Arthur glanced to his uncle with a look of dismay—but Uncle Mervyn simply looked up from his watch and shouted, "Begin!"

THE RECORD ATTEMPT

Arthur cocked back his arm, then snapped it downward. The tail of the whip shot out in front of him—but to his dread, it made no sound.

He brought the whip up again and snapped his arm down a second time—but again, the whip did not crack.

One of the audience members, an old Chinese man with a long white mustache—who happened to be the owner of the First Motorized Wheelchair Ever Assembled—slowly pivoted his antique wheelchair and inched his way toward the high-diving dog show.

Arthur began to panic. Had he completely forgotten how to crack a whip? What if he couldn't manage to crack it even once? What was he doing wrong?

He closed his eyes and tried to recall the fundamentals of whip cracking, as taught to him by his uncle.

"I trust you've learned," Uncle Mervyn had said, "that a sonic boom occurs when an object travels faster than the speed of sound—or roughly 761 miles per hour. I imagine you've even heard a sonic boom yourself once or twice when a jet plane has torn across the sky above you and broken the sound barrier. But what you might not have known, Arthur, is that common cows have been traveling faster than the speed of sound since the early Roman Empire—long before the First Jet Aeroplane was ever invented. You see, lad, the sound of a bullwhip cracking is actually the result of a small sonic boom. When properly handled, the tail end of a whip can reach speeds in excess of 760 miles per hour, thus breaking the sound barrier and creating the noise we hear as a whip 'crack.' And of course, bullwhips are made from leather, and leather is really just tanned cow hide. So, you see, contrary to popular belief, the race to achieve supersonic flight was not won by a man—but by a cow, some two thousand years ago when the First Leather Whip was cracked, and it took us humans till the mid-1940s just to catch up. Now of course, some might say this discrepancy in technological advancement is due to the fact that no cow has ever survived the flight, making it difficult for our scientists to question them about their methods. But I have other suspicions. . . ."

Indeed, Uncle Mervyn believed that some sort of magic

must be involved in order for common cows to succeed at such a complex endeavor. Which is why at Christmas he had presented Arthur with a magical bullwhip.

"But what makes it magical, Uncle Mervyn?" Arthur had asked.

"Well," replied his uncle, "how else could a cow break the speed of sound without being strapped to a rocket?"

As Arthur stood alone on stage, on the verge of disaster, his uncle's words now brought him clarity. Seeing as this was a magical bullwhip he was dealing with—why was he trying so hard to make it work? Surely, the whip had much greater powers than he had.

Arthur glanced again at Uncle Mervyn, who, despite the boy's rocky start, was grinning back at him and offering an encouraging thumbs-up. The boy closed his eyes and cleared his mind. He raised the bullwhip handle once more, and then—without giving it too much thought—brought the whip down with a *crack*.

Arthur let out a sigh of relief. *All right*, he said to himself. *Just 931 more cracks to go.*

• • •

The first hundred or so were a bit shaky, but by the 101st crack, Arthur had hit his whip-cracking stride. He was cracking the whip naturally and fluidly, without even having to think about what he was doing. So much so, that he began to focus his attention elsewhere.

Arthur soon realized what a ragtag bunch his audience actually was. The old wheelchair-bound Chinese man was halfway to the next stage by now, leaving behind five less-than-ideal specimens of spectatorship. It was clear the only reason they had stayed behind was that it required far less effort than walking the one hundred feet or so to get to the next act. Their eyes were glazed over, and their faces carried blank expressions.

With such unsupportive supporters, Arthur felt his momentum slipping away, his technique growing clunkier and clunkier with each crack. He found himself wondering how much easier this all would have been if he had just had a larger audience, with people who were somewhat interested in bullwhip cracking and milk-bottle balancing. He would not have to wonder for long.

• • •

Up at the next stage, the last of Mr. Mahankali's high-diving dogs executed a reverse triple somersault before plunging into the large portable diving pool with barely a splash—sending the surrounding crowd into a frenzy of applause. And this was only the warm-up round.

Dressed in a finely tailored dinner suit, the dogs' trainer—who, of course, had as much hair on his face and body as any of the beasts he cared for—had just turned to the diving platform to set the height for the actual record attempt, when he happened to glance toward Arthur's stage.

He was delighted at first to see the boy attempting another record, but it soon became clear, even from a hundred feet away, that Arthur was struggling—and that he was performing in front of what may have been the World's Worst Audience.

When Mr. Mahankali had finished his adjustments, he strode to the front of the diving pool and addressed the crowd. "Thank you, good people," he said. "The high-diving dogs will now be taking a fifteen-minute break before attempting their next world record. In the meantime, please join me in proceeding back to stage number 9, where one of the great Whipple children is in the process of breaking a world record of his own."

Then, in one swift motion, the uncommonly hairy man climbed onto the back of Shiva, his elephant transport, and took hold of the reins. As he started toward Arthur's stage, Mr. Mahankali called out to the mass of bewildered people behind him: "Come now. Follow me."

• • •

When Arthur noticed the elephant heading toward him and the throng of people following behind it, his heart swelled. Were all those people really coming to watch *him*?

Finally, his efforts would be fully appreciated by a crowd of sophisticated observers—some of whom might actually be whip-cracking enthusiasts. It was just what he needed to raise his spirits and rekindle his momentum. As the new arrivals shuffled in around Arthur's stage, his whip-cracking instincts returned.

Arthur had cracked the whip 699 times before the sheer magnitude of his new audience finally struck him.

He had been staring out at the night sky for most of the attempt, as he concentrated on keeping the milk bottle balanced. But when the crowd cheered at his seven-hundredth crack, he allowed himself a full view of his surroundings. The present crowd was well over ten times the size of his previous audience.

Suddenly Arthur felt incredibly small. Had all these people really come to watch *him*?

It was hard to believe he had ever hoped for anything beyond the benign little crowd he'd started with. He tried to forget they were there, but it was no use. There were simply too many of them. Then he remembered a bit of advice he had once heard—that if you get nervous in front of an audience, you should picture its members in their undergarments. He figured it was worth a try—but it did not have quite the effect he had anticipated.

As Arthur closed his eyes and imagined them all without clothes, he found it rather unsettling how well they were taking it. Here they had just lost all but a few scraps of their clothing, and they were acting like nothing had even happened. Arthur longed to have that kind of confidence. He wasn't half that self-assured with all of his clothes *on*.

More dismayed than encouraged, Arthur opened his eyes and wiped all thoughts of scantily clad audience members from his mind. He decided it was better to be stared at by a group of regular, fully clothed people, than by a bunch of strangely confident, half-naked ones.

Fortunately, the whole business of picturing the audience without clothes on and then pondering the implications of such a proposition, had in fact taken Arthur's mind off his anxiety for several moments. Before he knew it, the crowd was cheering again as he hit eight hundred whip cracks. The cheers were even louder this time, as Arthur neared the home stretch, with only 132 cracks to go.

All of Arthur's uneasiness seemed to magically lift from his shoulders. The finish line was pulling him now. All he had to do was go along for the ride.

At the 901st crack, Uncle Mervyn began counting down from thirty-two, and the audience quickly joined in.

"Thirty-two!" called out Uncle Mervyn.

Crack! went the whip.

"Thirty-one!"

Crack!

"Thirty!"

Crack!

Arthur began imagining what it would feel like to be hoisted onto the crowd's shoulders and paraded around the estate.

"Twenty-five!" shouted the audience.

Crack! went the whip.

They would carry him across the lawn and all the other guests would turn to each other and whisper, "Who is that?" And someone would exclaim, "Why, it's Arthur Whipple! He's finally done it! Oh, happy day!"

"Twenty!" shouted the audience.

Crack! went the whip.

They would set him down in front of his family, who would all be grinning with pride. His father would say, "Well done, my boy! I am proud to call you my son! You *are* a Whipple, after all!" His mother would cry, "Oh, Arthur, you are as good a son as any mother could hope for!" His brothers and sisters would argue over who would get to be Arthur's partner for the upcoming Table Tennis Tournament of Champions.

"Fifteen!" shouted the audience.

Crack! went the whip.

All of his dreams would come true. He would never feel like an outsider again.

As Arthur scanned the crowd, trying to determine which onlookers were most likely to storm the stage first, he was startled by a strangely familiar pair of sparkling green eyes staring up at him from the third row back.

The hopeful gears of his imagination ground to a halt as a rush of horror swept over him. There, only a few feet from the front of the stage, stood the ominous ghost girl from the Crosley estate.

She looked even more fearsome than he remembered. Her face was a ghastly shade of pale, her lips a deep dark red, nearly black—not unlike the color of her swirling wavy hair, which hovered about her shoulders like wisps of reddish inky smoke.

Arthur's breath caught in his throat. What insidious sort of spirit was this? As everybody knows, only the most powerful poltergeists are able to leave the confines of their designated haunting grounds—and here this one was standing on his own lawn.

He knew he would not escape a second time from such a determined demon, but he was not yet ready to die. Not when he was in the midst of his most successful world record attempt to date.

Please, he pleaded with the phantom, *let me finish this one last attempt so I don't die completely recordless.*

But Arthur's concentration had been shattered by the promise of certain death.

"Eleven!" shouted the audience.

Ffffft! went the whip.

The crowd gasped.

After 922 consecutive whip cracks while balancing a milk bottle on his head, Arthur's whip had ceased to crack, just ten cracks away from a new world record—and the fulfillment of all his dreams. Upon his impending demise, the *Grazelby Guide* would remain unmarked by Arthur's name for all eternity.

Having just had it so thoroughly crushed, Arthur could no longer see much use for his soul, and at that moment, he found himself longing for the wraith to come devour it—if in fact it was still interested. But when he searched the audience, he found the ghost girl had vanished.

Somehow, the specter's disappearance caused Arthur even more distress than its arrival had. Was he losing his mind? Had he just ruined his best chance at breaking a world record simply by being unable to control an overactive imagination?

There was an awkward silence as the audience came to grips with what they had just witnessed. The only audible sound was the steadily increasing whine of a dilapidated wheelchair motor as the old Chinese man finally made his way back to Arthur's stage. When the old man realized he had made the journey between stages twice now without witnessing a single record-breaking feat, he let out a sigh of indignation.

After a few more moments of disbelief, the silence was broken by the solitary sound of two hands clapping.

Still seated astride the elephant, Mr. Mahankali applauded Arthur's valiant effort—and decided to ignore the small matter of the boy's failure to succeed. Gradually, other members of the audience joined in the applause, but most were simply too dumbfounded to show any sort of response. Much of the crowd turned away and slowly headed back to the next stage.

Arthur removed the milk bottle and hung his head in despair. He had just achieved the best failure quotient of his life—a near-perfect 1.0108—but somehow this only made him feel worse.

Uncle Mervyn, however, seemed to feel otherwise. "Good show, Arthur!" he exclaimed as Arthur climbed down from the stage. "That was your best attempt yet! They don't come much closer than that, lad. It's only a matter of time before we'll be filling out the paperwork for your first world record!"

Although he had been hearing his uncle's pep talks for as long as he could remember, and not one of them had ever proved accurate, Arthur once again felt his disappointment begin to dissipate.

UNWELCOME GUESTS

As Arthur made his way toward the main stage with Uncle Mervyn and Mrs. Waite, he tried not to think about how close he had just come to achieving his one true goal in life. Fortunately, he would soon have the start of official birthday celebrations to occupy his mind.

After weaving their way through the gathering crowd, the boy and his chaperones found their places near the front of the towering stage at the festivities' center. Minutes later, the crackle of a microphone joined the *pop* of a spotlight as it cut through the night air and gleamed onto the curtain.

The crowd hushed as a short, balding man in a black tailcoat and white tie stepped up to the microphone. Arthur recognized him as "Nonstop" Norman Prattle, the popular radio personality who held the record for Most Logged Hours of Radio Airtime.

"Ladies and gentlemen, boys and girls," the man declared in a rich but nasally voice, "on behalf of Mr. and Mrs. Whipple, as well as the entire Whipple clan, it is my honor and privilege to welcome you to the Eighteenth Annual Whipple Family Birthday Extravaganza!"

The crowd broke into thunderous applause, filling Arthur with a deep sense of pride.

As the applause faded, Nonstop Norman continued. "And now, it is my great pleasure to introduce the musical entertainment for tonight's festivities. All the way from Chicago, Illinois, performing their hit song, 'All of Me,' please welcome—Johnny Stump and the Missing Limbs!"

Amidst another burst of applause, the master of ceremonies exited the stage as the curtain unveiled a dimly lit orchestra of nine musicians. Seated on a stool at the rear of the stage, the band's leader was lit by a spotlight, revealing a certain peculiar detail about him: the lower half of his body was completely missing.

Climbing down the stool, Johnny Stump sauntered to the front of the stage, his abbreviated torso swinging to and fro while his arms did the work of his nonexistent legs. As he hoisted himself onto the round pedestal beside the microphone, he flashed a charming smile to the audience, causing two young ladies in the front row to spontaneously swoon. When he started singing in his smooth, alluring voice, the crowd was completely enraptured:

All of me—why not take all of me?
Oh, can't you see?—I'm no good without you
Take my lips—I want to lose them
Take my arms—I'll never use them . . .

The back of the stage lit up as shafts of blue light illuminated the band. It was now clear the musicians themselves were just as extraordinary as their leader. They too were lacking appendages—their arms, to be exact. Indeed, they were all playing their instruments with their feet—and playing them so well, that no one ever would have known it simply by listening.

When Johnny Stump had sustained the song's final note for nearly half a minute, the audience cheered with hoots and whistles. He held it for another twenty-nine seconds (thus breaking the record for Longest Sustained Vocal Note), before a crash of cymbals from the armless percussionist signaled the end of the song. On the last beat, Johnny Stump bowed his head, and the stage went black. The crowd went wild.

A spotlight punched a hole in the darkness as Nonstop Norman walked back to the microphone. "Let's hear it for the Highest-Selling Limbless Orchestra of All Time! And now, ladies and gentlemen, it is my pleasure to introduce your host—the First Man to Climb Mount Kilimanjaro Entirely on Stilts—Mr. Charles Whipple!"

Amidst deafening applause, the curtain cracked open and Arthur's father walked onto the stage and up to the microphone.

"Thank you, thank you!" he cried. "Thank you all so much for coming. Welcome to Neverfall Hall and this year's Whipple Family Birthday Extravaganza, which has just now been certified the Largest Garden Party Ever Hosted at a Single-Family Residence—our one-thousandth record in two years!" He broke for another burst of applause, then added, "I am thrilled to report this latest record has officially made us eligible for this year's championships—so, with any luck, we'll be bringing home another cup before the year is through!"

At the thunderous applause that followed, Arthur couldn't help but imagine how it might have felt to have heard his own record credited with securing his family's championships hopes.

"Indeed," Mr. Whipple continued, "with this first step of eligibility out of the way, we are now free to focus all our energy on the upcoming Unsafe Sports Showdown, which has always been our most important event of the season. . . . But enough about us," he declared. "We are deeply honored to have such a fine group of guests joining us this evening. Please forgive me for pointing out just a few of you. Let's see . . . Over here to my right, we are honored by the presence of the grand duke of Luxembourg—the World's Youngest Monarch!"

A spotlight zigzagged through the crowd and then halted on a six-year-old boy in the front row who had been hoisted onto the shoulders of his royal advisor.

"Please welcome His Royal Highness Grand Duke Frederik Henri Albért Gabriel Félix Marie Guillaume, the Second!"

At this, His Royal Highness the Grand Duke—et cetera, et cetera—waved briefly at the cheering crowd, then tapped his advisor on the head with a jeweled scepter to signal he was ready to be put back down.

"Also with us tonight," continued Mr. Whipple, "the Detective with the Most Solved Cases in History—the illustrious Inspector Hadrian Smudge!"

The spotlight landed on a tall man with a square jaw and beak-like nose. At the mention of his name, he saluted the crowd.

"And," Mr. Whipple added, "I believe I saw Bianca Bainbridge earlier this evening. Are you here, Bianca? Where are you?"

The spotlight darted over the crowd again before finding a fur-clad woman clutching a slender cigarette holder between two fingers.

"Ah, there you are, my dear! Please welcome the star of *Cleopatra's Cats!*—the Shortest Running Broadway Show in History—whose enormous salary bankrupted the production and forced it to shut down halfway through Act I on opening night—Bianca Bainbridge, everyone—the World's Highest Paid Actress!"

As the coyly smiling stage star lowered her head and bowed, the face of the guest behind her was briefly revealed in the spotlight's gleam. It belonged to a man with chiseled cheekbones and impeccably straight teeth that sparkled as he grinned.

When Miss Bainbridge raised her head again, Mr. Whipple's demeanor had entirely changed.

"Oh dear. How has . . . Hmm . . ." he stammered.

His face had become white and cheerless—as if he had just seen a ghost. Arthur wondered if perhaps he himself wasn't the only one being tormented by spirits that evening.

"Well . . . so . . ." the shaken host continued, "anyhow . . . um . . . Please excuse me. Do enjoy the party."

And with that, he swiftly left the stage.

As Nonstop Norman did his best to recover from the host's bizarre exit by bringing Johnny Stump and the Missing Limbs out for an encore, Mr. Whipple headed straight toward his valet, Wilhelm, who was standing at the bottom of the steps on the side of the stage, next to Mrs. Whipple and the Whipple children.

"I wonder what's come over your father," Uncle Mervyn whispered to Arthur. "Let's go see if we can't find out, shall we?"

As they made their way toward the rest of his family, Arthur strained to hear his father's conversation.

"Vhat seems to be the matter, sir?" Wilhelm inquired in his thick German accent.

"There is a ghost in the audience who needs to be dealt with," Arthur heard his father say.

The boy's heart beat faster. Finally, he had something in common with his father. He, too, was seeing ghosts.

Unable to contain his excitement, Arthur ran to Mr. Whipple and blurted, "I've seen them too, Father!"

Mr. Whipple turned to his son and arched his brow.

"What the blazes are you on about, Arthur?" he snapped. "Seen whom?"

"The ghosts! They've come to devour our souls, haven't they?"

"Have you gone mad, boy? There are no ghosts here!"

"Oh. But I thought . . ." Arthur trailed off, confused and deflated by his father's rebuke.

Mr. Whipple turned back to Wilhelm. "As I was saying, there is a guest in the audience who needs to be dealt with. He is standing toward the back, near Bianca . . ."

But before Mr. Whipple could finish his instructions, he was addressed by a charming voice.

"Charles Whipple—is it really you?" called the voice.

Arthur and his family turned to see a certain chisel-cheeked, sparkle-toothed man striding toward them.

"Great Wall of China—it's good to see you again!" cried the stranger as he reached out both his arms, clutched Mr. Whipple's hand, and shook it thoroughly. "How have you been, Charlie? It's been ages, hasn't it?"

Mr. Whipple looked disoriented and more than a bit uncomfortable. His mouth opened slightly, but before he could speak, the stranger noticed Arthur's mother standing just behind her husband.

"Ah . . . and you must be the lovely Mrs. Whipple," smiled the stranger. Releasing his grasp on her husband, he offered his hand to Arthur's mother. "I've seen your photo countless times, of course, but I must say—you are even more radiant in person!"

With that, he raised her hand to his lips and gently kissed it.

"Rex Goldwin," he introduced himself. "You may recognize me from the latest issue of *The Amazing Ardmore Almanac of the Ridiculously Remarkable*. First time I've graced its pages in nearly twenty years—but I'm happy to say I've just signed a new, record-breaking sponsorship contract. It's no *Grazelby Guide*, of course—but we can't all be Whipples, now can we?" he winked with a chuckle.

Arthur was well aware of the *Ardmore Almanac*. It was the one book Mr. Whipple had prohibited his children from ever reading.

"Why, of course, Mr. Goldwin," Arthur's mother nodded. "I believe your picture was on the front page of *The Record* some weeks ago—though I'm afraid my husband forgot to mention he knew you. Not overly chatty about the past, this one. Honestly, I sometimes forget he ever had a life before I met him. . . ."

Mr. Whipple stepped forward. "I'm sorry, Mr. Goldwin," he said, "but are you sure you received an invitation?"

"Charles!" scolded his wife. "That's hardly hospitable behavior."

"Not at all, Mrs. Whipple," Rex Goldwin assured. "Your husband has every right to be selective about his guests." He reached into his jacket and retrieved a folded piece of parchment with silver lettering. "Really, it's my fault for not stopping in as soon as we received it. It *has* been a very long time since Charlie and I last spoke—and

I can hardly blame him for being a bit surprised to see me. In fact, I wasn't quite sure the invitation was meant for us when it was delivered to the new house—but then there it was, 'Dear Neighbor . . .'"

Just then, a voice called out from behind him.

"Rex, dear?"

The group turned to see a woman striding toward them in a glittering gold dress with blonde hair that had been pulled up into a glamorously gigantic beehive. Following behind her was a sizable cluster of smiling and well-groomed children.

"Where have you—" she began, but stopped short when she realized with whom Rex was conversing. "Oh, my," she gasped. "What an honor."

"Hello, darling," Rex greeted the woman. "Sorry for running off like that, but I just couldn't pass up the chance to finally say hello to our distinguished hosts. Charles, Eliza—allow me to introduce my wife, Rita. Rita—Charles and Eliza Whipple."

"It is such a privilege to finally meet you," gushed Rita Goldwin as she shook hands with a reluctant Mr. Whipple and his far more sociable wife. "We're all big fans," she confessed. Then, turning to the group of children behind her, she said gleefully, "Children, say hello to the Whipple family."

"Hello, Whipple family," beamed the children.

"We've been telling them stories about you ever since they were born," Rita explained, "and now, I must say, they've become quite the little record breakers themselves."

"Isn't that sweet, Charles?" cooed Mrs. Whipple.

Arthur's father offered no response.

Rita Goldwin turned again to her children. "Children, would you like to introduce yourselves?"

The children nodded enthusiastically.

"I'm Roland," declared the athletic-looking boy on the far end of the cluster. He appeared to be the oldest of the bunch. "Pleased to meet you," he said with a bow.

Next to introduce themselves were Rosalind and Roxy Goldwin, the eldest of the girls, whose lush, flowing hair was blonde and brunette, respectively. As they stepped out from behind their siblings and curtsied, Arthur noticed Henry and Simon's eyes bulge slightly.

It wasn't long before Roland, Rosalind, Rupert, Roxy, Rodney, Randolf, Radley, and Rowena—their ages ranging from around seventeen all the way down to four—had all stepped forward and given their introductions.

As button-nosed Rowena completed her curtsy, Mrs. Whipple clapped her hands and said, "What a delightful group of children!"

"Why, thank you, Mrs. Whipple," replied Rita Goldwin. "Hopefully you'll be able to meet the rest of them some day. It's a pity they all couldn't be here tonight. Our two eldest—the twins—are off studying abroad, traveling the world through the Clapford Fellowship. They'll be green with envy when they hear we got to meet you. And then there's little Rowan, who just had his first birthday and is with the nanny tonight. And then . . . Now, wait a minute—where on earth is Ruby? She ought to be here with us."

There was some shuffling amongst the Goldwin children, and then—as Arthur looked on in disbelief—from out of the cluster stepped the green-eyed ghost girl.

Arthur's heart began thumping against his ribcage—but it wasn't much more than a reflex. At this point, he was far too confused to be completely terrified.

The ghost girl held up the corners of her black V-neck dress between her black fingernails and curtsied, then stepped back into the crowd of children. When she glanced toward Arthur, the boy flinched in fright—but then, to his continued bewilderment, her mouth curled into an amiable smile. The smile lasted only a moment before she looked away again, leaving Arthur more confused than ever.

"Ahem," said Mrs. Goldwin. "Would you like to introduce yourself, young lady?"

The ghost girl stepped forward once more. "Oh, right. Sorry," she said. Executing a halfhearted second curtsy, she added, "Ruby," then returned to her previous position. Next to the others, she might well have been the illegitimate daughter of Dracula, sent to be raised by a family of fashion models.

"You'll have to forgive Ruby," explained Mrs. Goldwin. "As record-breaking children go, she's a bit . . . unpolished. And for some reason, she insists on dressing herself like a corpse these days. Powder and lipstick are meant to enhance your features, dear—not deaden them."

Ruby gave a strange, joyless smile, then shifted her eyes to the sky, as if halfheartedly searching for some distant heavenly body.

Arthur remained thoroughly perplexed. Apparently, he was not the only one who could see the ghost girl. Indeed, it seemed she was simply an odd-looking member of the Goldwin family. But how could this be possible when he had witnessed a figure bearing her exact likeness not long ago on the Crosley estate?

"Well, it certainly was a pleasure meeting you and your lovely children," Mrs. Whipple concluded. "We must arrange a joint outing sometime. Where was it you said you lived?"

"Just down the road, actually," said Rex Goldwin. "Would you believe we've just purchased the old Crosley estate?"

As a wave of realization swept over Arthur, he did not notice his father's face grow a shade paler, from something of an eggshell cream to more of a glacier white.

"Have you now?" said Mrs. Whipple. "My—that *is* close. I'm surprised we've never seen any movers."

"Well," Rex replied, "we've only just closed the deal this week, so we're still at the Dwellinger Grand for the present moment. But we've been visiting the grounds for over a month now with various architects and landscape designers; you can imagine the work we've got ahead of us to make the place halfway inhabitable. Still, we just couldn't pass up the opportunity to move to where the

106

action is—what with the International World Record Federation honoring your back-to-back wins at the championships by holding them in your city this year, alongside the Unsafe Sports Showdown. Seems this is the place to be for record breaking these days, eh? Luckily, the heavy machinery arrives tomorrow, so it won't be long before we're all moved in and joining you for neighborhood gatherings!"

"I say, that is exciting news," beamed Mrs. Whipple. "Do you intend on competing in any events now that you're here?"

Rex smiled bashfully. "We'd certainly be honored—if they'd have us. But of course, up till now, record breaking has only ever been a private hobby of ours. We've never publicly competed as a family before, and I myself haven't competed in years—so we're really only just getting our feet wet. For a while there, it did seem we might make the deadline for championships eligibility tonight, but I'm afraid we've ended up just a couple of records short of the required thousand."

"Well now," said Arthur's mother, "that's nothing to be sneezed at, Mr. Goldwin. We scarcely made that number ourselves! I'd say your record tally is absolutely spectacular for a family of beginners—even if you won't be eligible this year. I'm sure you'll have no trouble at all gaining eligibility for the next championships, if you keep at it. My," she chuckled, "we'll have to watch our backs, won't we, Charles?"

"Indeed," Mr. Whipple said gruffly. "Now, I do apologize, Mr. and Mrs. Goldwin, but we really must be getting back to the party. . . ."

"Oh, of course, Charlie," Rex replied. "And what a lovely party it is. Fine food, distinguished company . . . though I must say the band's a bit of an odd choice." Nodding at Johnny Stump, he chuckled, "Really, Charlie—I do hope you only paid *half* price!"

"Why, Mr. Goldwin!" laughed Arthur's mother. "I'll have to share that one with Mr. Stump—he gets quite a kick out of that sort of thing."

"Oh, but Mrs. Whipple," Rex grinned, "surely he doesn't do any *kicking* at all!"

"Ahem," Arthur's father scowled, curtailing any further laughter. "As I was saying, I'm afraid we are neglecting our other guests, as well as a number of vital birthday duties, so—"

"Say no more, Charlie," said Rex. "Again—terribly sorry about any mix-up with our invitation. I'd hate to cause any distress on your special day. Just say the word and we'll head straight back to the hotel."

"Oh, we wouldn't dream of it—would we, Charles?" Mrs. Whipple asked without looking at her husband.

Mr. Whipple sighed.

"Do stay," implored Mrs. Whipple.

"You are very gracious indeed," said Rex Goldwin. "Now, please—get back to your party. I'm sure we'll be seeing plenty of each other from now on—eh, neighbors?"

"Most certainly," Mrs. Whipple smiled. "Let us know as

soon as you're settled. Now enjoy the rest of your evening."

Mr. Whipple let out another tortured sigh. Mrs. Whipple shot him a stern glance.

Arthur's parents gathered up their birthday-celebrating children and led them off to perform their next vital birthday duty, leaving Arthur to wait awkwardly beside his uncle. He now stood only a few feet from Ruby Goldwin, who clearly was not, nor ever had been, a ghost—but merely a girl with peculiar fashion tastes whose parents had purchased the house down the street. The terror Arthur had once felt in her presence now turned to embarrassment.

But before he could persuade his uncle to take him somewhere—*anywhere*—else, Uncle Mervyn, who had been listening in just outside the conversation with the new neighbors, stepped forward and introduced himself to Rex Goldwin.

"Mervyn McCleary," said Arthur's uncle, shaking Rex's hand. "Adjudicator for the International World Record Federation, under contract with the *Grazelby Guide*—and the Whipples' primary officiator. Pleased to meet you. Afraid I'm not familiar with your earlier work, though I have read your recent profile in *The Record*. So, how are you liking it over at the *Almanac*? I've known quite a few certifiers over the years who've been contracted by Ardmore after earning their officiating licenses from the IWRF—but I've since lost touch with all of them. Bit of a secretive place, it seems. And what of their publishing policy regarding the Regrettable Records? I'm afraid I can't say I approve."

Rex nodded considerately. "Your concerns are perfectly valid, Mr. McCleary. I'm the first to admit the *Almanac* hasn't had the best reputation in the past—but we're trying to change all that. It might take some time—years maybe—but they assure me this is the start of a new era for Ardmore."

"Well, I'm certainly glad to hear it. Very few wrongs that can't be righted with the proper amount of effort."

"Indeed, Mr. McCleary," Rex said with a heartfelt smile, "I couldn't agree with you more."

"Very good, Mr. Goldwin," Uncle Mervyn smiled back. "So tell me about some of your recent records then. I'm always eager to hear what the rest of the record-breaking world is up to."

While Rex proceeded to describe his record for Largest Private Collection of Military Prototypes, Arthur continued to stare straight at the ground—and away from Ruby Goldwin—until he was overcome by a sudden fit of curiosity.

He glanced in Ruby's direction—and found she was already looking straight at him. Their eyes met for an uncomfortable moment, before Arthur quickly glanced away again.

After several more seconds of staring at the ground, he could no longer bear the awkwardness. "Mrs. Waite," said the boy, turning to his chaperone, "may I go browse the Grazelby exhibition for a bit?"

"I suppose, dear," the housekeeper replied, "but don't be too long. The ceremony begins in less than half an hour, and you know we can't start without you."

"Yes, ma'am—I won't be late," Arthur called over his shoulder, then hurried off toward the massive tent at the rear of the crowd.

• • •

The tent that contained the Grazelby exhibition was large enough to house a small circus, and when Arthur stepped through the draped entryway, he imagined himself its ringleader. Any thoughts of ghost girls—or of unpleasant neighbor children masquerading as ghost girls—vanished from his mind as he slipped into a state of wonder.

The tent was filled with assorted record-breaking exhibits, some belonging to the Whipple family and some on loan from the private collections of their guests—but all astonishing. And since most of the partygoers in the area were still out watching Johnny Stump and the Missing Limbs, Arthur practically had the place to himself.

Though he had seen his sister Cordelia's scale model of the Arc de Triomphe before, it never failed to fascinate him. It was over twelve feet tall and constructed entirely from standard playing cards. Despite a total lack of adhesives or fasteners, it was so well built, Cordelia assured him, that an entire rugby team could stand on its roof without causing the slightest structural damage.

Stepping through the giant archway, Arthur proceeded

down the first row of exhibits, pausing to marvel at each of them.

Soon the boy had reached the rear of the chamber, where a giant floor-length curtain spanned the full width of the tent. Following the velvet rope that ran along the front of the curtain, he came to a silver-plated sign that read:

PRIVATE.
AUTHORIZED PERSONS ONLY.
NO PEEKING.
THANK YOU.

Though most of the guests had no way of knowing what the sign was guarding, Arthur knew that behind this curtain sat dessert. The rear half of the tent was in fact being used as a holding bay for the World's Largest Birthday Cake, which was to be kept under wraps until the official unveiling—an event that held particular interest to Arthur that year.

Staring up at the giant curtain, Arthur dreamt about the colossal cake behind it. He was dying to get his first peek; he only hoped the wait didn't kill him first. With a wistful sigh, he stepped away from the curtain and returned to the exhibition.

As he headed down the center aisle, he suddenly stopped short. There, studying the pendulum on the World's Thinnest Working Grandfather Clock, stood Ruby Goldwin—

the one person Arthur had sought to avoid by entering the tent in the first place.

Now that he knew she was not an apparition but a living, breathing human girl, he could hardly decide which was worse: to have been put to death by a soul-swallowing specter—or to be constantly reminded how foolish he'd been to actually believe in soul-swallowing specters. It was beginning to seem that the ghost girl—in one form or another—would simply go on tormenting him forever.

Luckily for Arthur, she appeared to be unaware of his presence, so he quietly performed an about-face, then made his way around the corner. Proceeding down the next aisle, the boy peered constantly over his shoulder to make sure she was not following him.

When he felt confident he wasn't being trailed, he turned his head forward to locate the main exit—and nearly collided with the very girl he thought he was eluding.

He skidded to a halt—but this time, he did not escape her notice. Indeed, it seemed she had been watching him for some time.

"Hello," she smiled.

"Oh," gulped Arthur, startled by her proximity. "Hi."

This was the closest he had ever been to the ghost girl.

"So you've had enough of the crowd as well, eh?" she said. Arthur squinted. "Um . . . yeah."

"Excellent," smirked the girl, "we can be unsociable together then."

113

Arthur gave an awkward smile, then, not wanting to encourage her, turned away and pretended to browse the exhibits on his right. Briefly stopping at each display, he retreated down the aisle, back toward the enormous cake-concealing curtain at the rear of the tent. But as Arthur tried to move away, the girl simply followed him, examining each exhibit as soon as he had finished with it.

"I'm Ruby, by the way," said the girl, still smiling as she offered Arthur her right hand. "You know—in case you lost track in the never-ending onslaught of delightful Goldwin children. We keep running into each other, you and I, but we've never exactly met."

Not knowing what else to do, Arthur took the girl's hand and gave it a perfunctory shake. "Yep," he said, doing his best not to prolong an already awkward conversation.

For a moment, it seemed he had succeeded—but Ruby Goldwin would not give up so easily.

"You're Arthur, right?" she added after a brief silence, effectively taking on introductory duties for the both of them. He hadn't seen that one coming.

"Um. Yeah."

"Pleased to meet you, Arthur," she smiled.

"Yep," said the boy. "So . . . do you always dress like that?"

"What—this?" she replied, referring to her makeup and tatter-sleeved dress. "Oh, you know—just taking a stand against the oppressive grip of popular fashion. As one does."

"Oh, right," said Arthur. "Of course."

"Yeah," the girl frowned. "Not really sure it's my thing, to be honest. Just don't tell that to Rita. Wouldn't want her to think she'd broken me. . . ."

"Fair enough," Arthur said brusquely. "Well," he added, turning back toward the entrance, "I should probably get back. See you—"

"By the way," Ruby called, "your whip-cracking/milk-bottle-balancing act was very impressive, you know. I've never seen anything quite like it. You must have practiced for years to get so good."

Arthur turned back around. For some reason, he no longer felt quite so eager to leave the girl's presence.

"Thanks," he said, his chilly expression melting away. "It's not easy finding genuine whip-cracking/milk-bottle-balancing enthusiasts these days."

"Yeah—sorry for slipping off afterward like that. I really wanted to meet you, but I figured you might need a moment. You really were amazing, though."

The boy flashed a warm grin. He could hardly remember why he had been avoiding her in the first place.

But the girl hadn't finished.

"So," she said, "what records have you actually broken then?"

And there they were. The words Arthur lived in constant dread of hearing: *What records have you broken?* The words flew at him like daggers—but somehow, he managed not to flinch. He had been asked this question so many times by so many people, he had gradually devised a sort of verbal shield, which he could recite in such instances to keep the daggers from reaching his heart: "Well," he said, "I've come really close, but I haven't actually broken any records—yet. Any day now, though."

The girl scrunched her lips to one side. "Ahh—well, don't worry about it, Arthur. I was only trying to make conversation. Seems all anyone in this world ever wants to talk about is what records they've broken. But seriously, who needs their silly games anyway, right?"

"Well," Arthur replied with furrowed brow, "I don't know if I'd refer to world-record breaking as *silly* . . ."

"All right then, what *would* you refer to it as?"

"I don't know . . . well, *serious* at the very least—but also grand, significant, esteemed, revered . . . hallowed . . . and that's just scratching the surface, really."

"Wow. You've got quite the vocabulary when you choose to use it, haven't you?"

"Ever since I tried to break the record for Listing the Most Synonyms in One Hour, they just sort of come out sometimes. . . . So how many records have *you* broken?"

"Oh." Ruby's cheerful expression faded. "Just one—but it was a long time ago; it doesn't matter now. . . ."

"Doesn't matter? I don't think you understand what an honor that is." Arthur's voice filled with reverence as his father's words echoed in his mind. "You're a world-record holder; it doesn't matter how long ago you broke it—your

116

name will be forever immortalized in the World Record Archives!"

"Don't remind me."

"What do you mean? Why wouldn't you want to be reminded of the most important thing you've ever done in your life?"

"It's just not something I'm proud of."

Arthur nearly choked. "I don't understand. I've never met anyone who wasn't overjoyed to have their name in the record books. . . . Well, except maybe for Geoffrey Dwindle, the man who contracted the Most Aggressive Strain of Flesh-Eating Bacteria Ever Recorded—but come to think of it, I'm sure he was a lot happier than the man with the *second*-most aggressive strain; at least Mr. Dwindle got something in return for his troubles. . . . But anyway, I'm sure your record isn't nearly as awful as his."

Arthur was then struck by a troubling thought. "Wait—you haven't broken the record for Youngest Murderess to Escape from Prison or something terrible like that, have you?"

"I don't know; I might be proud of *that*. I imagine it takes a good deal of ingenuity to escape from prison."

"So, it's worse than murder, then?" Arthur gaped.

Ignoring the boy's last question, Ruby turned to the silver-plated sign ahead of them and said, "So what's behind the curtain?"

"It's a surprise," Arthur said hastily. "But—"

"Can we have a look?"

117

"Absolutely not. But you haven't answered—"

"Well what about *them*?" said Ruby, pointing to the far end of the curtain. "Why should they get a peek, while the rest of us are stuck out here in the Dullest Museum on Earth?"

With an exasperated gasp, Arthur glanced to where the girl was pointing—and promptly focused his gaze. Thirty feet to their left in the darkened corner of the room, where the curtain met the side of the tent, ripples had begun forming in the fabric. It appeared someone on the other side was hunting for the way out.

"That," explained Arthur, "would be my family's chef, Sammy the Spatula, simply adding some finishing touches before he presents the cake to—"

"It's a cake?!" blurted Ruby.

Arthur let out a defeated sigh. "You know," he said, "I've just thought of some questions I should ask Sammy before the unveiling—so if you'll excuse me . . ."

"Oh," said Ruby, her shoulders drooping slightly.

Arthur smiled with equal parts regret and relief. Intriguing as the girl had proved to be, he could hardly justify keeping company with someone who seemed to think so poorly of world-record breaking—and who, furthermore, would not deny committing a crime worse than murder.

Straightening his jacket, Arthur proceeded past Ruby and headed toward the rippling. But before the boy had taken two steps, a figure emerged from behind the curtain.

Arthur gasped. It was not Sammy the Spatula.

With all the fuss over failed record attempts and troublesome ghost girls, Arthur had nearly forgotten about the first pang of dread he had felt that evening.

It was the clown. The same tiny, smirking clown Arthur had tried to escape only one hour before.

THE CLOWNS

Startled and terrified, Arthur ducked behind the nearest exhibit. For a moment, Ruby looked at him as though he had lost his mind—but as soon as she saw the source of his fright, she dropped to her knees and hid behind the display in front of her. Despite her own rather morbid appearance, it seemed she was no fan of sinister-looking dwarf-clowns either.

The two children peered through cracks in their respective exhibits as the shadowy figure stepped into the room and looked stealthily from side to side.

When the dwarf seemed satisfied that the coast was clear, he turned and pulled gently on the edge of the fabric, creating a gap between the curtain and the side of the tent. Slowly, the lumbering form of the dwarf's giant companion stepped forth into the shadows.

The giant carried a large, black leather case with what appeared to be a dragon etched into its side. Arthur wondered what could be inside it. Perhaps this was where they kept the bones of the unsuspecting children who unwittingly invited them to their birthday parties.

Once the giant had fully emerged, he reached down with his free hand and scooped up the dwarf, then stepped out of the corner. The two men crossed into the light, slyly returning to their clown routine as they headed for a small exit on the side of the tent. The giant extended a massive arm, and the dwarf used his partner's upturned palm as the base for a handstand.

The children sat petrified, their eyes locked on the ghastly duo until, finally, the giant ducked through the opening, and the two clowns disappeared from view.

Without thinking, Arthur looked over at Ruby and found himself exchanging relieved glances with her.

"Who were those two?" whispered the girl. "And what were they doing back—"

Before she could finish, a voice called out behind them— and Arthur spun around to see Wilhelm standing at the main entrance.

"Master Arthur," the butler called. "It is time for you to take your position."

The boy leapt to his feet. If anyone could defeat a pair of diabolical devil-clowns, it was Wilhelm.

"Wilhelm!" he cried.

121

Glancing back to Ruby, Arthur shot the girl an uncommonly confident smile, then hurried off to report what they had just witnessed.

"Vhat is it, Master Arthur?" called the butler, his face filling with concern as he rushed down the aisle to meet him.

But now that Arthur finally had a grown-up to confide in, his memory grew foggy. As he replayed the incidents in his mind, his prior conclusions now struck him as rather improbable. Had the clowns really been staring at him earlier that evening—or had they merely been gazing in his general direction? Had they really been sneaking out from behind the curtain just then—or had they simply lost their way? Indeed, it was difficult to be certain of anything he had seen that night. He had, after all, recently mistaken the girl down the street for a ghoulish fiend from beyond the grave—and had subsequently made a fool of himself upon mentioning it to his father. Surely, he was mistaken about the clowns as well.

Recalling the sting of his father's last reproach, Arthur decided to wait for more proof of actual evildoing before risking ridicule a second time. He did his best to push any thoughts of the clowns and their supposedly suspicious behavior out of his mind—and focus on the fact that, at least for now, they were gone.

"Um," said Arthur as the butler approached, "so where exactly should I stand for the start of the ceremony?"

"Oh," said Wilhelm, surprised by the trivial nature of

Arthur's question after what seemed to be an urgent cry for help. "Vell, if you just go stand vith your uncle on the side of the stage, I vill find you there."

"Oh, right," said the boy. "Thanks, Wilhelm. See you soon."

"Yes. Okay. Godspeed, Master Arthur."

Wilhelm proceeded past him toward the curtain at the rear of the tent, and Arthur glanced back toward Ruby Goldwin. She wore a perplexed expression that seemed to say, *Why didn't you tell him about the clowns?!* but Arthur tried not to let it bother him. After all, it wasn't *her* reputation on the line here. And besides, he hardly had time for this sort of thing now. He had an honored and vital birthday duty to perform.

And so, with a quick wave to the bewildered girl, he turned and hurried for the exit.

Stepping out into the night air, he cautiously scanned his surroundings—and was pleased to find them devoid of all clown life. He drew a deep breath, then set out across the estate. By the time he had rejoined his uncle at the main stage, he had all but forgotten about his latest encounter with the mysterious duo.

• • •

"Now," grinned Nonstop Norman, "might we have all the birthday boys and girls up here on stage? I've got a special announcement for you."

Smiling and waving to the crowd, Arthur's parents led

123

his siblings up the stage steps, then clustered them together at center stage. The Whipple children grinned and wrung their hands in anticipation. They had waited all year for this.

"Boys and girls," said the announcer, "it's time . . . for cake!"

Six spotlights positioned on the sides of the stage snapped on, blinding the audience and forcing them to look in the opposite direction. There, at the rear of the crowd, was the cake.

Every year, the Whipple family birthday cake was bigger than the one before, and this year was no exception. The cake was almost twenty feet high—twenty-eight, if you counted the candles—and thirty feet in diameter.

Wilhelm trudged forward at its front, clutching a tow rope over each shoulder and cleaving a wide path through the crowd as he went. When he had reached the stage, the butler wiped his brow, and the cake lurched to a halt. The crowd gasped in amazement, then promptly filled in around it for a closer look.

The cake was iced in white buttercream with huge ribbons of lavender marzipan running down its sides, while fourteen giant candles jutted up around its top edge—one for each Whipple whose birthday it was.

As the band played their specially arranged intro of "Happy Birthday to You," Wilhelm wheeled a towering metal staircase up to the side of the cake.

Uncle Mervyn nudged Arthur and whispered, "It's time," then led the boy through the crowd.

Wilhelm greeted Arthur with a firm handshake and a warm smile, which helped to calm the boy's nerves—until, of course, Wilhelm handed him the blowtorch.

"Just like vee practiced, okay?" smiled the butler.

"Okay," said Arthur as he took the torch and turned to climb the stairs.

When the boy had reached the top step, Nonstop Norman addressed the crowd again, much to Arthur's surprise. "Performing the candle-lighting ceremony tonight: the only member of the Whipple family not to hold a single world record or to be born on the first of March—please give a generous round of applause for—I'm sure he could use all the applause he can get—Arthur Whipple!"

The audience obliged the announcer's request, but with a fair amount of bewilderment, as most of the guests were still unsure for whom exactly they were applauding.

Still, it was the most applause Arthur had ever received, and he couldn't help but blush. He looked down at Wilhelm, who replied with a smile and a nod, signaling the boy to begin his task.

This was it. The special honor he'd been preparing for. His parents had finally deemed him fit for the distinguished role of birthday-candle lighter. And though he knew the position had only fallen to him because he was the sole member of the family not celebrating his own birthday, he vowed he would not let them down.

Arthur raised the blowtorch over his head and touched the flame to the tip of the broad candlewick above him.

The next moment, a great roaring flame danced atop the four-foot-wide candle. Now lit, the wax monolith would have appeared more at home marking the entrance to an ancient temple than sticking out of a birthday cake.

One down . . . Arthur thought to himself.

Wilhelm grasped the carousel-like platform that provided the cake's base and, with a heaving grunt, rotated it a few yards to the left, positioning the next candle just in front of Arthur. The second candle lit as easily as the first.

Soon, the cake had come full circle and Arthur was holding the blowtorch to the last candle—when he happened to look across at one of the candles he'd already lit. A foot or so from the top of the candle, he noticed a tiny flame inching its way down the candle's back. It struck him as different from a normal flame, in that it seemed to sparkle as it burned. He scanned the other candles and saw they all had tiny sparkling flames inching down their backs as well.

But before he could give the matter much thought, the tip of the last candlewick ignited in a ball of flame—and the crowd gave a cheer so loud it nearly knocked Arthur backward.

The boy clutched the railing as Wilhelm wheeled the stairs away from the cake, and Arthur took the opportunity to admire his handiwork. The flaming pillars of wax cast a warm, flickering glow over the silvery surface of the cake. The only way it might have looked more beautiful was if it had been Arthur's own.

Surprisingly, the candle-lighting ceremony had gone off

without a hitch, which was really a first for Arthur. He was used to things going horribly wrong with any activity in which he was involved. Perhaps his luck was finally changing.

With the boy still perched atop the stairs, Wilhelm pushed the staircase up to the side of the stage and aligned its top step with the narrow, towering catwalk that stretched across to the stage's other side. As the butler stepped away, Arthur's family gathered at the bottom of the stairs and proceeded to climb them.

Mr. Whipple still seemed a bit dazed from his recent encounter with Rex Goldwin, but when he reached the top, he shook Arthur's hand and said, "Good work, Son."

"Thanks, Father," replied Arthur. "Happy birthday."

His mother bent down and kissed him on the cheek. "You were terrific up there, dear. Now be sure to get yourself an especially large piece of cake."

"I will. Happy birthday, Mother."

Following behind their parents, the Whipple children smiled and waved to their brother as they paraded past him. Arthur turned to watch as they filed out onto the catwalk, high above the stage.

"And now," declared Nonstop Norman, "as the birthday boys and girls prepare for the traditional candle-extinguishing ceremony, please join Johnny Stump in singing 'Happy Birthday.' Take it away, Johnny!"

The band piped up, and the whole crowd began to sing along.

Soon the Whipples had formed a single row along the

platform and stood shoulder to shoulder, facing the crowd behind a guardrail draped in black cloth.

"Happy birthday, dear Charles, Eliza, Henry, Simon, Cordelia, Penelope, Edward, Charlotte, Lenora, Franklin, Abigail, Beatrice, George, and Ivy. . . . Happy birthday to you!"

On the last note, the black cloth fell away, revealing a row of fourteen industrial-strength electric fans.

Arthur stepped forward and pressed the glowing green button on the steel post at the end of the platform. The row of fan motors sprang to life.

Grabbing hold of the handles built into each fan, the Whipples aimed their respective blowers at the flaming targets before them. From the stairs where Arthur stood, it looked like the Most Fun in All the World.

In a matter of moments, three of the candles closest to the platform had been blown out.

"I got the two on the right!" shouted Henry.

"No you didn't," retorted Simon. "I got at least one of them! Think I should know, seeing it was me who invented these candle snuffers. . . ."

"Stop bickering, you two," chimed in Cordelia. "We go through this every year; we'll blow them out much faster if we work together. See that one on the far right there? It won't be nearly as easy to blow out as those first three. But if we all aim for it at once, we'll be sure to get it on the first try."

The boys begrudgingly agreed, and the three siblings

pivoted their fans in the direction of the specified candle. As soon as their wind streams aligned, the roaring flame sputtered and went out.

"See," said Cordelia. "As usual, I'm the only one clever enough to recognize the importance of teamwork."

But then something happened that none of them had expected. There was a loud *pop*—accompanied by a small flash of light at the base of the candle. Chunks of icing shot out from the side of the cake and spattered several of the onlookers below.

Assuming it was merely part of the act or a practical joke of some kind, the affected guests cheerfully wiped the icing from their smiling faces.

When the candle began to fall, however, their smiles vanished.

The colossal column of wax wobbled slightly, then slowly leaned over the outer edge of the cake. Cries of laughter turned to shrieks of terror as molten wax poured from the top of the teetering candle onto the horrified crowd.

"What did you have us do, Cordelia?" cried Simon.

"I don't think *we* did that . . . did we?" stammered the girl.

The towering candle leaned further and further out-ward, and then, with a *crack*, completely broke away from the cake. As it tumbled toward the earth from twenty feet above, dozens of screaming partygoers ran for their lives.

9

WHAT HAPPENED NEXT

A **gaping hole formed** in the crowd as the guests scattered to get out from under the falling candle like a school of frightened fish dodging a hungry barracuda.

Whizzing past coattails and evening gowns, the column of wax crashed to earth with a *thunk*, gouging a deep crater in the lawn.

Screaming gave way to silence as the partygoers struggled to catch their breath and comprehend what had just occurred.

It was a wonder nobody had been killed.

"That was a close one, eh?!" exclaimed Nonstop Norman over the loudspeakers. "Sincere apologies to those of you who were almost crushed—I'm afraid that's just an occupational hazard of being a guest at the Whipple estate!

I can assure you everything is now under control, so do remain calm. Anyone with wax burns may report to the nurse's station and they'll get you fixed up just as soon as—"

But before he could finish his reassuring speech, he was cut off by another loud pop, accompanied by another flash of light—this time at the base of a candle on the stage side of the cake.

As the candle leaned menacingly toward the bandstand, Nonstop Norman looked up to see the flaming wax pillar looming directly over him, and discovered that—for the first time in his life—he had been struck completely speechless.

"Oh, God," Mr. Whipple gasped from the towering catwalk. "It's the curse. . . ." Then, turning to his family, he cried, "Everyone off the platform, now! To the stairs!"

And yet, even as the Whipples watched the candle tilt over the cake's edge, Arthur's baby sister, Ivy, remained still—gripping the fan in front of her as tightly as she could with one hand while clutching a party-hat-wearing stuffed bear in the other.

This would not have been half so problematic, had Ivy not been the youngest of the Whipple children and subsequently standing at the end of the row, nearest the stairs. Because the platform barely allowed for a single file line, the frightened little girl and her bear were inadvertently, yet effectively, blocking her family's only escape route.

"Ivy!" shouted Mr. Whipple. "Move! Now!"

But this only caused the terrified toddler to hold on tighter.

Realizing that if Ivy did not move out of the way very soon, his entire family would be trapped thirty feet in the air, Arthur braced himself against the staircase railing and reached out his arm toward her. "Come on, Ivy," he said. "Let Mr. Growls go. He'll be all right. You can do it. Just grab my hand . . ."

But it was too late. Before Ivy could be persuaded, the fiery column crashed into the stage.

Had Nonstop Norman followed his own advice and remained calm, he would have, at that moment, been smashed flatter than a French crepe. As Arthur soon realized, sometimes—no matter what anyone else says—remaining calm is simply not the appropriate response to a given situation. Sometimes, the appropriate response is to run like mad.

Luckily, the announcer recognized the situation for what it was—a time to run like mad; unfortunately, he took it to a rather extreme level. Instead of stopping when the immediate danger was over, Nonstop Norman kept running and running until the Whipple estate was completely behind him—leaving the rest of the endangered partygoers to fend for themselves. For this reason, Nonstop Norman Prattle was not present to witness one of the worst catastrophes in Whipple family history.

As the candle collided with the stage, it bounced off the floorboards—and promptly crashed into the tower of scaffolding at stage right. Regrettably, it was this tower that was responsible for holding up half the platform upon which the Whipples stood.

There was a long, hair-raising *creeeak*—and then, a sudden *crash*. Showing no regard for its distinguished occupants, the far side of the platform dropped out from under the Whipples' feet as the entire structure jolted forward.

Arthur's family clung to the handles of their fans, and Arthur felt the stair tower beneath him lurch sideways. His insides went suddenly squishy. As he watched in terror, the top step on which he stood sheared away from the catwalk—and began leaning over the horrified crowd below.

The tilting tower paused, as if weighing its options. Luckily, Arthur had the presence of mind not to wait around for a decision. Whirling about, the boy flung himself down the stairs as fast as his legs would carry him.

He had only descended three steps when the staircase made up its mind—and proceeded to topple.

As he felt the toppling tower pick up speed beneath him, Arthur ran faster. Over the railing to his right, he could see scores of screaming partygoers scurrying to get out of the tower's shadow.

There was, however, one partygoer who did not flee.

Making a beeline for the foot of the staircase, Wilhelm charged across the lawn into the falling tower's path. "Hang on, Master Arthur!" the butler shouted. "I've got you!"

As Wilhelm caught hold of the tower's base, Arthur felt a stutter in the tower's momentum. But some things, once set in motion, are simply too big to be stopped—even by the World's Strongest German. And so, after a brief hiccup in speed, the twenty-five-foot staircase continued to fall.

Arthur had only made it halfway down the stairs when he was thrown abruptly against the handrail.

There was a splintering *crunch* followed by a sharp shattering of glass as the staircase smashed through the cocktail bar that stood near the side of the stage.

With a rush of adrenaline, Arthur leapt free of the stairs and dove onto the lawn. Rolling into a skid, the boy gouged a muddy groove with his shoulder as the staircase crashed down behind him in a mess of tangled struts and twisted steel.

Arthur lay on the ground for only a moment, before staggering to his feet and turning toward the wreckage. "Wilhelm!" he cried, spotting the butler's body pinned beneath the edge of the structure that had once served as its base.

Limping to the spot as fast as he could, Arthur could see the unconscious butler stirring under the tower's weight. The boy strained to lift the mangled frame, but it would not budge.

The next thing Arthur knew, his uncle was at his shoulder, heaving at the staircase alongside him. But even with their combined strength, the structure barely shifted an inch.

"I'm afraid what we need, lad," Uncle Mervyn panted, "is another Wilhelm. And since we haven't got one of those, we'll have to wait for a crane or a jack or something with a bit more muscle than us mere mortals."

It immediately became clear, however, that they had no time to wait for anything.

As it happened, the cocktail bar that had been crushed in the fall had housed the World's Largest Hand-Blown Bottles of Brandy, Vodka, Whiskey, Rum, and Gin—the contents of which were currently gushing onto the surrounding grass.

In the past, Arthur had often heard concerned grown-ups warn underage citizens to stay away from alcohol. This had always seemed to him good advice, and indeed, it still did—though less because of alcohol's capacity to transform even the brightest individuals into blithering idiots, and more because of its high degree of flammability.

As another fiery candle fell from the cake and landed near the twisted staircase, the demolished bar—drenched in alcohol—burst into flames.

Arthur and his uncle looked at one another in horror.

Rivers of flaming liquor poured from the pile of debris in all directions—including that of the trapped butler.

"Oh no!" cried the boy.

"Come on, lad!" shouted Uncle Mervyn.

Clutching the staircase once again, the pair heaved with all their might—but still, they could not lift it. The heat stung Arthur's cheeks as the river of fire snaked its way to within inches of Wilhelm's head. The butler was about to be burned alive.

As the last drop of hope drained from Arthur's heart, the boy felt the ground begin to rumble beneath him. He spun his head around—and was confronted by an astonishing sight.

With flames reflecting in his dark eyes and wind coursing through his wild, abundant hair, the Panther-Man of Pandharpur bounded onto the scene atop a charging elephant, while Hamlet and the high-diving dogs raced in at their rear.

As Mr. Mahankali approached the blaze, he yanked back on Shiva's reins, bringing the hulking beast to a skid—and overturning the portable diving pool harnessed behind him. A massive blanket of water gushed forth, extinguishing the flames with a screeching *hiss* as billowing columns of steam and smoke escaped into the air above.

"Hold on, my friend!" cried the Panther-Man. "Shiva is here!"

Rushing to the base side of the staircase, the elephant grasped the bottom beam with his trunk and proceeded to lift. As the near side of the structure rose into the air, Hamlet and the other dogs joined Arthur and Uncle Mervyn in sliding Wilhelm's drenched but unburnt body out from underneath it. Once the butler was clear, Shiva sent the staircase crashing back to the ground.

Mrs. Waite rushed to Wilhelm's side as the dogs whined anxiously.

"He's still breathing," she gasped.

Just then, there was a sharp *clang* of metal from over the stage—followed by a harrowing chorus of screams.

136

Arthur turned to glimpse a nightmarish spectacle. High above the stage, his family clung for dear life to the fan platform, which now hung warped and lopsided—its far end several feet lower than the other, and barely attached to the mangled scaffold. From their precarious position on the opposite end, Arthur's parents and older siblings strained to reach the younger ones, but there was little they could do. Arthur heard his father shout, "Everybody—try not to move! Hold onto your fan handles as tight as you can! We've got to keep still or we will all surely perish. And don't panic!" Indeed, it was clear that any movement they made could dislodge the unstable steel frame from its supports—and send the whole thing crashing down.

This, however, was soon to become the least of their worries.

The next moment, the wooden stage beneath them burst into flames.

"Ahh!" cried Arthur—then promptly sprang into action.

He dashed around the fallen staircase toward the front of the stage, fighting his way through the blasting wind that rushed from the row of still-whirling fans overhead. As he struggled to look into the wind toward the unstable platform above, his eyes were met by a sight that made his heart stop.

The mangled platform twisted suddenly, and his youngest sister, Ivy—still grasping her stuffed bear—was flung over the front edge.

His mother let out a blood-curdling shriek and clutched

at the air as the little girl plummeted from the catwalk.

On the ground in front of the stage—thirty feet beneath his sister's launching point—Arthur stood paralyzed as the flailing figure fell straight toward him.

THE PARTY'S OVER

Arthur had less than a second to make one of the most critical decisions of his life. He felt fairly certain that if he attempted to catch his sister, the speed of her fall would kill them both. And yet, if he ensured his own survival by simply stepping out of the way, there was no question: his sister would definitely die. Was it worth the huge risk of being crushed himself for the minuscule chance that he might save his sister from breaking her back?

If he'd had more time to contemplate the pros and cons of each possible outcome, he might have decided on a different course of action—but in that moment, he figured his life henceforward would simply not be worth living, knowing he had had a chance—however tiny—to save his sister, and had chosen to ignore it.

So, with nothing else at his disposal, Arthur simply stuck out his arms and prepared to catch her.

As he glanced at his outstretched limbs, they seemed to him horribly thin and wobbly—hardly suited for catching a falling beach ball, much less a human being—but unfortunately, they were all that lay between his sister and the unforgiving ground below.

As Ivy grew closer and closer to impact, Arthur grew increasingly unsure of his chances for survival—yet increasingly resolute in his stance. Whatever happened, he would not let her fall.

Thank God for elephants.

Before Arthur could put his doomed plan into action, a long, leathery gray object entered the airspace above him, wrapping itself around the terrified toddler in midflight.

Ivy's continuous scream came to an abrupt end as she was plucked from the air by the strong and skillful trunk of the great elephant Shiva.

When the elephant delivered Ivy and her matching toy bear into the arms of Mr. Mahankali, Arthur finally exhaled. He was overjoyed to see his sister receive such a painless rescue, compared with the one he had planned himself.

As Mr. Mahankali handed the dazed little girl down to Arthur, Mrs. Whipple let out an emotional sob overhead, her tears of terror turning to tears of relief. But her family was far from safe.

The small stage fire had now become a blazing inferno,

accelerated by the constant rush of wind flowing from the underside of the platform. As it happened, the fans intended for blowing out the Whipples' birthday candles had shifted in the melee—and were now pointing straight downward, fanning the flames below them.

"Still proud of your 'candle snuffers' now, are you, Simon?" shouted Henry from his position amongst the other dangling Whipples in a tone that was equal parts playful and grim.

"Can't say I am," Simon shouted back over the fans' roar. "I knew I should've invented a candle-snuffer snuffer to go with them. If they keep blowing like this, Ivy's fall will seem a stroll in the park compared to what's in store for the rest of us!"

Until that moment, Arthur had not been aware of the bizarrely fine line between blowing out a fire and fueling it. He understood, more or less, that a burst of wind with enough force will push a flame away from its heat source and snuff it out (a technological discovery which made Diedrich Luftlippen—inventor of the World's First Birthday Candle—a very wealthy man), but he had never fully grasped the fact that—as fire requires oxygen to burn—any amount of wind with a degree of force less than needed to extinguish a fire will accelerate and spread it. The conclusion he came to now was that wind was more or less a double-dealing, backstabbing mercenary: it pretended to be your greatest ally when you went to blow out a birthday candle or navigate a sailing ship—but the moment you tried to stop an emerging inferno, wind suddenly turned on you and became your worst enemy. It seemed to Arthur that if anybody deserved to be hanged for treason, surely it was wind. If only wind had a neck.

Mr. Mahankali, in clear agreement, called down to him from the elephant's saddle. "We must do something about those fans, Master Arthur! How does one turn them off?"

"The switch is at the right end of the platform," Arthur pointed out. "But without the staircase, I don't see how we'll get to it!"

Scarcely waiting for Arthur to finish, Mr. Mahankali made for the far right side of the stage—then promptly rode his trusty steed up the stage steps onto a small unburnt patch of floor.

Now surrounded by a semicircle of lashing flames, Shiva stamped in agitation, but—drawing on his years of training—managed to keep all four of his feet within a flame-free area only sixty-five inches in diameter. This in itself was an incredible feat for such an enormous animal, but it was far from his best trick. With a quick command from Mr. Mahankali, Shiva raised his front feet off the ground and shifted his weight to his hind legs. As Arthur gazed up in amazement, the ponderous pachyderm continued to extend his hind legs and soon stood completely upright at the corner of the stage, against a backdrop of fire.

Clutching the elephant's sides between his legs to keep himself from falling off the now-vertical saddle, the Panther-Man issued a series of verbal commands—to which Shiva responded by tilting his head back and raising his trunk into the air.

The beast reached for the glowing red off button at the far right end of the platform—but even with his trunk fully extended, the World's Largest Indian Elephant was just a bit too short.

"No good," said Mr. Mahankali, bringing Shiva back to a four-footed stance. "Wait a minute," he added, calling down to Arthur. "Have you still got your magical bullwhip with you?"

"Yes," the boy replied, reaching into his jacket and retrieving a coil of braided black leather, "but what can I do with it?"

"Why, you must use your skills to flip the switch, of course!"

Arthur's heart sank. "But Mr. Mahankali, I'm not—"

"There is no time for 'buts,' Master Arthur—only time for actions."

"Yes, sir," Arthur nodded. He wanted desperately to help, but for his family's sake, it terrified him to think it had come to this—that *he* was their best hope for survival. It seemed they were in even bigger trouble than he had thought.

"How shall I get in range of the button?" he asked. "The whip isn't nearly long enough."

"Do not worry," the Panther-Man replied. "Shiva will help you." Climbing halfway down the elephant's side, he reached out his hair-covered hand and called, "Now, quickly—come to me."

143

Arthur set his little sister on the ground and squeezed her shoulders. "Ivy, you stay right here and keep Mr. Growls safe, all right?"

"All right, Arssur," she replied, squeezing her stuffed bear. "I do dat."

"Good girl," he said.

Leaving her with a quick hug, Arthur hurried up the stage steps and clutched the lowered arm of Mr. Mahankali, who promptly hoisted him onto the elephant's back, just behind the beast's gigantic head.

"I still don't think the whip will reach from here," Arthur worried aloud, "even if Shiva stands on his hind legs again."

"Of course not," said Mr. Mahankali. "You will have to stand on the top of his head." Then, noticing Arthur's troubled expression, he added, "But do not worry—he will not mind. Now, go!"

Before Arthur really knew what he was doing, he found himself scrambling—bullwhip in hand—up the back of the elephant's leathery neck, between the beast's massive draping ears—and onto the highest point of his skull.

It felt rather awkward, standing on someone else's head—whatever his species; luckily, as Mr. Mahankali had promised, the elephant was not bothered in the least.

The next moment, Shiva lurched upward, and Arthur's muscles strained to hold his body in place.

As the elephant's head halted at its maximum height—twenty-five feet above the ground—Arthur was nearly sent toppling backward. But Shiva quickly shifted his head, and the boy stayed put.

The elephant had done his part; now it was up to Arthur.

Rising to his feet on wobbly legs, the boy uncoiled the bullwhip and set his sights on the red button.

"Help us, Arthur!" cried George. "It isn't fun up here at all anymore!"

Several feet to the button's left, he and the other octuplets clung desperately to the twisted platform, the whirring fans pulling at their hair and lashing it against their faces.

"Don't worry, Georgie," Arthur called. "It'll be all right. You'll be down on the ground in no time. Just hold on tight while I try to turn off the fans, okay?"

"Okay, Arthur," replied George.

"Don't fall off!" Beatrice warned, her eyes wide with worry.

Arthur gave a nod to his sister and drew a deep breath. Then, imagining a milk bottle atop his head to aid his balance, he snapped his arm toward the glowing button.

With a *crack*, the tip of the whip stopped a foot short and two feet wide of the target.

Arthur, feeling the heat rising up from the flames below, wiped the sweat from his brow. He sent the lash shooting into the air once again—but once again, the whip fell short.

Unlike his ill-fated record attempt from earlier in the evening, all it would take to succeed this time was one well-placed crack—but Arthur now found himself longing for the carefree breeziness of nine hundred cracks placed entirely at random.

Over the course of seven tries, Arthur steadily closed in on his mark—but the button remained just out of range.

As he raised his arm the eighth time, a dreadful scream met his ears. Arthur looked left—and started in horror.

The sweet face of his little sister Lenora was now contorted and smashed up against the wire guard at the back of her fan. The large yellow ribbon in her hair had been sucked into the cage and now tugged mercilessly at her head. Spreading her fingers and pressing her palm against the wide-gapped guard, Lenora struggled to pry her face away from the whirling blade on the other side. Her neighboring siblings, Charlotte and Franklin, watched in helpless terror.

Arthur gasped. He was out of practice runs. If little Lenora was to remain unmaimed, his next crack would have to count.

The boy locked his eyes onto the smoldering crimson button.

With the force of not just his arm, but of his entire body, Arthur sent the whip hurtling toward its target.

The snakelike cord reared back its head, pausing a moment in midair—then lashed out and struck its prey with a fatal blow.

Arthur watched in delighted disbelief as the glaring red light went dark. The distinct sound of deceleration filled the air as the fan motors ground to a halt.

He had succeeded.

But before Arthur had time to properly celebrate, he was struck by an odd sensation. It was, in fact, the sensation of falling.

Having overstepped the edge of the elephant's cranium in his final lunge, Arthur now found himself plummeting toward the flaming floorboards below, his bullwhip trailing behind him like the World's Worst Parachute.

It soon became clear, however, that this was simply not his night to die. He felt a sudden pressure around his waist, and—though his insides were slow to get the message—his body was brought to an abrupt standstill five feet above the ground.

A quick inspection revealed an elephant's trunk wrapped around his midsection, and Arthur realized he had been delivered from death by the same method that had saved his youngest sister.

"Thanks, big fella," Arthur exhaled as he affectionately patted Shiva's trunk.

The elephant trumpeted in reply.

"Well done, Master Arthur!" shouted Mr. Mahankali from the elephant's back. "We can take it from here, my friend!"

Bringing his front feet to rest on the floorboards at the stage's corner, the elephant lowered the boy to the ground in front of the stage, setting him down beside his littlest sister.

As Arthur lifted Ivy into his arms, she chirped, "Whip-*crack*! Whip-*crack*!"

Giving the girl a squeeze, Arthur looked back up at the

platform. The spinning fan blades had slowed almost to a stop. Without the wind's goading, the flames had subsided considerably, leaving a narrow, fire-free strip at the stage's front edge.

Wasting no time, the Panther-Man led his elephantine steed along the front of the stage until they were directly beneath George, the rightmost octuplet. Once in position, Shiva reared up on his hind legs and stretched out his trunk toward the little boy. It still did not reach—so Mr. Mahankali ordered George to jump.

"Do not fear, Master George—Shiva will not let you fall."

Another hair-raising groan from the platform provided just the encouragement the boy needed; a moment later, he was scooped up in the elephant's trunk and then promptly retrieved by Mr. Mahankali.

Soon Beatrice had joined her little brother in the Panther-Man's waiting arms—and shortly after, Abigail.

As Arthur looked on with Ivy—who was busy repeating the phrase, "Elfunt, wooo!"—Shiva returned all four feet to the stage and lowered the first batch of rescued children to the ground.

Hamlet, the Whipples' Great Dane, who had been whimpering and pacing the ground below ever since arriving on the scene with Mr. Mahankali and Shiva, bounded over to Abigail and scooped her up onto his giant neck. She hugged him, and his tongue flapped gleefully from his mouth.

"You did it, Arthur!" shouted Beatrice.

"No," said Arthur. "Shiva did all the work. I couldn't have done it without him."

148

"Yes—but *he* couldn't have done it without *you*, Arthur."

Even though Beatrice was only five, and might not have completely understood, her compliment made Arthur feel more a part of the family than he ever had before.

Soon all of Arthur's siblings were standing beside him, with their mother in the grasp of the elephant's trunk.

The moment Mrs. Whipple's feet reached the ground, she ran to her children and wrapped her arms around each of them—reserving an extra large squeeze for Arthur. "Good work, Arthur—you saved us!" she cried. Then, retrieving Ivy from his arms and turning back toward the platform where her husband remained stranded, she added, "It's just a shame there weren't any world records for you in all that—or it might have been an absolute triumph."

Arthur would not have minded if his mother had stopped at "you saved us!"—but he had to agree with her. He could not imagine anything more triumphant than if, in the act of saving his family, he had somehow been able to pull off his first world record as well. Alas, there was no denying that a certain Mr. Kalpesh Sirahathi had managed three years earlier to flip a switch from the head of an elephant with a bullwhip—in a mere 2.24 seconds. Arthur only hoped his father would not be too disappointed in him when he finally made it to the ground.

As Arthur and the rescued Whipples looked on, Shiva rose to his hind legs one last time and offered his trunk to the stranded patriarch.

Dropping his feet over the edge of the platform, Mr.

Whipple gave a reassuring wave to his family and prepared himself to jump.

The elephant took a small step forward. And suddenly, what seemed to have been a happy ending in the making shifted to a scene from a nightmare.

Crrr-ack! The floorboards splintered beneath the elephant's foot. The cumbersome beast gave a trumpeting cry and tumbled sideways, Mr. Mahankali clinging helplessly to his back.

The elephant crashed through the floorboards, shattering the stage into an array of flying splinters and glowing embers. There was a tortured groan, followed by an earth-shaking thud, as Shiva and his master disappeared into the fiery chasm.

"No!" cried Arthur.

The force of the crash shook the towers of scaffolding at the sides of the stage, and in turn, the platform they supported. The catwalk tilted forward with a *screech*, nearly wrenching itself free from its supports. Mr. Whipple tumbled over the front edge—and dangled by one arm over the flaming death trap below.

"Charles!" screamed Mrs. Whipple.

Arthur's older brothers rushed forward and leapt onto the front of the stage—but even were they not cut off by a wall of flames, there was nothing they could have done to help him.

Arthur could scarcely breathe. He had watched as the brave Panther-Man and his noble steed were enveloped by fire, and now it seemed—without their help—he would watch the fire envelop his father as well. At that moment, he would have given anything to see the disappointment in his father's eyes once again—if only it meant the man was standing safely on the ground beside him.

Scattered screams rang out behind Arthur as some of the more adventurous party guests reconvened around the no longer exploding cake and glimpsed their host's horrifying predicament.

It was then that the boy began to detect a distinct, high-pitched roar rising above the pandemonium.

In an instant, the screams of horror turned to shouts of astonishment as something large and luminous streaked through the sky overhead.

It appeared to be a man in a rocket pack.

The next moment, Mr. Whipple lost his grip on the platform. But before he had fallen more than a few feet, the swooping airman caught him with one arm around the chest. The force of Mr. Whipple's fall caused the pair to dip unnervingly toward the flames, but a quick increase in the rocket pack's thrust corrected their path. Soon they were soaring away from the deadly platform as—with one final screech—the catwalk separated from its supports and plunged into the blaze below.

Circling back over the top of the crumbling cake, the pilot and his passenger promptly began their descent. A moment later they were alighting on the ground beside Arthur and the rest of his anxious family. The tightness in Arthur's throat became almost bearable again.

Now that they were so close, the boy was afforded a full view of his father's rocket-powered rescuer. Apart from the rocket pack, the formality of the man's jacket and tie was further contrasted by the dark-visored crash helmet that encased his head. Arthur could not remember being in the presence of a more awe-inspiring figure.

As the two men planted their feet firmly on the ground, Mr. Whipple staggered forward, practically doubling over with exhaustion—but his family rushed to his aid, throwing their arms around him and propping him up.

"Daddy, you're all right!" cried Lenora, her eyes filling with tears.

"That was a close one, eh Dad?" said Henry.

"We were so worried!" sobbed Penelope.

Arthur squeezed in amongst his family in their massive embrace, closing his eyes and inhaling through his nostrils. It seemed his father would indeed live to be disappointed by his recordless son another day—and Arthur could not have been happier for the opportunity.

"Thank you, children," panted Mr. Whipple. "I am exceedingly glad to be back on the ground with you all. But we've no time to waste—we must help Mr. Mahankali and Shiva!"

Arthur's father stepped away from the circle, but just as he started for the stage, Uncle Mervyn appeared at his back—and with him, the fire brigade.

A moment later, a team of firemen raced past with axes

and hoses in hand—and set about issuing streams of water onto the burning stage before them.

Mr. Whipple rushed to their chief and cried, "There is a man and an elephant in the midst of that mess who are both very dear to us. Please—you must bring them back alive!"

"We'll do our best, sir—but it doesn't look good from here."

Arthur's father returned to his family with his head hung low, and Mrs. Whipple put a comforting arm around her husband. "They'll be all right, dear," she said in the most reassuring voice she could muster. "When have they ever let us down before?"

As the fire brigade continued to douse the stage, Mr. Whipple turned to his rocket-pack-wearing rescuer, addressing him with the tone of a man recently reminded of his own mortality. "Thank God for you, Wilhelm—I was sure I was a goner. It's a good thing you convinced me to purchase that rocket pack—but how did you ever get it to work? Last I heard, you still couldn't get the blasted thing off the ground. . . ."

Before the man in the rocket pack could speak, a blackened and battered Wilhelm limped his way around the cake and into the gathering—much to Mr. Whipple's surprise, of course, as Arthur could plainly see. Some yards behind the butler trailed Mrs. Waite, who was clearly shocked as well—by how difficult it was keeping up with a man who had been completely unconscious just one minute earlier.

"Oh thank God you all are all right," Wilhelm raved to a very confused Mr. Whipple. "I came as soon as I voke up." His eyes scanning the scene as he spoke, Wilhelm seemed to notice something missing. "But vhere is Mahankali and Shiva? Mrs. Vaite says they saved my life."

Mr. Whipple was so taken aback by the unexpected appearance of a second Wilhelm that all he could get out was: "Um—er—they've fallen through the stage—the fire brigade is doing their best—but what are you . . . I thought . . ." His head now darted back and forth between the Wilhelm in front of him and the helmeted man with the rocket pack to his rear.

Upon hearing Mr. Whipple's fragmented, yet disturbing account, the *un*helmeted Wilhelm's mouth dropped open with deep concern and blurted, "I must help them!" Then, leaving his master in utter bewilderment, the battered butler took off hobbling toward the stage as fast as his injured legs would carry him (which was indeed much faster than most men can run on perfectly healthy legs). Rushing up the stage steps, Wilhelm grabbed an ax from one of the firemen and dashed through the spray of water and dwindling flames, fighting his way to the stage's center. Discovering an open gash in the floorboards, he promptly jumped through it, feet first—and disappeared from view.

"Godspeed, old boy," muttered Mr. Whipple, breaking free of his bewilderment to admire the butler's bravery.

With his best man on the job, there was little more Mr. Whipple could do to help, so he turned back to the mysterious man in the rocket pack. "My apologies for incorrectly addressing you earlier, good sir. You can see I am not altogether in my right mind this evening. Now, if you'll permit me—to whom does my family owe their deepest debt of gratitude for so courageously saving their father's life?"

As the man began to lift his helmet, he spoke for the first time.

"Sorry I couldn't get to you sooner there, but I had to pop out to the car and grab the old rocket pack. Good thing we've been taking it with us everywhere we go lately. You just never know when you might need a rocket pack these days, eh, Charlie?"

With his helmet fully removed, the man's chiseled features became visible, and Arthur instantly recognized him as Rex Goldwin, the Whipples' new neighbor—and Ruby Goldwin's father.

Having finally learned the girl's name, Arthur had thought he'd put an end to the mystery surrounding her—but now the Goldwin girl and her family seemed more mysterious than ever. Not even the Whipples kept a rocket pack in their car.

As Arthur's father stood speechless, Mrs. Whipple ran to Rex Goldwin, taking his hand in hers and shaking it vigorously. "Oh, you dear, dear man!" she cried. "You are one remarkable neighbor, Mr. Goldwin. We've only known you for a little over an hour—and here you've already saved my husband's life. I'm sure there is nothing we can ever do to fully repay such an act of selflessness, but if anything ever comes to mind, please do not hesitate to ask. We are deeply indebted to you for the rest of our lives!"

"Now don't get carried away, dear," her husband frowned.

"Why, what ever do you mean, Charles? You owe this man your very life, and I don't think you've so much as thanked him."

"Yes . . . of course," he sighed. "Thank you . . . Mr. Goldwin."

"Don't mention it, Charlie! What else are neighbors for, if not to lend a helping hand when needed?"

At that moment, Rita Goldwin and eight of her children rushed through the crowd and flocked around their father, hugging him and congratulating him for such a spectacular rescue.

Ruby, the ninth and final Goldwin child in attendance, shuffled in a moment later and immediately looked to Arthur, who returned her gaze with a subtle yet friendly smile. He could not hide the strange new connection he felt with her: it was because of her father's heroism that his own father was still alive.

The girl, however, did not smile back. Her dark-outlined eyes were filled with a peculiar unease that sapped the smile from Arthur's face and made him anxious all over again.

The two held their gaze for one brief moment—until Ruby's mother stepped between them to address Arthur's father.

"Charles," she said, "we can't tell you how glad we are you didn't fall into that terrible fire. How awful that would have been for you—and on your birthday! My Rex has been messing about with that ridiculous rocket pack for months now. Who knew it would end up saving a life as valuable as your own?"

"In fact, dear," said Rex Goldwin, "I believe that marks the First Human Rescue by Rocket Pack Ever Recorded— doesn't it, Mr. McCleary?"

"I . . . believe it does, Mr. Goldwin," Uncle Mervyn replied distractedly. He was busy staring at the disintegrating stage before them, into which two of his dear friends had disappeared.

"Hmm," Rex added, scrunching his brow, "I wonder if this doesn't present us with a certain groundbreaking opportunity here. Up till now, of course, no world record publication has ever published a record broken by someone sponsored by a competitor. But I know Ardmore has been hoping to collaborate for years—and seeing as it was Grazelby's biggest star whose life was saved, I'm sure the *Guide* will want to do something to commemorate the occasion . . . perhaps by jointly publishing the rocket-pack rescue record with the *Ardmore Almanac*?"

Mr. Whipple hardly had time to open his mouth before his wife gripped his arm and blurted, "Why, what an excellent idea, Mr. Goldwin. Don't you think it's an excellent idea, dear?"

Arthur's father just managed to get out a quick, "But

dear—" before Mrs. Whipple clamped her fingernails down on his arm. Mr. Whipple's face fell like a scolded child's. "Of course," he said. "What an excellent idea."

Uncle Mervyn, hearing agreement from both parties, nodded his consent. "Very well then. The International World Record Federation will no doubt be pleased to see cooperation between competing publications under its governance. I'll file the proposal first thing tomorrow morning."

"Oh my!" exclaimed Rex Goldwin. "I never dreamt the First Ever Collaboration between *Ardmore* and *Grazelby* would be for a record of *mine*—and for something so unexpected!" His eyes grew suddenly wide. "Hang on," he blurted, "what time is it?"

Uncle Mervyn glanced at his watch and then back at the stage. "Eleven forty-eight," he replied absentmindedly.

"So we haven't missed the eligibility deadline then?"

"No," said Uncle Mervyn. "It's not till midnight."

"Well then," said Rex, "I believe these two records have just brought my family's tally to the minimum thousand-record requirement."

"Do you wish to declare?" asked Uncle Mervyn.

"We do," said Rex. "Just give me the proper forms, and I'll see to it they're all filled out in the next twelve minutes."

"That won't be necessary," said the certifier. "You may send me your paperwork tomorrow. Once I verify the information, I'll simply backdate the forms, and then forward them on to the IWRF."

"Great Barrier Reef!" shouted Rex as he wrapped his arms around his family. "Well, kids—it looks like we'll be eligible for this year's championships after all! Don't ever let anybody tell you good things can't come out of tragedy."

Indeed, Arthur had never seen his father looking so tragic in all his life.

Soon, the stage fire had been reduced to a thick cloud of steam above the blackened floorboards. Members of the fire brigade rushed onto the stage and set about lowering a harness into the huge gash in the stage's center.

As the growing crowd looked on with anticipation, the intrepid Whipple butler emerged from the crevice, carrying a lifeless figure in his arms.

Though the bystanders who had witnessed the horrific crash knew that the body in Wilhelm's arms belonged to Mr. Mahankali, it scarcely seemed possible that it could be the same man. The right side of his suit was mostly missing, having been scorched clean through—and the silver-streaked hair that once covered his entire body now appeared to cover little more than half of it.

As Wilhelm carried the burnt figure down the stage steps and onto the lawn, the Whipple dogs flocked to their fallen master, whimpering with worry.

From this distance, Arthur and the other onlookers could see that Mr. Mahankali's face was devoid of life and badly burned. The hair around his right ear and lower jaw had all been singed away, so that his dark and blistering skin was exposed to the night air, probably for the first time in his life. Despite his rather gruesome wounds, Arthur was amazed at how peaceful the man looked, considering all the violence that had befallen him. The boy felt a sudden pang of dread. So this was what death looked like.

But just as the tears began to well up in Arthur's eyes, the dead man spoke.

"Shi-va . . ." muttered the Panther-Man in a weakened whisper, peering out through barely opened eyelids.

The crowd gasped. Upon hearing their master's voice, the dogs went wild, licking his face in jubilation. The Whipples rushed to Mr. Mahankali's side. Arthur's tears emerged as tears of joy.

Wilhelm was so overwhelmed with happiness to see his dear friend alive, he nearly dropped the man. "Mahankali!" he exclaimed. "You're not dead!"

"Shi-va . . ." repeated the mangled man.

"There is no need to vorry about the elephant. He is still breathing, and they are vorking very hard to free him," reassured Wilhelm. "Do not vorry, my friend. They vill have him out in no time. But now vee must get you to a hospital!"

With that, Wilhelm broke into a run and hurried off through the crowd toward the helipad on the other side of the estate.

Arthur could hardly process all he had experienced in the last few short hours. Between the bitter failures, terrifying encounters, and horrific catastrophes, there had been some major discoveries, great honors, and fantastic rescues.

But now, as his father gathered his family and led them off after their comrades, the boy could think of nothing else but the heroic gamekeeper who currently lingered at death's door.

"Poor Mahankali," Arthur overheard his father remark somberly to Uncle Mervyn. "He's immensely fortunate just to be alive, but with so much hair burned away, he will now most certainly lose his 'World's Hairiest' title to that awful Monkey-Man from Mongolia. I doubt our friend will feel very fortunate at all when he realizes what he has lost. It's hard to say which is worse—losing one's life, or losing one's greatest world record."

Then, with a sudden, hardened resolve, the Whipple patriarch declared, "I swear—if this curse has been aided by anyone on this mortal plane, I will not stop till I see the culprit hanged for what he has done to our dear Mr. Mahankali!"

It was a vow he would soon live to regret.

THE AFTERMATH

MORE MISHAPS AT WHIPPLE MANOR!

WHIPPLES SUFFER SECOND CRUSHING SCARE—AND ADD DEATH BY FIRE TO LIST OF HOUSEHOLD DANGERS

This year's so-called Whipple Family Birthday Extravaganza ended in disaster Saturday night when over a dozen thousand-pound birthday candles spontaneously fell from a twenty-foot-tall birthday cake and into a crowd of unsuspecting guests. After nearly crushing hundreds of horrified partygoers, the rogue candles set fire to an outdoor stage, stranding the entire Whipple family on a catwalk some forty feet in the air for over a quarter of an hour.

Several of the Whipples' employees were badly burned in the melee—including Phoolendu Mahankali (better known as the celebrated Panther-Man of Pandharpur) and his equally distinguished elephant sidekick, Shiva—who are both in critical condition at the time of this writing. (Once hailed as the World's Hairiest Living Man, Mahankali is not expected to retain his title, even if he does survive his injuries.)

Yet, despite its tragedies, the evening was not without its inspiring moments—largely provided by one Rex Goldwin, who, in the First Human Rescue by Rocket Pack, daringly saved Charles Whipple from falling to a fiery death.

The rescue capped off Goldwin's recent return to public record breaking—after a dazzling start to his career was followed by some two decades of relative obscurity. Though the feat is set to mark the First Ever Cosponsored Entry in the prestigious *Grazelby's Guide to World Records and Fantastic Feats*, Goldwin and his family have just declared their eligibility for this year's World Record World Championships under the sponsorship of *The Amazing Ardmore Almanac of the Ridiculously Remarkable*, one of Grazelby's less-respected competitors—a distinction, however, which may now be poised for reevaluation.

"Nonstop" Norman Prattle, the popular radio personality who served as master of ceremonies for the event, says he barely escaped with his life—and is quick to praise Goldwin's efforts.

"I rescued as many people as I could before I was

forced to evacuate," Prattle recounts, "but I just couldn't save them all. Dodging giant falling birthday candles was certainly never listed in the job description for emcee, I can tell you that! I hear the Whipples themselves would have been burnt to a crisp had this Rex Goldwin fellow not been there to save the day—I'm sure we'll be seeing a lot more of him in the future. I hate to say this, but I'm worried the Whipples may be losing their touch."

Saturday's "Birthday Cake Catastrophe" was not the first stain on the Whipple family's safety record. The incident is highly reminiscent of February's "French Toast Fiasco," in which one of the Whipple octuplets was nearly crushed to death by her breakfast.

After this second near-fatal incident at Neverfall Hall in as many months, some more excitable observers have drawn comparisons to the "Lyon's Curse"—the shadowy run of misfortune from the Whipples' distant past—but the Whipples have refused to comment on any such speculation. Meanwhile, other, more cynical pundits are simply accusing the Whipples of gross negligence—and argue the family's proposed involvement in next month's controversial Unsafe Sports Showdown is beyond the bounds of good taste.

The Whipples, for their part, have reportedly rejected all allegations of negligence, instead attributing the incident to "foul play" and procuring the services of the renowned detective, Inspector Hadrian Smudge.

Smudge, a guest of the Whipples during the incident, holds the record for Most Solved Cases in History. Though recently retired from Scotland Yard, Smudge now lends his services to various government agencies and select private individuals.

In a statement released late Saturday night, Smudge sent a warning to any possible perpetrators: "The Whipples have been the victims of a highly skilled saboteur—but not so skilled, I assure you, as to deceive the heightened senses of Sir Hadrian Smudge! The world may rest easily tonight in the knowledge that the criminal responsible for this heinous act will be swiftly and mercilessly brought to justice. Villains be vigilant—Inspector Hadrian Smudge is on the case!"

• • •

Arthur looked up from the photograph of the pointy-faced man defiantly holding up a sinewy finger on the front page of *The World Record*—and shifted his gaze to the man himself.

There, on the opposite side of the hospital waiting room, Inspector Smudge stood questioning one of the Whipple servants. With his thick, arching eyebrows and hooked nose, Smudge looked even more striking in person, and Arthur felt a wave of reassurance at the detective's decision to work on his family's case. If there was one man who could get to the bottom of the previous night's strange goings on, surely it was Hadrian Ulysses Smudge.

Setting down the paper, Arthur turned to find the octuplets at his left, quietly holding hands with their heads bowed, while farther down the row, his brothers Henry and Simon battled each other—solemnly yet vigorously—for the Fastest Lord's Prayer Ever Recited. Their parents, having so nearly lost their youngest daughter the night before, now sat to Arthur's right, cradling Ivy close to them—while Ivy did the same to her matching toy bear, Mr. Growls, who had had a rather close shave of his own. Arthur, feeling equally overcome with thankfulness and worry, followed the octuplets and bowed his head as well.

Half a minute later, the waiting room doors swung open, prodding Arthur and the rest of the anxious crowd to their feet as a bespectacled man in blue surgical scrubs entered the room. But before the man could speak, a second, much shorter surgeon stepped out from behind him and addressed the crowd.

"Mr. Mahankali is out of surgery," announced the undersized surgeon as she lowered her surgical mask, revealing the face of Arthur's eldest sister, Cordelia. Well on her way to becoming the World's Youngest Surgeon, Cordelia had recently accepted a provisional post at the hospital and had been called upon to assist in the Panther-Man's surgery. "It was touch and go for a while there," she continued, "but we are now anticipating a near-full recovery. . . ."

Cordelia's lip began quivering uncontrollably as her hardened professional exterior crumbled away and exposed the heartbroken girl beneath it.

The lead surgeon smiled and put a comforting hand on Cordelia's shoulder before cheerfully resuming the report. "I'm afraid Miss Whipple says '*near*-full,'" he chuckled, "because—though we did all we could—it seems Mr. Mahankali may never again reach the heights of his former hairiness." Then, noticing the grim expression on Mr. Whipple's face, he cleared his throat and added solemnly, "But, of course, most importantly, it does seem he will survive."

"Yes, of course, doctor," Mr. Whipple sighed. "May we see him?"

"Yes, may we?" interjected a shrewd voice from across the room.

Stepping forward, Inspector Smudge presented a burnished brass badge to the surgeon. "After my clients have had their visit, I should like a moment alone with the man."

"Very well then," the surgeon replied. "Come with me."

• • •

As the Whipples gathered around Mr. Mahankali's bed, Arthur grappled with conflicting emotions. Though he was overjoyed just to witness his hairy friend's chest rising and falling beneath the hospital sheets, he was equally horrified to see the proud Panther-Man in such a dreadful state, stripped of his most cherished world record and reduced to a matted mess of fur and bandages. With clumps of tangled hair poking out between strips of white gauze, Mr. Mahankali's unconscious face looked like something out of *Attack of the Mummy Werewolf*, a film which—however enjoyable it had been on screen—Arthur had no desire to see translated to real life.

Just then, the recovery room door burst open, and Sammy the Spatula barged into the room.

"Where is 'e?" the chef called to no one in particular. "I 'eard 'e's out of surgery." Then, noticing the unconscious figure in the hospital bed before him, he rushed to Mr. Mahankali's bedside—and broke down sobbing.

"What 'ave I done, mate?" he whimpered. "If I'd've known me best culinary creations would wind up nearly killing some of me best mates, I'd've dropped right out of cooking school. That's God's honest troof, that is."

Arthur hadn't thought it possible for anyone to appear more pathetic than the man in the hospital bed, but the chef's present state had promptly proved the boy wrong. It smelled as though Sammy the Spatula had recently taken a swim in the World's Largest Bottle of Scotch—but more likely, the chef had merely drunk it.

"Can you ever forgive me, mate?" the drunken man continued. "I'm sure I'll never forgive meself. . . ."

With that, Wilhelm stepped forward—his brow still streaked with ash from the preceding night's calamity—and gently patted Sammy's back. "There, there, my friend," he said. "This is not your fault."

The chef whirled his head around. "Innit, mate? It were me who baked the blasted fing, weren't it? And me who put the candles on top—and me who made the French toast what almost squashed a sweet little girl?"

At this, Mr. Whipple gingerly took the chef's arm and began leading him away from the bed. "Please, Sammy—be reasonable," he whispered. "Clearly, you've had nothing to do with these tragic incidents. You're the very best at what you do, my good man—and you were simply doing your job. . . ."

This apparently did not have the comforting effect Mr. Whipple had hoped for, as Sammy immediately yanked his arm away and turned to face him. "I just can't do it anymore, guv!" he blurted. "I made it froo two years in the clink wivvout givin' up on me cooking, but I reckon this 'as finally done it! I just can't bear to see nobody else 'armed by any more of me food. . . . It's been a pleasure working for you, Mr. Whipple—but please accept me resignation."

Mr. Whipple's eyes bulged in surprise. "Now, Sammy—you can't be serious! It's been a very long night, and I'm sure we could all do with a bit of sleep and a strong cup of coffee or two—so why don't you take the day off and we'll discuss this tomorrow."

"Sir, I—"

"Ah-ah-ah. I will not discuss the matter any further. As your employer, I order you to take the day off."

The chef sighed. "All right, sir," he said finally. "But don't fink it'll make me change me mind."

With that, Sammy stumbled for the doorway—but before he could grasp the handle, the door opened on its own, and Inspector Smudge stepped into the threshold. Nearly colliding with the man, Sammy glanced up at the inspector's face and took a startled step back—then hastily pushed past him through the doorway.

After watching the intoxicated chef stagger down the hallway and disappear from view, the inspector entered the room and made his way to the Panther-Man's bedside.

"How does your man seem to be getting on?" he inquired.

"They tell us he's stabilized," said Mrs. Whipple, "but that he won't be able to wake without severe pain for some days now."

"Most unfortunate," said the inspector. "I'm afraid, however, we haven't the luxury of waiting for the pain to subside. Alas, our duty to the truth must take precedence over any small amount of physical comfort."

Arthur's father nodded gravely. "Yes . . . of course, Inspector."

As Mr. Whipple ushered his family to the door, Inspector Smudge turned to the white-coated man in the corner of the room. "With your assistance, Doctor," he said, gesturing to the patient. "I shall make my inquiry as concise as possible."

The doctor nodded solemnly and walked toward the bed as the recovery room door closed behind Arthur and his family.

A moment later, an agonizing scream sounded through the door, sending shudders down Arthur's spine.

The Whipples waited for several harrowing minutes amongst the crowd of well-wishers gathered outside the

Panther-Man's room—until at last, the door opened and Inspector Smudge stepped into the hall.

"There is nothing left for me to do here," the inspector declared. "Unfortunately, Mr. Mahankali has little to add to the investigation, as he did not notice anything out of the ordinary prior to last night's disturbance."

While Arthur's heart sank to hear that Mr. Mahankali had been awoken in vain, the inspector's words sent the boy's mind racing. It was then that the image of the two suspicious clowns skulking through the shadows of the Grazelby tent leapt into his memory.

"And as there are no eyewitnesses to any wrongdoing," continued Inspector Smudge, "I'm afraid we'll be forced to rely solely on whatever *physical* evidence we may discover."

Arthur's pulse quickened. Surely the clowns had something to do with all this. And that made *him* an eyewitness. He could no longer remain silent.

The boy stepped forward. "Inspector, I—"

"Arthur, please," snapped his father. "Inspector Smudge has no time for your questions now."

"But I—"

"Really, Arthur," his father whispered crossly, "if you must get the inspector's autograph, at least wait till we're back at the house."

"Wh—? No," the boy stammered in confusion. "You don't—"

"Please, Mr. Whipple," the inspector grinned, "don't be too hard on the lad. This sort of thing is to be expected;

I am certainly no stranger to youthful adulation. But of course, your assessment of time is an accurate one." He gave a consoling little frown to Arthur and turned back toward the crowd. "Though I'm sure Mr. Mahankali has been thoroughly moved by everyone's presence here today, I believe we shall now do him more good elsewhere. Let us return at once to Neverfall Hall, where I may properly survey the crime scene and conduct further interviews. The sooner the investigation is resumed, the sooner Mr. Mahankali shall be avenged!"

An affirmative clamor arose from the crowd, and before Arthur could say anything more, he was swept off in the sea of departing well-wishers.

As the boy exited the hospital with his siblings and mounted the stairs of the triple-decker Hulls-Hoyst, which was both the Whipple family car and the Tallest Automobile on Earth, it seemed his chance to aid in the investigation had gone.

But then, as Arthur approached the car's second level, he happened to glance over his shoulder—and caught a glimpse of Inspector Smudge standing alone on the ground, less than five yards away.

His pulse quickening once again, the boy turned back to the stairs—and tried to convince himself he had no reason to speak to the man. He had, after all, already attempted to reveal his knowledge—only to be dismissed and ridiculed in the process. And besides, he reasoned, there was no *real* evidence that the clowns had had anything to do with the

Birthday Cake Catastrophe in the first place. In all likelihood, they were entirely innocent.

And yet—what if they weren't? What if Arthur's eyewitness account was the one missing piece in apprehending the villains behind his family's suffering? Surely it was worth risking any amount of ridicule for even the slightest possibility of cracking the case.

Arthur was nearly at the top level of the car when he suddenly stopped, causing a pile-up of Whipple children to his rear.

"Watch where you're stepping, Edward!" cried Penelope.

"Don't look at *me*," Edward grumbled. "I've climbed glaciers on five continents; I think I know how to climb a few stairs. . . ."

"Calm down, everybody," said Henry. "Arthur—what are you doing up there?"

"Sorry," said Arthur as he turned about and started back down the staircase. "I . . . I need to get down again. I'll just be a minute."

Amidst a chorus of irritated sighs, Arthur managed to make his way past his bewildered siblings and back onto the pavement.

Rushing over to the unsuspecting inspector, the boy skidded to a stop and blurted, "I beg your pardon Inspector Smudge but last night I'm pretty sure I saw two suspicious clowns sneaking around the birthday cake just before the candles started falling—they had a black dragon case—one was a dwarf, one was a giant—they probably had nothing to do with any of this but I just thought I should let you know . . . uh, sir."

Inspector Smudge barely had time to look up from the notebook he was studying before the boy had launched into his single-breath saga—but by the time Arthur had finished, the detective's interest had been visibly piqued. "My dear boy," he said, "if you are trying to submit a statement, I'm afraid you will have to speak much slower than that. Now, what is it you say you saw last night?"

"Clowns, sir," replied Arthur.

"Clowns? As in painted faces, brightly colored clothing, big shoes?"

"Yes, sir—something like that—but, um, creepy."

"I see," said the inspector. He flipped the page in his notebook and retrieved a pen from his pocket. "Do you think you might describe these clowns in a bit *finer* detail?"

"Um, yes, sir—I think so, sir. Um . . . well, one of them was the tallest man I've ever seen, and the other one was the shortest. I saw them step out from behind the curtain where the cake was sitting before Wilhelm rolled it out. The tall one was carrying a sort of big, black leather case, with um, a dragon on the side—and they seemed to be sort of, you know, *sneaking*. But it was probably nothing . . ."

There was an abrupt *honk* from the car, signaling his family's impatience.

"On the contrary, my boy," said the inspector, ignoring the horn and putting a sinewy hand on Arthur's shoulder.

"This might just be our best lead yet. Indeed, it seems you are the only person who saw anything at all last night. I must say, you possess quite a keen eye for someone of your abilities."

"Thank you, sir."

There was another impatient *honk* from the car.

"I'd better be going, sir," said Arthur.

"Yes, of course. I shall see you back at the estate, where we shall no doubt bring a swift resolution to this case— thanks in no small part to your illuminating account. In the meantime, we must keep the matter between ourselves. We wouldn't want your story finding its way into the wrong ears now; if our criminal quarry were to learn we're on their tails so soon, they might very well flee the country—and make our jobs unnecessarily difficult. Best not to frighten the fox before the hounds are ready to pounce, hmm?"

"Yes, of course, sir," Arthur nodded gleefully. "Thank you, sir."

Turning and scampering back toward the waiting car, Arthur could hardly believe how well his meeting with the inspector had gone. Far from being ridiculed or spurned, the boy had actually managed to become a secret partner in the investigation. His head brimmed with visions of stake-outs, hideouts, and shootouts.

"Really wanted that autograph, didn't we?" Henry remarked as his brother bounded through the car door and into his seat.

"What?" said Arthur, momentarily confused. "Oh, right. Yep—just couldn't help myself."

As Henry shrugged and turned away, Arthur failed to suppress a subtle smile. He could hardly wait to see the looks on his family's faces when they discovered he had played such an integral role in cracking the case and avenging their honor. Surely after seeing him awarded the title of World's Youngest Crime-Solving Sleuth by Inspector Smudge himself, they would never doubt him again.

• • •

Upon their return from the hospital, the servants promptly resumed their duties—as there was much to be done—while most of the Whipple children headed directly into the house and set about constructing the World's Largest Get Well Card for Mr. Mahankali and Shiva. Now that Arthur was part of the investigation, however, he had more important matters to attend to—like a survey of the crime scene. And so, as his parents and older brothers, Henry and Simon, accompanied Inspector Smudge out to the east lawn, Arthur tagged along a few steps behind them.

Peering across the sunlit grounds of Neverfall Hall, it was difficult to believe that something so terrible had taken place there hardly twelve hours earlier. Unless, of course, one noticed the cake.

The early morning sun had not been kind to the already disfigured dessert-turned-bringer-of-destruction. There was a massive sinkhole in the cake's upper surface and several glaring bare spots around its curving face, where slabs of hardened icing had sheared away from the cakey cliff underneath. The ground around its base was scattered with enormous fallen birthday candles, like a game of pick-up sticks abandoned by some frustrated giant child.

On the south side of the cake lay the ruins of a once spectacular stage, now reduced to a massive pile of splintered planks and twisted metal. A towering construction crane (the type that might be used to hoist an unconscious elephant out of a collapsed stage) stood motionless nearby, staring down at the carnage in silent judgment, no doubt thinking to itself, *For such tiny creatures, they certainly can make a mess.*

The entire area comprising the cake, the stage, and the crane was cordoned off by yellow tape that read **INVESTIGATION IN PROGRESS** in bold black letters. Positioned next to the wilting cake was a large wheeled staircase, similar to the one Arthur had stood upon the night before to light the wicks of fourteen doomed birthday candles. At the top of the stairs, a man stood hunched over the edge of the cake—and appeared to be sniffing it.

As Arthur's group approached the crime scene, the cake-sniffing man quickly stood up, brushed himself off, and started down the stairs. He was slightly thinner and shorter than average, with bright brown eyes and a pair of spectacles perched halfway down his narrow pointy nose, the tip of which was smeared with white icing.

"Inspector Smudge, look at this!" cried the man as he reached the ground, referring to some unseen object in his upturned palm—an object which he promptly proceeded to drop before anyone could catch a glimpse of it. "Oh dear," said the man, quickly dropping to his knees and proceeding to comb through the surrounding blades of grass with his fingers.

"Ahem," grumbled Inspector Smudge. "Allow me to introduce Detective Sergeant Callum Greenley, my *impeccable* assistant. D.S. Greenley—Mr. and Mrs. Whipple."

D.S. Greenley looked up from his foraging and held out a slightly grubby hand to Mr. Whipple. "Pleasure to meet you, sir," the sergeant smiled, vigorously shaking the Whipple patriarch's hand. "Big fan, big fan."

After holding onto Mr. Whipple's hand a moment or two too long, D.S. Greenley tipped his hat toward Mrs. Whipple and her sons, smiled, and said, "Ma'am. Lads," then returned to his search.

"You'll have to forgive D.S. Greenley," explained Inspector Smudge. "Since my retirement, Scotland Yard has asked me to personally train a select few of their *most promising* young detectives, allowing them to accompany me around the globe, observing my record-breaking investigation tactics and lending assistance when possible. It's hard to believe this is really the best the Yard has to offer these days. It's a wonder any crime in London gets solved at all—isn't it, Greenley?"

"Uh, yes sir. I suppose so, sir," the sergeant replied distractedly, still rooting about through the grass on his hands and knees. A moment later, he exclaimed, "Ah, here it is!" and, with one hand cupped over the other, slowly rose to his feet.

Drawn in by the suspense surrounding this mysterious object, Arthur joined his parents and brothers as they gathered around D.S. Greenley's outstretched hands.

"What do you make of *this*, Inspector?" inquired the sergeant as he removed his uppermost hand, revealing a thin clump of gray ash resting in the center of his palm. "It appears to be a used section of dynamite fuse, sir."

"I know what it is, Greenley," snapped Inspector Smudge. "Now tell me, where did you discover this?"

"There are bits of it on some of the candle stumps at the top of the cake—as well as on the sides of some of the severed candles on the ground. Here, sir—have a look."

The group followed D.S. Greenley as he scurried over to one of the fallen candles and began pointing out various sections of the wax pillar with giddy enthusiasm.

"See, there's a bit of burnt fuse stapled near the candlewick here, and then similar bits stapled every couple of feet or so down the side of the candle. It looks like—"

"Aha!" cried Inspector Smudge. After a quick glance at the burnt bits of fuse toward the top of the candle, he had darted down to the candle's other end. He now stood stooping forward with a magnifying glass, examining the circular cross section at the foot of the candle where the waxy pillar had been cleaved from its base. "Judging by this blackened stain here, it seems our saboteur started by boring a hole in the base of each candle, into which he then inserted some sort of explosive charge before running a length of slow-burning fuse from the charge all the way up to the tip of the wick—so that when the candle was lit, the fuse was lit as well."

Arthur suddenly remembered the tiny sparkling flames he had seen inching down the backs of the candles during the candle-lighting ceremony. If only he had been an aspiring junior detective back then, he might have realized what they really were.

Meanwhile, Inspector Smudge continued his examination of the evidence, relaying his findings to the rest of the crowd.

"And while the surface of the wax here at the candle's foot is rough on one side of the black mark—consistent with a sudden break—the wax is relatively smooth on the other side, showing signs of what appear to be saw marks. Our culprit no doubt sawed halfway through each candle, so that when the charges were detonated, the candles' weakened bases would snap, thus propelling their upper stalks over the edge of the cake. My, my. If it weren't so despicable, it might actually be quite clever. I trust you've arrived at a similar conclusion, Greenley?"

"Yes, sir. Something like that."

"Of course you have, Greenley," the inspector smirked. "So. We are looking for an individual or individuals in possession of some or all of the following items: one, dynamite fuse matching the residue stapled to the candles; two, a staple gun; three, some sort of saw, probably with candle wax in its teeth; four, a drill with a two-inch bit; and five, explosive charges. Furthermore," he added, winking slyly at Arthur, "certain information has come to light leading me to believe these items may be located in a large black leather case with the insignia of a dragon etched into the side."

"What an odd coincidence," Mrs. Whipple remarked with a smile. "Charles and I gave a set of knives to our chef, Sammy, in a case just like that for Christmas last year. Every now and then, I catch a glimpse of it when I venture into the kitchen."

Inspector Smudge cocked his head and arched his brow. "Really? Well that is an odd coincidence, isn't it now?"

Mrs. Whipple's eyes widened. "I mean," she added hastily, "I think it's a dragon—but you know, on second thought, it might actually be a winged dog—or perhaps a carnivorous goose. Yes that's it . . ."

Paying no attention to Mrs. Whipple's suddenly foggy memory, Inspector Smudge interrupted. "It's funny you should mention your chef in regard to this investigation, madam—because Mr. Smith has indeed been at the top of my list of suspects since the first candle fell."

Mr. and Mrs. Whipple gulped, while Henry and Simon traded dubious glances.

Arthur felt his heart drop.

"But surely, Inspector," cried Mrs. Whipple, "you can't sincerely believe our Sammy was involved in this?"

"I'm afraid I have very *good reason* to believe he was involved. You see, this is not the first time Sammy 'the Spatula' Smith and Inspector Hadrian Smudge have crossed paths. I, in fact, was chief inspector on the Caviar Case—the one that finally sent Mr. Smith to prison after years of unchallenged criminal activity. If you knew him like I do, you would not be shocked in the least by his involvement in this latest act of villainy."

"Inspector Smudge, I assure you," Mr. Whipple insisted, "Sammy has absolutely nothing to do with this. We trust him completely. He's been our personal chef for over seven years!"

"Ah yes, but what about his previous occupation?"

"Now, sir," replied Mr. Whipple, "we are well aware of the troubles he had with the law before he came to work for us—but that was a long time ago. He's truly a changed man."

"Really? Well that would be something. In the forty years I've been hunting criminals, I've yet to meet a single one who has suddenly woken up and decided toiling away for the rest of his life was a better way to attain the things he desired than simply taking them. Don't ever let anyone tell you crime doesn't pay. Crime pays loads. So much, in fact, these types are completely powerless to resist it—no matter how well they may convince you otherwise."

"But what would he possibly have to gain by sabotaging *us*?" asked Arthur's mother.

"Your naïveté is charming, Mrs. Whipple—but hardly methodical. Surely, given your family's current standing, there are many who would gladly pay to see the Whipple name tarnished, perhaps offering substantial *compensation* to an individual on the inside—an individual with access to information and facilities not available to outside parties. Such compensation might go a long way towards, say, paying off a certain record-breaking gambling debt?"

For the first time, Mr. and Mrs. Whipple offered no rebuttal. Seeing that he had dredged up doubt in his clients' minds, the inspector softened his tone.

"I'm afraid justice is not a pretty business, my dear Whipples. Many a trusting soul has found a loved one capable of unexpected evil. . . . Of course, then again, it is quite possible your friend had nothing at all to do with this dreadful business. But I'm afraid there is only one way to find out. So, if you wouldn't mind, please direct me to the kitchen."

• • •

Mr. and Mrs. Whipple reluctantly led the detectives through the house, where just outside the kitchen, the group was met by Mrs. Waite.

"Oh hello, Mr. and Mrs. Whipple. Inspector," said the housekeeper. "Just finished folding the spider-silk tablecloths from the extravaganza. Hard to get any work done at a time like this—but after last night, a bit of order might do us all some good. Any progress on the case?"

"Actually, Mrs. Waite," replied Mr. Whipple, "you may be able to assist us. Do you know where Sammy keeps his chief set of knives?"

"I believe he keeps them locked up in his secret-ingredient cupboard, sir. I can show you to it if you like."

183

"Please, Mrs. Waite."

The housekeeper led the group into the kitchen and directed them to a large pair of doors in the far corner, which were fastened together by a steel padlock.

"Ah, yes," the inspector noted. "You wouldn't happen to have a key to this cupboard, would you, Mrs. Waite?"

"Why, yes, sir. Sammy's been good enough to entrust me with a spare. If I hadn't sworn never to use it without asking him first, I'd gladly go and fetch it for you."

The inspector's polite smile faded. "Need I remind you, Mrs. Waite, that this is an official investigation?"

"I am sorry, sir," the housekeeper insisted. "I wish I could help, I really do, but official investigation or no—an oath is an oath."

"I see," sighed the inspector. "Well, no matter. It won't be the first time I've had to cut a lock in the name of Justice. Thank you for your help, ma'am."

"Please, sir," Mrs. Waite added, "I'm sure Sammy'd be more than happy to open it for you as soon as he returns to the house. I just know how much pride he takes in keeping the contents of that cupboard secret. One can only guess what rare, record-breaking items it contains. No other member of staff has ever been granted a peep, and I can only imagine how horrified he'd be to have a stranger—however official—rifling through it without him."

"Oh, but Mrs. Waite, Mr. Smith and I are hardly strangers. We are old chums really, he and I. I'm sure he will understand."

"I'm sorry sir, but it still doesn't seem right to me."

"Well, fortunately for your conscience, Mrs. Waite, it is not up to *you*. Your employers are determined to rule out Mr. Smith's involvement as quickly as possible—with or without his presence—and I'm afraid opening that cupboard may be the surest way to accomplish this. That *is* still your goal, is it not, Mr. and Mrs. Whipple?"

Arthur's parents paused a moment, and then, evading eye contact with Mrs. Waite, nodded silently.

"I'm afraid I must ask you to step aside, Mrs. Waite," smiled Inspector Smudge. "Put your conscience at ease, ma'am—Sammy will surely hear of your efforts to keep his secrets safe." Then, turning to his assistant he cried, "Greenley—cutters!"

After a brief startled look, D.S. Greenley removed a pair of bolt cutters from his coat and handed them to his superior.

Grasping the cutters with both hands, Inspector Smudge paused to savor the moment—and then, without a word, cut through the lock on the chef's cupboard.

Mrs. Waite stalked out of the room in protest.

Brushing aside the broken padlock, the inspector threw back the doors to reveal a deep closet brimming with bizarre foodstuffs. A thousand delicious smells hit Arthur's nostrils at once. The boy averted his eyes in an attempt to respect Sammy's privacy, but try as he might, he could not resist a few quick peeks.

Slipping on a pair of black gloves, Inspector Smudge promptly stepped into the cupboard and disappeared amongst the massive jars of pickled who-knows-what, strings of peculiar spices, and rows of burlap bags labeled in countless foreign languages.

A short time later, the inspector emerged carrying a large, black leather case with a dragon insignia on its side. At this distance, Arthur could see two words engraved below the emblem: *DRAKE® KNIVES*.

As Inspector Smudge placed the case on the kitchen table, he looked directly at Arthur. "Is this the case you saw the saboteurs in possession of as they sneaked about the cake, my boy?"

Arthur's family turned to him in shock.

"Um," said the boy. "Well, it does look slightly similar. . . ."

"What?!" gasped Arthur's father.

"But . . . it was rather dark at the time—so, I mean, I can't say for absolute certain. . . ."

"How did *you* know about this, Arthur?" his mother cried.

"Earlier this morning," explained the inspector, "your son came to me with information vital to this case. It seems he witnessed two suspicious individuals in the vicinity of the birthday cake just prior to the incident. According to the boy's report, they were dressed as clowns—and carrying a case identical to this one."

"Arthur, why didn't you come to us first?" cried Mrs. Whipple.

Arthur opened his mouth to explain, but no words came out.

"Don't worry, dear," Mr. Whipple assured his wife. "This doesn't prove anything yet."

"No, Mr. Whipple," replied the inspector. Having already undone the case's silver clasp, he now peered inside the narrow opening he had created at the case's top. "But I'm afraid *this* does."

With that, he splayed the case wide open to reveal its contents.

There in the open case lay a spool of dynamite fuse, a staple gun, a coiled up wire saw covered in flecks of what appeared to be candle wax, a hand drill with an extra-large bit, and the three largest firecrackers Arthur had ever seen.

A collective gasp escaped from all who were gathered in the kitchen—with the exception, of course, of Inspector Smudge, who did not seem at all surprised by this.

"As much as I am blessed to be consistently correct in my predictions," he sighed, "I must admit what a terrible burden it is to always be right. I'm afraid it's my lot in life. My deepest sympathies, Mr. and Mrs. Whipple—but I'm sure you will find it much better to have discovered Mr. Smith's treachery sooner rather than later."

Arthur's mouth hung open in shock. He had never imagined his account of the prior night's events would lead to *this*.

"But sir," pleaded the boy, "what about the clowns?"

"Just some of Mr. Smith's criminal associates, no doubt," Smudge explained. "Not hard to see why they might want revenge after your family's public refusal to participate in the IBCPC fundraiser last month."

"I've said it time and time again," Arthur's father growled, "we take no issue with clowns in general—but we will not support special treatment for them either. Clowns must be subjected to the same laws as the rest of us!"

"Please, Mr. Whipple," grinned the inspector. "You needn't tell this to me. But surely you can imagine how they might see things differently. And with the clowning profession in its current state of decline, everybody knows how desperate for money they all are. Mr. Smith no doubt offered them a cut of the payoff in exchange for—"

At that moment, Sammy the Spatula, carrying a small but ornately decorated cake, stepped through the kitchen door.

Arthur's mother went white.

"Wh—what are you doing here, Sammy?" asked Mr. Whipple.

"Just popping in to drop off Arfur's birfday cake, sir," the chef replied, oblivious to the recently discovered evidence against him. Holding up the cake, he turned to Arthur and smiled. "Told you I'd bake you anuvver one to make up for the prison cake—and well, here it is, mate—World's Tastiest, guaranteed by yours truly. Didn't want you to fink I'd forgot. . . ."

Arthur then noticed the cake's decoration. Tiny swirling bullwhips and miniature milk bottles dotted its surface in intricate patterns. The boy's heart sank. "Sammy—I . . ." he spluttered.

With that, Inspector Smudge turned about to face the chef.

"Wait . . ." Sammy gasped, the smile crumbling from his lips. "What's 'e doing 'ere?!"

"Still baking cakes, are we?" smirked the inspector. "I should have thought you'd outdone yourself with the last one. But perhaps you've another reason for coming here. Hmm?" he added, holding up the case full of explosives. "You weren't hoping to collect *this*, were you?"

It was then that Sammy noticed the open cupboard doors and the busted lock. He glanced at Arthur with a brokenhearted look that made the boy's chest feel hollow and then back to the inspector.

"What are you doing in me secret-ingredient cupboard," he cried, "and what 'ave you done wiv me knives?!"

"Greenley—arrest this man!" shrieked Inspector Smudge.

Arthur saw a glint of horrified confusion sweep across the chef's face, as D.S. Greenley glanced back to his superior for confirmation. Inspector Smudge's face had blossomed into a fierce shade of red that left little uncertainty as to his intentions.

D.S. Greenley turned and took a step toward the chef, retrieving a pair of handcuffs from his belt with one hand while holding up his other in an attempt at a calming gesture. "Now, Mr. Smith. Let's not make this any harder than—"

But before D.S. Greenley could restrain him, Sammy's left arm grabbed the sergeant by the shoulder and reeled him into a rigid choke hold while his right arm snatched a butcher knife from a nearby knife block and whisked it up to the sergeant's throat.

Arthur's birthday cake splattered to the floor.

"Don't move, Smudge!" the chef shouted desperately. "I ain't going back to prison, mate!"

"Sammy!" cried Arthur's mother.

"Sorry, Mrs. Whipple," slurred the chef. It was clear he had not completely sobered up since his appearance at the hospital. "I wish you lot didn't 'ave to see this . . . but I just can't 'ave these coppers locking me up again!"

"Perhaps," Inspector Smudge countered calmly, "you should have thought of *that* before you decided to blow up your employers' birthday cake, Mr. Smith. Because even if, by some chance, you are able to escape me now, your evil deeds will soon catch up to you—and the Law will follow shortly behind them. The Law does not like to be ridiculed, my criminal friend; it never forgets a name or a face. So no matter where you attempt to hide, the Law will lead me straight to you, and this I assure you, Mr. Smith—you shall not escape its shackles a second time."

"Spare me the speeches, mate," the chef shot back, trembling with fear and anger. "I'm sure your little stooge 'ere ain't interested in 'earing your sermons wiv this knife at 'is froat!"

"Oh, um, don't mind me, sir," D.S. Greenley interjected meekly from behind the razor-sharp blade. "I'm rather fond of your 'Noble Justice' speeches. You needn't stop on my account."

The chef gave his hostage a baffled look.

"Sammy, please!" implored Mr. Whipple. "Put the knife down! You'll only make it worse for yourself, man!"

"But I didn't do it on purpose, sir! You've gotta believe me! I can hardly live wiv meself knowing it were me who baked that bleedin' cake!"

Seeing that the chef was somewhat distracted in explaining himself to his employer, Inspector Smudge took a sly step forward.

"Don't come any closer, Smudge!" snapped the chef, his trembling hand tightening its grip on the knife and pressing the flat of the blade against D.S. Greenley's throat.

D.S. Greenley—who had taken his hostageship surprisingly well until this point—winced in pain, his face growing pale with panic.

"Well, I hate to say it, Mr. Smith," retorted the inspector, halting his advance, "but this is hardly the behavior of an innocent man. I have met scant few innocent men who enjoy holding butcher knives to the throats of police officers."

"You don't understand!" cried the chef.

"I understand perfectly, Mr. Smith," the inspector shot back. "Your gambling debts have made you a desperate man, and last night's disaster was simply the latest in a series of diabolical plots—perpetrated by you and the enemies of this family—to undermine and/or maim the Whipples and their loved ones!"

"No!"

"So you had nothing to do with the giant piece of French toast that nearly flattened a four-year-old girl?!"

"Th—that were an accident!"

"An accident involving a food item that you prepared, but then were conveniently absent from when that item turned murderous, no?"

"I don't know what you're talkin' about, mate!"

"Oh really? Then perhaps you can explain where you were during the party last night. You see, no one seems to remember seeing you anywhere near the cake when the candles started to fall. So what exactly were you doing while everyone else was under a brutal attack by one of your baked goods? Conveniently absent once again, were we?"

"I swear, I didn't even know anyfing 'ad gone wrong till it were all over! After I noticed your ugly mug in the crowd, I spent the rest of the night in the kitchen, mate!"

"Hmm. I'm fairly certain that 'running from authority' is generally the response of a *guilty* man, rather than an innocent one."

"Pardon me, sir, for not wanting to 'ave a chat wiv the filf who put me away!"

"Ah, yes. I did put you away, didn't I? What a fond memory. Shame the sentence didn't stick the first time. But don't worry, 'mate'—I'll make sure the next one does. And just think, once you're in prison, you'll no longer have to bother with all this culinary nonsense. They've got their own cooks there. Of course, their food might not be quite as tasty as yours—but at least there is no danger of being crushed by it!"

This last comment proved more than the record-breaking chef could bear. In a burst of rage, he yanked the knife away from D.S. Greenley's throat—and, raising the blade into the air, lunged at Inspector Smudge.

Mrs. Whipple screamed and pulled her three boys close, pressing up against the cupboard behind her while Mr. Whipple shielded his family.

Fortunately for the inspector, Sammy the Spatula's drunkenness had deprived him of the pinpoint precision with which he usually wielded a butcher knife. After a quick dodge and a simple jab to Sammy's wrist, Inspector Smudge swiftly disarmed the sluggish chef, leaving him off his guard and entirely vulnerable.

A moment later, the inspector had twisted Sammy's arm behind his back—and a moment after that, the two were on the floor, Inspector Smudge's knee firmly planted on Sammy's spine. A flash of the inspector's arm into his coat revealed a pair of handcuffs, which he promptly clapped onto the chef's wrists.

Just behind Inspector Smudge and his recent captive, D.S. Greenley slumped exhaustedly to the floor, clutching his throat with both hands and panting with relieved surprise that his head was still connected to his shoulders.

"*That*, Greenley, my man," informed the inspector, "is how one makes an arrest! Perhaps next time you won't make such a bumbling fool of yourself, will you?"

"No, sir. Of course not, sir."

Inspector Smudge returned his attention to his captive. "There we are, Mr. Smith," he goaded. "No use struggling now."

But it was clear that Sammy had no fight left in him. Dazed, disgraced, and helpless, the ordinarily gruff chef spontaneously began to weep. It was the most heartbreakingly pitiful sight Arthur had ever seen.

• • •

Inspector Smudge led the way as D.S. Greenley escorted a shackled Sammy the Spatula toward the black car in the Whipples' gigantic circular drive. Looming gray clouds blocked the sun overhead. Arthur, who had not left the chef's presence since his arrest, was gradually joined by other members of the Whipple family and staff as word of the confrontation made its way across the grounds.

Emerging from the front door and seeing his friend in handcuffs, the brave butler, Wilhelm, reflexively rushed forward but was halted by a gesture from Mr. Whipple's raised hand. Nothing could undo what had already been done.

The gatherers simply stood and stared, their faces full of surprise and sadness.

Still following a few steps behind the captive, Arthur caught a glimpse of Sammy's sniffling face and red, swollen eyes as the chef turned to D.S. Greenley.

"Sorry 'bout that business back there, mate," said

Sammy, his eyes darting between Greenley's face and the ground. "Nuffing personal."

"That's quite all right, Mr. Smith," the sergeant smiled. "You know, I've never been taken hostage before. It was rather exhilarating, actually. . . ."

"Greenley!" shouted Inspector Smudge, turning to face his assistant. "Don't ever converse with a criminal in custody! I mean, honestly, what *are* they teaching you at the academy these days? Now get the criminal in the car, and no matter what he says, not another word to him. Understand?"

"Yes, sir. Terribly sorry, sir," D.S. Greenley stammered as he quickly ushered Sammy into the back of the car then sat himself at the steering wheel.

Inspector Smudge paused outside the open passenger-side door and addressed Arthur's parents as they looked on in disbelief. "You are no doubt delighted, Mr. and Mrs. Whipple, to witness such timely justice here today. As promised, I have apprehended the mastermind behind these detestable acts of sabotage—in under twenty-four hours, no less—and I assure you, it will only be a matter of time, and perhaps a bit of rigorous interrogation, before Mr. Smith leads us to his accomplices, thereby bringing the case to a swift and tidy conclusion. Thank you all for cooperating during this investigation. Oh, and a special thanks to your son, there—what's his name—Angus, is it?"

"Arthur?"

"Yes. Arthur. It was his observant eye that ultimately led to Mr. Smith's arrest. I couldn't have done it without your help, my boy. I'm sure you'll make a fine detective some day."

Arthur had waited his whole life for this kind of recognition—but it did not have the effect he had expected. Instead of feeling proud or joyful or satisfied, he merely felt ill. Without even turning to look at them, Arthur could sense his family's disappointment searing into his temples.

"Now, do let me know if you find anything else that might help us track down Mr. Smith's henchmen," concluded Inspector Smudge as he removed his coat and entered the car. "I shall keep you posted from our end with details of the interrogation as it progresses. I can hardly wait to get started! I must say, this has been a monumental day for law-abiding citizens everywhere. Rest assured, dear Whipples—there is one less criminal free tonight to contaminate the world for the rest of us!"

"Thank you, Inspector," Mr. Whipple said emptily.

"No thanks necessary, my good man. *Justice* is my reward. . . . Well, justice and that figure we agreed upon when I was hired. I'll have Doris, my secretary, send out a bill. . . . Good day!"

With a final tip of his hat, the inspector pulled the door shut, sealing himself in with his prized captive. After an awkward moment and a muffled shout of "Drive, Greenley!" the car jerked into motion and headed down the long drive.

The row of stunned Whipples stood and watched the car until it turned the corner and vanished from sight.

"Do you really think Sammy had a part in all this?" Arthur heard his mother ask his father. "I mean, I know he has a bit of a dubious past, but this just doesn't seem like him at all!"

"I know, dear," Mr. Whipple sighed, "but it's hard to argue with Inspector Smudge's track record. He does hold the record for Most Solved Cases in History. I'm . . . I'm afraid he's done it again."

"Oh, Charles—it's all like some awful nightmare. I feel so betrayed, so heartbroken—it almost would have been better to never have discovered the culprit's identity at all than to find out it was our dear Sammy. . . ."

With that, Mrs. Whipple broke into tears.

Wrapping his arms around his wife, Mr. Whipple's face was solemn and weary as spontaneous sobs sprang up from their surrounding children.

Arthur had imagined quite a different outcome for his first case as a junior detective. One that included an honorary badge from Scotland Yard—or at least a proud word from his mother and father. The last thing he had expected was to see the trusted family chef hauled away in handcuffs, his family left traumatized and broken-hearted.

And yet, he now heard the call of his imaginary detective badge even louder than before. Despite Smudge's dogged insistence and his father's reluctant but eventual concession—not to mention the undeniable evidence—Arthur could not bring himself to believe Sammy the Spatula capable of such a bitter betrayal. And he would do whatever it took to prove it.

Even if it meant another encounter with a certain pair of clowns.

THE UNSAFE SPORTS SHOWDOWN

When the din of stomping feet and clattering chairs had grown to an almost unbearable peak, a booming, disembodied voice arose from the loudspeakers, reverberating through the outdoor arena. *"Ladies and gentlemen, boys and girls . . . welcome to Unsafe Sports Showdown Twenty-Seven!"*

The crowd issued forth a ground-shaking cheer, sending tangible vibrations through Arthur's bones as he paused to soak in the scene before joining in the clamor himself.

Eventually, the tumult began to fade, and the booming voice continued. *"Kicking off this year's Showdown, Cameroon battles Nepal for the Rhino Polo Intercontinental Cup!"*

Banners from both countries shot up across the stands as face-painted fans blew into faux rhino-horn trumpets and beat on drums resembling rhinoceros feet.

"And now, to perform the national anthem—along with the anthems of Cameroon and Nepal—the Youngest Singer Ever to Open the Unsafe Sports Showdown . . . Lenora Whipple!"

The crowd continued their applause, then hushed as Arthur's little sister approached the microphone at the center of the field.

But before Lenora could take her position, a small yet concentrated chorus of boos erupted from the stands.

"What in good Grazelby is *that*?!" cried Arthur's father.

"There!" shouted Simon, pointing to the stands below.

Arthur and the others turned to see a dozen people in the front row standing on their chairs and holding a banner that read: WHIPPLES + RECORD BREAKING = MENACE 2 ALL INNOCENT BYSTANDERS!

"The beasts!" cried Arthur's mother.

Just then, a team of security guards rushed in below, dragged the protestors from their seats, and escorted them back up the aisles.

The crowd cheered.

Being far too shrewd a performer to be put off by a few angry picketers, Lenora promptly stepped up to the microphone and started to sing.

The voice that filled the arena sounded more like a seasoned soprano's than a five-year-old girl's, as Arthur's sister belted out high notes with beautiful vibrato, transitioning effortlessly between three different languages.

On the last note of the Nepalese national anthem, the crowd roared in admiration of such a perfect performance, now frenzied with anticipation for the match to come.

Lenora bowed, humbly.

• • •

"And there you have it, folks—we are now officially under way! Absolutely mesmerizing voice that Lenora's got, eh, Chuck?"

"Positively, Ted. How anybody could boo an operatic angel like her is beyond me."

"Yep—hate to see it, Chuck. Quite a rocky time it's been for the Whipples as of late, wouldn't you say?"

"Oh, no question, Ted. First, there was that mishap with the World's Largest Piece of French Toast—and then the catastrophe of their birthday cake exploding and nearly making pancakes of their party guests. Just confirms my policy to never hire an ex-convict for a cooking position. Seems this Sammy 'the Spatula' Smith character was motivated by a record-breaking gambling debt, of all things. Luckily, due to the extreme nature of the crimes and the undeniable physical evidence, he has been denied bail and must await his trial behind bars."

"Luckily indeed, Chuck. And yet, even though these incidents have both been traced to their former chef, the Whipples have still managed to draw considerable fire from bystanders' rights groups and other assorted safety nuts for their supposed negligence."

201

"*Indeed they have, Ted. Thankfully—apart from the odd protestor—you'll not find many of those types here.*"

"*Thankfully not, Chuck. Still, the Whipples need to prove this recent run of bad luck is nothing more than a fluke if they hope to have a smooth championships season. The Unsafe Sports Showdown marks the final international world record tournament before the start of the World Record World Championships in just two months' time. It's vital that they go into the championships with as many records and as much confidence as possible, and this is their best chance to do that. If they can make a strong showing here today, as they're expected to do, their troubles may all be behind them.*"

"*I certainly hope so, Ted. . . . Oh, and here we are, folks—I believe I see the arena gates opening now!*"

• • •

Having since recovered from the minor pre-match incident, Arthur and his family watched from their private box as four unruly rhinoceroses emerged onto each side of the field, stamping their way into position. On the back of each rhino sat a rider holding the reins in his left hand—doing his best to control the bad-tempered beast beneath him—while grasping a long-handled mallet in his right.

When both teams had taken their places, the booming voice made a surprise announcement. "*And now, rolling the first ball into play, please welcome the former captain of the Indian National Team, Phoolendu Mahankali—and his elephant friend, Shiva!"*

At the center of the arena, a third gate opened—and out strode the Panther-Man, sitting proudly atop the elephant's back. Both were heavily bandaged—Mr. Mahankali with his arm in a sling and his head wrapped in gauze, Shiva with a brace on his front right leg and a huge bandage around his right ear.

Upon seeing the two famous figures enter the arena without assistance—battered but not broken—the entire crowd leapt to its feet, issuing an ovation louder than any it had yet given that day.

· · ·

It was a fine match—perhaps the best Arthur had ever seen. In the last minutes of the final chukker, Cameroon pulled out a long-shot victory over Nepal, with a final score of 8 to 7¾. What's more, there were only three tramplings and one goring this year—a substantial improvement over the previous year's final, which had earned the competing countries the record for Bloodiest Match Ever Played.

But despite being witness to such a fine game of rhino polo, seeing Mr. Mahankali and Shiva had reminded Arthur of the other great casualty of the Birthday Cake Catastrophe: Sammy the Spatula.

In the days since the chef's arrest, Arthur had done his best to uncover clues in the hopes of tracking down the mysterious clowns—but to little avail.

According to Gordon Carouser, the Whipple family's party planner, there was no record of the disparately sized duo ever being at the Birthday Extravaganza. Somehow, they had managed to sneak onto the estate without an invitation and then slip off unseen—hardly a simple task for such a conspicuous couple.

But whatever unholy magic lay behind their apparent teleportation, Arthur remained optimistic. Given their extreme sizes, he figured they would not be able to hide from him forever. Because, honestly, how hard could it be to find a nine-foot-tall giant clown? Surely, as long as they had not fled the country or gone completely underground, it was only a matter of time before the dwarf and the giant crossed Arthur's path again. And this time he'd be ready.

• • •

After filing out of the arena, the Whipples split off into two groups so that all the children might make their events on time. Mrs. Whipple and Mrs. Waite took Ivy and the octuplets off to compete in the Extreme Playground events— including extreme swing set, extreme seesaw, and extreme merry-go-round—while Mr. Whipple and Uncle Mervyn accompanied the older children as they made their way toward the Pogo Pavilion, where Arthur would be competing in his only event of the day: the junior division all-terrain rocket-stick race.

Though this marked the third year he had entered the competition, Arthur had not always been so familiar with this particular unsafe sport. Indeed, the first time he had climbed onto a rocket stick, he had learned the hard way that—though a rocket stick looks very much like a large pogo stick—it actually contains an internal combustion engine just above its foot pegs. When the foot of a rocket stick strikes the ground, it is driven like a piston into a combustion chamber, where fuel is compressed and ignited, causing a small but concentrated explosion. This fires the piston down again and—with the aid of a sophisticated spring system—launches the stick and rider as high as fifteen feet into the air. This had come as quite a shock to Arthur at the time, who—being only four years old—had mistaken the thing for his own bouncy play toy. Terrified as he was, however, the thrill proved habit-forming, and he had spent the next five years attempting to qualify for the official race.

The event itself, of course, is conducted on a large spiraling track, with the starting line on the outside of the spiral and wide enough to accommodate the entire row of competitors, while the finish line is at the center of the spiral and only three riders wide. Arthur had always thought the word "track" was used rather loosely here. Once it was filled with boulders, logs, pits, and swamps, it looked hardly like a track at all but more like a massive rock garden—in hell.

As Arthur stepped under the banner marking the Pogo Pavilion's entrance, he could no longer ignore the colony of killer butterflies that had begun to swarm in his stomach.

He had trained all year for this single race. Having competed in the event the previous two years with little success, he had much to prove that day—to himself, to his family, and to the world of unsafe sports.

In his first year of entry, Arthur had failed to complete the race at all, due to a nasty crash and a resulting equipment malfunction. The next year, he had not fared much better, ranking thirty-eighth out of thirty-nine participants—the only entrant behind him being Bonnie Prince Bobo, the pogo-sticking chimpanzee (who had subsequently vowed revenge on the boy for sending him to last place).

But this year would be different. Arthur had come a long way since his last defeat. He was another year older (a respectable 9 percent age increase over the prior year) and many of the top junior competitors had now graduated to the next division. Furthermore, he had since acquired new equipment (Henry's old HopRocket RDX), and in one of his latest trial runs, he had only been two seconds away from matching the current world record.

"Good luck, lad!" Uncle Mervyn called as the boy emerged from the equipment locker with his rocket stick. "I've got a feeling about this one; Arthur Whipple will not be a name these spectators soon forget!"

"Thanks, Uncle Mervyn," Arthur said with a nervous smile.

"Yes, Arthur," added Mr. Whipple, trying his best to be encouraging, "I am confident in the possibility of you finishing this race without severe bodily harm!"

"Thanks, Father," Arthur smiled again. Then, donning a beat-up crash helmet, he turned and headed toward the warm-up area.

• • •

As the competitors arranged themselves along the starting line, Arthur reached into his pocket and felt the corners of his magical domino. Rubbing the ebony tile for luck, the boy said a short prayer and promptly joined the others.

Looking about him, Arthur recognized many of his fellow contenders from previous years. Five riders to his left, at the center of the lineup, stood "Jump" Johnston—once the junior division's biggest star, until last year's race, when he had fractured his spine and been told he would never walk again. Fortunately, the prognosis hadn't mentioned anything about his ability to rocket-stick, and—by some miracle—though still unable to walk on his own, Jump had re-taught himself to *ride* just in time for this year's competition. Of course, he was only ranked thirty-second overall, but just to see him standing there on the starting line was truly an inspiring sight.

Six entrants to his right, Arthur spotted Andy Gravity—the rocket-stick prodigy poised to capture the crown from his debilitated predecessor. According to rocket-stick racing analysts, Andy was the one to beat.

Arthur looked at the next competitor—and shuddered. It was none other than his own simian nemesis: Bonnie Prince Bobo. Ever since he had bested the chimp in the previous year's race, Arthur had been receiving boxes of rotten banana peels through the post, with only a muddy monkey handprint for the return address. (Apparently, the Whipples' address had been filled in by Bobo's trainer, but it was hard to be too cross at *him*; if Arthur had managed to teach a chimpanzee to send things through the post, he'd probably not have been all that selective about what he sent out either.) Upon catching Arthur's glance, Bobo flashed a freaky set of chimpanzee teeth at the boy, as if to say, "This year, you're mine, chump!"

Arthur quickly looked past the primate toward the end of the line—at which point he noticed a girl who, though somehow familiar, he had not seen at any previous rocket-stick race. Recalling his own first experience in the event, Arthur couldn't help but pity her. She really had no idea what she was in for.

Arthur then realized why the girl looked familiar. She was one of the Goldwin children who had introduced themselves at the Birthday Extravaganza—one of the ghost girl's older sisters.

Suddenly struck by a related thought, Arthur shifted his gaze into the stands.

It took a few moments of scanning the crowd before he spotted her, but sure enough, there, leaning on the guard rail at the front of the steps, stood Ruby Goldwin. Her appearance, it seemed, had altered somehow since he'd last seen her—but as usual, she was already looking straight at him.

Even though he had almost expected to see her there, it proved no less of a shock. The last time he had seen Ruby Goldwin at one of his record attempts, it had caused him to spontaneously choke—though, to be fair, he *had* thought her a bloodthirsty poltergeist at the time. Since then, he had learned otherwise, and the two had actually shared some rather memorable moments together—but he still did not know exactly what to make of her. One thing was certain, however: this time, he would not let the Goldwin girl come between him and the finish line.

And so, as Arthur stood staring blankly back at Ruby—one foot on his rocket stick, one foot on the ground, unsure whether he was glad to see her or terrified, yet above all, determined not to be distracted by her once again—he was more than a bit dismayed to find himself the only entrant left at the starting line, suddenly engulfed in a cloud of dust.

Snapping his head to face forward, Arthur could just make out the flash of a green flag through a host of air-borne rocket-stick riders before him. Wasting no time, the boy planted both feet on the pegs of his HopRocket RDX and sprang into action, already half a bounce behind his competitors.

His lack of readiness offset by a flood of adrenaline, Arthur sailed through the air for several seconds before touching down on a large, craggy boulder that many of his opponents had wisely avoided. Fortunately, the boy managed to hit the rock at just the right angle, so that the resulting launch carried him over the heads of half a dozen riders at the rear of the pack and safely out of last place. Unfortunately, it also landed him within an arm's length of his arch rival, the dreaded Bonnie Prince Bobo.

Immediately sensing Arthur's presence, the chimp curled his lips into a menacing sneer, then burst into a flurry of unnerving grunts and shrieks. Arthur tried to remain calm—but he soon found himself under more than just a verbal attack.

As the two flew side by side through the air, the primate released the right side of his rocket-stick handle—and began swinging his free arm at the boy's head.

"Ahhh!" Arthur cried as the chimp's fingernails scraped against his helmet. (Hard as it was to accept at that moment, of course, Arthur knew the chimp's tactics were well within the rules of rocket-stick racing, as they did not involve firearms or blades over two inches in length.)

The assault persisted for nearly a hundred yards—until the chimp veered inexplicably to the right, leaving Arthur alone and unbothered for the first time.

Relieved to find that Bobo's battery attempts had finally ceased, the boy launched off a fallen tree—only to have the chimp pass directly in front of him a moment later, clipping his rocket stick and nearly wrenching it from his grasp.

The chimp, it seemed, was now determined to collide with him.

Touching down shakily on a thin slab of rock, the boy shot into the air once again—and found himself under the bitterest attack so far. Flying at him from the other side now, Bonnie Prince Bobo managed to unseat Arthur's left foot from its peg, filling the boy's ears with piercing shrieks as he hurtled past.

Scarcely managing to get his foot halfway onto the peg before touching down, Arthur took another precarious bounce, knowing full well it might be his last.

The chimp was waiting for him. Having honed his aim over the first two passes, Bobo did not fly past his target this time—but met the boy perfectly in midair.

Perhaps a bit *too* perfectly, as it turned out.

Instead of barreling into Arthur and knocking him out of the sky, the chimp matched the boy's trajectory so that both riders fell at the same rate and angle, with only a matter of inches between them. For a moment, their flight appeared almost synchronized, as if chimp and boy were in fact partners, performing some specialized stunt—but the illusion did not last long.

When Bobo realized his navigational error, he quickly resorted to his original strategy—namely, punching—and proceeded to wallop the boy.

Arthur did what he could to dodge the chimp's jabs, but at such close range, he had little choice but to brace himself and take the punches. After a thump to the ribcage, the boy suffered a crack to the back of his head, which rattled his brains and left his helmet dangerously cockeyed. He barely had time to breathe before another blow struck him square in the stomach.

Robbed of breath and racked with pain, Arthur clenched

the handle of his rocket stick and prayed for some sort of safe landing as he plummeted toward a disconcertingly jagged boulder.

In this disoriented state, Arthur was not entirely sure what happened next. All he knew was that a moment after he touched down, the attack abruptly ceased—and he was shooting through the air, faster and higher than ever before.

What had happened was this:

Moments earlier, as Arthur approached the rocky plateau beneath him, the chimp's abuse and proximity had grown so severe that by the time they touched down, the two rivals were practically occupying the same space. Reaching the rock a millisecond ahead of Arthur, Bobo prepared to deliver the knockout punch—just as the foot of Arthur's rocket-stick landed squarely on the exposed outer tip of the chimp's left peg.

Before either rider knew what was happening, the independent feet of their rocket sticks were compressing in tandem, one on top of the other, so that both pistons fired at precisely the same moment. The resulting burst of energy catapulted Arthur forward at nearly twice the velocity of a normal launch, while Bonnie Prince Bobo—deprived of thrust—smacked into the wall of rock ahead of him and slid into the greasy swamp below.

Barely detecting the sickening plop of his fallen nemesis, Arthur soared higher and higher, his chest growing increasingly hollow the further away the ground became. Then, for the first time since the race began, he noticed the roar of the crowd. Strangely, its intensity seemed to grow in proportion to his altitude. And then he realized: they were cheering for *him*.

Glancing downward, Arthur could see the tops of dozens of his competitors' helmets as he hurtled past them. He was no longer in the rear of the herd—in fact, he was swiftly advancing to its front.

Arthur found it difficult, however, to get too excited about this. For, as all things that go up must eventually do, he had begun to come down. Powerless to alter his dwindling momentum, the boy gripped his handlebars for dear life, his stomach floating toward his ribcage as the ground rushed up to meet him.

And yet, somehow, as the foot of his rocket stick struck the earth from that impossible height, Arthur did not splatter against the rocks, nor spontaneously combust, nor die in any way. Indeed, he managed to stay on his rocket-stick, and—despite a rather rough landing—merely bounced back into the race, as if he had planned the entire stunt all along.

Arthur allowed himself a moment to soak up the crowd's approval. It was slightly disconcerting that he had never received anywhere near as much applause for anything he'd actually planned, but he wasn't about to hush them now.

As Arthur surveyed the field, he found—to his astonishment—that there were only three riders ahead of him.

Leading the pack by several yards was none other than

Jump Johnston—the partially paralyzed rocket-sticking pioneer who required assistance just to walk, yet had managed not only to re-teach himself to ride, but apparently to win. If it had been inspiring to see him standing at the starting line, it was positively electrifying to see him now, a mere hundred yards from the gold medal.

The two competitors behind Jump were neck and neck in second place. Predictably, one of them was Andy Gravity, the up-and-coming hotshot who had been favored to win the entire race. The other rider's identity, however, took Arthur completely by surprise. It was Roxy Goldwin—the ghost girl's older sister—who, as far as Arthur knew, had never been in a rocket-stick race in her life.

Arthur then realized something even more surprising about the three frontrunners: he was gaining on them. The momentum from his last jump, it seemed, was carrying him forward at a faster rate than any of his competitors. As the gap closed between him and the second-place riders, a glimmer of hope arose in Arthur's mind.

I might actually win this thing, he thought.

And yet, before Arthur or the others could make any sort of dent in Jump's ten-yard lead, the finish line emerged around the spiral's last bend. As the track wound down, so too did Arthur's hopes of breaking away.

But then, it happened.

As Jump touched down on a rather unremarkable section of rock, his feet slipped from their pegs. In an instant, Jump's body crumpled and disappeared behind the boulder.

It was an unsettling sight—and yet, it provided Arthur just the opportunity he needed. Launching perfectly off a ridge of earth, the boy quickly found himself shoulder to shoulder with Andy Gravity and Roxy Goldwin. With the residual momentum Arthur still possessed, there was little doubt he would take the lead on the next bounce. He had as good as won.

If only as-good-as-winning was actually as good as winning.

Sailing over the boulder that had concealed Jump Johnston's fate, Arthur suddenly caught sight of the fallen front-runner—and the first glimpse of his own undoing.

There, splayed out in the rocky gap below, a battered Jump Johnston strained to climb out of the crevice, dragging himself inch by inch toward his rocket stick, which had landed on the ledge above him. It was only five feet up, but in Jump's impaired condition it may as well have been Mount Everest.

In the midst of his struggling, Jump glanced upward, and for a split second, Arthur caught his gaze. It was the most helpless, achingly tragic expression Arthur had ever seen—and in an instant, all the joy was sapped from his pending victory.

And then he realized: as important as the race was to himself, finishing first would never mean as much to him as merely *finishing* would mean to Jump. It was a bitter truth, but there was no denying it. He knew what he had to do.

Touching down alongside Andy Gravity and Roxy Goldwin, not twenty yards from the finish line, Arthur shifted his weight to his rear. As his competitors shot ahead toward the finish line, he shot away from it. The crowd gasped.

Pulling a backflip in midair, Arthur landed on the boulder that held Jump's rocket stick and quickly dismounted. His legs felt a bit like the World's Largest Spaghetti Noodles now that he was on solid ground, but he managed to steady himself. Grabbing a rocket stick in either hand, he scrambled into the cleft where Jump lay hopelessly inching forward on his belly. Arthur set the rocket sticks aside and crouched down beside him.

"Come on, Jump," he said, getting a shoulder underneath the other boy's arm. "Let's get out of here."

Jump looked dazed. "Who—who are you?"

"I'm Arthur Whipple. I'm a big fan. . . ."

Three riders zoomed past overhead, taking with them any chance of a medal for Arthur.

"Can you stand?"

"I think so."

Another rider shot past.

Jump leaned his back against the wall while Arthur fetched the veteran's rocket stick and stood it before him. Clutching the handles, Jump agonizingly hoisted his feet onto the pegs—then leaned away from the rock. Balancing himself unaided on the idling rocket stick, Jump turned to Arthur, who clambered onto his own HopRocket. "Thank you," he said, his eyes watering unexpectedly.

Arthur nodded.

Composing himself, Jump added, "All right, Arthur—let's go."

With that, the two boys shot upward, touching down side by side on the boulder's crest as they sprang back into the race.

● ● ●

"Unbelievable! Newcomer Roxy Goldwin has taken the gold and set a new speed record in the process! What an upset! And what a crushing blow to Andy Gravity! First, to be outpaced for most of the race by a debilitated Jump Johnston—who wasn't even expected to crack the top thirty—and then to be edged out at the last second by a total novice. . . . What do you say, Chuck, do you think he still has a shot at replacing Jump as the new face of rocket-stick racing?"

"I don't know, Ted—not if this Goldwin girl continues to perform anything like she has today. . . . And I've got to say it doesn't seem Jump is willing to give up that role just yet anyhow. His performance today was nothing short of amazing. Leading the race until the very end, and then finishing eighth when he was only ranked thirty-second—after all he's been through, he's proved today he truly has the heart of a champion."

"Absolutely, Chuck. But let's not forget about Arthur Whipple! What an incredible race he had today."

"That he did, Ted. You know, it's one thing to be bested by fierce competition as Andy Gravity was, but to willingly

*throw away a guaranteed medal—possibly even the gold—
in some misguided outburst of compassion . . . well, it's
more than I can comprehend."*

*"Absolutely, Chuck. In my days as a rocket-stick racer,
it never would have crossed my mind to do something so
foolish. Honestly, I don't know what he was thinking."*

*"Hard to believe he's from the same family as his broth-
ers and sisters, isn't it, Ted?"*

"Indeed it is, Chuck. Indeed it is."

• • •

Arthur suddenly wished the radio broadcast had not been
aired over the locker room PA system while he and the
other riders were still inside. Though his ears had perked up
with pride when the announcers first mentioned his name,
it quickly became clear that pride was the wrong response
to what they had to say about him.

Trying to escape the snickering of the other boys as soon
as possible, Arthur swiftly stuffed his balled-up, mud-caked
socks into his gym bag. *He* felt a bit like *they* smelt.

But disappointed as he was by his own loss, he couldn't
help but be just a bit happy for Roxy Goldwin. It must
have been truly thrilling to win the gold medal in an event
she had never even entered before. How proud her parents
must be. Though it was sure to be the only event the Goldwins would win that day, at least their first Unsafe Sports
Showdown had not been a total loss. For as well as Roxy
had performed in the rocket-stick race, she had only won,

of course, because none of Arthur's brothers or sisters had been competing against her. Surely, the rest of the Goldwins would not fare so well when they went up against the *real* Whipples.

As Arthur emerged from the changing room, Uncle Mervyn and Mr. Whipple were waiting with his older siblings to greet him. Henry and Simon attempted to smile, but try as they might, they could not hide their utter bafflement with their brother's performance. Cordelia simply stood with her arms crossed and glared at him.

Luckily, Uncle Mervyn got to Arthur before his sister could. "Nicely done, lad!" he exclaimed. "It's nothing short of incredible how much you've improved in just one year. You would have certainly won the whole thing, if you weren't so hopelessly decent—but thank God you are, lad, thank God you are."

"Yes, Arthur," added Mr. Whipple. "How remarkable you've only lost by eight places this year. Really, your failure quotient hardly looks bad at all, when compared to your last race. It's certainly better than we expected; we're used to seeing you do *much* worse!"

At once honored and injured by his father's best attempt at a compliment, Arthur smiled awkwardly up at the man— as an increasingly familiar figure approached from behind Mr. Whipple.

"That was some race, eh, Arthur?" Rex Goldwin interjected as he clapped the boy's startled father on the back. "You almost had it there for a moment or two, didn't you?

But I'm afraid there's just no beating my little Roxy. Maybe if your old dad had taught you a few of his own rocket-stick moves, you might've had a chance; I guess you'll just have to watch him in the premier division race later on today—you *are* competing, aren't you, Charlie?"

"Actually, Mr. Goldwin," Arthur's father said through arched eyebrows, "extreme croquet is my event."

"Ah, playing it safe, eh? Come on, Charlie—we can't let the youngsters have all the fun, can we?"

Mr. Whipple's eyes filled with fire. "Extreme croquet can hardly be considered *safe*, Mr. Goldwin!" he snapped. "Just try telling that to Wailin' Waylan Martinson's widow, who only last year lost her husband—one of the most respected extreme croqueters of our time—to the crocodile trap!"

"Whoa, there—easy, Charlie!" Rex chuckled. "Only a bit of a joke, old boy! My apologies. If I'd have known it was such a sensitive subject, I never would have mentioned it. Can't be good for the heart at your age, getting so riled up like that. . . ."

The fire in Mr. Whipple's eyes had gone from orange to blue and now, to white—but before the fire could consume his entire head, the changing room door opened again, and out stepped Roxy Goldwin—the recent rocket-sticking record breaker. The instant the girl crossed the threshold, she was rushed by a herd of reporters.

"Ah, there she is!" Rex grinned. "I'd better go congratulate the girl. It's been a pleasure. Gentlemen. Miss."

Saluting the boys and tipping his hat to Cordelia, Rex

Goldwin hurried off toward the nearby mob, leaving the Whipples with their mouths agape.

"Quite a character, that Mr. Goldwin—eh, Charles?" said Uncle Mervyn.

"Indeed," grumbled Mr. Whipple.

"Don't worry, Dad," said Henry. "We'll show him. I doubt he'll be so smiley when his family loses the rest of their events. I mean—no disrespect to Arthur—but we haven't really put our best foot forward, now have we? Wait till they see what we can *really* do!"

"Yeah," said Simon, "they won't even know what hit them!"

"They'll cry themselves to sleep tonight!" added Cordelia.

"Yes," Arthur chimed in, unable to resist, "we'll beat them so badly their self-esteem will be injured for an entire week!"

Arthur's surrounding family members stared at him blankly. There were many things at which Arthur knew he was not the best; it seemed he could safely add "trash-talking" to the list.

After a terribly awkward silence, Mr. Whipple finally spoke up. "Yes, well, I appreciate your resolve, children— and I look forward to watching you obliterate the competition, just as you always do. Now, let us go find your mother so we might congratulate the little ones on the heap of medals they have no doubt won this morning."

• • •

When the group spotted Mrs. Whipple and the octuplets just outside the Pogo Pavilion, Arthur instantly noticed an unfamiliar expression on the faces of his younger siblings—an expression that apparently went undetected by his father.

"So, Mrs. Whipple," Arthur's father grinned, "how many records have we broken so far?"

"Nine, in all," she replied.

"Splendid!" Mr. Whipple beamed. "Well done, children!"

It was another moment before it struck him that his children were not beaming back. "Now hold on there—why so glum? It seems you've broken a record in every event you entered, so where are your smiles, children?"

"Unfortunately," Mrs. Whipple replied, "eight of those records were broken again by other competitors . . . all of whom happened to be members of the Goldwin family."

Mr. Whipple's smile vanished.

"I'm afraid Beatrice was the only one to win her event. . . ."

For a brief moment, Mr. Whipple seemed to perk up a bit. "Well at least we've beaten them at something then."

"Not exactly, dear. Since no one from the Goldwin family actually entered the extreme hopscotch event, we weren't technically competing against them in that one."

"I see."

"You've got to hand it to them, Charles—those Goldwins are rather remarkable."

222

This proved too much for her husband to handle.

"No, Eliza," snapped Mr. Whipple, "I will not hand it to them—this is an outrage! Just who do they think they are, showing up out of the blue and robbing us of our records?"

"Charles!" Mrs. Whipple shot back. "This is hardly the sort of example you should be setting for the children. I'll not have them learning such dreadful sportsmanship from their own father. The Goldwins beat us fair and square in every event this morning—and furthermore, they have been nothing but nice to us ever since they moved into the neighborhood. Need I remind you that Mr. Goldwin went so far as to save your very life?"

Over the course of his wife's lecture, Mr. Whipple had been steadily drained of air, so that when she had finished, he resembled a wilted red balloon that had been left out in the sun too long. "No, dear," he moaned.

"I thought not. Now, that's the last unsportsmanlike comment I want to hear from you for the rest of the day—understand?"

"Yes, dear."

"Good. All right, dear—you needn't be so gloomy. There are plenty of opportunities left today to show the Goldwins what we Whipples are made of. . . . Speaking of which, how did Arthur's event go?"

As if the wilting red balloon had finally been popped, Mr. Whipple let out a feeble, dispirited sigh.

Requiring no further explanation, Mrs. Whipple quickly changed the subject. "Well, no matter; the day has only begun. Come, children—we don't want to miss our check-in for mother/child knife throwing!"

●　●　●

As Arthur tagged along behind his newly reunited family, he began to develop the strange sense that someone was tagging along behind *him*. He turned to confront his follower—and found himself standing face to face with Ruby Goldwin.

"Hello," said the girl. "Headed over to mother/child knife throwing?"

"Oh," said Arthur, stumbling backward at her abrupt address. "Um . . . yeah."

He now saw why the girl had looked different to him when he'd seen her at the start of the race. Indeed, her appearance had changed rather drastically since his first encounters with her. Her complexion was not nearly so pale, and her lips no longer looked the color of dried blood. In place of her previous gothic attire, she wore a drab knitted pullover and cropped trousers. Her dark, red-tinged hair, once spilling down the sides of her face like some demonic fountain, was unceremoniously pulled back in a ponytail. And yet, somehow, Arthur found her no less terrifying.

"Perfect," she replied. "I'm heading there myself; I'll walk with you."

"Oh," said the boy.

Turning and proceeding in his original direction, Arthur

picked up his pace a bit in the hopes of catching up with his family—and of making as little eye contact with the girl as possible.

Apparently Ruby did not get the hint, because the next moment she was walking alongside, half a step ahead of him. "Nice work in the rocket-stick race," she smiled. "That double-jump thing you did was incredible. I don't think I've ever seen anybody jump that high before."

"Thanks," said Arthur, slowing his pace ever so slightly. "Actually, Jump Johnston still holds the height record."

"You know," Ruby added, "if you want to win next time, you probably shouldn't stop to help your competition in the middle of the race. I'm no expert on rocket-stick racing—or on any sport, for that matter—but I think that sort of defeats the purpose of competing, doesn't it?"

"Well," said Arthur, "I . . ."

"I mean, personally," Ruby continued, "I wouldn't be caught dead in any of these races—but if you're going to play their game, you might as well play by their rules, right? Not to worry, though—you've learned your lesson. You'll get 'em next time, won't you?"

There was a break in the girl's speech, and Arthur realized she was actually waiting for a response.

"Yeah . . . I—I guess so," he stammered.

"Of course you will," Ruby smiled.

Arthur walked alongside her in confused silence for a few paces before his curiosity finally got the best of him and he couldn't help but ask, "So what happened to your fight against 'the oppression of popular fashion' or whatever it was? I almost didn't recognize you at first."

"Ah—just a phase, you know. It was fun while it lasted, but I'm over it now. Realized I was spending far too much time obsessing about fashion in order to make the statement that I don't really care about fashion. The only reason it lasted so long, I think, was I didn't want Rita to think she was getting her way. Just wasn't me in the end, though. I mean, it was all a bit creepy, don't you think?"

Arthur nodded. "Yep. Just a bit."

"Yeah, well, I'm not saying I won't break out the eyeliner and nail polish for full moons every now and then. . . . But anyway—speaking of creepy," Ruby added, her eyes bulging with ghoulish excitement, "I hear your family is *cursed . . .*"

"What?" gasped Arthur, stopping in his tracks.

"You know—this whole thing about your family's recent mishaps actually being a continuation of this age-old Lyon's Curse, or whatever it's called. Riveting, isn't it?"

Arthur frowned. "Maybe for you it is."

"I'm not trying to be insensitive," Ruby explained. "I'm just not used to this sort of real-life intrigue. It's just so, well, you know—*intriguing*. Oh—and what about your chef? How they arrested him for masterminding that business with the birthday cake and trying to murder your family and so forth—shocking stuff, right?"

Arthur's frown deepened as he slowly resumed his stride. "Yeah, well, they've got the wrong man."

"How do you figure?"

"Well, I haven't exactly got proof, but I think Sammy was framed. And I'm pretty sure those clowns we saw in the Grazelby tent have something to do with it."

"You don't say," said Ruby, with what sounded to Arthur a lot like sarcasm. "So what are we going to do about it, then?"

Arthur ignored the word *we*. "Since no one in my family seems to believe me, I'm going to have to catch the clowns in the act. It's just turning out to be a bit more difficult than I'd thought."

"I see," said the girl. "Now tell me again why you didn't just point out the clowns to your big butler friend when we saw them sneaking through the tent? It was obvious then that they were up to no good."

"It wasn't *completely* obvious," Arthur scowled.

"Please, Arthur. When have you ever known *any* clowns—especially looking the way those two did—to be driven by anything other than pure evil?"

"Come on, now—that's not really fair, is it? I don't think you should judge an entire group of people based on the faults of a few. Obviously, there are plenty of clowns in the world who are quite the opposite of evil."

"Name one."

"Well . . . what about Spokes McGee—the First Clown to Unicycle around the Globe While Juggling? Surely *he* isn't evil. The man's brought nothing but joy to millions of people."

"Strangled his entire family with one of his novelty bow ties."

"He didn't."

"I'm afraid so," said Ruby. "The IBCPC did their best to cover it up, but they couldn't conceal it forever. Big article on it in *The Record* last month. You really should read more often."

"Hmm," Arthur frowned. "Well . . . I'm pretty sure you've just made that up. But either way, it doesn't change the fact that we never actually saw those clowns doing anything wrong. My family had a lot on their minds that evening, and I didn't want to trouble them with some silly hunch that would probably just turn out to be nothing—so I decided to keep it to myself until I found some kind of proof. Is that really so terrible?"

Ruby didn't answer, but Arthur could tell by her expression that she was less than convinced. He couldn't really blame her. He was hardly convinced himself.

Suddenly flustered, he snapped, "Look, you wouldn't understand, all right?"

"Clearly," smirked the girl. Then, before Arthur could say anything more, she stopped abruptly and added, "Well, here we are."

The boy looked about him and saw that they had indeed reached the gates to the knife-throwing arena. It was hard to believe that such a long walk had passed so quickly.

"I'd better go find my family—not that they'll be looking for *me*," Ruby said cryptically as she and Arthur stepped through the gates. "Anyway, see you around."

"Oh. Right," said Arthur, caught off guard by the girl's abrupt farewell. Apparently, she conducted her goodbyes in the same manner as her hellos.

"See ya," he added with a half-wave.

Ruby smiled and waved back—then turned and dashed off into the stands.

As he watched the girl make her way through the crowd of eager spectators, Arthur couldn't help but feel just a bit relieved. He had never met someone so contrary in all his life.

And yet, as Ruby disappeared from view, the boy found himself filled with a strange sense of sadness for which he could find no explanation.

Ghost or not, the girl clearly had supernatural powers.

13

FRIENDLY COMPETITION

Having located his family in the stands, Arthur watched as his mother led his younger siblings onto the arena floor.

Upon reaching the white painted line at the center of the arena, Mrs. Whipple halted her advance and waved to the crowd, while the octuplets filed in against the wooden backboard ten feet behind her. There, they set about forming a human pyramid.

After George, the last octuplet, had climbed up to form the third level, Mrs. Whipple hoisted two-year-old Ivy into his arms. As George lifted his sister's feet onto his shoulders, she straddled the top of his head to form the pyramid's capstone.

With a nod, Arthur's mother returned to the baseline

and faced the pyramid, her back to the hushed crowd.

Next, Uncle Mervyn—who was officiating the event—wheeled in a narrow, cloth-covered table and brought it to rest in front of Mrs. Whipple. There, he removed the cloth to reveal a long row of razor-edged knives—and began carefully inspecting each blade. When he was satisfied all were up to regulation standards, the record certifier nodded to the contender and left the field of play.

Taking a moment to gather her focus, the woman drew a deep breath—and reached for the table. It was then that Mrs. Whipple began throwing knives at her children.

There were those, of course, who might have argued this was rather irresponsible behavior for a mother to engage in, and indeed, they might have had a valid point—that is, had Mrs. Whipple not been such a skilled knife thrower.

One by one, the deadly blades dug into the backboard, each of them mere inches from a smiling Whipple child and various vital organs. Outlining the pyramid's edges with surgical precision, Mrs. Whipple then proceeded to land knives in the spaces between each child. When every gap had been filled, she hurled her final blade at the pyramid's tip—and skewered the bow on top of Ivy's head.

The crowd roared.

After Uncle Mervyn had inspected the children to make sure there had been no rule infractions—such as pretending not to be stabbed by an errant blade (which, sadly, had become an all too common practice in mother/child knife throwing)—he gave a thumbs-up to the announcer booth.

A moment later, a voice filled the arena.

"At 17.682 seconds for thirty-two knives, Eliza Whipple and her children have just set a new world record!"

Still in pyramid formation, Ivy and the octuplets waved whatever free arms they had toward the screaming crowd.

Upon dispersing, the Whipple children promptly joined their mother for a victory bow. There were only three teams left to compete before they would be officially awarded the gold medal.

Despite a couple of superficial knife wounds and one fainting little boy, the next two mother/child teams made strong showings—but ultimately proved no contest for Mrs. Whipple's knife-throwing abilities.

Soon it was time for the last set of contenders to perform.

As Rita Goldwin and nine of her children strode into the arena, the crowd cheered almost as loudly as they had for Arthur's mother. Word had spread quickly, it seemed, of the Goldwins' long-shot victories earlier that morning.

Arthur glanced at the seats beside him. While Simon, Cordelia, and Henry rolled their eyes and feigned respectful applause, their father's face was still and serious, his hands folded tightly in his lap.

By this time, Rowena, Radley, Randolf, Rodney, Roxy, Rupert, Rosalind, and Roland had formed a single-file line perpendicular to the backboard in age order—with little Rowena at the front, carrying baby Rowan in a forward-facing harness. Noticeably absent from the lineup was Ruby.

Mrs. Goldwin nodded to the officials, signaling that her children were satisfactorily in position.

The crowd stirred. *This* was the Goldwins' final setup? It was hardly an impressive formation—by any standard—and Arthur couldn't help but feel a bit embarrassed for his family's new competitors. They were obviously out of their depth.

Uncle Mervyn wheeled the knife table into position, inspecting the blades as usual—but as he turned to leave, Mrs. Goldwin stopped him and appeared to ask a question. After a brief exchange of words, during which there was much murmuring from the crowd, Uncle Mervyn took the cloth from the table, folded it in two and held it up to his eyes.

The crowd was now completely baffled. What purpose did the cloth have, other than keeping the knives clean and dry?

They would not have to wait long for an answer.

The next moment, Uncle Mervyn wrapped the cloth around Mrs. Goldwin's head and tied it in the back, effectively covering her eyes and face. Rita Goldwin had requested a blindfold.

The crowd gasped. They had not witnessed a blindfolded round of mother/child knife throwing since Fannie "Infanticide" Jenkins had earned her nickname.

As Mrs. Goldwin plucked the first knife from the table, a hush fell over the crowd.

There was a flurry of flying steel, followed by several moments of dreadful silence.

The only movement came from Uncle Mervyn as he strode to the backboard. After a tense inspection of the area, the officiator gestured to Roland—the eldest Goldwin child—who promptly called out a drill command to his siblings. At this, the line broke into a staggered formation, each child stepping out to the left or to the right and raising one arm into the air—their final pose proving that no one had been pierced by their mother's knives.

The crowd leapt to its feet.

"*Unbelievable!*" shouted the announcer. "*At 17.639 seconds for thirty-two knives, the Goldwins have not only broken the record for Timed Mother/Child Knife Throwing, but the record for Timed Mother/Child Knife Throwing while Blindfolded, as well!*"

Casting aside her blindfold, Rita Goldwin blew kisses to her impassioned admirers.

Four seats down from Arthur, Mr. Whipple simply stared.

• • •

Outside the mother/child knife-throwing arena, Arthur stood with his older siblings and their father as they waited for their recently defeated mother and younger siblings to emerge. Cordelia, Simon, and Henry busied themselves plotting sweet revenge on the Goldwins, but Mr. Whipple stood silently, his face devoid of emotion, his mind apparently in another place altogether.

Arthur, being unused to such behavior from his father,

was not sure how to act in his presence. And so, after a few awkward moments, he turned to the man and said, "Father, may I have some money for a candied jellyfish?"

Mr. Whipple gave no response.

"Father?" the boy asked again.

"What?" the man replied dazedly. "Oh. Right."

He reached into his pocket and retrieved a handful of coins.

Usually, when Arthur asked to purchase a concessionary item, his father spent a fair amount of breath reminding him to see how many of the items he could eat in thirty seconds or how many he could juggle into his mouth—but this time, Mr. Whipple simply dropped the coins into Arthur's hand without so much as a word.

Grateful to be out of his father's strange company, Arthur hurried over to the candied jellyfish stand, which was several yards away. There, beneath a sign that read, THE SIGNATURE SNACK OF UNSAFE SPORTS!, he made his purchase.

"Good luck, lad," said the man behind the counter. "You never know—this just might be one with its stinging tentacles still attached. One out of twenty-five, guaranteed! Just had a boy—not unlike yourself—carted off by ambulance hardly five minutes ago!"

"Really?" Arthur said excitedly.

He studied the wrapper as he walked away, reading the slogans: *Free adrenaline rush included in every pouch!*™ and *So good, you won't mind risking severe pain and pos-*

sible hospitalization just to have one!™ Then he tore off the wrapper and nervously raised the sugar-coated confection to his mouth.

After the first adrenaline-charged bite, Arthur was mildly disappointed to find that it was of the standard stingerless variety, but this did not prevent him from enjoying it anyway. Though regular candied jellyfish was not nearly as exciting as its stinging counterpart, it was no less tasty.

Just then, Ruby emerged from a cluster of milling bystanders.

"There you are," she smiled.

"Oh, hi," replied Arthur in between bites of jellyfish. Her arrival had come as a bit of a surprise—but perhaps more surprising was that, for the first time, he almost felt glad to see her.

"I was afraid you were avoiding me," said the girl. "You know, since my family beat yours. Sorry about that. The Goldwins are pretty good knife throwers."

"That's all right," Arthur smiled. "I thought *my* family was good, but your family is *incredible*. You must be very proud. So—do you compete in any of their other group events?"

"Not really."

"Oh," said the boy. "Why not?"

"I don't know," Ruby shrugged. "Why don't *you* compete in *your* family's group events?"

Arthur sighed. "I've been barred from family competitions ever since I cost us the record for baby tossing when I was four months old. . . . But *you*—you're a world-record holder. Surely you'd be an asset to any team."

"Look, Arthur, you've got to stop with this 'world-record holder' nonsense. You'll find the Goldwins do just fine without me."

Punctuating Ruby's last sentence, there was an abrupt commotion near the arena's outer gates. Looking over his shoulder, Arthur could see Mrs. Goldwin and her children emerging from the arena—to much applause and popping of flashbulbs.

"Let's go see them!" he cried, suddenly caught up in the fervor.

The boy scurried back to the place where he had left his family, with Ruby trudging along behind him.

As the pair reached the small mob, Mrs. Goldwin was answering a question from an exceptionally eager reporter. "Well, we didn't get this good overnight, I can tell you that," she smiled. "No, it wasn't until day *three* that we had it completely mastered! I'm sure the kids could show you some nasty nicks from that first day, though—couldn't you, kids?"

The children all nodded enthusiastically.

"Mrs. Goldwin," another reporter chimed in, "how do you feel about knocking the Whipples out of nearly every competition they've entered so far today?"

"The Whipples are fine competitors—legends really— and it is truly an honor to defeat them. What a remarkable legacy they've left behind. We're immensely fortunate to call them friends—and we wish them all the best during this difficult time . . . of being, you know, conquered by us. If there is ever anything they need, we want them to know our door is always open—and conveniently located just down the street from theirs."

At that moment, Arthur's mother and her younger children emerged through the gates.

"Ah, here they are now!" Rita exclaimed. She walked over and wrapped her arms around a very surprised Mrs. Whipple, the mob following her every move. "Well done, Lizzie," Rita smiled as she released her grip on Arthur's mother. "Congratulations on your silver medal—you were nearly as good as we were. We'll have to watch our backs next year. If you work really hard, you might just beat us!"

"Thank you, Mrs. Goldwin," replied Mrs. Whipple, still slightly shaken by the sudden encounter. "But I think you are the one to be congratulated. That was truly some sensational knife throwing."

"Ahhh, what an honor that is coming from you, Lizzie—the former Mother/Child Knife-Throwing Champion of the World! You know, most people who have just been trounced by a relatively unknown competitor would be angry and bitter—but you somehow manage to remain complimentary. Bravo, Lizzie. Bra-vo."

Arthur's mother must have been altogether too touched to say any more—because at Mrs. Goldwin's last comment, she simply smiled and led her children away from the reporters.

Arthur had never seen his mother moved to speechlessness before. He turned to Ruby in astonishment. "Your mother really is incredible, isn't she?"

"Ehh," said the girl. "Rita's all right."

• • •

With only three events left in which both families were competing, the Whipples' chances to show the world they had not been entirely superseded by the Goldwins were dwindling fast.

Next up was the rocket-kart race.

Simon had been perfecting his rocket kart for several years now, having collected a steady stream of speed records in the process.

As a rocket kart is essentially a wheeled soap box with a rocket engine strapped to its back, the key to improving the general design is to use as large an engine as possible without it blasting through the kart's flimsy frame and instantly obliterating the driver. (This last consideration, of course, was to comply with the rather obnoxious rule that the driver of the rocket kart indeed be alive upon crossing the finish line.) Simon had gone through a great many dummy test drivers to arrive at his current design, which he felt was the perfect blend of power and unlethality.

And yet somehow, Rupert Goldwin's rocket-kart design proved to be just a bit better.

Though Simon held a wide lead for most of the race, the Goldwin boy nosed ahead of him just before the finish line—and promptly scored another world record for the Goldwin family.

Arthur noticed his brothers and sisters were no longer so vocal about their plans for revenge. His father remained silent.

Next, it was on to the Archery Area, where Cordelia would be competing in the foot archery event.

Despite Arthur's familiarity with this celebrated sport—in which competitors use only their feet to loose arrows from a bow toward a specified target—he had only recently learned of its somewhat dubious origins. According to Chinese legend, foot archery got its start in the late Jin Dynasty as a rather unpleasant method of capital punishment. Reserved only for the most despised criminals, foot archery was employed by the emperor when death by conventional archery struck him as too humane. Unfortunately for the executionee, it took much longer for the royal archers to hit the proper targets when they were made to use their feet. Instead of three or four arrows to put the poor wretch out of his misery, it typically required between seventy-five and one hundred—which soon led to the Great Chinese Arrow Shortage of 1214, and hence, the Mongolian victory and subsequent invasion at the Battle of Beijing in 1215. Of course, with the popularization of foot archery as a sport over the following centuries, foot archers had gained enough accuracy that in modern contests, only about one in fifteen arrows completely missed the target and flew into the surrounding crowd.

Cordelia, who held the records for Longest Distance to

Shoot a Bull's-Eye by Foot and Most International Tournament Wins, was truly a master foot archer. But so, it seemed, was Rosalind Goldwin.

Not surprisingly, as the end of competition drew near, it was down again to one member from each of their families.

For the tiebreaking round, both girls would shoot three arrows into the same target, and the competitor with the arrow nearest to center would win. For Cordelia, this would increase her record for Most International Tournament Wins to an even twenty; for Rosalind, it would make her the First Tenderfoot Ever to Win Gold in Target Foot Archery.

Favored by the coin toss, Rosalind chose to shoot first. After her first two arrows landed several inches from center, it was looking to be an easy victory for Cordelia—but Rosalind must have merely been gaining her bearings, because her final arrow landed dead center, with a heartbreaking *thunk*.

Unlike the crowd, the Whipples were less than ecstatic. For Cordelia to force a double tiebreaker and remain in the competition, there was only one shot she could make—and it was near impossible.

Cordelia started off strong, her first and second arrows landing well within the gold center circle—much better than Rosalind's first two shots—but still an inch or so from perfect center.

The Whipples' honor now hinged on Cordelia's last arrow.

Lying back on her specialized foot-archery recliner, Cordelia drew back the bowstring with her leg, the feathered end of the arrow snugly gripped between her toes. She held it there for an extended moment, biting her bottom lip in serious concentration as the crowd held its breath. And then, she let go.

As Arthur watched the arrow leave his sister's bowstring, he couldn't help but reflect on one of his all-time favorite heroes. Ever since he was a small boy, he had been thrilled by stories of the benevolent outlaw Robin Hood, who had lived in Sherwood Forest and—in order to impress a girl—had won an archery competition by skillfully splitting his opponent's arrow with an arrow of his own. Cordelia, however, had frequently assured her brother this was utter nonsense. "First of all," she'd explained, "you don't win an archery competition by making the exact same shot as your opponent—you force a *draw*. And second," she'd added, "if Mr. Hood actually had split an arrow in two, I'm sure he was just as surprised by it as anybody else. The way the story gets told, you'd think he went around splitting six arrows every day before breakfast. But believe me, Arthur, that's just not something you do much more than once or twice in your lifetime, no matter how skilled an archer you are, or however badly you want to impress a girl. The odds are entirely too low. If you want to go on listening to silly stories, be my guest—but you'll hear no such nonsense from me."

In the end, it seemed his sister was right about Robin

Hood. At least, it would be hard to argue with her after what happened next.

A moment later, Arthur watched Cordelia's arrow sink into the target, just left of Rosalind's—and another record for the Goldwins was secured.

• • •

The Whipples were all but silent as they trudged toward the Cycle Sector, where Arthur's eldest brother, Henry, would be competing in their family's final event against the Gold-wins: the penny-farthing stunt park.

As Arthur had learned from Dr. Bracket, his Early Bicycle History tutor, a penny-farthing (or high-wheel bicycle, as it is sometimes called) is marked by its two disparately sized wheels—the front being as large as five feet in diameter, and the rear being as tiny as five inches. Its name, Arthur had learned, had been derived from two British coins in circulation at the time of its invention: the penny and the farthing—the penny, of course, being worth a hundredth of a pound, and the farthing, a quarter of a penny. Apparently, upon seeing the bicycle in profile, somebody had thought it looked like a penny and a farthing standing side-by-side, since a penny was so much larger than a farthing, and since all some people can ever think about is money.

Even though the invention of the chain drive had long since replaced the need for such a large front wheel, the penny-farthing was still the vehicle of choice for true bicycle purists—or "wheelmen," as they preferred to be identified—

and Arthur's eldest brother considered himself one of them.

Henry was an expert wheelman. Not only had he executed the First Rear Tornado Whip-Twist in Competition, he was also the undisputed record holder for Most Gold Medals in the Penny-Farthing Stunt Park Event. And yet, with the Goldwins around, it seemed all prior awards had been virtually rendered meaningless.

Luckily, Henry thrived on pressure. It was widely rumored he would be unveiling a brand new trick at this year's Showdown, with experts speculating it could even be the elusive "Ten-Eighty"—the holy grail of spin moves, long thought to be humanly impossible by even the most seasoned wheelmen—in which the rider launches into the air and completes three full rotations before landing.

And so, despite his family's recent losses, Henry approached the stunt park with an uncommon air of confidence.

* * *

The stunt park itself was quite a marvel of recreational engineering. Squarish in shape, it was over fifty yards across, with all manner of ramps, rails, bridges, ledges, pools, and loops packed within its perimeter.

One by one, each rider entered to face it alone.

Halfway through the lineup, Roland Goldwin took to the park. As good as the previous competitors had been, Roland's superiority was instantly clear. Riding with more energy, more skill, and more style than anyone before him, the Goldwin boy soared to first place.

It was hard to imagine Henry coming even close to matching such a flawless performance. But when the eldest Whipple boy finally dropped in at the end of round one, Arthur felt ashamed for his momentary lack of faith. As ever, Henry was phenomenal.

When he had finished his run, all eyes turned to the scoreboard. A moment of tension, and there it was: 9.55— edging Henry into first by two-tenths of a point.

The Whipples cheered with joy and relief—but with two rounds to go, the competition was far from over.

As the second round commenced, it quickly became clear that Roland and Henry were in a class to themselves. While the other riders generally performed slightly worse than their own initial runs, the two frontrunners only seemed to improve upon theirs.

Adding an Extended Front Wheelie to his routine, Roland executed nearly half of his run without allowing his rear wheel to touch the ground. A score of 9.61 deftly moved him to the top of the board.

But then Henry pulled off triple consecutive Nine-Hundreds—completing two and a half rotations each time he launched off the lip of the half-pipe—reclaiming his lead with a lofty score of 9.67, much to the Whipples' delight.

And so, as the competing wheelmen headed into the third and final round, all the pressure landed squarely on the shoulders of Roland Goldwin. Since only the best run from each rider would be counted, even if Henry failed to finish the round, it would still take a near-perfect run from Roland to dethrone him.

Unfortunately, it seemed the Goldwin boy shared Henry's penchant for pressure. This time, in addition to the Extended Front Wheelie, he added an Extended *Rear* Wheelie as well, expertly transferring his balance from fore to aft, lifting the large wheel off the ground while stabilizing himself over the tiny one. He was on his way to his best run yet.

And then, it happened. Roland had just completed a routine Triple Tail-Whip, when his rear wheel slipped out from under him, sending the boy and his bicycle toppling inconceivably to one side.

Amidst a gasp from the crowd, Roland released his left handlebar and pushed against the ground with his free arm, managing to reverse his fall just before he hit the park floor. It was an impressive save—but it was too late. With a wobble like that, the Goldwin boy's chances of matching Henry's score were virtually nil.

Arthur and his family struggled to contain themselves (as it would have bordered on tactlessness to cheer for an opponent's misfortune), but even a cursory glance at their faces would have given away their excitement. After a long, harrowing day of defeat, here was their first glimmer of hope.

Sadly—for the time being—it was to remain but a glimmer.

Recovering from his near fall, Roland pedaled furiously to the drop that led to the Ghost-Maker—the highest launch ramp in the park. Picking up immense speed as he careened down the hill, the Goldwin boy charged up the ramp and rocketed off the lip, spinning himself violently through the air.

With each airborne revolution, the Whipples' faces dropped a bit more, so that when Roland clinched a clean landing after his third complete spin, the prior moment's hope had all but vanished from their eyes.

Meanwhile, the rest of the crowd had leapt to their feet.

Roland Goldwin—Unsafe Sports unknown and penny-farthing stunt park novice—had performed the First Ten-Eighty Ever Executed in Competition, before the reigning champion had even attempted it. Regardless of one's allegiances, the accomplishment could not be ignored.

Roland finished his run without further flaw, earning him an unbelievable score of 9.78 and pushing Henry into second place. But it wasn't over yet.

Though Henry had already lost one world record to his rival, the Whipple boy still had a chance at the gold and furthering his own record for stunt park wins—though it was hard to imagine a Ten-Eightyless run earning him the victory. Of course, if he had planned on surprising the crowd with the trick in his final run, only to be beaten to it by his opponent, pulling off a Ten-Eighty would not be impossible for Henry. But if he had planned it to be an icing-on-the-cake sort of trick, it had now become a *cake*-on-the-cake sort of trick: completely crucial—and somehow, infinitely more difficult.

Most riders would have buckled under the pressure, but Henry was not one to give up easily—or gruelingly, for that matter. And so, when it came time for the final run, he dropped into the park with the composure of someone with much less to lose.

Henry tore across the park, hitting all of his previous tricks with even more punch than before as he launched from ramp to pool to rail in a frenzied defense of his title. Executing one death-defying stunt after another, the eldest Whipple boy rode like his life depended on it. And it very nearly did.

When he had accomplished all he could on the lower park, he made his way toward the Ghost-Maker, with sixty seconds to spare. Dive-bombing down the slope, Henry reached the ramp at a higher speed than any other rider that day. It was a perfect launch.

As their eldest brother began his spin sequence, the Whipples began to mouth the number of rotations.

One . . . Two . . . Th—

Suddenly, a small, almost undetectable blur zipped across the sky toward Henry. As the boy headed into his final revolution, the path of the mysterious blur met his own.

Without warning, Henry's body convulsed, then seized up altogether, his momentum stalling in midair.

The horrified crowd struggled to make sense of what

248

they were watching. And then they realized. The blur had come from the Archery Area.

Arthur leapt to his feet alongside his family. He could hardly believe what was happening. His brother, it seemed, had been shot by a stray arrow from another foot archery event—and was now falling lifelessly toward the ground.

Then, by some miracle, Henry seemed to snap out of his paralysis. Managing to hit the downside of the ramp at a forty-five degree angle, he eked out a last-second land-ing—as a sigh of relief rose up from the crowd. He had survived. Now he could end his run and receive proper medical attention.

But Henry had other plans. Having fallen a few degrees short of a full Ten-Eighty, he had only managed to com-plete a measly Ten-Thirty-Five. It was a failure he refused to accept.

And so to the crowd's utter shock, as soon as he had regained his balance, the boy began pedaling harder than ever before, barreling around the park, pulling backflips and landing aerials, all the while circling back toward the Ghost-Maker.

No longer comfortable with their son's calculated risk now that he seemed to have an arrow lodged in his body, Mr. and Mrs. Whipple dashed down through the stands toward the competitors' entrance, with Arthur and his sib-lings just behind them.

"What is he doing?" shouted Cordelia. "With penetrat-ing trauma like that, he's likely to kill himself!"

"Come on, Henry," pleaded Simon. "Let it go, just this once. I don't want to have to perform your funeral march, Brother. . . ."

"Don't be a hero!" cried George.

Arthur and his family promptly arrived at the gate, but they could only stand and watch as Henry hurtled himself up and over the massive launch ramp one last time.

It was clear from the moment he left the ramp that something was not right. Instead of cutting cleanly through the air in his usual born-to-fly sort of way, his present action could only be described as floundering. Henry spun lopsidedly toward the ground and clumsily crash-landed on the ramp's backside after less than two rotations, his feet thrown from the pedals by the impact. As the clock ran down, he rolled haphazardly across the slope, swerving back and forth in unpredictable serpentine movements, his speed decreasing steadily until it was violently curtailed by the outer wall of the park.

Mrs. Whipple screamed.

Henry crumpled to the ground, his contorted limbs intertwined with the twisted frame of his bicycle. He did not move.

There was a great collective gasp—and the crowd fell silent. Even in the world of Unsafe Sports, death was a solemn matter.

But then, a hint of movement. A twitch of his shoulder—and Henry was wrenching his arm from the mangled spokes.

Mr. Whipple threw open the gate, and the Whipples leapt onto the park floor, racing to the aid of their fallen brother. But before anyone could help him up, Henry was already on his feet. As the battered boy staggered toward them, Arthur could see the feathered shaft of an arrow jutting out from behind his brother's shoulder.

And then, to the relief of all, Henry spoke.

"Sorry, Dad. I just couldn't pull it off. . . . If that bird hadn't run into me on my first Ten-Eighty attempt, I know I'd've made it—but it must've dislocated my shoulder or something, because my upper body's been completely stiff ever—"

"Henry," Mr. Whipple interrupted urgently, "that was no bird. Son . . . you have an arrow sticking out of your back."

Henry's brow furrowed in confusion as he turned his head to locate the offending object—but in his disoriented state, he merely pivoted his body away from his gaze and began stepping in a circle, like a dog determined to find its own tail.

"No, Henry. Don't move . . ."

"Coming through!" shouted a woman wearing a red cross on a white armband as she rushed into the cluster of concerned Whipples. "All right," she addressed Henry, "now hold still while we have a look." After a brief inspection, she declared, "Yes, you do indeed have an arrow sticking out of your back. We'll need to cut away the surrounding cloth to determine the damage."

251

Mr. Whipple nodded in consent. Retrieving an enormous pair of shears from her first aid kit, the woman removed the back of Henry's shirt—and uncovered the site of the wound.

The tip of the arrow entered horizontally, just beneath Henry's right shoulder blade, then exited near his spine, its point jutting out under the shoulder blade at the other side. It reminded Arthur of a simple sewing needle—but piercing flesh instead of fabric. This, of course, only made it all the more disturbing.

Thankfully, the medic's prognosis was not nearly so grim.

"It seems you are in luck, young man," she informed Henry. "The wound appears to be wholly superficial."

"Oh, thank God!" cried Mrs. Whipple.

"If I could just borrow a few of your tools," Cordelia offered to the medic, "I could have the intruding object out in no time."

"Umm," said the medic, "that's very kind of you, miss— but I do think it would be best to have the procedure done at a proper hospital, just in case."

"What, and dishonor my family name?" snapped Henry. "Did Lance Pierson need a hospital when he skewered his foot in the Vertical Javelin Toss? No, ma'am. I say we get it over with right here."

Mr. Whipple shrugged in a lack of protest.

"If you insist," said the medic. She removed a pair of bolt-cutters from the first aid kit and handed them to Henry's sister.

Cordelia promptly snipped off the arrow's tip, then grasped the feathered end and, without delay, slid it smoothly out of her brother's back. After cleaning and bandaging the twin puncture holes it had left behind, she offered both pieces of the arrow to Henry. "A souvenir, Brother," she smiled, "for your troubles."

The boy's eyes lit up as he took it. "Thanks, Cord," he grinned. Looking up into the stands for the first time, he raised the arrow over his head, as if to announce his triumph over the deadly projectile.

At the sight of an undeniably alive Henry Whipple, the crowd—whose murmuring had steadily increased since the medic's arrival—gave an explosive cheer.

• • •

As the boy and his family returned to the sidelines, the announcer's voice filled the arena.

"*Scoring a 9.72 in his final run, Henry Whipple has just missed the high score, halting his Streak of Consecutive Stunt Park Gold Medals at four—and confirming Roland Goldwin as this year's champion!*"

The Whipples hung their heads as the announcer continued to sprinkle salt on their wounds.

"*Goldwin's incredible winning run included the First Ten-Eighty Ever Performed in Competition—a world record that Whipple himself was expected to break . . .*"

Henry raised a hand to his brow in regret.

"*But it seems our silver medalist won't be going home*

empty-handed after all—as he has just become the First Entrant Ever to Complete the Stunt Park Event with an Arrow Lodged in His Body!"

There came a spontaneous cheer from the crowd, and Arthur's heart swelled with happiness for his brother. Indeed, Arthur recalled, the last entrant to have an arrow lodged in his body had not actually completed the event, due to loss of blood. The Unsafe Sports planning committee had scheduled an emergency meeting to discuss moving the foot archery event to a more remote location, but just before the meeting was to take place, the head of the committee had been struck by a stray arrow himself, and the meeting had been cancelled.

The Whipples turned to one another in delighted astonishment. Henry's unfortunate accident had proved to be their one defense against complete annihilation by the Goldwins that day.

The irony was not lost on Rex Goldwin.

"Tough break, son," Rex cooed to Henry as the Goldwins approached the competitors' gate, "to be struck by an arrow and nearly killed in the middle of your run. . . . Or," he chuckled, "should I say *lucky* break? Seems this whole Lyon's Curse business has its upside as well, does it not?"

Catching a stern glance from Mr. Whipple, Rex promptly changed the subject. "But honestly, it's been a pleasure competing with you all today. Looks like we've got the makings of a solid, friendly rivalry brewing here, eh? Like I always say, nothing breeds perfection like a bit of healthy competition—am I right?"

"Right you are, Mr. Goldwin," Arthur's mother replied. "It seems we've been resting a bit too heavily on our laurels lately—and we've got you to thank for bringing it to our attention. You truly have an amazing family."

"Please, Lizzie," Rita Goldwin cried as she and her children stepped up alongside her husband, "you're making me blush! I cannot tell you what a dream come true it is to hear you say that. . . . So, no hard feelings then?"

"Nothing beyond a bit of amicable competitive spirit, I'm sure."

"Splendid! You know, we really should all have dinner sometime. Be nice to get to know each other as *neighbors* as well as competitors, wouldn't it, Lizzie?"

Arthur's mother paused a moment, then said, "Of course it would, Mrs. Goldwin. Why, we've still not officially welcomed you to the neighborhood, have we? We'd be delighted if you'd help us remedy that by accepting our invitation to dinner this week—Friday, perhaps?"

Mr. Whipple turned to his wife in utter disbelief.

"Ah, that'll be fantastic!" Rex Goldwin beamed. "What do you say, Charlie?"

"Oh—well . . . I'm afraid we've got that *thing* on Friday—haven't we, dear?"

Mr. Whipple's wife responded with an icy glare in his direction.

"Never mind," he sighed. "It seems we'd be delighted."

"Perfect!" exclaimed Rex Goldwin. "We'll be looking forward to it, Mrs. Whipple."

Just then, there was some commotion at the gate to their rear, and Arthur turned to see a now common sight: a rabid pack of reporters swarming around the latest member of the Goldwin family to break a world record against a Whipple. Flash bulbs glinted off Roland's teeth as the penny-farthing champion smiled for the cameras.

"All right then," Rex Goldwin announced. "More interviews to give, I'm afraid. But do enjoy the rest of your day—and good luck in your remaining events. . . . Shame we won't be there to spur you on to your best anymore—but at least you'll be able to *win* a few before you leave, eh?"

Mrs. Whipple managed a polite smile. Her husband did not.

As Rex and Rita turned to face the reporters, Arthur noticed Ruby standing near the gate, a few yards from her brothers and sisters. Detecting the boy's gaze, she waved to him with an expression that seemed to say, *Sorry about your brother being shot with a misfired arrow and failing to win his event. Hope he's all right.*

Arthur appreciated her sentiment, but before he could wave back, a panting, gray-suited man scurried through the gate and approached his father.

"Mr. Whipple?" the man inquired, wiping his brow.

"Yes?"

"Benjamin Quivers—head of the Foot Archery Committee. I came as soon as I heard. Please accept my sincere apologies regarding the stray arrow. Usually, when one gets away from us, it merely hits a wall or—at the very worst—a bystander, but to hit an athlete in the middle of his event . . . I am truly sorry."

"It's quite all right, Mr. Quivers. Though it certainly gave us a scare for a moment or two, Henry was able to turn the incident to his advantage and pull out a world record anyway."

"Yes. That must have been quite a relief after being shut out all day by those Goldwins. At least *someone* in your family was able to break a record against them."

Mr. Whipple clearly did not find this comforting—but Mr. Quivers did not seem to notice.

"Yep," he added. "It's a good thing your boy knows how to take an arrow properly—he really saved your necks today. To be honest, I'm shocked he wasn't hurt any worse. You should've seen the size of this fellow who shot the arrow. Must've been nine feet tall . . ."

Arthur's ears perked up as a chill ran down his spine.

"Really, it's a wonder the arrow didn't go straight *through* your boy."

"Yes, we're very lucky," Mr. Whipple said curtly. "Thank you for your concern, Mr. Quivers, but I'd better get back to my family."

"Oh, yes. Please do. Hope to see you next year—if you're still competing in the world records game, of course."

There was a slight hiccup in Mr. Whipple's cordial

expression, but he quickly regained his composure, then turned and walked away—affording Arthur a moment alone with the committee head.

"Um—pardon me, sir?" the boy asked timidly.

"Yes?"

"The man who shot the arrow—he didn't happen to be wearing any, um, unusual clothing, did he?"

"What exactly do you mean by *unusual*?"

"Oh, I don't know. Like maybe a clown suit?"

"Nope. No clown suit."

"Oh. Well . . . did you happen to get his name?"

"I'm afraid not, my boy. The incident occurred during warm-ups for the amateur speed-shooting challenge, and in the end, he declined to compete—before his name had even made the roster. The event's just finished, I believe—but you might still catch him, if you'd like to have a chat with him about clown clothing. Last I saw him, he was hanging around with this really short fellow. Rather unpleasant looking chap. You really can't miss them."

Another chill met the boy's spine.

As the man turned and walked away, Arthur glanced over at Ruby. She'd heard the whole thing—and seemed to know as well as he did what it meant. The dwarf and the giant were there—and apparently up to their old tricks.

Ruby gave Arthur a look that said, *What are you going to do?*

As much as Arthur wanted to inform his parents of his suspicions, he had learned the hard way not to open his mouth without the proof to back it up. Before he presented his case, he would have to do some investigating.

"Father," the boy asked, making his way toward Mr. Whipple, "may I go watch the amateur foot archer speed-shooting challenge?"

"Hmm? Oh. Yes, that's fine. But don't be gone too long. Extreme croquet is coming up soon, you know."

"Yes sir," Arthur replied. "I won't be long."

Then, without so much as a word to each other, Arthur and Ruby walked side by side to the stairs that overlooked the Archery Area—and promptly began the descent.

• • •

Unfortunately, there was no sign of the oddly sized suspects at the foot archery field. Indeed, there was no sign of anyone. The participants and spectators of the recently concluded amateur speed-shooting challenge had all since dispersed, leaving behind only abandoned targets and concessions wrappers.

With a disgruntled sigh, Arthur set about scouring the area.

"Now, what exactly are we hoping to find here?" asked Ruby. "I mean, I thought we were after the clowns from the party—without the clown suits, apparently—but since they're obviously not here, what is there to look for?"

"Clues," replied Arthur, not looking up.

"Oh, right. Clues. Of course."

Ruby began staring casually at the ground. "So—I mean, I hate to say I told you so—but now that they've started shooting arrows at your family members, are you willing to admit that clowns might be just a little bit evil?"

"An isolated incident," muttered Arthur. "Their chosen profession has nothing to do with it."

"We'll have to agree to disagree on that one," said Ruby. "But I still say you should have told somebody about them."

"Noted," said Arthur.

The two continued their search in silence. But the more Arthur thought about it, the less he could focus on finding clues. Just who did this girl think she was, anyway? Telling him what he should and shouldn't do. *She* didn't have the pressure of trying to belong in *her* family. *She* already was a world-record holder—and she didn't even seem to appreciate it. After several seconds of stewing, he could no longer hide his indignation.

"You know, you've got a lot of—"

"Wait, Arthur—look at this!" Ruby cried, pointing at the ground in front of her.

As Arthur hunched over for a closer look, he forgot all about his intended tirade. There in the mud was an enormous shoeprint.

The two exchanged dumbstruck glances, then crouched down to examine their find more closely. The impression was over twenty inches in length and nearly eight inches across.

"Do you think this counts as a clue?" whispered Ruby.

"Well, I've never really found one before," Arthur admitted. "But yes, I'm pretty sure this counts."

Upon further inspection, it became clear that the print was not simply an orphan. Every five feet or so, the children found another matching shoeprint, so that a traceable path in the mud was soon revealed. If there had been any doubt as to who had left the prints, the children's next discovery instantly confirmed their suspicions.

"Whoa—look at these," Arthur gawked.

Running alongside the first set of prints was a barely noticeable second set, made up of shoeprints so tiny and so faint that they could only have been left by a toddler—or a very small dwarf.

"So, what now?" asked the girl.

"I guess we try to follow the footprints and see if they lead us to our suspects," replied Arthur.

"And after we track down this nine-foot giant assassin and his stealthy sidekick, then what?"

Arthur shrugged. "We apprehend them?"

Ruby shot the boy a skeptical look.

"I don't know," said Arthur. "I'm still pretty new at this detective stuff. We'll figure that out when we get there, I guess. But for now, I think the proper detective thing to do is to just follow the clues where they lead."

"So we're detectives now, are we?"

Arthur suddenly felt immensely embarrassed for saying that part out loud. He had forgotten that his junior detective credentials were mostly in his head.

"I just thought . . . I mean, if you don't want—"

"No, no—'detectives' is good," Ruby cut him off.

"As long as I get to be the hard-boiled private eye who's addicted to the job almost as much as he's addicted to the bottle. Oh, and at some point, I get to wear a trench coat."

"Uh . . . sure," said Arthur, surprisingly encouraged. She seemed even more into this than he was.

"All right," Ruby declared, "so what are we waiting for? Lead the way, Detective Whipple!"

ON THE SHOULDERS OF GIANTS;
OR, WHERE THE CLUES LED

Arthur and Ruby followed the trail nearly fifty yards, until it disappeared into the dense grove that divided the Archery Area from the extreme croquet lawn. Halting just outside the trees, Arthur stared into the gloomy woodland, then glanced to his partner for encouragement—or, preferably, restraint. But Ruby would not be so easily intimidated.

"After you," she smiled.

Upon entering the grove, the duo found the tracks increasingly difficult to follow. While fallen leaves obscured the ground underfoot, the canopy overhead blocked out the fading daylight—as well as whatever slight warmth it had provided.

"This must be how they avoided unnecessary attention," Arthur suggested, breathing into his hands and rubbing them together. "These trees are the only things tall enough around here to provide cover for a giant."

"True," said Ruby, "or it could be a trap. They could be hiding in here still, knowing no one will be around to stop them from brutally murdering us."

The sound of leaves crunching beneath Arthur's feet suddenly took on a rather ominous quality. "I suppose that's another possibility," he admitted, hoping the girl didn't notice his sudden increase in pace.

When Arthur glanced up to gain his bearings a short while later, he was relieved to see light poking through the thinning trees ahead of them. Only a hundred feet left to go amongst the trees, and they'd be able to continue tracking in the open again—where there was far less chance of being ambushed by vicious off-duty clowns. Things were looking up.

At that moment, it began to rain.

Soon the children's ears were filled with what sounded like the World's Largest Batch of Popcorn being popped directly over their heads. Arthur felt a cold pinprick on the back of his neck. And then another. And another—until there were too many to distinguish one from the next. He was quickly becoming drenched.

Looking back at Ruby, he couldn't help but smile at their ridiculous circumstances—but as he returned his gaze to the ground, he noticed the water pooling up in one of the giant shoeprints.

A terrible thought struck him. Soon the tracks would be

completely washed away—and with them, their first and only lead.

"Run!" cried Ruby, apparently arriving at a similar conclusion.

Arthur spun back around and charged forward, doing his best to follow the dissolving trail of muddy shoeprints through the undergrowth. But soon, there was nothing left to track.

In their haste, the children had failed to notice the trail veer sharply to the right and curve behind an enormous oak tree. As a result, they also failed to notice the two pairs of eyes—one unusually large, the other unusually small—peering out at them through the crook of a tree branch. Had they noticed this, of course, more than just their mission might have ended right then and there.

Unaware of their recent brush with death, Arthur and Ruby scrambled onward. Moments later, they burst out of the trees and onto a swampy stretch of lawn.

"Wow," said Ruby, rain pouring off her nose. "Good work keeping to the trail through all that. I lost it a long time ago."

"Well, actually," said Arthur, "so did I."

"Oh," said Ruby.

"I thought I'd be able to pick it up again once we were out of the trees," Arthur gasped, rainwater spilling down his face, "but it seems it's been completely washed away—and now we've lost our one chance at finding the clowns and setting things right."

Ruby put a hand on the boy's sopping shoulder. "Don't worry yourself, Arthur. We're bound to find them sooner or later. But first—let's try to get out of this rain, shall we?"

Arthur drew a breath, then wiped his brow and nodded.

Surveying the area, the pair found that the lawn sloped down from the trees and butted into a paved thoroughfare some thirty yards ahead of them. There, streams of pedestrians made their way across the Unsafe Sports Complex—some of them carrying umbrellas, others darting from shelter to shelter.

They then noticed a medium-sized snack stand on the far side of the road, complete with patio tables and a large awning—under which several umbrellaless pedestrians currently huddled.

At once, the pair set off sloshing toward it.

By the time they had ducked in under the overhang, their teeth were thoroughly chattering. Exhausted in body and spirit, Arthur collapsed into a patio chair, while Ruby continued toward the concessions window.

A minute later, the girl pulled up a chair beside Arthur and placed a steaming paper cup on the table in front of him.

"ExploCocoa?" she offered.

"Thanks," replied the boy, managing a brief smile as he took it.

Casually pulling the tab from the top of the lid, Arthur raised the cup to his lips and began blowing frantically through the opening. He now had two minutes to drink the beverage before a tiny explosive charge was detonated at the base of the cup, spattering scalding hot cocoa onto his face and hands. On any other day, the challenge would have given Arthur an immense thrill, but in his current mood, the usual joys of ExploCocoa were entirely lost on him. At least it was keeping him warm.

"Cheer up, Arthur," said Ruby. "We'll get 'em next time."

"I don't know," the boy sighed in between breathy sips. "It's hard to imagine a better opportunity than the one we just—"

But before the words had even left his mouth, Arthur was forced to rethink them. There on the pathway before him, jutting out above the heads of passersby, emerged the upper portion of an extraordinarily tall man. Seated on the man's shoulder, holding an umbrella over both of their heads, was a dwarf.

Arthur glanced at Ruby—and found she shared his shock.

Thinking quickly, the girl grabbed two snack menus from the center of the table and held them in front of their faces.

Peering over the tops of their paper shields, the junior detectives surveyed their suspects as they passed in front of the snack stand. Far from their previous carnival attire, the oddly sized pair now wore matching burgundy blazers. It was almost creepier.

Suddenly, the dwarf turned his head in the children's direction. Having ventured a bit too boldly above their foldable hiding spots, Arthur and Ruby's faces were exposed from their noses upward—and for an instant, the miniature man's eyes seemed to lock onto them. Hearts suddenly racing with the dread of being discovered, the children ducked back behind their menus.

Clamping his eyes shut, Arthur longed to return to a simpler time—a time when he had yet to learn that closing his own eyes had no effect on the ability of others to see him. But it was no use. He was not invisible. He could practically feel the giant assassin towering over him—ready to render him permanently speechless.

"Psst—Arthur," Ruby whispered, to the boy's surprise. "They've nearly passed."

Cautiously opening his eyes, Arthur peered around the menu—and caught a glimpse of the giant's back as it exited his field of view.

By some miracle, they had escaped discovery after all.

"Come on," said Ruby, rising to her feet. "We don't want to lose them again."

Gasping with relief, Arthur joined his partner, and the two hurried off toward the bustling thoroughfare, not noticing as their abandoned cups abruptly burst behind them—two quick *pops* leaving the table covered in steaming hot chocolate.

• • •

Crowded as the pathway was, the young trackers had little trouble following their newly found suspects, as the back of

268

the giant's enormous head consistently hovered several feet above everyone else's.

"Where do you think they're headed?" asked Ruby as the giant and dwarf turned a corner and briefly disappeared from view.

"Maybe they're on their way to another sabotage," Arthur replied, "and we can catch them in the act."

But as the children ventured around the bend, it became clear their suspects had far simpler plans—starting with fleeing the scene of the crime. The pathway ahead was intersected by a series of gates, each leading off the grounds of the Unsafe Sports Complex.

While Arthur and Ruby looked on, the giant squeezed through the center exit and ducked through the gate, the dwarf still seated on his shoulder as he lumbered toward the adjoining roadway.

"What do we do now?" whispered Ruby.

"I guess we get our hands stamped," said Arthur. "I mean, it hardly seems right to just let them get away after all that."

"Hardly."

As the pair approached the gate, they each offered a hand to the attendant for a return stamp, then stepped through the turnstile.

• • •

Arriving at Unsafe Sports Street, the children caught a glimpse of their suspects rounding the next corner.

269

"There they go!" Ruby shouted, then broke into a run, with Arthur following just behind her.

Fearing the fugitives would disappear into the dark recesses of the city before they could reach them, the children splashed onward, burrowing through the perpetual wall of rain.

When they got to the corner, Arthur and Ruby peered around the Unsafe Sports Complex's outer wall—and could scarcely believe what they saw. Far from vanishing into the maze of city streets, their suspects stood less than fifty feet away, patiently waiting for the signal at the nearest pedestrian crossing—with hardly a vehicle on the road.

It was quite a disconcerting sight. What sort of criminals had no qualms about sabotage and murder, but saw fit to obey even the most trivial traffic laws? With each new trait, these villains only grew creepier and creepier.

The next moment, the light changed, and the umbrella-carrying duo made their move to cross.

Edging around the corner, the children tiptoed down the pavement in silent pursuit. Once their suspects' backs were completely turned to them, Arthur and Ruby darted across the empty street, effectively committing the very violation at which the assassins appeared to draw the line.

The young detectives proceeded to follow their marks onto Chancy Lane, then Hazard Street, and then Death-trap Road, all the while ducking behind various stoops and waste bins to avoid detection, narrowly dodging sudden backward glances from the dwarf on numerous occasions.

The next series of turns led them through a patchwork of increasingly dwindling and darkening alleyways, the likes of which neither Arthur nor Ruby would ever have had the courage to venture down alone.

It was becoming more and more difficult to remain undetected in such cramped surroundings, so it was much to the children's relief that the alleyway finally opened out onto a proper street, despite its being a rather deserted one.

By this time, Arthur and Ruby had lost any notion of their whereabouts within the city, but they surmised by the backdrop of boxy gray buildings before them that they had been led into some sort of commercial district.

Peering out from behind a crate of moldy cabbages, the children breathed through their mouths as they watched the dwarf-carrying giant trudge across the street and onto the rear lot of what appeared to be a large warehouse. The two men took shelter beneath an overhang, and the dwarf collapsed his umbrella as the giant lowered him to the ground. Then, retrieving a shiny cigarette case from his jacket, the giant removed two cigarettes—placing one in his own mouth and handing the other down to the dwarf. After hunching almost completely over to light the dwarf's cigarette, the giant lit his own, extinguished the match, and then checked his watch.

For the next several minutes, the sinister twosome simply stood against the wall of the warehouse, exchanging a few inaudible words in between puffs of smoke and periodic watch checks.

"This must be the rendezvous point," whispered Ruby. "The place where they get instructions from the boss."

"Right," said Arthur. "So we should probably wait till they make contact—and then apprehend the lot of 'em. . . . Any ideas on how we might do that?"

Ruby shrugged. "We really could use some backup right about now."

As much as Arthur had imagined single-handedly hauling the culprits down to the police station, he had to agree with Ruby. Though they might have been able to handle the dwarf, the giant was well out of their weight class.

Just as he started to worry their showdown had ended before it had even begun, Arthur spied one of the city's signature plum-colored telephone kiosks on the street corner across the alleyway.

"Wait here," he whispered. "I'm going to try and call this in."

• • •

Making sure the giant and the dwarf were looking away, Arthur slipped across the alley and hid behind a stack of discarded boxes on the other side. He crouched there a few moments while he collected his courage, then took a deep breath and scampered around the corner, opening the phone box door and stepping inside in one swift motion. With the rain's constant patter helping to camouflage the sound of the door clapping shut, Arthur felt confident he had remained undetected.

He yanked the receiver to his ear and dialed Emergency.

"Yes. Hello. I must speak to Inspector Hadrian Smudge. I have urgent information concerning suspects involved with the Whipple Birthday Cake Catastrophe. Lives are in danger. . . . Yes, I can hold."

After what seemed to be a never-ending stream of the World's Schmaltziest Hold Music (which provided a rather bizarre contrast to the otherwise cloak-and-dagger setting), a man's voice finally crackled through the receiver.

"D.S. Greenley speaking . . ."

"Oh. D.S. Greenley. Is Inspector Smudge with you?"

"Ah—unfortunately, the inspector is across town receiving the Golden Magnifying Glass Award from the Academy of Qualified Award Givers—but can I help you?"

Arthur was rather disappointed to hear the record-breaking detective would not be available to witness what was likely to be the boy's crowning achievement in crime fighting. D.S. Greenley seemed a nice enough fellow—he had, after all, treated Sammy the Spatula with respect and mercy during his arrest—but then again, Greenley hadn't exactly displayed the most effective suspect-apprehension skills on that day either. This worried Arthur. If the man had not been able to properly take custody of a drunken chef, whom Arthur knew to be harmless, how would he handle two bloodthirsty assassins, one of them a giant, no less? But of course, Arthur did not have access to an alternative army of record-breaking detectives, so D.S. Greenley would have to do.

273

"Well, yes," the boy replied, the urgency returning to his voice. "This is Arthur Whipple . . ."

"Oh, hi-ya, Arthur," Greenley interjected, jovially. "Haven't seen you since that unfortunate business with the chef. Poor bloke. . . . So what seems to be the problem?"

"Well, earlier today, at the Unsafe Sports Showdown, this girl Ruby and I saw the same giant and dwarf I reported seeing at the Birthday Extravaganza—the ones suspected in the cake catastrophe. They tried to kill my brother Henry by sabotaging his event—I mean, somebody saw a giant and a dwarf shoot an arrow toward the Penny-Farthing Stunt Park during his run—but we found them, and we followed them to . . . Hold on a second." Arthur gingerly cracked the door open so he could get a peak at a nearby street sign. "Dankly Avenue and Bleak Street, it looks like. We've got them pinned down outside an abandoned warehouse. . . . Well, they don't actually know they're pinned down, so they could conceivably leave at any moment—so maybe 'pinned down' isn't completely accurate. But they've been standing in the same spot for several minutes now, and we've been watching them real hardlike."

"Good work, Arthur," commended a noticeably impressed D.S. Greenley. "Now just stay put. I'm on my way."

"Right," said the boy. "We'll just keep standing here, watching them as hard as we can until you get here."

"Don't you worry, Arthur. We'll get them this time— thanks to your exceptional detective work. Now, don't make a move till I get there—I shouldn't be more than ten minutes."

"Yes, sir."

The line went dead, and Arthur found himself alone again inside the rain-battered phone box.

Not wanting to put the operation at risk by stepping out into the open a second time, Arthur cracked the door and stealthily extended his arm through the resulting gap. He then gave a thumbs-up, followed by two flashes of five fingers, hoping Ruby would know that he meant: *Hang on, backup is coming in ten minutes*—and not: *Proceed north, fifty-five degrees*—or: *Thumb fingers fingers*, which would have been very confusing. They really should have come up with a standardized set of signals before the stakeout, but it was too late for that now.

Retreating back into the relative cover of the phone box compartment, Arthur resolved to sit and wait. It was not yet nighttime, but the sky was dark with thunderheads, and light was scarce. Through the rain-distorted glass, he could see the glowing tips of the saboteurs' cigarettes as the giant and the dwarf continued their cryptic conversation against the warehouse wall.

• • •

Several minutes passed, and the barrage of raindrops on the phone box roof gradually slowed to a drizzle, affording Arthur a slightly clearer view. Fortunately, the suspects had neither altered their position, nor seemed to suspect being under surveillance.

275

D.S. Greenley would be arriving any moment now, and the assassins would be taken away in shackles, thereby absolving Sammy the Spatula of all wrongdoing. Arthur's heart leapt at the thought of it.

He traded another round of thumbs-ups with Ruby from her position in the alley, then shifted his eyes back to the suspects. Everything was going according to plan.

Until it didn't.

Before Arthur knew what was happening, the giant and the dwarf extinguished their cigarettes and stepped out from underneath the overhang, where the giant began fiddling with something on the wall. The next moment, the loading bay door to their left began to open, its massive steel-sectioned face hoisted upward by some unseen motor.

Arthur leapt to his feet. His first stakeout as a junior detective was crumbling before his eyes. If his suspects were to enter the warehouse, there was no telling where they might disappear to, making it unlikely for even the police to find them. He had to do something.

Throwing the phone box door open, Arthur burst out into the misty air and charged across the street, the wild-eyed look of a man possessed carved into his face.

"Aieeeeeyah!" came the boy's involuntary battle cry.

As the baffled giant and dwarf turned to see what sort of wounded animal was hurtling toward them, Arthur realized he had no idea what he was going to do once he reached them.

His battle cry fading into self-conscious silence, Arthur skidded to a stop a few yards in front of his suspects, where he stared up at the giant for one uneasy moment—and then down at the dwarf for another. Both men's eyes were filled with equal parts bewilderment, annoyance, and rage, prompting Arthur to take a stumbling step backward in an abrupt bid for retreat.

"Get 'em, Arthur!" called a voice behind him.

The boy turned to find Ruby standing a few paces to his rear, her eyebrows arched in defiance. As glad as he was to see that she supported his half-baked plan, her vocal encouragement had now rendered it impossible to abandon.

Arthur turned to face his foes once again—and found that their expressions had grown even more hostile. "I . . ." he stammered, floundering for either a brave word—or an excuse.

The giant cut the boy off with a loud grunt, and then, covering half the distance between them in one gargantuan stride, moved menacingly toward Arthur, raising his right arm into the air. Now trembling, the boy held his hand to his face in a pathetic attempt to shield himself.

But before the crushing force of the giant's fist could reach Arthur's skull, there came a howl of sirens.

The next moment, two police cars screeched onto the lot on either side of them, effectively halting the giant in his tracks. The car doors flew open, and four men leapt out—three of them in full police uniform, the fourth in a gray trench coat.

"Freeze!" shouted the plain-clothed officer. "Step away from the boy!"

Exceedingly thankful for his timely arrival, Arthur immediately recognized Detective Sergeant Greenley.

"On the ground—now, now, now!" barked the sergeant.

For a moment, the giant and the dwarf simply stood there, knees half-bent and hands half-raised, seemingly stunned by the officers' abrupt arrival. Without delay, the three uniformed men swooped in to enforce Greenley's command, the smallest of them going for the dwarf, while the other two tackled the giant. Soon, both suspects had been brought to the ground, where they proceeded to writhe and squirm with cries of protest.

"Let me go!" squealed the dwarf.

"Hands behind your head, now!" ordered Greenley.

"You're making a mistake!" growled the giant.

"We'll see about that," said Greenley as the uniformed officers clapped handcuffs onto their detainees.

Now, the series of events leading up to that moment— from Arthur leaving the phone box to the police arriving and restraining the giant and the dwarf—had taken place in a mere matter of seconds, so that the loading bay door, which had been set in motion prior to the giant's incapacitation, was only just reaching its halfway point as Greenley uttered that soon-to-be-regretted phrase. A moment later, the bottom of the massive metal door had reached eye level, and the warehouse's shocking interior was revealed.

It was a boardroom.

At the room's center was an enormously long table, behind which hung a series of ornately framed painted portraits of aging men in burgundy blazers. But far stranger than the existence of such a polished meeting chamber inside so grimy an exterior were the chamber's occupants.

In the high-backed chairs surrounding the table sat two dozen men, all wearing the same matching burgundy blazers—half of them giants and half of them dwarves.

Arthur turned to D.S. Greenley in time to see his eyes bulge in terror.

"Police! All of you—stay where you are!" cried the sergeant, knowing full well that if they decided to do otherwise, he and his men would be unable to stop them.

Fortunately, the blazered men appeared to be heeding his orders—at least for the time being—and simply sat silently glaring outward.

It was a bizarre sight indeed. Arthur had the sickening sense that he and his comrades had stumbled upon some clandestine death cult—the sort that could make a couple of children and four policemen disappear in minutes without a trace. But as the dwarf coldly addressed D.S. Greenley, an even more unexpected explanation was offered.

"You, sir, have just handcuffed the newly elected co-presidents of the Global Guild of Dwarves and Giants, on their way to deliver their inaugural speeches, no less! Congratulations, officer—this must be some sort of world record for police stupidity!"

Arthur could see that D.S. Greenley shared his own confusion.

"But—you were going for the boy!" cried Greenley, pointing his finger at the giant. "I saw you! How do you explain *that*?"

"I simply wished to give the lad a leaflet on dwarf/giant sensitivity. Check my breast pocket. There's a stack of them in there. You might want to give one to him and his friend there—they both could badly use some education on the subject."

Greenley nodded to his partners, who promptly hoisted the two men to their feet, their once tidy jackets now sullied and wet from the rain-slicked pavement. Standing on pointed toes, one of the officers searched the giant's pocket, uncovering a small stack of leaflets, thereby substantiating the giant's claim.

Not sure what to make of this, Greenley turned to the dwarf. "Where were you on the night of March the first?"

"I don't know—do you see a calendar stitched to my sleeve?"

Greenley shot the dwarf a stern look, and he reconsidered.

"Probably a hundred miles away at the old headquarters, packing boxes. We've only just moved to this new location a week and a half ago. As you can see, we haven't even had time to paint or put up the proper signage."

"So you weren't anywhere near the Whipple estate, then?"

"Ahh, that was the night of that self-indulgent birthday binge they host every year, wasn't it?"

Greenley nodded.

"Weren't invited," replied the dwarf. "Apparently it doesn't matter to them that we're the leaders of one of the most respected branches of the World-Record Breakers Union, so long as we haven't broken any world records ourselves. Some of us have more important business to attend to than constantly trying to make ourselves feel special—such as protecting the rights of exceptionally sized people everywhere! And anyway, after what ended up taking place at this year's debacle, I'd say we owe them a debt of gratitude for *not* inviting us. As it stands now, I wouldn't go near that house if they paid me."

His face filling with desperation, D.S. Greenley abandoned all subtlety and blurted, "These children—one of whom is in fact Arthur Whipple—say they witnessed you leaving the scene of a murder attempt today, after two men matching your descriptions were witnessed perpetrating an act of sabotage!"

"Oh," the giant countered calmly, "you mean the children who have been blatantly stalking us for the past half hour?"

Arthur gulped and glanced at Ruby, who widened her eyes and pulled the corner of her mouth to one side in the widely accepted expression for "oops." It seemed they hadn't been nearly as stealthy as they had thought.

"I mean, we're used to having children stare at us every now and then, living in this narrow-minded society of ours, but to be tracked like animals through the city after volunteering at an Exceptional-Size Awareness booth . . . I guess that'll teach us to try and get involved with community sporting events from now on."

"And as for these preposterous claims," added the dwarf, "that we were somehow involved in sabotage and attempted murder simply because we match some vague description—well, clearly, we're not the only exceptionally sized people on the planet." He motioned to the boardroom behind him. "It could have been anyone."

At this, one of the dwarves at the table, a tan-faced, silver-haired man, rose to stand on his chair. "Officer," he started in an oddly deep voice, "if I may—" But he was promptly cut short.

"I'll do the talking here, Mr. Lowe!" snapped the tiny co-president. "I won the vote fair and square, despite your shameful smear campaign; if you want to be the voice of the GGDG, you'll have to do a far sight better at the next election!"

The silver-haired dwarf hung his shoulders, muttered something under his breath, then returned to his seat.

"Now," sighed the dwarf in handcuffs, turning again to Greenley, "where was I? Ah, yes. Your glaring mistreatment of this guild's members!"

"Indeed," the giant concurred. "I truly hope you're not suggesting we all look the same—or that it should be considered strange for two persons of contrasting sizes to socialize!"

It was at that moment Arthur noticed the giant was significantly shorter than he remembered him being at the party. The man presently standing before him couldn't have been over eight feet tall, but the giant he had seen at the Birthday Extravaganza had measured nine feet, at least. Likewise, the dwarf now appeared significantly taller— standing almost three feet high, where the clown from the party had measured only two. Suddenly sick to his stomach, Arthur realized that he and Ruby had indeed followed the wrong giant/dwarf duo.

"I hate to say it," concluded the dwarf, "but this sounds like a case of size-profiling in the worst degree. Not all dwarves are baby-thieves and witch servants, you know!"

"Yeah," added the giant. "And not all giants make their bread from ground-up human bones!"

"Well," replied the dwarf, turning unexpectedly to face his lofty companion, "let's be honest, Stuart. That does still happen a lot more than it should. You giants do love your bone bread. I've actually been meaning to talk to you about this—and I wish you didn't have to find out about it this way, but it's already been added to the agenda for the next meeting, because frankly, it looks bad for everyone in the GGDG that you still insist on baking that stuff. Even if you have largely limited the ingredients to animal bones, we believe it's an insensitive practice which needs to stop."

"Who's we?"

"The dwarves."

"I see. Well, I never would have voted for the merger if

I'd known this is how we giants would be treated! Because, as you know, Brian, the art of bone-bread baking is an ancient giant tradition passed down through countless generations, not unlike your ridiculous custom of sneaking into people's houses and fixing their shoes."

"Look, Stuart, we've been over this before; undercover shoe cobbling is a benevolent service to the community!"

At that moment, another car screeched onto the lot. Before it had even reached a complete stop, the rear door opened, and a man in a white bow tie and black overcoat leapt out. Still clutching a glistening golden trophy in the shape of an oversized magnifying glass, Inspector Smudge sprang forward.

"Where are they?!" demanded the inspector in the split second before he noticed the large giant and tiny dwarf standing before him in handcuffs. "Ah, what do we have here?" he smirked, stepping toward them in taunting triumph.

"Um, sir," D.S. Greenley muttered through his teeth, putting a hand on Smudge's shoulder and delicately pulling him aside, "I'm afraid these are not our suspects. Apparently, they are the co-presidents of the Global Guild of Dwarves and Giants, which has recently relocated its offices to this ramshackle warehouse. It seems the boy and his friend saw them at the Unsafe Sports Showdown today after another possible sabotage attempt, and assumed they were the same men he'd seen at the party."

The smugness in the inspector's voice promptly shifted

to seething anger. "Do you mean to tell me I rushed out of the Golden Magnifying Glass Awards banquet for nothing? Do you think the Academy of Qualified Award Givers gives out awards willy-nilly?!"

"Of course not, sir."

"Well, I guess I've only got myself to blame for thinking you'd actually made a break in the case. I don't have to tell you how valuable it would have been to collar a co-conspirator who could testify against Mr. Smith for us, since the man himself is proving so difficult to break. Honestly, after the amount of interrogation he's been through, you'd think he'd have confessed to the crime by now, or at least given up his accomplices. Very frustrating indeed. Not that any jury will find him innocent—but as an agent of the law, it is my duty to make their job as easy as possible. . . . Of course, most agents of the law are not constantly hindered by inept assistants—are they, Greenley?"

"No, sir," said the sergeant, hanging his head in shame.

"All right, Greenley—clean up this mess. I'll be in the car, imagining I'm still being applauded by powerful men and beautiful women in a seven-star hotel—instead of sur-rounded by incompetent cops in the bowels of the city. . . . And as for you, Angus," Smudge continued, shifting his attention to Arthur, "I'm afraid you've got a long, long way to go before any reputable law enforcement agency ever dreams of considering you an honorary detective. You had a promising start, but it seems you've outlasted your use-fulness to this investigation. I'd have kept to the solo work, if I were you. Your judgment, it would appear, has been ill affected by the company you keep." He nodded his nose to Ruby. "Indeed, if I ever catch you conspiring with this girl again, I shall have no choice but to arrest you both for obstruction of justice—a charge of which you will almost certainly be convicted. And good luck ever doing anything in law enforcement with a criminal record to your name. Surely, that's not the sort of *record* you're after, is it, boy?"

"No, sir."

"I thought as much. Now, why don't we leave it to the professionals from now on—and stay out of their way, so they can get some *real* police work done, hmm?"

Then, with a flurry of overcoat that momentarily smothered Arthur and nearly knocked the boy backward, Inspector Smudge turned and stomped off to the car, slamming the door behind him.

Arthur, finding himself unable to look at Ruby after being so thoroughly and humiliatingly chastised, simply stared at the ground.

Detective Sergeant Greenley recomposed himself with a deep breath, then returned to his detainees—and found that the giant and the dwarf had resumed their discussion on the intricacies of inner-guild politics.

"Ogre!" shouted the dwarf.

"Toad!" bellowed the giant.

"I hate to interrupt," said D.S. Greenley, "but if you'll just answer one more question for us, we'll be able to release you, so you can get back to your meeting."

"What is it?" the giant barked.

"Do any of your members happen to be employed as clowns?"

"Oh, only about half of them," snapped the dwarf. "How else do you expect us to find work in such a discriminatory world?!"

"I see," Greenley sighed, retrieving a set of keys from his pocket.

As the detective proceeded to free the men from their shackles, Arthur felt the full weight of his failed stakeout. He was as far away now from freeing Sammy as he ever had been.

"My apologies for the misunderstanding," Greenley said earnestly, while the two men grumbled and rubbed their wrists.

Clearly unsatisfied with the sergeant's apology, the dwarf offered one final diatribe. "You know, when we moved our headquarters to the city, we thought we would finally be able to break free from the blatant sizeism of our previous small-town police force, but it seems we were mistaken. Rest assured, Detective. The union will be conducting a full inquiry into this miscarriage of justice!"

And with that, the co-presidents of the Global Guild of Dwarves & Giants sharply turned their backs and strode into the bizarre boardroom, claiming their positions at the head of the table. As the loading bay door began to close in front of them, Stuart and Brian turned again to face the four policemen and two children, joining their fellow committee members in what may have been the Largest Synchronized Evil-Eyed Stare Ever Executed.

Amidst the whine of the motorized door, Arthur and Ruby heard the squealing of tires behind them and turned to catch a glimpse of Inspector Smudge's car as it sped off indignantly down the street, disappearing into the gray light of the city.

When the metal door had finally sealed in its oddly sized occupants, D.S. Greenley broke the clumsy silence. "Well," he said, struggling to conceal traces of disappointment and disgrace from his otherwise cheerful expression, "looks like this wasn't our day—eh, Arthur?" Turning to Ruby, he extended his hand and added, "Don't believe I've had the pleasure, miss. Detective Sergeant Greenley."

"Ruby," said the girl through chattering teeth, holding up a trembling arm to take the sergeant's hand.

"Ah, look at you, poor girl!" Greenley declared, his face filling with compassion. "Out in the rain with no coat—you must be freezing." Removing his trench coat, he promptly draped it around the shivering girl. "Hope this helps, miss. There are blankets in the car as well if you need them. Arthur?"

"Thank you, sir," replied the boy, only briefly glancing up, "but I'm sure I'll be fine."

"All right then," Greenley concluded, opening the rear door of the car. "I'll take the pair of you back to the Unsafe Sports Complex. Your parents have no doubt begun to worry."

•••

As the car wound its way through the dingy streets of the city, Arthur sat silently in the back seat, staring out the window at passing gray buildings. Meanwhile, D.S. Greenley and the officer behind the wheel immersed themselves in a comprehensive discussion of some new model of police truncheon: the JusticeStick 2K-O.

Though Ruby sat a mere two feet away on the other end of the back seat, Arthur couldn't bear to even look in her direction. After all his talk about gathering clues and doing the "proper detective thing," his so-called detective work had only managed to harass two innocent men, enrage the World's Greatest Sleuth, and shame the amiable policeman who had believed in him. What a fool he must have seemed.

Just then, he felt a tug on his shirt. He tried to ignore it, but the first was soon followed by another. Risking a timid glance to his right, Arthur found Ruby looking at him with a strange smirk.

The girl promptly pulled back the right side of her borrowed coat. There, under Ruby's arm, resting on her soggy pullover, was a golden magnifying-glass-shaped trophy.

"Where—How did you get that?!" the boy whispered in shock.

Ruby leaned in toward him. "Smudge set it down on Greenley's car while he was lecturing you. Must have been too busy ordering his driver to peel out at us to realize he'd left it behind."

"You know that's stealing, don't you? And from Inspector Hadrian Smudge, no less—I mean, he's one of the world's most respected record holders!"

"I don't know if you've noticed, Arthur, but he's also sort of a swine. And besides, I have every intention of returning it. First thing tomorrow, I'll have it forwarded straight back to him . . . by way of Beirut."

"What?!"

"Serves him right for talking to you that way," Ruby said matter-of-factly.

Arthur opened his mouth to insist she return the trophy as quickly as possible—but merely sighed instead. As much as he disapproved of Ruby's revenge plot, he was strangely flattered by it. No one had ever shown so much interest in him that they were willing to break postal regulations just to avenge his honor.

"Look," he said, after a stretch of silence, "I'm sorry for wasting your time today—and for being such a lousy detective partner."

Ruby cocked her head in puzzlement. "Are you joking? This has been one of the best days of my life! I mean, today I found my first clue in a criminal investigation, I went on my first stakeout, I got to stay out in the rain without being forced indoors. . . . And you make a *great* partner. Look at me—I've tagged along with you less than a day and I'm already wearing an authentic police trench coat." At this, she flipped up the coat's collar, which was so large that it jutted up over the top of her head, causing her to look simultaneously like a hard-boiled detective and an alien overlord. "Not to mention the developments we've made in the case. In just a few hours of working together, we've already eliminated two suspects. We can now safely cross Stuart and Brian of the GGDG off our list. So that's two less people in the world we need to investigate, isn't it?"

The girl had a point, but Arthur still wasn't convinced the day had not been a complete waste. "But now that Smudge has taken us off the case, does that even matter anymore?"

"Have you never read a detective novel? This is the part where the renegade detective and his loyal partner are thrown off the case by their domineering superior officer and forced to work outside the system. This is usually when they do their best work, actually. Oh yes, Detective Whipple—our investigation has only just begun."

The boy was surprised to find a faint smile sneaking into the corners of his mouth. Though he had failed yet another record attempt and lost the mysterious clowns once again, Arthur couldn't help but feel he had gained something that day as well.

A MATTER OF GRAVE IMPORTANCE

When Mrs. Whipple called him to the study the morning after the most disappointing Unsafe Sports Showdown in his family's history, Arthur could have guessed neither the reason for his summons nor how profoundly it would prove to shape his future.

"Ah yes—there you are, dear," his mother said as he met her outside the study door. "It seems you have a telephone call."

"It does?" said Arthur. He could scarcely remember the last time anyone had telephoned specifically to speak to him.

He was then struck by a sudden thought. *Could it be Ruby?*

After returning from the GGDG to the Unsafe Sports

Complex, Arthur had not seen the girl again for the rest of the evening. It had barely been twelve hours since they had parted—but somehow it seemed to him quite a bit longer.

Mrs. Whipple shrugged. "Try not to be too long now," she said. "I'm expecting a call from the Culinary Genius Placement Agency. Of course they would choose today not to send the weekly candidate for Sammy's old position. Just the sort of thing I'd like to be worrying about after a day like yesterday. . . ."

Arthur nodded, smiling with equal parts sympathy and regret, then strode into the study.

Upon approaching the desk at the rear of the room, he picked up the receiver from its resting place and raised it to his ear. "Hello?" he said.

A hushed, distorted voice crackled over the line.

"Is this Arthur Whipple?"

Unless Ruby had contracted a truly horrific throat disease since their last meeting, this was not her.

"Yes," replied Arthur. "Er . . . who is this?"

After a short pause, the voice answered.

"Somebody who may have some useful information for you . . . regarding the Cake Catastrophe case . . ."

Arthur gasped. "What? But how—?"

"Meet me at midnight at the Undertakers' Graveyard. And come alone . . ."

"Hang on," spluttered Arthur. "How will I know—?"

But the line was already dead.

After replacing the receiver, Arthur stood and stared

at the telephone for several moments. What had just happened? To whom had he spoken? Was he really to meet this person in a graveyard at midnight? And honestly, what sort of person scheduled meetings in a graveyard at midnight anyway? Surely, there were much better meeting places. Lunch at a local café would have been nice. Or a picnic on a park bench—that would have been fine. But no. He had to get an informant who preferred to do business amongst crypts and corpses.

And yet, the more Arthur thought about it, the more he knew he had to go.

For a moment, he wondered if he ought to tell his parents or involve the police, but when he recalled the debacle he'd created at the GGDG with D.S. Greenley and Inspector Smudge, he immediately decided against it.

He then began contemplating the best way to contact Ruby, only to be sidetracked a moment later by the memory of Smudge's warning—and the threat of what would happen to them if they were ever caught working on the case together. As fine a team as Arthur felt he and Ruby had wound up making, the thought of disobeying such a revered world-record holder suddenly gave him pause.

As for his *own* involvement, he could hardly cancel the graveyard appointment *now*; he had no idea how to contact the man—and failing to turn up to a scheduled meeting without first notifying the other party was surely a breach of informer etiquette. Bringing Ruby along, however—after Smudge had expressly prohibited it—was another matter entirely. The boy had no desire to pick up a conviction for obstruction of justice; he could not imagine Ruby had any either. And of course, the voice on the telephone *had* told him to come alone; the last thing he wanted to do was lose his informant's trust before the man had even told him anything.

And besides, he thought, Ruby probably wouldn't have wanted to come with him anyway. It had all sounded nice at the time, what she'd said to him in Greenley's squad car—but looking back now, he couldn't help but wonder if she hadn't merely said those things out of pity. Surely, she hadn't *really* cared about the investigation, had she?

No, he concluded. This time, he was on his own. If somehow Ruby was still interested, he could fill her in on the details the next time he saw her, without needlessly bothering her or endangering her life or reputation.

His mind made up, Arthur drew a deep breath and proceeded to the study door.

"What was that all about, dear?" his mother asked as he emerged from the room.

"Oh . . . nothing," he replied, hurrying past her as nonchalantly as possible. "Just, um, an encyclopedia salesman—after the record for Most Volumes Sold. You know how pushy those guys can be. Well—all right then. See you at lunch. . . ."

He had just reached the stairs when his mother's voice stopped him in his tracks.

"Arthur?" she called in an unmistakably suspicious tone.

The boy turned his head, his heart beating suddenly faster. "Yes?"

His mother glared at him through arching eyebrows. "You haven't bought anything, have you?"

Arthur let out a pent-up breath. "Oh, no," he said. "I, uh, told him our encyclopedia needs are all well taken care of."

"Good," his mother nodded. "We're still receiving volumes from that *101 Steps to Record Breaking Success* series you signed up for last year."

"Oh yeah," said Arthur with further relief. "Sorry about that. I should've realized it wasn't for me at Step 2: 'Become a *101 Steps* Salesman and Convince Your Friends and Family to Buy This Life-Changing Book Series.' Somehow, my sales pitch was never even close to as good as the guy who sold it to *me*. Probably would have helped if I'd bought the companion series, *101 Steps to the Perfect Sales Pitch*, like Step 3 recommended."

"Well," said his mother, "At least you're learning from your mistakes."

"Yep," Arthur smiled as he started up the stairs. "Oh, by the way," he added, "on a completely unrelated topic— apparently, there have been some . . . sightings . . . of an exceedingly rare bird in the area. The, um, Great Stripy-Eared Musk Owl, I believe. I thought I might have a go at the First Successful Live Capture—you know, before somebody else nabs one. Now, of course, they only come out after dark, so, you know—if it's all right with you—I'd like to leave the house for a few hours this evening . . . at around, say, midnight?"

• • •

Gripping a lantern in one hand and a flimsy butterfly net in the other, Arthur approached the towering pair of wrought iron gates and peered up at the sign overhead. In the lantern's soft glow, he could just make out the words **UNDERTAKERS GRAVEYARD** sculpted in the metal. This was the place.

From Neverfall Hall to the graveyard gates, it had been half an hour's walk, the first ten minutes of which, Arthur had felt compelled to make stripy-eared-owl calls and actively search the foliage for fluttering feathers, just in case anyone was watching. Once or twice, he'd sworn he'd glimpsed the bird's characteristic brown-and-white-striped ears and polka-dotted plumage—until, of course, he'd remembered the bird was merely an invention of his own imagination and did not in fact exist.

As awful as Arthur felt lying to his mother, he figured it would all be worth it if that night's meeting contributed in any way to solving the mystery of the Cake Catastrophe and clearing Sammy's name. Indeed, had another approach occurred to him, he would have gladly taken it, but it seemed the only way to get to the truth in this case was to tell a lie. He was pretty sure this was that "moral gray area" crime-fighters were always referring to. Still, he knew it wasn't something to be taken lightly. This time, it was fibbing to his mother about bird catching; next, he'd be planting evidence and forcing false confessions. Clearly, it was a slippery slope. If he wanted to keep that moral gray area from turning charcoal, he would have to be careful.

Arthur checked his watch. Two minutes past midnight. He looked about him, but saw no sign of anyone. Surely, he wasn't meant to actually *enter* the graveyard? That did not seem practical at all. Clearly, the best course of action was to station himself outside the gates and wait for his contact to arrive.

After five minutes of this, however, with no such encounter, Arthur decided he would at least have to give the inside a look.

It would be the first time he had ever done so—despite living within walking distance of the graveyard—due largely to his father's rather strong feelings on the matter. "Intolerable places, graveyards," Mr. Whipple had told his children. "They're full of *graves*. We've had more than enough burials in our family; we don't need to be reminded of any others." Arthur had thought this sounded reasonable at the time, whatever it meant, and had always kept away from the place—but then, he'd never had a reason to do otherwise.

As he pushed on the iron bars, the gate opened with a long, slow *creak* that pierced the silence and made him wonder if creaky hinges were simply a standard option at the cemetery gate factory. Unfortunately, the thought made the sound no less unnerving.

Swallowing hard, Arthur crept underneath the graveyard sign and into the graveyard itself.

Once inside the gates, he found himself at the edge of a weathered cobblestone square. It contained no visible signs of life, but at its center, he could just make out an imposing statue with outstretched angel's wings. Somehow, it made him feel just a bit better about his murky situation to see an angel was watching over him. As he raised his lantern and approached the statue, however, it soon became clear this was no angel—or at least not the sort of angel he would ever want to have as a guardian.

The figure carved into the stone was in fact a sunken-cheeked, sullen-faced man, wearing an old-fashioned suit and ascot tie. His straight, shoulder-length hair was capped with a towering top hat, and in his outstretched palms, he cradled a single human skull.

With the discovery of this final detail, the broad, feathery wings that extended from the figure's back no longer gave the least bit of comfort to Arthur. While it was always nice to think that angels were able to get to him anywhere their wings could carry them, it was not half so pleasant thinking the same of this fellow.

Arthur gulped and shifted his attention to the large monument that served as the statue's base, where he proceeded to read the following inscription:

HERE LIES
OBEDIAH DIGBY LOWE
"DR. DOORNAIL"

FATHER OF MODERN UNDERTAKING
&
BREAKER OF NUMEROUS
UNDERTAKING WORLD RECORDS

PREPARED AND BURIED TWENTY-SIX CORPSES
IN A SINGLE DAY—YET IN THE END,
COULD NOT PREPARE HIMSELF

"QUI SEPULTUS MORTUI NUNC SEPULTUS"

Arthur had just read the last word of the closing epigram (which he might have understood to mean, literally: "Who Buried the Dead, Now Buried," had he spent less time doing things like loitering in graveyards and more time studying his Latin, as his Dead Languages tutor, Dr. Verbabel, had instructed), when the cemetery gate screeched shut behind him. He whirled about—but saw no one.

"Hello?" he called out to the darkness.

There was no reply.

Another standard option at the cemetery gate factory, he thought to himself. *Always slam shut when you least expect it.*

His heart beating faster now, he slowly turned back to the monument, and—in the hopes of occupying his restless mind—began browsing the nearby headstones.

This would prove to be a rather bad idea.

Each tomb, he discovered, belonged to another notable

or record-breaking undertaker. According to one monument, here lay Richard Bawkes, designer of the World's Most Expensive Coffin; according to another, this was the eternal resting place of Mortimer Curtens, director of the World's Largest Private Non-Mafia Family Funeral. As Arthur went from one grim record holder to the next, his morbid curiosity quickly got the better of him—and before he knew it, he had wandered deep into the graveyard.

At the tomb of Gideon Balmer, who had achieved the Shortest Time after Death to Prepare and Bury a Single Corpse, Arthur began to wonder again at the sort of person who would choose this for a meeting place. Not only was it a graveyard—it had to be the *Creepiest* Graveyard on the Planet. Top ten, at the very least.

By the time he'd arrived at the gravestone for Jules Drayner, holder of the record for Most Blood Collected from Exsanguinated Corpses in One Year, Arthur's morbid curiosity had turned to genuine disgust.

Just then, a nearby rustling noise whirled him around a second time.

"Hello?" he called.

Again, there came no answer. Holding his breath, he crept toward the noise.

As he slowly peered around a shovel-shaped grave marker, the source of the noise was revealed, though it took Arthur a moment to discern precisely what it was he was looking at. Two dark shapes shuffled atop the lichen-covered tombstone before him. One of them proved to be a malformed, greasy-feathered raven, the other, a large black rat—and they appeared to be fighting over something. But what exactly was it? Chalky and slender and—Ah yes, of course: a human finger bone.

Suddenly queasy, Arthur was struck by an overwhelming urge to leave the Undertakers' Graveyard as soon as possible—at any cost.

Turning away from the battling vermin, he dashed off in what he believed to be the direction of the entrance, scrambling past crooked headstones and crumbling tombs.

He had not traveled ten yards when a low voice stopped him dead in his tracks.

"Thou canst not escape death," it bellowed. *"Why dost thou flee?"*

Arthur's blood turned to ice. His eyes darted to and fro. It seemed the voice was in fact emanating from the decrepit headstone in front of him.

The boy closed his eyes in terror. "I—I would like to leave now," he stammered.

"But thou hast not completed thy task."

"I—I'm sorry," Arthur pleaded, "but what task do you mean exactly—um, sir?"

"That thou shouldst pass not twixt yon gates, ere thou speak'st with that selfsame soul who bade thee journey hither. . . ."

Arthur opened his mouth to reply, then stopped short.

"Wait. What was that now?"

"Blast," cursed the voice. *"What I mean to say is—you*

really can't leave before you talk to the person you came here to meet. Sorry about that. Graveyard voice. Force of habit."

"What?" cried Arthur.

At that moment, a tiny figure stepped out from behind the gravestone.

A rush of horror gripped Arthur as he realized: it was a dwarf.

"Ahh!" the boy shrieked—then swung his butterfly net at the dwarf's head and bolted in the opposite direction.

Before he could make his escape, however, Arthur's toe caught on the corner of an unearthed coffin lid—and he was sent crashing to the ground, barely six feet away.

Fumbling for his lantern, Arthur rolled onto his back and began scouring the shadows for the dwarf's giant companion. He knew he had but a moment before the towering brute emerged and came forth to destroy him.

And yet, as the boy lay clutching his lantern, paralyzed with fright, no such person appeared.

"Ow!" cried the dwarf, stumbling forward as he rubbed the side of his head.

"D-don't come any closer!" Arthur warned, brandishing his butterfly net. "I haven't forgotten how to use this!"

"Argh," the little man groaned, feeling his scalp for a lump. "Why'd you do that?"

In the lantern's light, Arthur examined his tiny adversary. Dressed in a dark suit with an ascot tie, he had tan skin and thick, silvery hair. The boy couldn't quite place it, but he felt as though he had seen the man's face before.

"I'm—I'm sorry if I hurt you, sir," Arthur said cautiously. "I—I thought you were the dwarf who's been terrorizing my family. Well, I mean—*are* you the dwarf who's been terrorizing my family?"

"I should've known," sighed the dwarf, shaking his head. "Seems our dear co-presidents were right about something for once in their lives: you really could use some exceptional-size sensitivity training."

"Wait," said Arthur. "Co-presidents? As in Stuart and Brian? Of the GGDG?" It was then Arthur remembered the tan-faced, silver-haired, deep-voiced dwarf standing on his chair in the GGDG boardroom, being rebuked by the tiny co-president. "Hang on," he blurted, "you're—"

"Thornton Lowe—at your service," said the dwarf, and, stepping forward, offered the boy his hand.

Arthur promptly accepted it and, with a bit of huffing and puffing on both their parts, staggered to his feet. "Thank you, Mr. Lowe," said the boy. "Now, um, just to be clear—and I'm sorry if I'm showing poor exceptional-size sensitivity here, but I can't help but feel I've had run-ins with an extraordinary number of dwarves lately, and I'm just a bit confused. So, anyhow—you're sure you're not trying to harm my family in any way?"

"Quite the contrary," replied the dwarf, rubbing his head again. "I thought I was clear about that on the telephone."

"Yes, I guess you were," Arthur nodded. "Pleased to meet you, Mr. Lowe. I really am sorry about the head. Afraid it's got me a little on edge, this place. I mean, honestly—what ever made you want to meet *here*?"

Mr. Lowe's brow wrinkled. "What exactly are you trying to say? That you don't like the Undertakers' Graveyard? Now, I might be able to forgive the unprovoked brutality, but if you think I'll let you insult this sacred ground, well, then you are sorely—"

"Oh no, no—it's not that," Arthur lied. "It's lovely, really, the graveyard. I just, um, wondered if you might have a particular connection to it or something—that's all."

"Oh. Hmm," said the dwarf, his expression softening. "Well, yes—as a matter of fact I do. You see, apart from serving on the board of the GGDG, I happen to be director of Lowe and Sons Funeral Company. Started by my great-great-great grandfather, Obediah Digby Lowe—Dr. Doornail himself. Perhaps you saw his statue?"

"Oh, yeah," Arthur nodded. "I knew that name sounded familiar."

"Yep," Mr. Lowe continued. "Always been one of my favorite places, this. All the greats are laid here. Philip Valtz. Justin Hume. Solomon Kroker. They just don't bury 'em like they used to, do they?"

"I guess not," shrugged the boy.

"Nope. Come here whenever I get the chance, just to clear my head—and commune with the icons of undertaking's past. You're lucky you live so close; *you* can visit anytime you like! I'd move out here in a heartbeat, myself—but there just aren't enough people dying in the countryside,

I'm afraid. Nope—apart from a lucky outbreak of swine flu here and there—it's much better for business in the city."

"Hmm," said Arthur, his queasiness returning slightly. "Makes sense, I guess. . . . But, um, well—what was it you called me here to tell me? Something about the Cake Catastrophe case, was it?"

"Oh, right—of course," Mr. Lowe chuckled. "Get me talking about undertaking, and I'll rattle on for days. But we've got graver matters to discuss, haven't we?"

A devilish grin formed across the dwarf's lips.

"We have?" Arthur gulped.

Mr. Lowe nodded. "So, let's see here. Where to begin? Ah yes. The election. As you may have deduced from your little visit to the GGDG, I recently ran for the office of co-president, against Brian Carmine, the dwarf you had the pleasure of meeting yesterday, along with his giant crony, Stuart Fisch. Pleasant chap, that Carmine—wouldn't you say?"

"No," said Arthur. "I don't think I would."

"Well, that's only because he's a snidey, self-important little tapeworm. But we shouldn't hold that against him, should we?"

"Hmm," said Arthur. "I take it you don't like him very much."

"Like him? Oh, I *like* him all right—as a potential customer for Lowe and Sons. Why, there's nobody I'd like to work with more. Indeed, I would consider it my honor, and a boon to the whole exceptional-size community—as well

306

as every other community—to get him behind my doors. A couple of tyrants, Carmine and Fisch. Silence anybody who speaks out against them or tries to paint any of our members in a less than favorable light. Why, with his ties to the Dwarven Brotherhood, Carmine's really nothing more than a gangster with a gavel. Constantly having me followed by his criminal cronies to make sure I don't speak out of turn. Good thing I managed to give them the slip tonight. They'd no doubt beat us both to a bloody pulp for what I'm about to tell you. . . ."

Up until that moment, Arthur had been feeling fairly comfortable with his present situation, despite the grim surroundings—but now all of his prior uneasiness came rushing back. "They would?" he said, his eyes unconsciously searching the shadows again.

"Oh, most definitely," Mr. Lowe nodded casually. "Now where was I? Ah yes. The election. Right. So, anyway—on the night I was outvoted by that no-good cockroach, I took myself off to the Mountain and Molehill, the local dwarf/giant tavern, to drown my sorrows. Must have been the day after your family's Cake Catastrophe, because it was all over the news that night. *Whipple Chef Bakes Birthday Bomb*, they were all saying. So, there I am, minding my own business, trying to forget I'd just lost the vote to a talking termite, and the dwarf at the table next to me tries to strike up a conversation. Clearly had one too many, this fellow—and by one too many, I mean: one drink total. Doesn't take much for us little folk, you understand. Honestly, if it weren't for the giants, the Mountain and

Molehill would barely break even. But anyhow, he leans over to me and says, 'Funny about that exploding birthday cake, isn't it, friend?' Now, as I've mentioned, I was in a bit of a bad temper, so I reply, 'How should I know? I wasn't there.' 'Ah,' he says, 'but *I* was.' 'Were you?' I say. 'Are you a friend of the Whipples, then?' '*Friend?*' he scoffs. 'To those simpletons? Hardly. No, no—my associate and I attended as part of the, um, *entertainment*.' At this, he gestures to the corner behind him and the huge giant seated there in the shadows, who I had previously failed to notice. 'Say no more,' I reply. 'It's our lot in life, us exceptional sizes. Never invited anywhere unless it's to be put onstage and gawked at, are we?' 'Oh no,' he says. 'I assure you, friend—it was *us* running the show this time. Why, with only a few simple improvements to that silly family's birthday cake, we orchestrated the main attraction itself. And though we may have been dressed as clowns, it was *us* doing the gawking—at all those screaming fools running for their lives.' Now at this point, the drink is really doing its work on me, and I can hardly follow him. 'What was that now?' I say. 'I don't quite understand. Do you mean you were on the Whipple party-planning committee or something?' At this, he gets rather snippy and says, 'What I mean is: *we* blew up the Whipple birthday cake. But don't think you'll ever read about us in the papers; we've already succeeded in stitching up the Whipples' poor half-witted chef—so we'll never be blamed for any of it.' By this time, I've had about enough. 'Goodness,' I say. 'And to think I've been seated next to a criminal mastermind all this time. Well, I'd best be off now. Good luck in all

your future sabotage plots. Sounds like you're off to a smash-
ing start.' And with that, I got up and left."

Arthur's mouth hung open. He could scarcely believe
all he had just heard. "And—and what happened next?" he
spluttered. "Did you see where they went?"

"No," said the dwarf, shaking his head. "That was it. I
went home, poured myself an ill-considered second drink
and promptly passed out. I've been back to the Mountain
and Molehill many times since, I'm sorry to say—but I've
never seen those two again."

"Well," said Arthur, "let's see here: a giant and a dwarf,
dressed as clowns, who claim to have blown up my family's
birthday cake, and pinned it on our chef. Yep. I'm pretty
sure these are our guys. So, what exactly did they look
like?"

"Didn't get much of a look, I'm afraid. Rather a min-
imalist lighting scheme they've got at the Mountain and
Molehill."

"Hmm," the boy sighed. "And you didn't happen to
catch either of their names?"

"Afraid not. Really didn't think much of it at the time—
there'd been no mention of a dwarf or a giant even being
suspected in the Whipple Cake Catastrophe. Seemed he was
just after a bit of attention, this fellow—and, well, the way
we dwarves get treated by you average sizes, I could hardly
blame him, could I? But when you and your friends came
sniffing about the GGDG office yesterday, looking for a
dwarf and a giant in connection with your family's recent

mishaps, it struck me this fellow might have been telling the truth—and my conscience would no longer allow me to remain silent. . . . Not to mention I'd give anything just to see that worm, Carmine, squirm a bit. If he wants to be co-president, let *him* deal with the public outrage when two of our members are charged with sabotage and attempted murder!"

"Ah," said Arthur with a nod. "Well, you know, whatever the reason, I'm really glad you came forward with this. Although, if what you say is true about Mr. Carmine, aren't you worried he might have you—well, you know—*silenced*?"

"Ha!" snapped Mr. Lowe. "Let him try it! We undertakers don't scare so easily. What's the worst he can do—kill me? Death is how I make my living; I don't fear death—I welcome it. . . ."

There was a sudden howl of wind, followed by what sounded like the eerie cry of some nearby nocturnal creature, and Arthur couldn't stop his spine from tingling.

He was just about to chalk it up to some deluxe add-on feature from the cemetery gate factory, when he looked up at the towering stone monument to his right—and saw the call's actual source.

There, leaning over the column's top edge, two tiny human faces looked down at him, while a pair of hefty wooden mallets glinted beside them in the moonlight.

Arthur hardly had time to yell "Look out!" before the two dwarves had leapt from their perch and were flying at the boy and the undertaker with weapons raised.

In a fit of terror, Arthur dropped his lantern and gripped his butterfly net at both ends, just in time to block the first dwarf's hammer—which was nearly as long as its wielder was tall. Funny as the pairing appeared, however, the crushing force of the dwarf's blow was no laughing matter.

"Mr. Carmine says hello!" the second dwarf cried as he swung his mallet at Mr. Lowe.

The little undertaker dodged to one side, causing his attacker to overextend himself.

"Send him my regards!" Mr. Lowe cried back, and on the last syllable, punched the man in the mouth before he could raise his mallet again.

Seeing his partner hurt, the first dwarf turned back to Arthur with a menacing snarl.

Similar to his partner's, the dwarf's thick, tattooed arms, rolled-sleeved shirt, and greasy dungarees suggested a rough career in either the circus or rail industries, or possibly in the circus rail industry. Incidentally, it was the workers from precisely these three industries whom Arthur would have last chosen to face in hand-to-hand combat.

His first block had been lucky—but the boy was no match for such a hard-bitten opponent.

"This ain't your fight, boy," growled the dwarf. "No need for you to get hurt too bad—if you just stay down. . . ." With that, he pressed the top of his mallet into Arthur's chest and shoved the boy backward.

Before Arthur could catch himself, he tripped over a gravestone and tumbled to the ground.

The man gave a crooked smile, then turned and walked toward the other two dwarves, who were now grappling at close quarters.

"How did Carmine end up with you two anyway?" the undertaker barked. "Were all the other sewer rats already booked for the night?"

While Mr. Lowe's arms were tied up in his struggle with the second dwarf, the first dwarf casually approached and smashed him in the nose with his mallet.

As the stunned little undertaker stumbled backward, the second dwarf extended a toe to trip him—and Mr. Lowe crashed to the ground on his back.

Arthur pulled himself to his feet and watched helplessly as the two thugs closed in on their prey.

"Always got something to say, haven't you, Mr. Lowe?" the first dwarf smirked as he thumped his hammerhead against his palm.

The winded undertaker struggled to sit up, but the second dwarf pressed him down with his mallet and boot.

"No need to get up, Mr. Lowe," the first dwarf sneered. "You're just where we want you. We're about to do a little experiment, see—to find out if you still talk so much after you've had your jaw broke."

"Just you try it!" wheezed Mr. Lowe. "No broken jaw's going to shut me up!"

"Oh, I see," said the dwarf. "I was sort of hoping you'd say that. I guess we'll just have to break *more* of you then, won't we?"

He took a step forward and raised his mallet into the air.

From several paces away, Arthur saw a flash of fear in Mr. Lowe's face—before the undertaker banished it again behind a glare of defiance.

The boy could stand back no longer. Without thinking, he strode straight for the dwarves, picking up his fallen lantern on the way.

As the dwarf lunged at his defenseless victim, Arthur brought his butterfly net down around the man's head, the metal ring catching him at the throat and stopping him mid-lunge. His hammer fell harmlessly to the earth.

Before the dwarf could free himself from the net's grasp, the boy bashed him about the skull with the lantern.

As shattered glass rained down upon his shoulders, the dwarf went limp and crumpled to the ground, motionless beside the astonished undertaker.

For a moment, Arthur felt a great surge of satisfaction course through his veins—but it was promptly replaced by the far more typical surge of terror.

"You little scab," hissed the second dwarf in disbelief.

He lifted his hammer from Mr. Lowe's chest and turned it toward Arthur.

Before the boy could backtrack two strides, the dwarf was upon him.

With one powerful swipe of his mallet, he knocked the butterfly net from Arthur's grasp—and with a second, knocked the boy's feet out from under him.

Arthur struck the earth with his shoulder. As the pain

shot through his arm, he looked up to see the dwarf towering over him.

"Ain't nobody never told you to pick on somebody your own size?" said the dwarf. "This oughtta teach you . . ."

With a cruel grin, the dwarf hoisted his hammer over his head.

Arthur held up his trembling hand in feeble defense. He wondered what his mother would think when she learned he had lied about hunting stripy-eared owls after she found his battered body in the middle of the graveyard.

The dwarf swung the hammer down.

As Arthur winced in horror, there came a heavy *thump*. But the hammer's blow never reached him. His attacker went blank in the face and inexplicably toppled forward. The hammer struck the ground a foot to Arthur's right, just before the dwarf fell face-first on top of it.

Breathless, Arthur looked up. Where his attacker had once been, Mr. Lowe now stood, clutching a giant mallet in his hands.

"Nasty little vermin," the undertaker grumbled, "degrading a sacred, soothing place like this. . . . So, I guess I hadn't quite given them the slip after all, had I? My mistake."

Arthur struggled to catch his breath. "That's quite all right," he panted. "I'm just happy I'm still in one piece. Thanks for—you know—helping me keep it that way."

"My pleasure," said Mr. Lowe, wiping a trickling of blood from his nostrils.

"How's your nose?" asked Arthur.

"Still attached, thanks to you—and that's good enough for me. Not always the case in my business."

When he had helped Arthur up, Mr. Lowe knelt down and held two fingers to the lifeless dwarf's throat—then strode over to the other and did the same.

"Are they . . . ?" the boy asked somberly.

"Not yet, I'm afraid," Mr. Lowe replied. "Though I certainly don't envy them their position. Of course, it would have been us face-down in the dirt had you not possessed such singular butterfly-netting skills. Right then. If you'll just help me drag these two out to the old hearse, we can be on our way before they wake up. We're parked in the coffin-unloading zone, just around back."

"You're not going to . . . *undertake* them, are you?"

"What, before they're dead? What a morbid lad you are. Don't you know the Undertaker's Oath? '*No embalming shall be started, till the client's soul has parted. . . .*' Not that I wouldn't love to help their souls along, of course—it's certainly no less than they deserve. But no—I thought I'd just put them in a couple of body bags and drop them in a field somewhere for the evening. Always unsettling to wake up in one of those. Take it from me, the minute or so before they manage to find the zipper is absolutely priceless!"

Arthur gave an uneasy chuckle, then cleared his throat and said, "I can only imagine. But—are you sure we shouldn't just call the police?"

Mr. Lowe scrunched up his face. "Please, Arthur. Why do you think I came to you instead of the police in the first place? Because as much as I detest Carmine for his views on just about everything else, I do share his opinion of law enforcement. There's no more sizeist an institution than the police. The last thing I want is to have to deal with those vultures."

"But you *are* willing to testify, aren't you?" pleaded Arthur. "About the dwarf and the giant at the Mountain and Molehill? I mean, it may be our only shot at getting Sammy out of jail."

"Well, how else am I going to make Carmine pay for this? Just put me in touch with Sammy's lawyers, and we'll see if we can't get the judge to grant us a special preliminary hearing."

"Really?" gasped Arthur. "Oh, wow—thank you, Mr. Lowe. I'll ring them first thing in the morning."

"See, Arthur?" the dwarf smiled. "How's *that* for win-win? *You* get to help your chef—and *I* get some well-deserved revenge on my arch enemy. Not as good as having his body on a slab, of course—but I'm a patient man. Two people nobody can escape in this life: the lawyer and the undertaker. And if the first one doesn't get you, the second one certainly will."

• • •

Arthur looked across the courtroom to the place where Sammy the Spatula Smith was seated, his wrists bound in shackles and his large frame shrouded in loose-fitting prison clothes. At the start of the hearing, the man seated there had borne little resemblance to the jovial chef Arthur had once known—but over the course of Mr. Lowe's testimony, the boy had watched a hopeful glow emerge on Sammy's face.

"And what, Mr. Lowe," said the judge at the center of the room, "did you do after the dwarf in question professed that he and his giant associate had sabotaged the Whipples' cake and then framed the accused for the crime?"

"It was then, Your Honor," replied Mr. Lowe, dressed in his finest undertaker's suit, "that I got up and left the establishment. After paying my bill, of course. Always settle our accounts, we undertakers."

"And have you seen either of these men since?"

"No, Your Honor, I have not."

"And why, may I ask," the judge added, furrowing his brow, "have you waited until now to come forward with this evidence?"

"The truth, Your Honor, is that I didn't even know it *was* evidence until four days ago. And then, it was only due to the efforts of one remarkably determined boy."

The courtroom rustled with curiosity.

Arthur's heart stalled in his chest.

"And which boy would this be, Mr. Lowe?" said the judge.

"Why, that's him right there, Your Honor," the dwarf replied, pointing to the twelve-year-old boy seated amongst the Whipple family in the front row of the audience. "Arthur Whipple."

317

The crowd gasped.

Arthur's family turned to him in astonishment.

Across the courtroom, Inspector Smudge glared at him with a scowl so deep his face looked in serious danger of imploding.

When the stirring had subsided slightly, Mr. Lowe continued. "Just the other day," he explained, "Arthur followed two of my, er, *colleagues*—a dwarf and a giant—to the GGDG offices, suspecting they were responsible for the attacks on his family. It was the first I'd heard of any exceptionally sized persons being suspected in that case. It was then I realized the fellow from the Mountain and Molehill wasn't just talking nonsense. Indeed, if it weren't for Arthur, I'd never have come forward at all. Just wish I'd have known about his deftness with a butterfly net before I asked to meet with him." Mr. Lowe rubbed the fading bruise on the side of his forehead. "Vicious forearm he's got, that lad. Can't complain too much, though. He did use it to rescue me from a band of bloodthirsty ruffians in the end. I must say, without that boy and his butterfly net, I should not be in this courtroom now—nor likely anywhere else, for that matter. . . ."

The crowd whispered in wonderment.

Unable to contain his outrage any longer, Inspector Smudge leapt from his seat. "Forgive me, Your Honor," he blurted, "but you can't be taking this man seriously! Clearly, this so-called *evidence* is nothing but unsubstantiated hearsay—and ought to be thrown out at once!"

"Inspector Smudge," the judge barked, "it is only because of your impeccable commitment to justice that I do not have *you* thrown out! In this courtroom, I'll have you leave the judgment to *me*!"

"Yes—of course, Your Honor," Smudge nodded, returning to his seat in frustration. "My sincerest apologies."

"Thank you, Inspector," said the judge. "But, of course— you are correct. Compelling as Mr. Lowe's testimony may be, it is strictly hearsay, and as such, is inadmissible as evidence at Mr. Smith's trial."

Inspector Smudge grinned with the self-satisfaction of a full-bellied crocodile.

The hopeful glow escaped from Sammy's face. The Whipples sighed in despair.

"It's just not right," whispered Simon.

"It's a miscarriage of justice, is what it is," grumbled George.

Arthur felt his heart begin to wilt. All he had worked for, it seemed, had come to nothing. Sammy would not be returning home as the boy had dreamed.

But the judge hadn't finished.

"However," he added, "given the thorough nature of Mr. Lowe's allegedly witnessed confession, this court is compelled to believe there may be some truth in it. Inasmuch as this lessens the probability of Mr. Smith's guilt, as well as the likelihood he will flee, this court sees fit to overturn its denial of bail to the defendant. Bail shall be set at fifty thousand. Mr. Smith, you are not to leave the country and must check in with Inspector Smudge once a week—but upon payment of bail, you shall be released from custody, and need not appear at court until start of trial in two months' time. Do you understand the terms of your bail, Mr. Smith?"

Sammy could hardly contain his excitement. "Indeed, I most certainly do, Your Honor," he nodded.

"Very well then. This court is adjourned."

Arthur closed his eyes and exhaled.

The Whipples jumped to their feet and cheered.

"Justice lives!" cried George.

Across the room, Inspector Smudge stamped his boot to the floor as another scowl threatened to cause a cave-in of his features. Just beside him, however, Detective Sergeant Greenley sprang from his seat and clapped his hands together.

"Sit down, Greenley!" the inspector snarled.

"Of course, sir," said the sergeant as he promptly returned to his seat. "Terribly sorry, sir." But try as he might, he could not entirely expunge the smile from his face.

As soon as Arthur had risen to his feet, he was rushed by his siblings.

"Why didn't you tell us, Arthur?" Simon laughed, clapping his brother on the back.

"Really, brother!" agreed Henry, gripping the boy's shoulder. "Here you've been gathering evidence of Sammy's innocence and meticulously planning his release for weeks now, and we've never known a thing about it!"

"Well," Arthur smiled bashfully, "I don't know if *meticulous* is quite the right—"

Just then, Cordelia clapped him on the back so hard, it made him gasp. "Hoping to keep all the fun to yourself, were you?" she said with a sly, yet unmistakably warm smirk. "Save some ruffians for the rest of us next time."

The octuplets swarmed about him and wrapped their arms around his waist.

"You did it, Arthur!" cried Beatrice, beaming proudly up at him. She had uttered that phrase more than once since he'd saved her from a certain treacherous breakfast, but Arthur never tired of hearing it from her.

It was then his parents stepped forward.

"Indeed you did, my dear," his mother beamed as she embraced him. "Well done!"

"Yes—well done indeed," smiled his father, grasping the boy's hand. "My my—what a fine detective you've ended up making! Why, I'd not be surprised if you've finally found your true calling in life. Rest assured, Arthur—you shall have our full support in this endeavor. Now that we know Sammy's innocent, I'll be hiring the offices of Bleader and Leach to clear him of these ridiculous charges. And with the work you've already done on the case, I've no doubt I can convince them to hire you on as a private detective. How would you like that, Arthur—working cases for the Winningest Legal Team in the World?"

"That," Arthur gaped, "would be *amazing*."

"I figured as much," grinned his father. "Who knows what fantastic sleuthing records you'll break if you keep on like this, at a place like *that*? Goodness, Arthur. Your failure quotients are getting so near a perfect 1, I can scarcely see the use in charting them any further. Hmm. . . . What would you say to throwing your old charts on the fire just as soon as we get home?"

Arthur had never considered such a prospect, but it suddenly sounded to him like the Most Exhilarating Thing in the World. He nodded excitedly.

"Very good," his father smiled. "I'll let you light the match. . . . Now—I'd best go congratulate Sammy before they escort him off again. Hope he'll let me make up for not believing in him by paying his bail. Wish me luck. Oh, and Arthur—"

"Yes?"

"Excellent work, Son."

"Thanks, Father," the boy replied, then watched as the man turned and strode off toward the family chef.

When Arthur thought back to the terror he had felt at the Undertakers' Graveyard just a few days earlier, or his embarrassment at the GGDG, or his guilt at Sammy's arrest, it was hard to believe those events had ever managed to lead him *here*. Yes, there was more work to be done— but he had set out to have an innocent man released from jail, and he had succeeded.

Arthur stood about telling stories to his eager siblings of his encounters with Stuart and Brian, co-presidents of the

GGDG, and his clash with the dwarven thugs they had sent to silence Mr. Lowe in the Undertakers' Graveyard.

He looked up to see his father shaking hands with an undeniably grateful-looking Sammy the Spatula, then watched as a pair of court officials came to escort the chef out.

Just before Sammy left the courtroom, however, the chef turned and looked straight at Arthur. He opened his mouth as if to speak, but tears promptly filled his eyes. Wiping them away with his shoulder, Sammy smiled and gave an amiable wink, then turned away again and exited the room.

And suddenly, all of Arthur's recent troubles no longer seemed to him like troubles at all.

THE TROUBLES ARE OVER

Through a porthole on the Whipple family frigate, Arthur watched the last sliver of sun disappear over the shimmering horizon—and breathed a sigh of content.

At the sound of a nearby door opening, he turned to see Sammy the Spatula emerge from the galley and into the large, dark-wooded cabin where the boy stood with his father, Mr. Mahankali, and seven-eighths of the octuplets. (Franklin, being the nautical expert of the family, was occupied above deck, manning the ship's helm. Having recently turned five, he was thrilled to be finally allowed to navigate all by himself.)

"Sammy!" cried Mr. Whipple from his position at the bar to Arthur's right. "You've been a free man all of eight hours and I believe you've spent seven of those in the kitchen! Come out here and enjoy yourself, man!" And with that, he popped the cork from a large bottle of champagne.

"Sorry 'bout that, guv," Sammy smiled. "The thought of cooking for you lot again were the only fing stopped me going barmy in that place. And, well—it's the only way I know how to say fank you for what you and Arfur done for me." He turned to face the boy. "That's right, lad. A decade's worth of cooking your favorites won't 'ardly begin to repay such kindness and courage—but it'll not stop me trying."

Arthur blushed. "Ah, come on, Sammy," he said. "It's just good to see you back in your chef's clothes and, you know, out of that *other* uniform."

"Quite right," agreed Mr. Whipple, holding up the champagne bottle. "Can I pour you a glass, old boy? World's Bubbliest, this."

"No fanks, guv," Sammy smiled. "After what happened the last time I had a drink, I fink I'll be sticking wiv milk for a while now."

"Glad to hear it," Arthur's father smiled back. "In that case, I believe we have a fine vintage for you. Mahankali?"

The Panther-Man—who had now shed all his bandages except the sling that held his right arm—promptly retrieved a bottle of milk from behind the bar and measured it into a martini glass. With a warm smile, he handed the glass to the chef.

"Here you are, Mr. Sammy. I have extracted it this very morning from the World's Creamiest Cow."

Upon receiving the glass, Sammy clutched Mr. Mahankali's good hand and looked him in the eye. "Cheers, mate," he said. "I can't tell you how glad I am to see you out of that 'ospital bed. Gave me quite a scare there, you did . . ."

"I am so very glad to see you as well, my friend," said the Panther-Man. "The animals have missed your exquisite cooking. I have not known what to tell them."

"Tell 'em I missed them too," said the chef. "They're a fousand times more pleasant to be 'round than the animals I 'ad to live wiv this past month."

Sammy smiled and took a long drink of milk, then gave a satisfied *ahhh* and turned to Mr. Whipple. "Good to be back, guv," he grinned.

The octuplets, who had just finished setting the thirty-foot dining table at the center of the cabin, scurried over to their newly freed chef and tugged playfully at his apron.

"So, tell us Sammy," said George with deep interest, "what was it like on *the inside*?"

"Did you have to shiv anybody?" asked Charlotte.

"No shivving, fank goodness," Sammy chuckled. "Though I did 'ave to hit a bloke wiv a soup ladle once."

"Oooh," the octuplets murmured in awe.

Just then, the ornately carved main doors opened, and in stepped Arthur's mother and older siblings—followed by the entire Goldwin family.

Arthur's father gave a heavy sigh—and promptly downed his drink.

"And this," explained Mrs. Whipple, "is where we shall be dining this evening: the Sea-Level Ballroom, converted some years ago from the ship's original gun decks."

"Good to know we're on a pleasure cruiser and not a warship," smirked Rex Goldwin. "Left our muskets and cutlasses back at the house, I'm afraid."

Arthur's eye immediately went to the rear of the group, where, trailing behind the others with her nose planted in an old, cloth-bound book, strode Ruby. Though he had been trying to get the girl's attention ever since she and her family had boarded the boat a half hour earlier, his efforts thus far had proved bafflingly unsuccessful.

"Ah—and here he is," declared Mrs. Whipple as the group approached the bar, "our man of the moment: Sammy the Spatula Smith! Sammy, meet the Goldwins."

Rex stepped forward and took the chef's hand. "Such a pleasure to finally meet you, Sammy," he beamed. "Congratulations on your recent unfettering. So glad you could be here tonight—instead of *elsewhere*."

Sammy nodded enthusiastically. "So am I, Mr. Goldwin—so am I. Pleasure."

"Yes," added Arthur's mother, "and not only is Sammy our guest of honor this evening, but—at his own insistence— he'll also be our chef for tonight's feast. Again, Mr. and Mrs. Goldwin, thank you for allowing us to combine these two gatherings into one. With Sammy being discharged this morning, we wanted to be sure to give him an unforgettable release party, but then, we'd already asked your family to dinner tonight. Seemed the perfect time to take the family frigate out for a cruise. I do hope you don't mind."

"Please, Lizzie," cried Rita Goldwin, "don't say another

word about it! What an honor it is to be included in such a personal and momentous occasion. How truly gracious of you and your husband!"

"Really, Mrs. Goldwin," said Arthur's father, his buoyant demeanor having flattened considerably since the Goldwins' entrance, "all credit *must* go to my wife."

Mrs. Whipple gave a subtle elbow to her husband's ribs.

"But of course," he added, forcing a smile, "we are all pleased to welcome you aboard the *Current Champion*."

"Ah," said Rex, "now there's a name for a ship, eh Charlie? I only hope you aren't forced to change it on our account—given our performance this past weekend at the Unsafe Sports Showdown. Everyone knows what bad luck it is to rechristen a boat."

Mr. Whipple's smile faded. "Your concern is most appreciated, Mr. Goldwin. I assure you, we shall do all we can to avoid such a blunder. . . ."

"Yes, well," his wife said with a nervous chuckle, "I know I could do with a bit of dancing. What do you say, dear—shall we reconvene on the lower deck?"

Not waiting for a reply, Arthur's mother ushered the party to the railing at the front edge of the ballroom. There, a flight of stairs descended through an unenclosed atrium onto an expansive mirrored floor. When she flipped a switch at the top of the staircase, however, the mirrored floor suddenly became transparent as rows of lights beneath the ship lit up the sea below.

Shimmering schools of fish darted past lumbering sea

turtles and slowly drifting seahorses, against a backdrop of plump corals and purple anemones.

Arthur glanced at Ruby, and found her mouth hanging open at the sight. The instant she noticed his gaze, however, the girl clamped her jaw shut and snapped her eyes back to her book, leaving the boy more baffled than ever. Though it seemed he had been right to question her commitment to the investigation, he couldn't help but be a bit taken aback by her sudden iciness toward him.

"And here we have the Glimmer Gallery," Mrs. Whipple declared, "our newest addition to the *Current Champion*—whose crystal keel effectively makes her the Largest Glass-Bottom Vessel on the Sea. And makes a rather fine dance floor as well."

"Ooh," Rex said, dazzled. "Most impressive. Seems this old wooden dinosaur just might be worth keeping around after all, eh Charlie?"

Before Mr. Whipple could respond, his wife hastily interjected. "Very well then. Let's get these festivities properly under way, shall we?"

• • •

As Cordelia played the pipe organ built into the ship's wall, Henry and Simon challenged Rosalind and Roxy Goldwin to a flamenco dance duel, while their families swayed and twirled about them. Arthur, joining in the festivities with an improvised Irish step dance at the corner of the floor, peered through the dancers to the opposite corner, where Ruby stood alone, still reading her book. Strangely, the more he watched his brothers twirl her sisters across the dance floor, the more he felt compelled to go approach Ruby herself.

And so, when he had worked up the necessary nerve, he strode around the floor's perimeter to where the girl stood, and promptly addressed her.

"Oh—hi, Ruby," he said over the music as nonchalantly as possible. "Funny, I don't think we've said two words to each other tonight. And, well, after the talk we had the last time—you know, after the GGDG incident—I sort of figured—"

Ruby looked up from her book. "I suppose you've come to ask me to dance then," she said curtly. "Typical."

Arthur frowned in confusion. "Oh, no," he said, "I thought we could talk detective work—you know, about the case. Perfect time with everybody else out dancing, don't you think? Not much of a dancer myself—I mean, I once attempted the Longest Continuous Box Step, but I ended up breaking my ankle a couple of hours in. Haven't really tried it since."

"Oh," said the girl, her face falling slightly. "Well go ahead then. What did you want to tell me?"

"Oh, right," said Arthur. "Okay. So, um—I don't know if you've heard—but, well, I sort of made the break in the case that got Sammy out of jail. I mean, he's only out on bail, so he'll still have to stand trial—and, of course, we still haven't managed to capture the real dwarf and giant—but, you know, some people think it's a pretty big deal, actually."

"I see," said Ruby. "So I guess we're working alone now then, are we?"

"What?" said Arthur, scrunching his brow. "No—"

"Funny, I'd have thought *partners* would include each other in missions utterly vital to the case they're working on."

"No. That's not what I was. . . . It was the witness—Mr. Lowe—he told me to come alone. I didn't think I ought to argue with him—I mean, he was pretty clear on the matter."

Ruby closed her eyes halfway and shook her head. "They always tell you to come alone, Arthur—but no good detective ever actually *does* it. I mean, what if it had been an ambush? He could have been waiting there to tie you up and lower you into a vat of boiling acid or something, and nobody would have been there to rescue you—or at least to identify your remains."

"A pair of hammer-wielding dwarf-thugs did try to beat the living daylights out of me," Arthur admitted.

"My point exactly," said Ruby. "Wait," she added, "Mr. Lowe, or the 'dwarf and giant' dwarf?"

"Neither, actually. Two associates of Brian Carmine, the GGDG co-president. Both of them were too tall to be our man. Believe me, I checked."

"Gee. It's a full-time job just keeping track of the dwarves in this case—let alone avoiding being murdered by them. Another reason no good detective in your position would ever leave his partner behind."

"Hard to argue with you there," said Arthur.

331

He scratched the back of his head and shuffled his feet, while Simon and Roxy whirled past in the background. "But, well," he added, "besides all that—I mean, I have to admit: I might still have been *kind of* worried about Smudge catching us working together."

"What?" Ruby gasped.

"I know, I know," replied the boy. "But even if he is a bit of a swine, he's still one of the most respected record breakers of our time—and I just don't think I can cross him."

Ruby sighed and shook her head again. "You've got to get past this, Arthur. I mean, just because somebody's given Smudge a few gaudy trophies—"

"Four hundred and two, actually," corrected Arthur, "the Highest Number of Trophies Ever Received by a Law-Enforcement Agent."

"Whatever," scowled Ruby. "The point is: a man's trophies don't make him any more qualified to judge what is right and wrong. And from what I can tell, they might even make him *less* so."

"Well, I don't know about *that*," said Arthur as Henry landed a front aerial behind him, followed by a triple back tuck from Rosalind. "But I see what you're saying. It's possible I maybe shouldn't follow *every* order of Inspector Smudge's—despite his amazing collection of world records. . . ."

"Honestly, Arthur—all the records in the world couldn't buy him the instincts you've got. You just have to learn to trust them, that's all."

"You think so? Okay, I'll try. I'm sorry I didn't tell you about the meeting. Afraid I wasn't thinking clearly. It's all new to me, you know, this detective business. I, um—I won't let it happen again."

"You'd better not."

"I won't," Arthur insisted. "Honestly—I didn't realize you cared. But now, I give you my word: next time I'm summoned to a graveyard at midnight by a mysterious stranger who turns out to be the dwarfish descendant of the World's Creepiest Undertaker—as well as the target of pygmy thugs hired by a corrupt union boss—I'll be sure to invite you along."

Finally, a hint of a smile crossed Ruby's lips. "Fair enough, Detective Whipple," she said. "Man. I can't believe you went to a graveyard at midnight without me. That'll be a tough one to beat."

Arthur held out his hand. "Partners?" he said.

Ruby gave a melodramatic sigh, then .took the boy's hand in hers. "Partners," she replied.

As the two shook hands, Ruby looked to the center of the glass floor they were standing on, and the dancers busy upon it—while a pod of dolphins glided past underneath.

"Really is beautiful, this dance floor," she said. "Like we're citizens of Atlantis or something. Sure you don't want to dance?"

Arthur scrunched his brow again. "What? Like together? With you? Really?"

"Well, yeah," said Ruby.

333

Arthur shrugged. "All right. If you really want to."

"Well, come on then," said the girl, leading him out onto the floor. "Show me this box step I've heard so much about."

When she had found an available spot, Ruby turned back to Arthur and gave a smile and a curtsy. The boy bowed in response, then raised his elbows in the air—but before he could proceed any further, the music abruptly ended.

At the center of the floor, Henry, Simon, Rosalind, and Roxy struck their final poses, and everyone cheered.

Just then, a loud *booong* rang out from above, and the party turned to see Sammy standing at the top of the staircase with a dinner gong in his hand.

"Ladies and gents," he grinned, "if you would like to join me upstairs, dinner will be served shortly."

Ruby turned to Arthur. "Guess you'll just have to save your famous dance moves until after dinner."

Arthur gave a good-natured scowl. "I'm pretty sure you're mocking my dance moves now."

When the party had moved back to the dining area, Wilhelm poured champagne and ginger ale for the guests, while Sammy grabbed the bottle of milk from behind the bar and addressed the crowd.

"Before we eat, I'd just like to say a few fings. First of all, fanks to the Whipples for paying me bail and springing me from the clink—and for frowing me this fabulous party 'ere. Absolute class, you lot. I couldn't be prouder to be your 'umble chef. You keep letting me in your kitchen, and I'll keep cooking for you. . . . And as for you Goldwins, well—

any family who can give the Whipples a run for their money must be a fine family indeed. I'm pleased to know you."

Sammy then turned to the bar and retrieved an empty glass. "And now," he said, "let me pour a drink for the *true* man of the hour—me best mate, Arfur."

As Sammy filled the glass from his bottle of milk, Arthur couldn't help but be reminded of the milk bottle he had balanced on his head during one of the most heartbreaking failures of his life—and marvel at all that had happened since.

Looking to Arthur with sparkling eyes, Sammy handed him the glass of milk. "Fanks for believing in me, mate. Not only 'ave you proved yourself a brilliant detective, but a true friend as well. In honor of your dedication and 'ard work, we'll be 'aving your favorite pasta dish tonight: cannelloni colossale. A bit of a challenge, I must say, preparing thirty-foot pasta on a boat—but it were well worf it, mate. What you done for me were nuffing short of extraordinary—and, well—it means more to me than I can say. . . . So there you 'ave it." He wiped the corner of his eye with the heel of his palm and raised his milk bottle. "To old friends and new ones. And to Arfur Whipple—the truest friend of all."

The others hooted and whistled, and everybody drank.

As Arthur savored his glass of milk, Sammy's words echoed in his mind—and for the first time in his life, he felt he had truly succeeded in something.

Unfortunately, the feeling would not last long.

Thrusting the milk bottle back into the air after his first drink, Sammy then added, "Take that, Lyon's Curse! 'Ave to do a good bit better if you want to do away wiv Sammy and the Whipples!"

The others cheered and raised their glasses in salute.

"Hear, hear!" shouted Rex Goldwin.

Though Arthur's father raised his glass as well, the boy noticed he did not do it quite so enthusiastically.

"Cheers!" cried Sammy, and tipped back his milk bottle.

"Cheers!" replied the others, and tipped back their glasses.

When Sammy had had several gulps of his drink of choice, he wiped his mouth on his sleeve and declared, "Right then—to dinner. Let me just pop into the galley and see what's keeping Mrs. Waite. Should be out any—"

But before the chef had even finished, the main doors flew open, and the Whipples' housekeeper burst into the room.

From where Arthur stood, he could see the woman's face was pale and splotched with pink—a detail Sammy apparently failed to notice.

"Ah," the chef smiled, "there you are, luv. Where have—"

"We've been boarded!" cried Mrs. Waite. "I'm sorry, Mr. Whipple—I tried to stop him, but—"

At that moment, a tall, beak-nosed man pushed past her and barged into the ballroom.

The smiles fell from the Whipples' faces. Sammy's eyes filled with terror.

"Well, isn't this a lovely little soiree?" Inspector Smudge grinned. "I do hope I'm not interrupting."

Mr. Whipple stepped forward. "Well . . . of course not,

Inspector," he said cautiously. "Though I must say your entrance comes as a bit of a shock. I trust nothing is the matter? Surely Sammy could not have infringed upon the judge's orders so soon. . . ."

"Please, Mr. Whipple," the inspector grinned, "why should you think anything was the matter? I have merely come to deliver a bit of news—news so good, in fact, that I simply could not wait for your return to share it."

Mr. Whipple's cautious scowl deepened. "And to what exactly does this news pertain, Inspector?"

"Why"—the inspector beamed—"only to the solving of every crime against your family—and to the utter restoration of the Whipple name!"

Mr. Whipple glanced at his wife, then back to Inspector Smudge. "Well then, Inspector—please go on."

"Indeed, Mr. Whipple. But I wonder if the news might be more potent coming from someone besides myself. I trust you will not mind if we invite a few more guests to our party?" The inspector stepped to the left side of the doorway then shouted into the dimly lit corridor behind him, "Gentlemen—send in our guests!"

At this, the voices of what must have been Smudge's men echoed out in the darkness. "Go on then!" one of them called gruffly.

Arthur peered into the corridor. It seemed the shadows themselves were moving toward him.

Slowly, inexorably, a giant figure emerged from the doorway.

Arthur's breath froze.

The figure wore a plain gray suit and tie—but its face was smeared with thick pasty makeup and a cracking crimson smile.

Arthur lunged backward. He glanced to Ruby and shared a look of horror, then shouted, "Everybody look out! He's come to murder us all!"

But before anyone could run for cover, Inspector Smudge raised his hand sharply and said, "Please. There shall be no murders by this man tonight. Despite his enormous size and strength, this unspeaking ogre is well within my power, I assure you."

It was then that Arthur noticed the shackles on the giant's wrists and ankles. But where, he wondered, was the giant's partner?

The hunching giant promptly attempted to stand, only to strike the back of his skull on the ballroom ceiling, which was a foot too low for his head. He grunted loudly in annoyance, but said nothing.

Just then, an impossibly tiny man wearing similar attire and face paint stepped out from behind the giant.

Rita Goldwin let out a shriek. "Goodness, Rex!" she cried. "What sort of party is this?"

Rex pulled his wife close to him, his face full of disgust. "Your guess is as good as mine, dear. Never can tell *what* will turn up at a Whipple gathering, can you?"

Arthur's father took another step forward. "Please, Inspector," he said, "what is the meaning of this?"

"Really, Mr. Whipple," Smudge replied, "I should have thought you of all people would like a word with the elusive culprits behind the Cake Catastrophe Case. Allow me to introduce: Messrs. Overkill and Undercut."

The shock on Mr. Whipple's face intensified. "But how—?"

"Simple really. Directly after the hearing yesterday, I stationed an undercover unit outside the Mountain and Molehill with orders to detain any suspicious parties who might arrive. Indeed, it only took the interrogations of five other giant/dwarf duos before we arrived at the guilty pair. In the end, it was the makeup that gave them away—ridiculous creatures, clowns—and they quickly confessed to everything."

"They did?"

"Like schoolboys. Far more easily, in fact, than I had expected for such conniving criminals—but then, of course, there are scant few who can endure the interrogations of Inspector Hadrian Smudge. Still, I should never have obtained any sort of confession at all, had I not found the culprits to begin with. And for that, Mr. Whipple, it would seem some recognition is due—to that rather fidgety son of yours there." He nodded at Arthur. "As it turns out, what I thought was merely impudent meddling on his part has proved to be the deciding factor in solving the entire case!"

Arthur stood staring at Smudge with his mouth wide open.

There was a moment of silent disbelief before his father

turned to him and cried, "Good Grazelby, Arthur—you've done it! Not only have you freed Sammy, you've had him acquitted as well!" Letting out a relieved sigh, Mr. Whipple turned to Sammy and smiled. Sammy, who had stood petrified ever since Smudge's appearance, relaxed his shoulders and chanced a grin at the corner of his mouth.

Arthur felt his heart begin to swell. What he failed to notice, however, was the smirk on Inspector Smudge's face.

"Not so fast, Mr. Whipple," called the inspector. "I'm afraid no one has said anything about Mr. Smith yet."

Arthur's heart stopped its swelling. The Whipples' smiles grew uneasy.

"Perhaps," continued Smudge, turning to the scowling, shackled dwarf beside him, "Mr. Undercut will be so kind as to oblige. Indeed, he has insisted on speaking with you Whipples since the moment of his confession."

At this, the dwarf stepped forward—and looked directly at Sammy.

"No use pretending any furvver, boss," he said in a voice that sounded like a strange, high-pitched version of Sammy's own. "It's all over."

The dread returned to Sammy's face. "What?" he gasped.

"It were a good try," continued the dwarf, "feeding that story to Mr. Lowe like you told us to do, to get you sprung from the clink—but it's all gone pear-shaped now, 'asn't it? Reckon Overkill and me shouldn't have gone back to the Mountain and Molehill after that business—but then, *you* try entertaining a roomful of screaming, cake-eating kids whilst wearing shoes ten sizes too big and see if you don't need a stiff drink afterwards. Of course, you're not usually one to pass up a drink yourself, are you, boss?"

"Stop calling me 'boss'!" spluttered Sammy. "I ain't never seen neivver one of you in all me life!"

"Really, boss," said the dwarf, "ain't no good denying it now. After them Whipples snubbed the IBCPC and showed their clear hatred for us clowning folk, we was 'appy to 'elp you try and murder them at their birfday party, but, you see, the inspector's offered me and Overkill reduced time if we come clean now—so I'm afraid we'll 'ave to stop you before you carry out plan B and finish them off. You do understand, don't you, boss?"

Mr. Whipple's face turned grim. "What's going on here, Sammy?" he said. "What's he talking about?"

"I—I swear I don't know, sir."

The dwarf sighed. "It's a real shame, of course. We were really looking forward to stealing their fortune with you after you'd *poisoned* them all tonight. . . ."

The room gasped and turned to Sammy in shock.

"It's not true!" cried Sammy.

"Oh, isn't it, Mr. Smith?" snapped the inspector. "Then perhaps you might explain how I came to find *this* in the galley amongst your spices not three minutes ago—just where Mr. Undercut said it would be." Opening his coat, he whisked out a small black bottle with a skull and cross-bones on its label. "A rather unusual ingredient, even for you, Mr. Smith—wouldn't you say?"

Everyone gasped again and glanced at the dining table.

"What?" cried Sammy. "No—it's not mine!"

"Of course it's not," smirked the inspector. "It never is, is it?" He returned the bottle to his coat. "Well, my dear Whipples—what do you think of your chef now, hmm? Clearly, he's been in league with this giant and dwarf pair from the very start. And tonight, he's endeavored to murder you once again. I believe that makes three times now, does it not? Surely you can see now—it's best if Mr. Smith comes with me."

Sammy's gaze darted between the confused and concerned faces of the nearby Whipples. "No," cried the chef, "I've got nuffing to do wiv any of this, I swear! Why should I ever want to 'arm any of you?"

"*Why*, indeed, Mr. Smith?" the inspector sneered. "Surely even someone with your limited intellect can imagine what a gambling addict with record-breaking debts might do with a stolen family fortune?"

Mr. Whipple opened his mouth to speak, but stopped short.

"Please, sir," Sammy begged his boss. "Don't listen to this rubbish. I—I don't know what's going on here."

As Arthur's father stood in silent contemplation, Inspector Smudge shook his head and sighed. "I am sorry," he said, "to have to reveal Mr. Smith's true nature to you a second time—but then, if you and your boy had listened to me in the first place, we should not be in this situation again, now should we?"

Mr. Whipple lowered his head, then looked up at Sammy with a heartbroken expression. "You," he said softly, "you had better go with him, Sammy."

"Sir—no," the chef pleaded. "You 'ave got to believe me. I—"

"You heard the man," Smudge said as he took a step forward. "The game is up, Mr. Smith. You're going away for good this time. Come along now—and let's not have any fuss about it. You've nowhere to go—and you'll not be taking any hostages *tonight*. I've learned my lesson from your last arrest and left that fool Greenley out of it this time. Allow me to introduce my new associates. Gentlemen!"

On his command, four brawny policemen stepped into the room and flanked Inspector Smudge beside their exceptionally sized prisoners. Each of the officers carried a different firearm—twin pistols, rifle, shotgun, and machine gun, respectively.

"Mr. Smith," said Smudge, "meet the Commissioner's Execution Squad. Execution Squad, Mr. Smith."

"Pleasure," said the man with the machine gun.

"*Execution* Squad?" cried Arthur's mother. "Surely, as damning as the evidence may be, Sammy still has the right to a trial?"

"Oh, it's not *that* sort of execution squad, Mrs. Whipple," chuckled the inspector. "Not *execution* in the sense of putting criminals to death, you understand—but *execution*, in the sense of getting things done. Executing *orders* and *tasks* and such."

343

"Righto," said the man with the machine gun. "Nobody better at executing orders than the Execution Squad. More Successful Arrests per Member Than Any Other Law Enforcement Unit on the Planet. . . . Of course, we do also hold the record for Most Suspects Terminated While Resisting Arrest—so I can see how some people might get confused about the name. But in our defense, we always give our suspects the choice of which record they'd like to contribute to."

"Most generous indeed," said the inspector. "So, which one will it be for you then, Mr. Smith?"

Any last trace of hope in Sammy's face completely drained away. Arthur could see the contents of the milk bottle that dangled from his left arm beginning to quiver.

"Well, I don't know, Inspector," said the chef in a stony voice. "'Ard to tell which is worse these days, innit? If I'm ever proved not guilty, I reckon you'll only make somefing else up—or find some uvver lying jackals to slander me—in order to put me away again." At the word "jackals," the dwarf put on an affronted expression, but Sammy paid no mind. "Seems there's only one way to truly be free of you, eh, Inspector?" he continued. "And I fink I may be ready for that. They're good shots, these blokes, are they? Won't make it too painful, will they?"

"Sammy, please," said Mr. Whipple, "just go with them. Whatever you've done, I don't want to see you hurt."

"Appreciate the sentiment, guv—but I'd ravver end fings on me own terms *now* than to rest me fate in *his* hands anuvver minute." The chef gave a mournful smile to Arthur's father, then slowly turned away.

By the time he'd turned back to Inspector Smudge, a mad twinkle had appeared in Sammy's eye. "So tell me, Inspector," he said, "you'd consider a milk bottle a deadly weapon, wouldn't you? Plenty of blokes from the old days wiv missing teef who certainly would, I reckon. Smashed a pumpkin from fifty paces once, I did—and that's a much smaller target than your head, innit, Inspector?"

His hand trembling, Sammy began to raise the bottle.

The Execution Squad aimed and cocked their weapons.

"Sammy, no!" cried Arthur's mother.

"Goodness me, boss," said Mr. Undercut, wringing his shackled hands together. "What ever are you doing?"

Mr. Overkill simply stared.

"Put the milk bottle down, Mr. Smith," Inspector Smudge ordered, but he could hardly keep the smile from his lips.

The milk sloshed against the sides of the bottle as Sammy lifted his quivering arm past his waist.

Arthur stood looking on powerlessly from two yards away. Everything he had accomplished was crashing down before his eyes. Whatever the dwarf claimed, he could not imagine Sammy plotting to kill a *mouse*, much less his entire family. He *knew* Sammy, and this was not him. There had to be some other explanation.

As he watched the Execution Squad tighten their trigger fingers, Arthur decided his only choice was to take his friend at his word. If Sammy was telling the truth, and he did nothing to help him, he would have to answer someday for his inaction. If Sammy was lying, that was *his* problem; Sammy would have to answer for that himself. And that was none of Arthur's business.

Unfortunately, there was still the matter of Sammy's rapidly impending demise to contend with. If only Arthur could stop time, then maybe he could find a way to save Sammy's life.

Then it struck him. Perhaps stopping time wasn't quite as impossible as it seemed. But could he really stand up to Inspector Smudge?

Arthur glanced to Ruby.

Her expression told him what he had to do.

He took a deep breath. Then, as casually as he could manage, Arthur stepped between the Execution Squad's guns and the trembling chef.

"Arthur!" cried his mother.

"What are you doing, boy?" the inspector shrieked. "Get out of the way! Do you want to be shot?"

Arthur tried to keep his voice from shaking. "So sorry to interrupt, officers—it's just that I'd really like to assist with Sammy's arrest, seeing as it was me who unwittingly helped to free him. Now that I realize what a mistake that was, I would hate to make another one. And I feel it would be a mistake not to inform you about the slight flaw I've noticed in your plan."

"What?!" scoffed the inspector. "*You've* noticed a flaw in *my* plan? Preposterous!"

"Please, Inspector. You've got to listen to me. From what I can tell, your plan hinges on Mr. Smith being trapped in the ship's cabin with no way out but the passage you and your men are currently standing in front of. But I'm afraid you've overlooked a possible alternative escape route. Perhaps you haven't noticed how much weight Sammy has lost in jail—what with the questionable quality of the food there—but at his current size, he might just be able to squeeze out that porthole he's standing next to. Your men could try and shoot him, of course—but then, what if one of the children got in the way? Record-breaking though the Execution Squad may be, I can't imagine they'd want to add child murder to their list of achievements. I mean, what would the commissioner think about that?"

"You fool!" screeched the inspector. "Can't you see you've got in our way yourself!"

Arthur gasped and put on his most convincing frown. "Oh no," he muttered. "I have, haven't I?"

With a quick backward glance, the boy shot an urgent look to Sammy. As the chef's eyes narrowed from desperation to resolve, Arthur turned back to face the officers.

"I can't believe I've done it again," he whimpered, raising his hands in submission. "Why do I keep making such dreadful mistakes? Please don't let them shoot me, Inspector!"

"Shut up, boy!" the inspector snarled. "Out of our way, now!"

"I can't," cried Arthur, his lips and limbs trembling.

Looking down the barrels of five firearms, each of them trained in the direction of his head, he hardly had to embellish his reaction. "My feet won't budge!"

At that moment, Arthur detected a small *thud* behind him, not unlike the sound of a milk bottle dropping onto a wooden deck.

"He's going for it, lads!" cried the man with the machine gun.

"Boss, come back!" squealed the dwarf. "Inspector, you've got to stop him!"

What happened next was a blur.

Arthur heard the scuffling of feet to his rear, and the next thing he knew, Inspector Smudge and the Execution Squad were rushing at him.

"Don't let him get out!" shouted Smudge.

Just before the man with the shotgun knocked Arthur to the floor, the boy heard the squeal of hinges, followed by a distant splash. Twisting about on the floor, Arthur craned his neck to see the man with the pistols, the man with the rifle, and the man with the machine gun all run to the open porthole, point their weapons through the opening, and open fire on the water below.

The octuplets screamed.

Arthur's heart pounded in his chest. "Come on, Sammy . . ." he whispered to himself.

After the three men had emptied their magazines on the unsuspecting sea, the man with the shotgun traded positions with his colleagues and added one final blast to the barrage.

348

When the shooting had ceased, Smudge turned to Arthur with rage in his eyes. "You imbecile!" he shrieked. "How dare you interfere with my investigation! If not for certain recent laws against it, I'd have you flogged before this entire ship!"

"Oh, you needn't worry about *him*, Inspector," said the man with the rifle. "Takes more than a dimwitted boy to thwart the Execution Squad. I got your man, despite the distraction." He patted his rifle barrel. "Put one straight through him with Miss Veronica here."

"Rubbish," said the man with the pistols, brandishing his weapons. "When his body washes ashore, I think you'll find his skull's been ventilated by matching revolver shots."

"Care to make a bullet bet on that, lads?" said the man with the machine gun. "Fifty pounds I've got says I filled him with so much lead, he goes straight to the sea floor."

"I'll take your wager," said the man with the rifle. "Always gets her man, my Veronica."

"Very well," said the man with the pistols. "But let's get one thing straight—in the case of multiple hits, the pot goes to the kill shot, as determined in an official autopsy. And no trying to bribe the coroner this time, either."

"Yeah," said the man with the shotgun, "let's try and be civil about our bullet bet this time. Absolute murder on my digestion, all that bickering."

Arthur began to feel his own digestion might fail him at any moment.

"Gentlemen, please," Mr. Whipple interrupted. "Traitor as the man may be, we have all grown extremely fond of Sammy over the years, and the thought of his death is utterly sickening to me. So, I should appreciate it if you'd kindly postpone your morbid wagering until after you're off our boat."

"Not a fan of gambling, are you, sir?" said the man with the machine gun. "Say no more." He made a gesture as if buttoning his lip, but promptly turned to the man with the rifle and whispered, "What's with him?"

The man with the rifle shrugged.

"My apologies, Mr. Whipple," said Inspector Smudge. "Public relations is not one of the Execution Squad's specialties, I'm afraid. But, of course, they'd have had no opportunity for such vulgar speculation had your boy not complicated the situation by—"

"Hey, look!" cried Rupert Goldwin.

While everybody else stood frozen around the dining table, Rupert was leaning himself over the ballroom railing and pointing excitedly to the glass floor below.

Everybody darted to the railing and peered over the edge.

There, in the water beneath the glass, illuminated by the ship's lights amidst the coral and sea creatures and kelp, was Sammy the Spatula.

He was doing the breaststroke.

"Sammy!" cried Arthur, unable to hold back his relief.

The boy quickly realized, however, that relief was not exactly the appropriate emotion.

"He's getting away!" shouted Rupert.

The faces of the Execution Squad filled with disbelieving outrage.

"What the devil!" cried the man with the rifle.

"Not a scratch on him," the man with the pistols gasped.

"Well, I'll be scuppered," grumbled the man with the machine gun. "Thinks he can escape the Execution Squad, does he? We'll see about that, we will."

And with that, the Execution Squad pointed their weapons over the railing.

"No!" Mr. Whipple cried as he lunged toward them.

But it was too late. Without delay, the four men opened fire on the swimming fugitive below—and the glass floor above him.

The party dove for cover as bullets ricocheted in every direction.

Only after they had used up all their ammunition did the Execution Squad cease fire.

"What have you done?" cried Arthur's father.

In the ringing silence, the party peered cautiously over the edge.

At the middle of the floor, there was but one tiny crack, no bigger than a foot in length.

The crowd gave a collective sigh of relief.

Mr. Whipple turned to the man with the machine gun. "What were you thinking?" he demanded. "You could have—"

He was cut off by a loud crunching noise.

Arthur turned back to the floor to see that the tiny crack now stretched from one end of the floor to the other. Before he could comment, the first crack was joined by a second—and then third—and then fourth—until the floor resembled little more than a giant crystal spiderweb.

Screams rang out from the crowd.

"All hands on deck!" shouted Arthur's father.

As the crowd scurried for the door, Arthur hesitated just a moment—unable to take his eyes off the fracturing floor below.

"Arthur—come on!" Ruby called out behind him.

Arthur whirled about and ran toward the girl and the crowded doorway.

But before he could reach them, a tiny man in fading clown makeup stepped in front of him.

"Going somewhere?" squealed the dwarf. He held up a shiny handcuff key, and Arthur noticed the two sets of shackles that now lay discarded on the floor. "Come on, Overkill—let's make sure our persistent little friend here doesn't die from *drowning*."

Arthur looked up to see the giant reaching an enormous hand for his neck.

At that moment, the Glimmer Gallery exploded at his rear. The ship lurched, sending the giant—as well as Arthur and all the others—tumbling to the floor.

Arthur turned to see a wall of water gushing toward him.

And then, the world went black.

352

• • •

When Arthur came to, he found himself coughing up water on the deck of an unfamiliar boat.

"There, there, Master Arthur," said a voice above him. "I've got you. You vill not be drowning tonight."

Arthur looked up to see the Whipple butler leaning over him. "Thanks, Wilhelm," he spluttered. "Where are we?"

"Welcome aboard the *Swift Justice*," replied Inspector Smudge, walking up behind him. "Good thing I had the presence of mind to board your sinking ship, wouldn't you say?"

Looking about him as he rose to his feet, Arthur found he was aboard a police boat crowded with the former passengers of the *Current Champion*. He felt a sudden pang of dread, sending his eyes darting from one corner of the vessel to the next. But he was relieved to find no sign of the clowns anywhere. The only member of his family not accounted for was his five-year-old brother, Franklin, whom he promptly noticed five yards off the *Swift Justice*'s starboard bow, clinging to the top of the frigate's mast—the only part of the *Current Champion* still visible.

Arthur's mother and father, leaning themselves over the police boat's rails, were currently engaged in a maritime dispute with the young sailor.

"Franklin," his father commanded, "get down here at once!"

"A captain always goes down with his ship!" the little boy shouted.

"You can go down with the ship when you're older!" cried his mother. "Until then, you shall come aboard the rescue boat with the rest of us!"

"But maritime law clearly states—"

"There is one thing a captain must always obey, even before maritime law: a captain's parents. Unless, of course, that captain wants to lose his sailing privileges for an entire year!"

Franklin looked suddenly aggrieved. "An entire year?" he cried. "Ah, come on—that's not fair at all!"

"Must we take away cartography privileges as well?!" his father bellowed.

"No, sir," Franklin sighed.

"Then you had better get yourself off that mast and into our boat this instant, young man!"

"Yes, sir," said Franklin—and followed his father's orders.

"Is that everyone, then?" said Inspector Smudge when Franklin was safely aboard the police boat.

Using an emergency blanket to dry his hair—which somehow looked just as perfect as ever—Rex Goldwin gave an eager smile and said, "All accounted for here, Inspector."

"Yes," panted Arthur's father, "I believe that's everyone."

The survivors watched as the last inch of the *Current Champion*'s mast sunk beneath the surface and disappeared into the still, black water.

Arthur noticed three massive, cream-colored tubes float-ing amongst the debris where the ship once stood, each of them thirty feet long and over a foot in diameter. His heart sank when he realized: it was his favorite pasta dish—can-nelloni colossale—the World's Largest Tube Pasta.

His father let out a low, mournful sigh. "Everyone," he added, "except for Sammy."

"Well, yes," said the inspector, "and his oddly sized henchmen, of course. But you needn't worry about those villains anymore. I should have liked to bring the three of them back to face trial, but no matter—Justice always catches up to those who offend her, one way or another. Hard as I tried to offer Mr. Smith the civil course, his crimi-nal heart was bent on taking the violent one. And now it seems his criminal heart beats no more."

"I'll say," said the man with the shotgun. "Nobody can hold their breath that long."

"No, they can't," said the man with the machine gun. "Gentlemen—the bullet bet is back on."

The members of the Execution Squad grinned.

"And for that," the man with the machine gun con-tinued, "I reckon we've got this observant young man to thank." He turned to Rupert Goldwin and patted him on the back. "If not for his keen eye, Mr. Smith might've actu-ally got away. Good lad you've got here, Mr. Whipple. Sort of makes up for that other one—the daft one with the death wish—doesn't he? Funny, that—how completely opposite brothers can be to each other, eh? Got a brother myself who's a Franciscan friar, if you can believe it. Makes for rather awkward dinner conversation at the holidays, it does. . . ."

Rex Goldwin chuckled. "Oh, Rupert's not Charlie's boy, officer. Though I can think of no better compliment you might offer me or my son. Hard to believe, eh, Charlie? People are mistaking my kids for yours now! Goodness, what a night. Shame about your chef trying to murder you again and your boat sinking, of course—but I must say, this evening's not turning out too badly after all!"

"Yes," agreed Rita Goldwin, "we'll have to do it again sometime soon. And perhaps we'll actually have *dinner* at the next dinner party, eh, Lizzie? What do you say *we* host next time—our house, a week from tonight? If you like, we can go to your house for dessert—I mean, if it's not too much for you. Should be enough time to find yourselves a new chef, shouldn't it?"

"Yes," said Mrs. Whipple, wiping the corner of her eye to conceal a sudden tear. "I'm sure it should, Mrs. Goldwin."

"Friday next it is then," smiled Rita. "We'll try and keep our house afloat until we've at least finished dinner!"

"Now, dear," scolded Rex, "let's not be insensitive—they can't help it that they're eternally plagued by a horrific family curse, can they?" He turned to Arthur's father with a pitying smile. "We really are sorry about the boat, Charlie—but look on the bright side: at least you won't have to worry about renaming it anymore. Now you can get yourself a brand new boat and christen it with a name a bit more appropriate for the future. The *Fading Star*, perhaps? I mean, I trust you've got frigate insurance?"

The man with the machine gun snorted. "Hope for your boy's sake your policy doesn't include a *stupidity* clause."

The Goldwins and the Execution Squad snickered.

Arthur gave a mortified smile, then, catching Ruby's glance, lowered his eyes to the deck.

As the snickering died down, he heard Ruby's voice speaking clearly out over the others.

"You know," said the girl, "sometimes stupidity and bravery are pretty much the same thing."

There was a moment's pause as the snickerers looked at her blankly—before they all burst into wild laughter.

"Sure they are, luv!" cracked the man with the machine gun. "And koalas and killer whales are the same class of animal! Great Gatling, that's a good one!"

Of course, had the man with the machine gun known as much about zoology as he did about, well, machine guns, he would have known that koalas and killer whales are indeed the same class of animal: specifically, class *Mammalia*. Arthur was himself well aware of this fact, but he was in no mood to point out the mistake. (Of course, given the man with the machine gun's *actual* area of expertise, Arthur likely would not have corrected him anyway.)

Mr. Whipple cleared his throat. "Well then," he scowled, "now that you've all had a good giggle at my family's expense, perhaps we might get back to shore—before one of you geniuses decides to shoot a hole in *this* boat as well."

The giggling stopped.

As the police boat circled round and headed back toward the harbor, Ruby touched her hand to Arthur's shoulder. "Never mind them, Arthur," she said. "Sometimes stupidity and bravery *are* the same thing. And if that's the case here, then what you did was the *stupidest* thing I've ever seen."

Arthur sighed and looked up. "Thanks," he said. "I think."

"You're welcome," said Ruby. "Every reasonable person knows you can never trust a clown—especially one who admits to trying to murder you, like that nasty Mr. Undercut. So, despite what anybody else may say—I think your instincts were *right*. I didn't know Sammy like you did, but I've got a feeling wherever he is—in this world or the next—he's grateful."

Arthur tried to smile, but couldn't quite manage it. In the end, despite all his hard work, he had been utterly unable to help Sammy.

Surely, in a life overflowing with failure, this was his biggest failure yet.

THE TROUBLES ARE NOT OVER

There was no breakfast at the Whipple estate the next morning. As the harsh light of day stabbed through Arthur's window, the boy pulled the covers over his head. After what had happened the night before, he never wanted to get out of bed again.

He succeeded at this endeavor another three hours, before there came a knock at his door.

"Yes?" groaned the boy.

The door cracked open, and Mr. Whipple poked his head in. "I know it was a rough night, son—but you can't stay in bed forever."

Arthur rubbed his eyes and sat up. "'Inert' Burt Torpidson stayed in bed fifty-three years and eighty-one days," he yawned. "I'm pretty sure I can beat it."

"I don't know, Arthur. Not really your style, is it?"

Arthur sighed. "What's my style again?"

"Well," his father replied, "it's certainly never been to hide from trouble, that's for sure."

"Yeah," said Arthur. "I guess you're right."

The boy's eyes suddenly grew watery. "But . . . Sammy . . . he—he was our friend."

"I know, Son."

"But if I hadn't put my nose where it didn't belong—I mean, he'd still be in jail, but then Smudge would never have found the clowns, and at least Sammy wouldn't be . . ."

"Don't blame yourself, Arthur. He fooled us all, the poor wretch. Seems the drinking and the gambling had a tighter grip on him than any of us knew. . . ."

The boy hung his head. "How can I *not* blame myself?" he said softly. "I mean, what with my constant failures— and now Sammy—it seems . . . it seems this Lyon's Curse is all my fault somehow. Father—am I . . . *cursed?*"

Mr. Whipple stepped into the room.

"No, Son," he said. "Please—you mustn't think such things. This curse has nothing to do with you. No, I—I'm afraid *I* am the one who has brought this upon us."

Arthur looked up with a puzzled expression.

His father let out a deep sigh. "You have asked about the Lyon's Curse before," he said, "but I have not told you the whole story. I told you your grandfather did not survive the curse—but what I did not tell you is that . . . it was *me* who killed him."

"What?" cried Arthur in shock.

Mr. Whipple held up his hand to calm him. "Now, technically, it was not my hand that put him to death—but it may as well have been. When I was younger, you see, I failed to achieve a certain world record which previously had been in our family for years—and my father took it upon himself to win that record back. He was on his way to the attempt—to make up for my failure—when the curse brought his plane down . . . and there were no survivors. He died . . . because I failed." Mr. Whipple's voice was distant and hollow. "You see, Son—you are not the first person in this family to fail. And all your trifling failures combined will never add up to the one failure I shall always regret. You are not cursed, Son. *I* am."

As the man gazed silently out the window, Arthur stared into his father's eyes. He never would have dreamt his father capable of such failure—nor that the two of them could possibly have anything—even remotely—in common.

Arthur was just gathering the words to express his profound sympathy when his father collected himself with a sudden sniff, then clapped his hands together and turned back to face him.

"Of course," Mr. Whipple added, the usual vigor returning to his voice, "this is all the more reason to fight failure with all that is within us. And, despite what happened with Sammy, there's no denying you did some fantastic detective work before the unfortunate end. No failure there, Son. A bit of an odd tactic, perhaps, stepping in front of the Execution Squad like that—but overall, truly excellent stuff. Now, I'm afraid we *will* have to rethink that private detective job with Bleader and Leach, given the outcome here—but not to worry, Son. I'm sure it won't take half so long to find another field you excel in. Now you've had a taste of excellence, you'll be all the more hungry for the next—and we Whipples can't stay excellent at something too long before we become the very best at it. So, pick your head up, Son. Your first world record could very well happen any day now. I'd say ten years, tops."

Any trace of the broken man tormented by past regret had now gone, leaving in its place the same purposeful patriarch Arthur had always known.

"Thanks, Father," said the boy.

"Yep," said Mr. Whipple with a warm nod. "Now let's get ourselves dressed and downstairs, so we can help your brothers and sisters with the day's attempts, shall we? Don't want to have to see those Goldwins again before we've added some new records to the books, now do we?"

"No sir," said Arthur.

"Right then. I'll see you in one hour."

Mr. Whipple turned to leave but stopped just outside the doorway. "Oh—I almost forgot," he added, reaching down to retrieve something around the corner. "It seems you've got a delivery here."

He held up a square box wrapped in brown paper, about eighteen inches in each dimension, and carried it across the room to Arthur's bed. "Left by private courier just a few minutes ago. Quite heavy, really—but no mention of the sender that I can find. Certainly doesn't look like Bonnie Prince Bobo's handwriting, this. Another one of those book clubs you've signed up for, perhaps?"

"Yeah," Arthur nodded as he took the package. "Probably."

"Very well, Son. Enjoy your delivery, whatever it is. And then back to work—understand?"

"Yes, sir."

For an instant, Arthur thought he caught a further glimpse of regret peeking out from behind the sparkle in his father's eyes—but it was promptly obscured by a broad, confident smile, just before the man turned and closed the door behind him.

Finding himself alone again, Arthur rose from his bed and placed the parcel on his dressing table. He tore off the paper to reveal a large white box with a removable lid.

Just the right size for a letter bomb, he figured—or perhaps a human head.

But as he could not imagine things getting much worse than they already were, he gripped the edges of the lid and promptly lifted it from the box.

The contents were even more shocking than he had imagined.

It was a birthday cake.

At its center, set off against a backdrop of dark chocolate, white letters spelled out the following:

Happy Birthday, Arthur!
(Better Late Than Never, Eh Mate?)

It then struck the boy that, spaced around the cake's circumference, sculpted in gold leaf and glaze, were twelve tiny portholes.

Arthur's heart leapt at the sight.

Sammy was alive.

The Execution Squad would not be pleased.

Scarcely able to believe what he was seeing, Arthur examined the pick that stuck out from the top of the cake. There, he found the following description:

CERTIFIED: WORLD'S TASTIEST
(WITH EXTRA-SPECIAL FILLING)

He then noticed the shiny butcher's knife tied with a white bow to the inside wall of the box. With ever-growing enthusiasm, Arthur untied the knife and cut into the cake.

After removing a wedge-shaped piece and placing it on the large saucer that had been fastened against the box's opposite wall, he noticed a vertical streak of gold at the center of the cake. Using the knife point to prise at the slender, metallic object buried at the cake's core, he soon removed a shiny brass cigar tube.

Hastily cleaning it on his sleeve, he unscrewed the cap and slid out a rolled-up scrap of paper. With trembling hands, he unfurled the tiny scroll.

It was a letter. And it was addressed to him.
His heart raced as he began to read.

Dear Arthur,

Thanks for what you done on the boat,
mate. That's twice in two days you've saved
me life, I reckon. Brings a tear to me eye
when I think about it, it does. Nobody
never done nothing like that for old Sammy
before. If not for you and that well-placed
porthole—as well as them unoficial records
for underwater breath-holding and treading
water I happen to hold from that time
'Barracuda' Barry tried to put the cement
shoes on me—I'd be a dead man for sure.
Didn't hurt either, of course, that favorite
pasta dish of yours just so happens to make
a right good flotation device as well.
　　Wish I could have delivered this in
person—but I can't take any chances, now I'm
a fujitive ghost. Better your family think me
dead than a traiter, I'm sorry to say. Hard to
blame them for not trusting me, of course,
what with all the evidense keeps turning
up against me and now them filthy clowns
saying I were they're boss. Not everybody's as
optomistic as you are mate—and I reckon even

you may have your doubts. All I can say is, you've got to believe me—I'm innosent as the Queen herself. Somebody's trying to frame me for things I never done—and Smudge has clearly got it in for me. Sorry for losing it on the boat there for a minute, but if I'd have let him put me away again I'd have never seen the outside of a jail in me life. And that just ain't something I can live with.

If I'm ever to come out of hiding, I've got to clear me name somehow—and your the only one I can trust. I know you already done so much for me, but I've got nobody else to turn to. Its down to you to find the real cullprets what done this. And my money's on them giant and dwarf devils.

Now, I must warn you: I never knew what happened to them two after the boat went under, but I had the strange feeling another one of them big pasta tubes were following me to shore. Didn't think much of it at the time, as I reckoned them clowns had made it back into Smudge's police boat, but with the paper this morning saying their 'presumed drowned,' I'm afraid we've not seen the last of 'Messrs Overkill and Undercut.' If their still out there, its only a matter of time before they strike again—and you've got to be

366

ready for them when they do. You've got to find out who they are and why there after your family. Its the only way to protect you Whipples and clear me name.

Right then. Afraid I'll not be able to risk writing you again whilst I'm in hiding but I'll be thinking of you and saying me prayers all the while. Stay strong, mate. Your all the hope I've got in this world.

Until we meet again . . .

Your Greatful Freind,
Sammy

P.S. Enjoy the birthday cake, mate. With any luck you and me will be sharing your next one together . . .

Arthur lowered the note and stared out the window. His jaw hung open in disbelief.

He was back on the case—and now, it was more vital than ever. Sammy had entrusted him with his very life—and he would not let him down.

Whatever had caused the Lyon's Curse to return, he would not stand by and watch it destroy his family. If Overkill and Undercut were still alive somewhere, plotting another attack, it was up to him to stop them. Who knew what rules—or records—he would have to break in the process?

Setting the note on the table, Arthur carved off a sliver of cake and raised it to his lips. It was, without a doubt, the best cake he had ever tasted. Beneath the layers of chocolate ganache, vanilla custard, and hazelnut mousse, he distinguished dark undertones of danger and dread—followed by delicate notes of courage and hope.

It tasted like adventure.

And this was only his first bite.

ACKNOWLEDGMENTS

To my family and friends: thanks for your amazing, bordering-on-unreasonable supportiveness—especially to those of you who let me sleep at your house for a year or three, and those of you who lent me money despite the historically dire repayment rate of struggling novelists, and those of you who were always eager to read more of the story, even if some of you grew three inches taller between chapters. (And thanks specifically to my wife's family for not kidnapping her when she announced I was going to quit my job and sell our house to "try and be a writer.") If not for all your help and encouragement, dear family, this book would not exist (and would now vanish before your eyes in three, two, one). . . .

To my mom: thanks for being a rabid fan of all my endeavors—and for not letting me not finish the endeavors I start (however much I may grumble about it at the time).

To my dad: thanks for encouraging and inspiring me to be creative for as long as I can remember—though I'm afraid I will never re-create the magic of your legendary "Boy & His Daddy" stories.

To my brother, Jake: thanks for giving me the appreciation for competitive sport essential to the Whipples' world—and for sitting through all my school plays when you probably would rather have been out kicking a ball. (Then again, you now know all the lyrics to *Les Misérables*, and I know all the current standings for the Barclays Premier League. I think they call that a win-win.)

To my sister, Courtney: thanks for being a Whipple fan from the start. And thanks for always believing in me, even when I don't quite believe in me. There will always be a cushion on our couch reserved for you. (Just not the one I've worn the groove into. That one's mine. Sit on it at your peril.)

To all the dearly departed writers who created worlds from which I myself never wanted to depart (e.g., C.S. Lewis, T.H. White, E. Nesbit, Roald Dahl, Howard Pyle, Arthur Conan Doyle, Joan Aiken, Dr. Seuss): thanks for showing me what wonder looks like. Hope they have "meet the author" events in Writer Heaven. (Also, hope they let me into Writer Heaven.)

To all the living writers who have done the same: sorry if my hands shake a bit if I ever get to meet you before we get to Writer Heaven. (Fingers still crossed about Writer Heaven.)

To Kathy Treat, Carolyn Ebner, Amy Cordileone, and everyone at the Lincoln City Fellowship: thanks for carrying me in the end, so I could cast the ring into the fires of Mount Doom (so to speak).

To my agents, Laura Rennert and Lara Perkins: thanks for your constant support and your amazing skills in the arts of both business and, well, art. Laura, thanks for believing in the book when it was only 72 pages long—and for sticking with it when it was 650. Lara, thanks for the inspiring story chats and for the voodoo magic you worked on the manuscript so that it is not still 650 pages long.

To my editors, Ben Schrank and Gillian Levinson, my designer, Danielle Delaney, my illustrator, James Gilleard, and everyone at Penguin/Razorbill: thanks for turning my ridiculous pipe dreams into beautiful book reality. Ben, thanks for taking a chance on

Arthur Whipple and me, despite our glaring recordlessness. Gillian, thanks for making the book better with every pass and for your astounding ability to keep track of the story when I can hardly keep track of it myself.

To my boys, Henry and Miles: thanks for making the world a truly magical place. Henry, thanks for all the times you've told me to "stop working, Daddy," so we could go wrestle or make waffles or play invisibility cloak. You are one extraordinary kid, and there is nothing that makes me prouder or happier than being your dad. Miles, at the time I write this, I haven't quite met you yet (apart from a few transbelly high-fives), but it somehow feels as though you've been with us all along. I can't wait to show you around this fantastic world of ours—and promptly sign you up for the Ward wrestling team.

Finally, to my wife, Wendie: thanks for listening to me ramble about the Whipples for the past fifteen years—and for all the times you rambled along with me. It's no secret to anyone who knows our story: I could never have done it without you. I just wish I could find the words to properly express my undying love and gratitude. (Hmm. Undying? Sounds a bit Dracula-esque, don't you think? Man. I'd really love to bounce some ideas off you here, just like we've done for every other part of this book. Good thing the acknowledgments section is pretty much the only subject on earth I don't have the privilege of discussing with you—or I would clearly be lost.) But I guess what I'm trying to say is: in writing and in life, everything is better with you. Thanks for being my best friend and partner in crime-fighting. Thanks for being my Ruby. There's nobody in this world with whom I'd rather go adventuring. . . .

And above all, to God: thanks for making all other thank yous possible.

SELECTIONS FROM THE WORLD RECORD ARCHIVES

BIRTHS

HIGHEST NUMBER OF SHARED COINCIDENTAL BIRTH DATES IN A SINGLE FAMILY: 14

Held by Charles & Eliza Whipple and twelve of their thirteen children: Henry, Simon, Cordelia, Penelope, Edward, Charlotte, Lenora, Franklin, Abigail, Beatrice, George, and Ivy. Though Charles and Eliza were no doubt fond of each other before they discovered they shared the same birth date, the prospect of conquering the prestigious coincidental birth date record together can hardly have hindered their decision to wed.

MOST TEETH AT BIRTH FOR A HUMAN BABY: 16

Held by Abel Denton. Sadly, Abel's mother was forced to switch her child to bottle-feeding after only seventeen minutes, an effort for which she still bears the scars.

HEAVIEST HUMAN NEWBORN: 22 LBS., 7 OZ.

Held by Roberto Babosa. Birthed by Gabriela Babosa. RIP Gabriela Babosa.

HUMAN ODDITIES

HAIRIEST HUMAN EVER RECORDED: 78.6% SKIN COVERAGE

Held by Phoolendu Mahankali (a.k.a. the Panther-Man of Pandharpur). Fortunately for his humble family, little Phoolendu was able to use his Grazelby sponsorship money to help offset the crushing cost of haircuts. He eventually went on to study medicine but ultimately opted for a position as a lion tamer, because he found putting his head inside a hungry lion's mouth had fewer devastating side effects than most doctors' prescriptions.

HAIRIEST LIVING HUMAN: 74.3% SKIN COVERAGE

Held by Nergüi Khünbish (a.k.a. the Monkey-Man of Mongolia). It has only been a matter of weeks since the Monkey-Man secured the Hairiest Living Human title and gained the respect that such a title affords. Six years ago, in response to a lifetime of taunting from his normally follicled peers, he founded the "Hair Khan Cult," whose exceptionally hairy members proclaim to be the true descendants of Genghis Khan and the rightful heirs to the Mongolian Empire. They have hatched numerous plots to overthrow the current government, but as the cult consists solely of Nergüi and his cousin Ordu (who bases his claim to exceptional hairiness solely on a slightly longer-than-average mustache), the Mongolian government has thus far remained intact.

ORGANIZED COMPETITION & UNSAFE SPORTS

MOST NATIONAL STRONGMAN COMPETITIONS WON BY A SINGLE GERMAN: 16
Held by Wilhelm von Kleve. Competitors at Muskelmannspiele (the German Strongman Games) are tested in dozens of traditional events, including Holstein-cow hoisting, schnitzel shoveling, and beer-barrel balancing.

LONGEST INDOOR HORSE RACE RUN IN A SINGLE FAMILY RESIDENCE: 489 YDS., 2 FT., 9 IN.
Held by Henry and Simon Whipple at the First Annual Neverfall Hall Indoor Classic. After their parents took stock of the damage, the First Annual Neverfall Hall Indoor Classic also became the Last Annual Neverfall Hall Indoor Classic.

BLOODIEST RHINO POLO MATCH EVER PLAYED: 18 TRAMPLINGS AND 11 GORINGS
Held by the Rhino Polo Intercontinental Cup Final, between Borneo and Zambia, at Unsafe Sports Showdown XXVI. Though Borneo managed to claim the victory in the end, only three members of the squad were physically capable of hobbling over to the winners' podium to accept the trophy at the following awards ceremony.

OLDEST PLAYER TO BE EATEN BY CROCODILES IN AN EXTREME CROQUET MATCH: 66 YRS., 284 DAYS
RIP Wailin' Waylan Martinson. * Perhaps making Mr. Martinson's death even more

tragic, extreme croquet officials believe the attack could have been prevented had Mr. Martinson not always insisted on carrying four freshly severed rabbit's feet from his belt for good luck. ***NOTE:** Half of all proceeds for this Regrettable Record have been paid to Mr. Martinson's widow by Grazelby Publications.

MOST POISON DARTS DODGED IN A SINGLE GAME OF EXTREME HOPSCOTCH: 73

Held by Beatrice Whipple. To prevent antidote-hoarding, the antitoxin is now distributed after all competitors have completed their runs.

FIRST EVER BLINDFOLDED ROUND OF MOTHER/CHILD KNIFE THROWING

Held by Fannie "Infanticide" Jenkins, Unsafe Sports Showdown XI. (Donations to the Timothy Jenkins Memorial Fund may be sent to the World Record Archives offices and will be forwarded to the proper address.)

FASTEST ROCKET-KART RACE FINISH: 49.583 SEC.

Held by Rupert Goldwin. If not for the rule that the driver be alive upon crossing the finish line, the record would have gone to Leonard "Flash" Fletcher for his unbelievable time of 26.392 seconds. RIP Leonard "Flash" Fletcher.

OBJECTS & STRUCTURES

FIRST LEATHER WHIP: 132 A.D.

Invented by Tergus Acerbus. After experimenting with various whip-making substances, including lambswool, peacock feathers, and dried grass, Tergus Acerbus finally arrived at tanned cowhide as being the most durable—and painful—material for whip production.

WORLD'S QUIETEST NOISEMAKER: .6 DBA

Manufactured by No-Noise Toys. Voted "Best Toy Company on Earth" by the League of Curmudgeonly Neighbors.

FIRST NUCLEAR POWER PLANT

Held by Tranquil Towers, Seascale, England. Upon its opening, Tranquil Towers held a second world record, for Cleanest, Safest

Radioactive Energy Producer on the Planet. That record, however, was short-lived.

FIRST NUCLEAR REACTOR LEAK

Held by Tranquil Towers, Seascale, England. Promptly renamed to "Mostly Tranquil Towers" after the incident.

FIRST WALL TO SURPASS 5,000 MILES IN LENGTH

Held by the Great Wall of China (at 5,500.254 miles). The Great Wall, which spans nearly the full width of China, was gradually built over more than two millennia to be the ultimate defense against foreign invaders. Upon its completion at the start of the 17th century, China's rulers could breathe easily at last. In a cruel twist of fate, however, the capital city of Beijing was promptly sacked by an army of rebellious peasants—all of whom were resident Chinese citizens. Unfortunately for the old rulers, the giant wall they had built made it much harder for them to flee their now-hostile homeland, and they were all summarily executed.

LONGEST WALL EVER BUILT: 5,501.102 MILES

Held by the Greatest Wall of China. Not to be outdone by his predecessors, the Kangxi Emperor (Longest-Reigning Chinese Emperor in History) commissioned the Greatest Wall near the start of the Qing Dynasty to overshadow the ancient Great Wall. The two walls run side-by-side across the country—but the Greatest Wall stretches roughly one mile farther.

WORLD'S FIRST BIRTHDAY CANDLE: AUGUST 12, 1808

Invented by Diedrich Luftlippen. Herr Luftlippen originally devised the idea for the birthday candle in order to win a bar bet, in which he was wagered a hundred Deutschmarks that he couldn't get a roomful of party guests to eat a cake with someone else's spit all over it.

WORLD'S LARGEST GET WELL CARD: 10'8" x 1'4" (OPEN)

Made by Cordelia, Penelope, Edward, Charlotte, Lenora, Franklin, Abigail, Beatrice, George, and Ivy Whipple for Phoolendu Mahankali (a.k.a. the Panther-Man of Pandharpur) and their elephant, Shiva. The Whipple children were careful to grip the card tightly upon presenting it to Mr. Mahankali, so as not to repeat the incident with the former Largest Get Well Card, whose recipient (a Mrs. Constance Aiken) was forced to spend six more weeks in intensive care when her children forgot to wipe their hands after eating buttered toast.

VEHICLES & TRAVEL

FIRST MOTORIZED WHEELCHAIR EVER ASSEMBLED: 1916

In the private collection of Lâo Bàoyuàn. Originally devised by military engineers during the Lesser World War, as a method of getting wounded soldiers back onto the battlefield as quickly as possible.

FIRST JET AEROPLANE: 1937, THE "DERRING DART"

Engineered by Sir Frank Derring. A compulsive gambler (as nearly every jet pilot after him has proved to be), Sir Frank had the misfortune of living a hundred miles from the nearest casino and invented the First Jet Aeroplane to get himself to the roulette tables in the fastest conceivable time.

FIRST SUPERSONIC JET: 1946, THE BOLT XLR-8, MANUFACTURED BY BOLT AVIATION

Piloted by Commander Chance "Zippy" Keen. Also a compulsive gambler, Commander Keen piloted the First Supersonic Jet to get himself to the roulette tables just a little bit faster.

TALLEST AUTOMOBILE ON EARTH: 11 FT., 9 IN., TOWERING SHADOW TTT

Manufactured by the Hulls-Hoyst Motor Company. Commissioned and owned by Charles & Eliza Whipple. The Hulls-Hoyst Motor Company was formed when the Hulls Engine and Hoyst Ladder companies merged in 1907. It has remained the leader in the luxury oversized-motor-car market ever since.

WILD WONDERS

THICKEST TREE LIMB EVER RECORDED: 12 FT., 9 IN. DIAMETER
Held by "Thor's Arm," a branch on the giant sequoia "Thunder God." Ironically, the limb was severed by a lightning strike during Lightning Storm Larry, the Most Powerful Lightning Storm in Recorded History.

YOUNGEST PERSON TO SUMMIT KANCHENJUNGA (WORLD'S THIRD-HIGHEST MOUNTAIN): 4 YRS., 5 MOS., 28 DAYS OLD
Held by Edward Whipple. "Though the climb up was rather grueling, sliding down was much more fun," Edward reported after completing the descent.

YOUNGEST INDIVIDUAL TO LIVE A MONTH WITH A WOLF PACK (VOLUNTARY): 4 YRS., 11 MOS., 12 DAYS
Held by Abigail Whipple. In a never-before-documented oddity of wolf behavior, the pack leader seemed to offer Abigail a permanent place in the pack. She was, however, forced to decline, citing "interspecies differences," though not without tears.

WORLD'S OLDEST LIVING MAPLE TREE: 534 YRS.
Held by "Old Sweet Bruce," a sugar maple in Pelham, Ontario, Canada. Heavily armed Mounties are stationed around Old Sweet Bruce twenty-four hours a day to ward off syrup-smugglers.

LARGEST EVER EXPEDITION TO SOUTH POLE VIA ICE CREAM VAN: 26 VANS
Sponsored by the Freezy-Creemy Ice Cream Company. Expedition led by Alfred Peregrine Congelati. The expedition hit an unexpected snag when its leader realized a group of stowaway children had left the transport ship and instinctively proceeded to chase after the ice-cream-van convoy as it ventured across the icy wasteland. The expedition was forced to double back in order to return the children to the safety of the ship. Though many of the stowaways suffered from severe frostbite, all of them claimed the journey was worth it, as they were each given a Choco-Rocket in return for their troubles.

MOST CHILDREN SWALLOWED BY A SINGLE FOREST: 38

Held by the Black Forest, Germany. Some observers have wondered why anybody would choose to live near such a dangerous place for children, but local parents have been known to use its reputation as a highly effective scare tactic. As such, children in the Black Forest region have been certified to keep the Cleanest Rooms of Any Region on Earth.

BREATHTAKING BEASTS

LARGEST COMMON HOUSEFLY EVER RECORDED: 25/32 IN. LONG

Captured in the wild by Penelope Whipple (who narrowly rescued it from her brother George's attempt at the Most Flies Swatted in One Hour).

TALLEST DOG IN THE WORLD: 45 13/16 IN.

Held by Hamlet, a Great Dane in the care of the Whipple family. Though he and Shiva, the World's Largest Indian Elephant, are fond friends, Hamlet received a nasty shock when he mistook one of Shiva's tusks for one of his oversized chewing bones. He has not made the same mistake since.

FIRST ANIMAL IN SPACE:

Held by Boris the bear, Leningradsky Zoopark, Leningrad, USSR. Carried aboard Sputnik 2 ½, launched by Soviet Space Program. Though the capsule contained only a few days' worth of food and oxygen, and though it has been confirmed with near certainty that Sputnik 2 ½ burned up in Earth's atmosphere three weeks after launch, Soviet officials insist that Boris is still orbiting the earth and conducting "extensive outer space research." Indeed, whenever a shooting star crosses the sky, Russian fathers routinely raise their arms in salute and tell their children to "wave to Boris."

WORLD'S SMALLEST MOOSE: 26 LBS., 7 OZ. (FULL GROWN)

Held by Little Monty, a pygmy moose on exhibit at the Anchorage Animal Refuge of Alaska, until his untimely death. Taxidermal remains in the private collection of

Charles & Eliza Whipple. Unfortunately for Little Monty, one of the other animals on exhibit was the World's Largest Eagle.

WORLD'S LARGEST MOUSE: 11 LBS., 2 OZ.

Held by Big Stanley, the cheese thief of New South Wales. Taxidermal remains in the private collection of Charles & Eliza Whipple. The date of Big Stanley's capture is still celebrated as "End-of-Tyranny Tuesday" in cheese shops across southeastern Australia.

HIGHEST HAMSTER-PILOTED MODEL-ROCKET LAUNCH EVER RECORDED: 1,732 FT.

Rocket built by Simon and Cordelia Whipple. Hamster training and rocket launch by Cordelia and Abigail Whipple. Piloted by Corporal Whiskerton, a hamster in the care of the Whipple family. Corporal Whiskerton is currently undergoing therapy for post-traumatic stress disorder.

MOST FIREFLIES EMPLOYED IN SPELLING OUT A FLOATING MESSAGE: 2,591

Insect-wrangled by Penelope Whipple. (Message: HAPPY BIRTHDAY TO US!) The art of firefly wrangling is notoriously difficult, as all training must take place at night, in order for the trainer to see her performers—and to comply with the strict firefly-labor laws recently initiated by the SPLI (Society for the Protection of Luminous Insects).

WORLD'S CREAMIEST COW: 5.24% AVERAGE MILK FAT

Held by "Ample" Agnes, a Jersey cow in the care of Charles & Eliza Whipple. The Whipples have reported several attempts by so-called cream fiends to steal their prized cow, but the suspects have all been quickly captured due to the slow foot-speed, shortness of breath, and difficulty squeezing through car doors that is commonly attributed to cream addicts.

FABULOUS FOODS

MOST FRANKFURTERS EATEN IN ONE MINUTE: 7

Held by Beatrice Whipple. According to current regulations, both frankfurter and bun must be eaten, though they need not be eaten at the same time. Pureeing the two together and drinking the mixture through a funnel, however, is now strictly prohibited in light of Dan "Chug-it" Chugston's stomach rupture at 'Furter Fest XIV.

LARGEST BOWL OF MUESLI BROUGHT TO TABLE BY ELEPHANTS: 3,247 GALLONS

Cereal prepared by Samuel (Sammy "the Spatula") Smith. Elephant team led by Phoolendu Mahankali and his elephant associate, Shiva. Commissioned by Charles & Eliza Whipple. During the hectic training season leading up to the Synchronized Swimming Masters, this time-saving contrivance allowed the Whipples to combine their morning breakfast with their morning swim.

MOST GRAVY DROPPED BY CROP-DUSTER AT ONE TIME: 852 GALLONS

Gravy prepared by Samuel (Sammy "the Spatula") Smith. *Dropped from aircraft by Wilhelm von Kleve. Commissioned by Charles & Eliza Whipple.* After its role in their Christmas dinner, the Whipples returned the cropduster to the farmer they had borrowed it from, who went on to harvest the best-selling potato crop of his farm's hundred-year history. Unfortunately, he was never able to replicate the subtle yet distinctive gravy-flavor of those potatoes, and business promptly fell off again.

LARGEST SINGLE PIECE OF FRENCH TOAST: 15'2" x 13'8" x 1'5.5"

Prepared by Samuel (Sammy "the Spatula") Smith. Lowered from aircraft by Wilhelm von Kleve. Commissioned by Charles & Eliza Whipple. Agent of the Whipples' infamous "French Toast Fiasco" and possible harbinger of the deadly "Lyon's Curse," but reportedly delicious.

For more selections from the World Record Archives, visit **FANTASTICFAMILYWHIPPLE.COM**

Turn the page for a peek

at the record-breaking

battles to come in...

WHAT REMAINS TO BE SEEN

It **was unclear** how the human thigh bone came to be sticking out of the seventeenth turret on the World's Largest Sandcastle. It was, however, looking more and more likely that its builder would be disqualified.

The world-record certifier for the twelfth annual Castle Classic snapped his rulebook shut, then trudged off across the beach to determine just how the bone had entered the sand supply. After examining all the sand-removal sites in view, he followed the builder's wheelbarrow tracks to an opening in the cliffside and disappeared within.

The crowd of sandcastle spectators murmured. There was no doubt the builder, now distraught at the prospect of forfeiting his hard-won record, had scooped up the bone by accident in his frenzy to finish construction in the allotted time. But the bone's origin remained a mystery. The common consensus was that the femur had simply washed ashore after a routine raid on a bone smuggler's boat, as random bones had been known to do in the area.

This theory, however, was quickly proved wrong when the certifier burst from the cave screaming.

The police were promptly called to the scene.

"Coming through!" barked the beak-nosed man in the thick, black overcoat as he pushed past the crowd at the cave opening, hardly glancing at the multi-spired fortress of sand that towered twenty-five feet over his head between the surf and the cliffside. "Let me see him! Where is he?"

The man charged into the shallow cavern now bustling with police and made his way to the place where three officers crouched over the floor with brushes and small metal implements in their hands.

Embedded in the ground between them lay a human skeleton, completely intact, apart from its right femur bone. On its left index finger, it wore a heavy gold ring.

"Ah yes, Inspector Smudge," started a policeman with what looked to be a high-ranking hat. "I'm—"

As Inspector Smudge took in the scene, the hopeful smirk fell from his face like a man from a cliff. "What is the meaning of this?!" he cried. "These aren't the remains of our fugitive. These bones have clearly been here for years, and Mr. Smith only disappeared off the Whipples' boat last night!"

"Yes, Inspector," said the high-ranking-hatted officer.

"I'm afraid the call to you may have been a bit premature. The first officer to arrive thought this may have been your man—this Sammy 'the Spatula' character—seeing as how the Whipple shipwreck occurred less than a mile offshore from here. Apparently thought his body might've washed up overnight and provided a bit of a buffet for the local sea life."

"Ha!" sneered the inspector. "I've seen shore crabs do quite a number on seawater stiffs before, but never anything like this. Looks decades old, this one. Surely just some other would-be gangster who got what was coming to him. Cases usually go unsolved of course. But who am I to stand in the way if these hoodlums want to kill each other off? As much as I'd love to further my record for Most Solved Cases, I shall happily sacrifice if it means a few less criminals in this world."

A medium-built, spry-looking man in a gray trench coat stepped out from behind Inspector Smudge and pointed at the skeleton's left hand.

"What do you think about the ring, Inspector?" he said brightly. "Interesting markings there, aren't they?"

"Ahh, Greenley," said the inspector, closing his eyes and rubbing his temples. "Interesting though it may be, the ring is a distraction. It'll no doubt aid in the identification of this unlucky individual, but as we have established this is not our man, that information is utterly irrelevant to us. Any other dazzling insights, Detective Sergeant?"

"No, sir," replied D.S. Greenley, less brightly.

"Well," the inspector sighed, "this has been a disappointment. I had hoped the tip we got this morning from the man in that coastal cookery shop claiming to see Mr. Smith alive was a mistake, but now it seems we must regard it as a legitimate sighting." He returned his dark, broad-brimmed hat to his head. "All right, Greenley. Let's leave it to the local police to sort out this mess, shall we? What we need to do is get ourselves back to Saltcliffe Station and wait for Mr. Smith to make his move. If he is indeed alive, that train will be his only way out of the area. We'll catch him there as he attempts to flee, and he'll be back in shackles before teatime."

• • •

Arthur Whipple had the misfortune of being nearest the doorway when the knock came.

He had hardly been able to sleep that night and had crept from his bedroom just prior to sunrise, before anyone else in the house had risen. As he wandered past the entry hall on his way to the kitchen, he was nearly startled out of his slippers by a violent thumping at the front door.

Upon collecting his wits, he decided the knocking sounded far too urgent to wait for Wilhelm—the Whipples' butler and World's Strongest German—to answer it. So he walked to the door and opened it himself.

He immediately wished he hadn't.

It did not seem possible that the man outside the door could look any angrier. But then the man realized who it was that had opened the door for him.

"Ah!" cried Inspector Smudge, throwing up his arms in

exasperation. "I can't stand to look at him, Greenley! Get him out of my sight!"

"Really sir?" said Greenley with a yawn. The typically wide-eyed detective looked as though he had not slept in some time.

"Out of my sight—now!" ordered Smudge.

"Yes, sir," said Detective Sergeant Greenley.

Inspector Smudge whirled about and stormed off down the steps.

The sergeant turned to Arthur with an apologetic smile. "Pardon us, Arthur—nice to see you again, by the way— but would you mind fetching your parents? The inspector would like a word."

"Of course, D.S. Greenley," said Arthur. "I believe they're still in bed, but . . ."

The sergeant sighed. "I'm afraid nothing short of the grave will stop the inspector this morning."

"Right," said Arthur.

He returned two minutes later with his mother and father, strategically positioning himself behind his parents as Smudge stamped back up to the doorway.

"Good morning, Inspector," said Arthur's father, Charles, with half-open eyelids. "A bit early for a friendly visit I'd say. What seems to be the trouble?"

"Oh nothing, Mr. Whipple," Smudge grumbled. "Just thought I'd stop in to deliver the morning paper in case you'd missed it." With that, he removed a bulging newspaper from his coat and hurled it at Arthur's father.

Mr. Whipple caught the paper with a grimace, then held it up to the light.

Spanning *The World Record*'s front page was a photograph of Inspector Smudge and a dozen policemen holding spatulas next to a stack of barrels at a train station.

It looked to Arthur like any of the other record-breaking property-seizure photos that typically graced the pages of *The Record*—except for one small detail. Over Smudge's shoulder in the top left corner, a circular section of the background had been enlarged to show a dark figure suspended in midair, dangling from the handles of what appeared to be a rolling pin. The figure wore an all-black chef's uniform—complete with puffy, black chef's hat—like some sort of culinary cat burglar. The rolling pin in the figure's grasp straddled a taut stretch of rope, which the figure was using as a zip line to glide toward an open door on the side of a steaming freight train.

The headline above screamed: treacherous whipple chef alive and on the run!

"Sammy?" gasped Arthur's father.

"Oh, Charles," cried his mother.

A sudden, relieved smile formed on Arthur's face—but he quickly hid it behind his hand.

Luckily, Smudge failed to notice. "Indeed," the inspector snarled, "it would seem your chef has cheated both death and justice yet again. First, he manages not to have his body wash up in a cave yesterday morning, and then last night he stages a spatula-smuggling operation to divert law enforcement from a brazen train getaway!" Noticing the confused expressions on the Whipples' faces, the inspector threw up his hand in a dismissive gesture. "I hope it makes you happy knowing you and your son have unleashed a dangerous criminal into the world. After his numerous attempts on your lives and now his blatant fleeing of the law, I trust you harbor no further delusions as to Mr. Smith's innocence. But fear not, dear Whipples—however you may hinder her course, Justice shall prevail in the end!"

Arthur's parents stood clutching the newspaper, unable to look away from the photograph.

"Come on, Greenley," snapped the inspector. "We haven't an hour of daylight to spare."

"Yes, sir," yawned the sergeant. He tipped his hat to Arthur and his parents and said, "Morning, Whipples," then turned to follow the inspector, who had already stormed back down the front steps.

Mr. Whipple closed the door behind the detectives and put his hand on his son's shoulder. "You see, Arthur?" he said, pressing the newspaper into the boy's chest. "Chin up. Sammy may have betrayed us, but at least he's not dead. We must count our blessings. Now go rouse your brothers and sisters. We've got to get on with our lives and get back to work."

When his parents had left the room, Arthur unfolded the newspaper and stared once more at the grainy blown-up image of Sammy the Spatula. He smiled to himself and started flipping to the section where the story continued.

His progress, however, was soon halted by a certain striking photograph on page 2.

There at the top of the page was a picture of a grinning skeleton, half-buried in sand. Below it was a small close-up of the skeleton's bony fingers, one of which wore a distinctive metal ring. The accompanying headline read:

BURIED TREASURER!

Grim curiosity getting the better of him, Arthur couldn't help but take a peek at the article below:

> A human skeleton discovered in a coastal cave by a record certifier at the Castle Classic sandcastle-building competition on Saturday has been identified as the remains of Bartholomew Niven, former treasurer for the Ardmore Association Board of Directors.

Arthur squinted at the last words of the opening sentence. He had heard the Ardmore Association mentioned before, but he had never learned much about the organization beyond its name. He knew it was somehow involved with the publication of the *Amazing Ardmore Almanac of the Ridiculously Remarkable* and the certification of certain world records not listed in *Grazelby's Guide to World Records and Fantastic Feats*, the publication that sponsored his own family's record breaking. But since Mr. Whipple had prohibited any of his children from ever reading it, this knowledge was of little use. Arthur gnawed his lip and continued the article.

> There was some preliminary speculation that the skeleton could be the crab-eaten remains of the Whipple family's former chef, escaped convict Sammy "the Spatula" Smith, after he jumped off the family's frigate just before it sank to the sea floor on Friday (in yet another apparent example of the so-called Lyon's Curse that has plagued that family in recent weeks).

Arthur shuddered. It was hard to believe it had been less than two days since the Current Champion had sunk. *They couldn't sink Sammy, though, could they?* he thought. *Guess that's what Inspector Smudge meant about Sammy's body not washing up in a cave. Seems the Lyon's Curse hasn't completely caught up to us after all then, doesn't it?* He tried to sound confident when he said this in his mind, but he only shuddered again when he thought about just how close the curse had come. He went back to reading.

> Smith, however, was quickly ruled out when the coroner determined the man in question had been deceased for over twenty years. (Furthermore, Smith would be seen alive on more than one occasion that day. SEE FRONT PAGE.)
>
> The ring on the skeleton's hand, which features the Ardmore treasurer's seal, ultimately led to the discovery of the man's identity.

Arthur re-examined the photograph of the skeleton's ring. At the center of its broad, rounded face the ring bore the emblem of a jeweled, five-pointed crown. Each of the crown's points, however, ended in a sharp, curving flame, so that the crown appeared to be made of fire.

Pretty, Arthur thought, *but certainly not the Most* Practical *Piece of Headgear Ever Invented*. He traced the symbol with his finger, then returned to the article.

> The evidence of the ring was quickly corroborated by aging dental records, confirming the skeleton to be none other than Bartholomew Niven, the lost Ardmore treasurer. Cause of death has yet to be determined.
>
> Niven was last seen alive some twenty-five years ago, just before he and the rest of the Ardmore Board of Directors seemingly vanished without a trace. Though the disappearance of the entire board, which had been public at the time, proved something of a mystery, it seemed to solve itself a month later, when the Ardmore Almanac appeared on newsstands across the globe as it had always done before. The public assumed the board had simply gone underground to avoid the pressures of such a highly competitive field. But the discovery of Niven suggests there has been a new treasurer on the Ardmore board for some time.
>
> Indeed, with the deep and active treasury the Ardmore Association clearly possesses (evidenced not least by its new, record-breaking contract with the Goldwins, who broke more records at last week's Unsafe Sports Showdown than any other family), a successor to Niven would

surely be required for the management of its finances. The identities of any such board members, however, remain a secret. Ardmore's chief legal representative, Malcolm Boyle, gave a brief statement regarding the organization's current governance by this unnamed shadow board: "The Association feels that separating its board of directors from its record-publishing pursuits pulls the spotlight from its leadership and places it on the amazing world-record breakers it sponsors, where the spotlight belongs."

And so, despite the discovery of Niven's remains, it seems the identity of the current treasurer may never be revealed.

Arthur gulped and looked at the photo of the skeleton again. He did not know what to make of what he'd just read, which involved events occurring long before he was born and an organization he knew next to nothing about. What Arthur did know was how very glad he was that the skeleton in the photo was not Sammy the Spatula's. His father had been right about counting his blessings.

Arthur closed the newspaper and glanced about him to make sure no one was watching. Then he reached into his pocket and slid out the secret message he'd received inside a birthday cake one day earlier. He unfolded the letter and began reading its closing lines for the tenth time that morning:

Stay strong, mate. Your all the hope I've got in this world.

Until we meet again . . .

Your Greatful Freind,
Sammy

Arthur stood staring at the words another moment, then—with a sharp breath—returned the letter to his pocket and went to fetch the others.